The Girl Who Lost Her Way

Also by Georg Engel from K A Nitz:

Thy Neighbour's Wife

The Famine Village and Other Tales

Sorceress Circe: A Berlin Romance

The Burden

The Fear Before the Wife

Tales of the Forbidden

The Rider on the Rainbow

The People of Moorluke

The Girl Who Lost Her Way

Georg Engel

K A Nitz
ALBANY, NEW ZEALAND

Die verirrte Magd first published
in German 1911

This translation into New Zealand English
Copyright © K A Nitz 2017
All rights reserved

ISBN: 978-0-473-42194-6

To the mothers.

To you, dear mother, is devoted that lesson which you taught me unobtrusively and by example, of how the eternal divinity, near and remote at the same time, giving, and yet constant, weaves a goal in women.

It is also dedicated to you, to the greater mother, the home town washed by the sea, and the arable land which so often appears gloriously in my dreams.

But I give this book also to the others, to all those countless women who have ever been embraced lovingly by a child's arms. For, when the mothers listen and nod seriously to me, the straying German girls will find their way again.

BOOK ONE

1

Surr, surr. Thus the scrawny, emaciated little man pushed his cart through the nocturnal streets of the little seaside town. The crashing sea foamed and swept over the crumbling stone walls which had formerly served the seaside stronghold as defence and shelter, and when such a skimming cloud of foam splattered before the cart of the old gardener Jochen Tobis, the little man then shook the white strands of hair which straggled out from under his old soldier's cap between his forehead and ears, and then he coughed to himself, "Cold — ice-cold. That's bad for my flower garden, and for people."

And then he rolled his cart along so that the single wheel groaned loudly through the night, surr — surr.

All the little one-level houses of Domstraße slept veiled in the darkness of night. No light dawned from the curtained windows onto the lonely wanderer, and only the moon, which chased through the black valleys of clouds with uncanny speed like a silvery ball swung by a giant fist, sometimes up, sometimes down, occasionally tossed a sparkling shimmer on the low row of windows of the soundless street.

Deep below, the whistling sea wind wailed over the bumpy cobblestones, and tousled the pitiful clumps of grass which spent their existence brown and decayed between the cobbles.

Surr — surr.

"It must be here", old Tobis finally perked up anew, as he released with a groan the braces of the cart from his shoulders to set it down. "Yes, yes", he continued, as he directed his ice-grey head upwards. "Up there a light is burning. And now the ill woman shall be having her hyacinths. For I know well, she is waiting for whether the roots take or not. That is what all the people do. It lies in the blood. It comes down to the roots."

With that, amidst renewed wheezing and laments, he lifted a series of tall hyacinth glasses from his box, em-bedded the clinking things carefully in his arms, and then crept cautiously up both steps of the antiquated house which had been erected in the severe style of the great Prussian king.

The bell did not ring.

It had been removed from the green, protruding en-tablature of the front door. The man was able to enter into the hallway unhindered. And at once the steps creaked under the steps of the man toddling up them. Quite quietly, quite distantly. It sounded as if the wood-worms were tapping in rotten beams.

Tick — tick.

"Don't you hear something?", Mrs Mathilde Boddin inquired at this moment, and sat up a little in her pil-lows. "Don't you hear something, Hertha?", she asked once more of the delicate blond girl who was resting at the other end of the cosy room, stretched out long and clothed on a chaise longue. "Is the wind dragging over the floorboards, or does someone want to visit me so late? Who can it be?"

Hardly had the words been uttered than the young creature jerked up. Her eyelids, overwhelmed by sleep, opened up, and a pair of large, sparkling blue eyes in which life flashed directed themselves inquiringly and tensely at the speaker.

Only for a moment, then the supple figure, which in her close-fitting, delicate blue dress recalled a porcelain figure — likewise from the time of the great king — slid down from her place of rest, and now stood as lightly and buoyantly on her feet, not as if she had stepped up to an invalid's bed, but rather as if these charming ankle boots intended soon, very soon, to spin into a whirling dance.

Strangely, even in these black shoes which the blue dress left free, the erratic, demanding life twitched and stirred.

With a few gentle movements, the daughter had hurried to the window. Now she pushed the antiquated half-length curtains to the side, and sent her sharp gaze down onto the black, soundless street.

Was she really able to recognise the little cart in the heavy darkness?

"Mother," Hertha turned back straight afterwards, and her lightly veiled voice, which always shook a little as if some passion or covetousness were only arduously restrained in it, trembled in quiet triumph. "Mother, you know what I see down there? Jochen Tobis's cart stands before our door. And watch out, now the old man will soon be bringing you your flowers which you yearned for so much."

"Really?" the mother repeated. "Oh, that is good, my daughter, that is very good. See, I have simply such a belief in sun and flowers, in short in everything which you find in the south. You were also born down there, in the warm lands. Come, my child, sit down with me. Today I am as well and easy as I haven't been in a long time. And hence I would like to talk to you about what I have been dreaming about constantly, and always in the bad and long days of illness. Come, sit down on my bed."

Only, the little one did not comply with her wishes. She shook her head definitely, and tossed out the reply, "No, mother, not so near. Professor Jahn expressly forbade me that just this morning, and it constricts you too. See, this here is the sort of low ottoman on which I always rock myself so pleasingly. Do you see, like this. And now speak, mother."

The rococo figurine had settled down so lightly and cheerfully. And when the gaze of the invalid flew over the pliant creature whose abundant, golden head of hair sparkled and flashed in the reflection of the light as if golden threads from the Christmas tree were strewn on her head, a half contented, half poignant trait played about the lips of the mother. She grasped for the slender, cool hand of her daughter, and after she had clasped this with her damp fingers, she closed her eyes as if in thought.

Tick — tick, the woodworms bored from the stairs. Or was it the steps of the gardener bringing the flowers?

And as if the tense listening of the invalid had somehow hurt her, she placed one hand on her heart quite abruptly, and breathed in and out deeply a few times.

"Mother, what's wrong?", Hertha inquired, as she bent over the suffering woman. But even this hasty movement did not spare that rococo grace with which the entire blue figurine seemed brought to life. "Are you lacking something?"

"No, no, my child," Mrs Mathilde comforted her, whilst, despite her smile, a delicate cough forced itself over her bloodless lips. "Nothing at all. Seriously, I feel much better. It seems to me today constantly as if I were strolling along the shore of the Ligurian Sea with your dear father during our honeymoon. He had just received his commission as a captain at the time, and although he hung onto his military profession with body and soul, and often enthused to me about how I would quite cer- tainly be someday called the wife of a general, or even Her Excellency, oh my child, it was delightful for me though to observe how the precious blue waters, with their reddish brown, shimmering mountains all around exuding the colour of autumn vine leaves, how they weaved their effect on the dear painter's eyes of your father. He was so happy, often I had to fling a long and colourful artist's cravat around his neck half in jest, and I see him in my memory then, how he sits on a gently undulating little hill under the shadows of pines before his easel to capture on the canvas with drunken gaze all the trembling and transitory beauty. Yes, yes, my dearest," — here Colonel Boddin's wife sighed to herself lost in thought, but straightaway she passed the white handkerchief to her mouth again. And then — as if she had something to hide — she was suddenly convulsed, as if in hidden shock at the cloth in her fist. But this quick movement did not remain hidden nevertheless from her daughter's eyes. Over the beautiful oval of the girl's countenance, a snowy pallor came chasing. Only for a second, then the delicate, blood-red lips could smile again.

"Continue, mother."

The white-haired lady turned about in her pillows, and after she had propped her head on her hand, she again let her gaze glide worriedly, in an almost evaluat- ing way, over the figure of the slender creature. At the same time, she shook her head quite gently and with distress.

An audible crunching came from the stairs. The woodworms which ticked so persistently seemed to have crept a small stretch of the way closer.

"Yes, see my child," the suffering woman continued, and at the same time, her large dark eyes were spellbound all of a sudden in deep recollection, sweeping far back to the painted wreaths and garlands of the ceiling. "In that, yes, directly in all the inexhaustible happiness which I enjoyed in living together with your father, in that lay the little, but unrelenting sorrow of my existence. Your father considered himself namely — you will surely also recall it, my child — in spite of all strictures, to be one of those dictatorial natures who are able to master life according to their will, even according to their command. To knead fate, prepare it, and force it into a fixed form, that was for him, I believe, precisely the art most worth striving for. That is why, my child, he was also incapable of bending and buckling, often not before his superiors, in no way, however, before the alternating conditions of politics or even before the demands of a small town. He kicked at every obtrusive corner with his imperious artist's nature."

As the mother spoke thus, the forehead of the blue porcelain figurine twisted so that three narrow, enchanting creases formed over her brow, and then she opened her lips a little until you could see her firmly clenched white teeth. Even her eyes sprayed out a hard defiance before she burst out, throwing her blond head back, "In that, father acted quite rightly, not kowtowing. Before whom then? Do the small and small-minded people here perhaps merit it?"

At the same time, she laughed curtly, and whipped one of her slender ankle boots a little. Then the recumbent woman nodded, and stroked the girl gently on the hand.

"Child," she whispered, barely audible to herself, "my sorrow arises directly from that. So much of your late father has passed into you. And if I should ever dwell far away, though it will hopefully last some time yet", she added with hasty defiance, for she felt very well how the cool hand twitched almost imperceptibly in her own, "but if I ever should dwell far away, then you will stay behind here alone. A soldier's child without pension, and without means. And as your only foothold, I leave you only your sister who as the wife of a high school teacher would also only be able to protect you slightly and pitiably from the hardship of life."

Again Hertha creased her golden brow. What terrible words the illness was supplying her mother with. Hardship! Oh, ugh! It would certainly never dare approach her, never! With a quick gesture of the hand, she tried to cast from herself this word and all the adversity tied to it into some corner. And really, as she thought this, she in fact performed that hasty gesture as if she had grasped a disturbing insect from the air and killed it.

Away!

But the ill woman continued speaking. Her weak spirit, girding itself for the ascent, described more and more distinctly and objectively the dangers, the deprivations, and the bitter tears which stream from the sorrowful wells of a withered existence to all those left behind. Then everything became distinct and visible. And gradually the broad room, which had previously dozed so comfortably in the light of the white ceiling lamp, filled with black figures. They climbed out of the floor, with giant, awkward limbs, and clubs in their fists. They crept out of the walls; black, shadowy, with bloody knives from which fresh drops ran. And then they sat before the shivering little one on the sofa, on the fauteuil and cane chairs, yes, they even let swaying legs swing down from the dark mahogany wardrobe to beat the rhythm there according to the words of the suffering woman which were barely still comprehensible.

"Do you hear," one of them whispered, "I am the renunciation."

And from here and there it rang out, "And pain, and restraint, and hardship, envy, illness, and friendless old age."

Oh, it was quite horrific. It beset the chest, it squeezed the breath back. No, no, it must never come true. And as little Hertha with her wide-open bright eyes, in which fear and horror had thrown something black, precisely as if two frightened moths were fluttering there, as the shivering girl stared at all the shadow folk who, ever more numerous and grotesque, moved closer and closer to her, it suddenly arose before her proud mind that, according to the judgment of all, and also from her own self-consciousness, she should be in possession of the power to push all such ridiculous bourgeois afflictions away from herself. Oh certainly, quite certainly! She seemingly trembled for such imperious, joyful struggles in which she would show what innate beauty and intellectual talents accustomed to winning were able to achieve. Quite clearly, she would prostrate numerous before herself, men who would marvel, begging and kneeling to her, at her luminous and yet cold face, as well as women who would have to realise enviously the supremacy of the little one.

Yes, yes, she would be capable of all that. Did not the tall mahogany mirror gleam and reveal its silvery light over there? And following an irresistible force, she jerked up, straightened, and now stood before the darkly luminous glass. She instinctively nodded contentedly when she perceived her delicate and yet so firmly staunch figure in the image.

Then there was a gentle knock at the door, and when Hertha opened it, there she saw standing on the dark stair landing the old white-haired Jochen Tobis.

"Good evening, Mademoiselle," the little man wished her, whereby he let his hyacinth glasses, which he had carefully embedded in his black military coat from 1866, tinkle against each other more clearly. "I have brought them now. Three white and three red. And they have a scent, Miss", he added, waggling his head, as he was already moving forward with his shuffling steps into the light to send a peering glance over to the invalid's bed, "a scent like from paradise itself. They are really not the usual bulbs. Smell one!"

He raised one of the white umbels up, and looked at it tenderly. For a moment, the room was filled by a gentle, pleasant aroma. Even the ill woman, who had lain for so long with closed eyes, seemed to sense the sweetness of the air surging forward. She opened with astonishment her lacklustre dark eyes, and then she gave an almost imperceptible sign that the old gardener was permitted to approach. Did she surely think at this moment of how, over many years during her long stay in the small insignificant garrison town, she had been, in consequence of her preference for flowering plants, the best customer of old Tobis? Again and ever again, she had liked to adorn her residence with colourful flowers, and thereby bring a shimmer and splendour into her life. Now she nodded at the scent-bringing bulbs, which the old man had carefully placed on the window sill, with a contented, relieved smile.

"Now it will go better for me, old Tobis," she then murmured.

And the old man, who had sat down in his black coat in a corner of the room directly next to the large brown grandfather clock, nodded his head, and replied, chewing strangely with his toothless mouth, "Yes, yes, Madam, that I well believe. When the flowers grow so beautifully tall, it is a sign. Then it goes uphill. But here, Madam," he continued and brought forth from his coat yet one last glass which he had carefully hidden until then, "here I have one more. Just look, it raises itself up snow white. And all that without a single root having taken in the water. What surely will happen with it, Mrs Boddin? It is like a miracle. For it comes down to the roots. And all creatures themselves know internally where they must stretch their fibres too. Hence I thought to myself —".

Only, Jochen Tobis would not reach the end.

Once more, hasty, powerful steps could be heard on the stairs, and before Hertha, who had already read off in astonishment the ninth hour from the brown grandfather clock, could spring up, you could hear how there was a knock on the door of the adjoining room.

"Go and see who it is", the ill woman requested with her dull, creeping breath. And then she added weakly, "A visit so late still?"

"Yes", the gardener agreed in his corner grumpily. "It surprises me, we could conclude things here alone."

"What did you say?", Mathilde Boddin straightened up, a little shocked at this expression.

Only, the old man, who held the glass with the white hyacinth motionless between his knees, just murmured indifferently, "I only thought so, Mrs Boddin."

Then it went quiet in the invalid's room again. Only the air was filled by the sweet, wavering, ever increasing scent.

**

"Is that you, Heinrich?", it fell from Hertha's lips in surprise when she became aware unexpectedly of a tall, broad-shouldered male figure in the adjoining room, which was only lit by a single candle. "Is it you? What brings you, dear friend?"

But she would not have needed to inquire at all, for her bright eyes had long since recognised that the tall ponderous appearance, who lingered motionless before her in a ragged fleece jacket and with tall farmer's boots, was carrying in his right hand, which was clothed in a woolen mitt, a shot hare which hung down stiffly almost to the white floor.

"Here", the young, barely 28 year old farmer began, whereby any impartial observer could have established already now how the awkward giant fell into an ever increasing embarrassment before this blue porcelain figurine who looked at him so steadily and surely. "Here, Hertha," he began once more, as he shook the hare awkwardly so that the animal's ears seemed to move slightly, almost with the appearance of life. "Look, I shot him this morning at our hunt in Werrahn. And think, he went running almost as far our farm. Then my mother thought I should give it to her dear friend, Mrs Boddin, because she is not in quite good health —".

The little one swung her foot impatiently.

"So you would like to show my mother," she then interrupted this awkward speech, "a little attentiveness certainly. Right, Heinrich Kalsow, isn't that what you wanted to say?"

"Yes, yes, of course," the ragged grey-fleeced man stuttered in some relief. "You are right there. That is what I wanted. And since I anyway had to buy winter seed in town, you understand, my mother thought it would perhaps not be too late if I —".

This time, a half amused, half disparaging smile slid over the lips of the little one. It was remarkable though that she had almost never heard this giant man complete a thought. Could he perhaps probably even bring the simplest sentence to an end at all?

"Well, give it here," she helped him out more promptly, whereby she was already taking the gift from his hands. "It is terribly nice of your mother that she so often thinks of the friend from her youth who is ill."

"Yes," Heinrich concurred, "and she also wanted it said that it was such a pity that we, that is, she, my mother, had seen so little of you recently. But you know,

Hertha, the old lady does not let the business out of her hands. And since we have now begun milking —".

"There she certainly toils the entire day," the girl concluded, puckering her white brow.

No really, this old Mrs Kalsow, whom she had never seen in living memory except with glasses on her nose and a pencil in her hand, she was also portrayed in her memory not exactly as a charming model of femininity. Oh, it was though very awful when women had to trouble themselves in such a way over their daily up-keep. And again the sombre thoughts which the ill woman had invoked in her just before forced them-selves on the girl, and such a fright shivered through her at the same time that she instinctively clasped the ragged sleeve of her visitor as if she wanted to seek with his presence succour and help from flesh and bone.

"Heinrich," she stuttered, and at this moment, her words sounded much more sympathetic and ingratiat-ing than ever before. "You are certainly very busy!"

"Oh, it goes okay — it goes okay," the giant stammered as if he had to fend all praise from himself.

"No, I know," the little one persisted, "you do rarely begrudge yourself rest. And here I find it actually won-derfully nice of you that you still seek us out so late in the evening. Have you at least got your wagon with you for the trip back?"

"No, Hertha. That doesn't matter at all though. One of our draught horses actually has — let me think now — gotten a stone in the front hoof. And then my mother suggested —".

"Yes, what did she suggest then?", it burst out hastily from his listener. "What did the old lady suggest then again?"

"Oh, she was merely suggesting," the young farmer replied, confused a little by her vehemence, "that in our circumstances, the way would be much easier on my legs than those of our sick mare. And then I must also say though, the old lady is perfectly right again. Don't you think?" Here he laughed quietly to himself, and looked benevolently down at his tall turned-down boots. "But my God," he added in shock, "I am forgetting entirely to ask how it is going with your mother? Look, Hertha, when I see you in particular, then —".

He broke off, and his honest grey eyes, which had sought the floor for so long, rose to the splendour of Hertha's blond hair, which seemed in this half-dark space to be filled with an inner light.

It sparkled and glistened. Little glow worms in the dark bushes could not twinkle more surprisingly on Saint John the Baptist's Day[*].

The giant was thinking of that at this moment in the half-dark room. Yes, his good mood even forgot for the moment that in the adjoining room an invalid was languishing. One — two — three of Saint John's little glow worms. Thus he counted. My God, how glorious and strange those golden wavy, silken threads were.

But the girl thus admired did not like to endure his everlasting silence.

"What happens when you see me?", she guided him again back onto the track he had left. "And why are you looking at my hair so persistently? Do you see something in it?", she added with a graceful turn of her charming head.

Only, now the giant was so embarrassed that he could only stammer out incoherent sounds. Hertha then decided to prepare a quick end for this get-together. With a bold grip, she shoved her arm under his, and as she pulled the balking man with gentle force to the ill woman's room, she whispered to him, "Because you are so gallant, Heinrich, you shall also get to see my mother. You know that she is very attached to you. Much more

---

[*]   24th June.

than you deserve, you big, awkward man. And now come."

With that she led the farmer, who in his bashfulness no longer attempted to offer her any resistance, over the threshold.

But how strange! In the broad room through which the ceiling lamp poured such a bright, friendly shimmer, it had meanwhile become ever stiller and more soundless. The old gardener crouched motionlessly by the grandfather clock, the white hyacinth pressed firmly between his knees, and his incessantly moving lips seemed to count the gliding back and forth of the pendulum. Only from time to time was his white ragged head seen to bend down deeper to the glass with the white flower, as if he intended to establish in quiet curiosity whether the wondrous bulb had not struck a root in the meantime.

"For it comes down to that."

"Mother," the girl called with her rousing voice, "Heinrich Kalsow is here. The big tall son of your friend from Werrahn with whom you sat on a school bench. See, here he is. And he has brought with him a hare that he has shot for you. Will you not like to thank him for it?"

But what did that signify? Mrs Boddin did not stir. Surely her departing powers of understanding seemed to have caught the familiar sounds. But the dark eyes remained wearily and weakly directed at both the arrivals, and without any special astonishment at the sudden entrance of the visitor, it poured mutely over her strangely shaking lips, "How it smells, Hertha. And the beautiful pure air. And the great, wide garden full of red and white hyacinths."

"Yes, Madam," the wizened little man rasped from by the brown grandfather clock. "How well you can see that. Thus have I actually planted the beds in my garden. There it is working out very well."

"Mother," the blue rococo figurine cried suddenly, shaken by fear, as she drew back step by step, and, without knowing it, clasped at the same time the hand of her companion in a tight grip, "Mother! Do you not see Heinrich?"

"Oh yes," the recumbent woman whispered without stirring. And her jerking breath occasionally cut through the erupting voice. "Heinrich — I know well — he brings goodness. But what use is all that? When I am gone now, then they will all invade through the doors, and want to carry you away, my poor child!"

"Me, mother? Who then?"

"Oh, poverty. That ugly black poverty. See, she is sitting there by the clock and holding a crust of bread in her hand. Haven't you noticed?"

When both the young people turned to the corner in suddenly climbing horror, they saw there how Jochen Tobis slowly raised his head to peer at the clock face.

"Yes, yes," he murmured at the same time to himself, drawing the black, creased military coat somewhat closer about himself, "now it will soon be time for me."

In the quiet space, you could distinctly hear the heavy action of the clockwork. It sounded as if something invisible were striding with soft soles over the floor.

But the ill woman continued speaking. Sensible and incomprehensible things merged in confusion.

"Heinrich," she slurred, "my good boy. You cannot understand it. But how will it be? What can the future bring her if the tender thing should straightaway struggle with hardship and deprivation? Oh, that murderous ghost! It sits on my chest, Heinrich, because it wants to squeeze my throat shut. And do you not see at all how it stretches out its gaunt, fleshless bony hand to

tousle the bright, golden hair of my child? Oh, how I always liked tending to it! Heinrich — Hertha," she cried
out, "I am scared!"

Did something cold really skim over the young,
powerful man, making his limbs shudder as if with a
chill? Or did the powerful tremors and shaking which
penetrated the giant before this bed signify only sympathy and pity for the girl who wordlessly held his arm
clasped as if she must never ever release this last hold.
Fitfully, and with a haste which was usually foreign to
him, the farmer drew his companion to the half-length
curtains of the window, and they both surely did not
know that he had stretched out to the helpless girl both
paws in which she had nestled her delicate hands dully
and without consciousness.

"Hertha, it isn't going well for your dear mother."

"But that must not be, must not," the little one
stammered, and kicked her foot out without consideration for her surroundings. And without preliminaries, as
if chased, she added yet, "Heinrich, you aren't going
now, are you? You won't leave me here alone?"

"No, no, Hertha! How can you think that? And especially when so many awful things are now clustering
around you," he stuttered awkwardly afterwards. "See, I
know it is not the time for it now, but my dear child, I
should ask you — that is, my mother suggested it as it
were — whether it would not be proper if you later —.
No, no," he excused himself as if shocked before one of
her flashing glances. "No misfortune will occur, quite
certainly not."

"Do you want to offer me perhaps a favour?", the
blue porcelain figurine filled with indignation as she
tore her hand from him half unwillingly. But as they
both quarreled with one another, the broken voice again
rose from the white pillows, "How will I save my youngest from hardship? How will I protect my youngest from

poverty? Jochen Tobis," the ill woman suddenly rattled from her stiffening chest, "why are you putting out glaring white hyacinths about me? They are growing higher and higher. Quite high, like snow covered trees. Oh, how good it smells — snow — sweetly scented snow."

But by the window, another voice cried out at the same moment shrilly and in whipped-up fear, "Do you hear, Heinrich? Did you hear that? No, no, I don't want to sink into poverty. I don't want to fall back into hardship. How will I protect myself from it? Tell me, how in all the world?"

Then the giant, who had striven through all the years of his childhood for this one high, unreachable dream, indulged in all the gravity and strength of an unspent nature, then the tough steady man, who towered so hulking in his tall farmer's boots, then it was up with him. With his large fists, he seized both arms of the girl in an overflowing, rising feeling which almost made him sob. These full taut arms which barely gave under the pressure.

She cried out wildly.

"What do you want, Heinrich?"

"Oh, Hertha, dear little Hertha," he stammered, "you should come to us, my mother wanted to tell you. And then — and then — if you want, if you really would make me so happy — — It is not the hour for that now, but you can believe me — I would — I would —. I swear to you, Hertha, you could be so without worry, for see, my dear little child — I would do everything to —".

Only, again the words of the giant would swirl away unfinished.

Look though, look, both of you by the window!

How pale and outstretched the woman lies there with her delicate, spiritually marked countenance. And why does the old gardener rise quite suddenly from his corner, why does he tilt his white shaggy head, and speak to himself, nodding his head and like someone who has long expected something, "I note it well, now she has struck roots. But where, where, that we men do not know. And over that we brood. For it all comes down to the roots. Everything in our incomprehensible life. Yes, yes, Madam, so it is. And now adieu."

And with that he again nestled his white flower under his black creased coat, and shuffled slowly out of the desolate room.

But behind him, the silence remained heavy and impenetrable.

2

This is the living room of Mrs Lotte Kalsow in Werrahn.

It is a large broad room placed at ground level so that the three windows which peer forth behind black and white printed cotton curtains rise barely a metre above the spacious, poorly cobbled farmyard strewn with straw, equipment, and all sorts of manure heaps. If you stand in the middle of the shiny white floor in the massive room, then the male friends of Mrs Lotte, but especially the tall gaunt sexton Vierarm who sits at the moment right opposite the old lady on the window sill by her small mahogany sewing table, are surprised ever anew over why both the enormous beams, covered with a light blue wallpaper, and sinking year by year somewhat lower from the ceiling, why both these faithful supports of the house have not long since dared to make the attempt to look at the world from below. Only, both the venerable house guardians have like all the other things in the small farm of Werrahn assumed, through the constant traffic with Mrs Lotte, such a sterling quality and so much sense of duty that they would certainly never ever bring to fruition such a rebellious plan, at least as long as mother Kalsow is calculating with her pencil under them.

No, that would really be out of the question.

And as Mrs Lotte moistens the pencil a little with her tongue, and at the same time sends a calculating look away over her sharp glasses at the ceiling, both the light blue giants look down as deferentially and ready to be of service to the delicate busy woman in the large white farm apron as if they wanted to strengthen again and again the tiny wizened lady's trust with the succinct sentences, "You, Mrs Lotte, and we. We keep the house. We with our load-bearing, and you with your pencil. And that we have aged a bit together is of no matter, the years make us fast. Stay firm."

And the blessing of the house in Werrahn perhaps consists in that.

A small taste of this well-tried house maxim is also placed before the sexton Vierarm on this morning where the mist rolls across the yard in grey, hazy masses. He is just reaching for the warm cup of coffee which is sending out its steam in broad leisureliness before him on the sewing table. Then he listens for a moment to the dull bellowing of the cows which rings drawn out and clear through the impenetrable mist. And as his thread-like figure shivers a little, he peers, turning his beardless head back, once more at the vigorously crackling fire which hisses and flickers over there in the humble, green tiled stove.

"Do you allow, Mrs Lotte Kalsow of Werrahn," he begins with a sort of reverent solemnity which must have been poured into him probably by his clerical office. "Don't resent me it, Mrs Lotte Kalsow of Werrahn, if I suggest to you — in all modesty of course — that such a cup of coffee for a man's stomach when it is three degrees below zero, — — well yes, you comprehend surely — —. I don't want perhaps to challenge your hospitality. No, that lies far from me. But I would like to maintain, Mrs Lotte Kalsow, that a glass of grog, in particular with a prevailing temperature of three degrees below zero, appears digestible to the human body, and also not unwholesome to the upper brain attributes. As said, do not misunderstand me, I will also drink this. But it is yet something different. And I was just thinking."

Only, his slender opposite just shook her head severely and dismissively. Her white bonnet with its black velvet ribbons trembled at the same time as if gripped by inner ire, and the hooked nose of the little lady appeared to point somewhat more sharply, before its owner now bent forward vigorously to tap the table top warningly with her finger.

"Young folk — young folk," she disagreed with displeasure, whereby it did not trouble her further that the youngster of a sexton who sat opposite her in a shabby brown frock coat had long since shut the door of youthful folly behind himself. He might number sixty. But that was of no matter, for these words formed a favourite expression of mother Lotte, and also suppressed the testimony of an inwardly benevolent mood. "It is terrible," she continued, "what habits the young folk of today become addicted to." At the same time, her gleaming brown eyes stabbed about furiously at the motionless, venerable countenance of her visitor. "Are you not at all ashamed, sexton Vierarm, that you cannot keep away from the vice of alcohol, just like all the other young folk here in the district? I think," she continued more ferociously, and moved her glasses up onto her wizened forehead, "you believe in the devil incarnate? Yes, you even think you have seen him several times already with your own eyes? And of that I have no doubt at all either. For you are a spiritual man, and have occupied yourself much with ghosts and such things. But don't you also think that the incarnate one sits very well in a spirit bottle, and, as soon as it is uncorked, can climb out to push its fists into the neck of such a de-fenceless man-child, and then away with him — march, march — in misery and sorrow?"

"Whether it can do that?" —

The sexton Vierarm felt himself seized by his favourite idea, for he considered himself quite truthfully and in reality to be an exorciser of devils and invoker of spirits, and every man in Werrahn knew that the Prince of Hell with claws, horns, and sulfurous haze had once already sat on the sofa opposite the clerical gentleman in the sexton's room, and later, riding on a sow, had gone out the window. Admittedly, Christian Vierarm, as he himself admitted, had entertained his distinguished visitor that evening with grog. — When the sexton felt reminded of that most august mission of his, he forgot for a moment both his freezing limbs and the meek, en-ticing desire for the golden yellow drink, and enthused completely in the tone of one of the lesser prophets.

"Mrs Lotte Kalsow of Werrahn," he perked up, and at the same time, he raised his bushy, black eyebrows, which formed a strange contrast with his tousled, iron-grey mane, frightfully high. "Yes, it is true, the devil skulks about the countryside, and spits hellish phlegm into the souls of youth. You can believe me, I have met him in all possible forms recently. He has shoved him-

self into the middle of everything. With the gentlemen
officers, he sits in a shiny bright uniform at table in the
mess, and clinks champagne glasses with them. For he
does not do it under this noble drink in such excellent
company. And in the businessmen's clubs, and in the
captains' associations within the city, he sits there behind the table, and plays left and right. You know
already, "God's Blessing at Cohn" and "My Aunt, Your
Aunt." For our business folk call such exciting things
these days their recreation. And with the young girls of
today, God it's lamented, there he goes now straight in
and out. He has himself engaged by them as a maid, and
makes mad hairdos for them so that you'd think the
stork has built his nest on the back of their head by mistake. Yes, yes, Mrs Lotte Kalsow of Werrahn, do not be
amazed, my eyes take note of all that, for they are spiritually sharpened. And if then the young ladies want to
have themselves dressed by him, yes, cheers, do you
think perhaps that he really dresses them? Eh where!
Everywhere you see instead the pure, bright godly flesh
peering out. He then dubs it style and naturalness, the
hellish swindler. And what remains worst of all, when
the poor seduced things then go to bed in the evening
after they have chattered all sorts of blasphemous nonsense during the day, then the delicate maid pushes for
them such books under the pillow as will finish off the
unwise, perverted heads. There the devil in fact has a
whole series of writer fellows which they now call philo-
sophers. Mrs Lotte Kalsow of Werrahn, I am though
also a philosopher, and Pastor Fielitz even said recently
to me that I represent the transcendental viewpoint.
What do you say to that? The intellectual man honoured
me so greatly! But this new philosophy by which the
young folk shall be allowed everything, but also purely
everything, for example, that they no longer honour the
proper registry office, or get straight any of their own

religion — well that is then also such a fine sort of religion — and that they declare tradition and modesty to
be blatant nonsense, no, I do not engage myself with the
new sort of philosophy. But as said, Mrs Lotte Kalsow of
Werrahn, don't take it the wrong way, the worst of all,
the true emissaries of Satan, that remains the women.
Excuse me, you are not one at all. I mean of the sort described. But the proper women, Mrs Lotte, they are
assessed like the parable of the girl who lost her way, so
that you would like to plonk a tree in their path to call to
them, 'Stop, for your feet are walking the path of shame
and your hands are snares."

After these expositions, the sexton poured a great
quantity of his hot coffee down, shook as a result of the
unaccustomed drink, and gasped a few times. The mistress of the large farm, however, adjusted her glasses,
and after she had made a knot in the threads with which
she was just then wanting to sew, she threw from her
narrow brown eyes a penetrating look at the tall man.

"Listen to me please, Mr Vierarm," she spoke distinctly and forthrightly, as was her way, "do you perhaps
mean someone specific perhaps with this young girl?"

"A specific one? No, why should I?", the visitor
replied, seeking in vain to fathom the meaning of the
question. "I don't know at all —".

"Oh, I just thought that", the tiny woman continued,
avidly sewing again, "you had possibly heard tell here in
the house that we perhaps had received an addition.
Hertha Boddin. You know her from before. For, in the
event the Colonel's wife in town should perhaps be
taken from us, may God preserve her, —"

"Yes," the sexton inserted unctuously in-between,
"who counts the days of man?"

"Then, dear friend, I decided — that is, understand
me right, I just intended it temporarily — that I would

then like to take in the daughter of my childhood friend."

"Miss Hertha?", the sexton now started. "The creature with the sinful golden hair?"

"That is just tattle," the mother cut him off, creasing her furrowed brow. "How can the little girl help having a beautiful head of hair? But I wanted to ask you now, dear friend, since I place great value on your knowledge of human nature, whether you believe that the little thing would fit without difficulty for herself, but mainly also without disturbance for us, into our circle and particularly into our entire being and way of life? What do you make of her?"

"What do I make of her?" The sexton rose, and his tall figure stretched up so alarmingly that his listener had to lean back so as not to lose the man's iron-grey hair from her sight. Then he flailed his arms excitedly.

"Mrs Lotte Kalsow of Werrahn," the questioned man began with an extremely deep voice. "You want to know about this little one? Now, then I will tell you, in her sits one of the thousand demons which unfortunately our Lord and Saviour could not drive out from this beautiful earth."

"Are you not also mistaken?", mother Kalsow interrupted doubtfully.

"No, Madam, there can be no talk of a mistake at all. Look, how she back as an eight year old thing, when she was out here visiting you at Werrahn — you will well remember — then she once ran up to me in church on Sunday with short skirt and bare legs. For she came straight from catching crabs out of the Schwarzbach stream. And when I had pointed out to her this wanton behaviour, and forbade her it, what do you surely think happened then? Did she perhaps run home ashamed to you, Mrs Lotte? Not a trace. After the service in fact, it had to happen to me that I saw the godless thing sitting up in the branches of the cherry tree which hung over right there next to the churchyard wall. There she was sitting quite cheerfully on a swaying branch, and think, she was swinging her bare, unclothed feet still, although your own son, namely our Mr Heinrich, was standing under her, and she was throwing one red cherry after another at his head. See, Mrs Lotte, and then my inner voice was already speaking loudly to me at the time, 'this little one is lacking dear shame, and she also has that unconscious and innate defiance.' Such creatures I know. And if you ask me, 'shall I take into my house the young lady with the formerly bare legs?', then I will answer you in all truthfulness, 'No, Mrs Lotte Kalsow of Werrahn, don't do that, for you have a clean house, and no proper place is to be found with you for such a demon with its sinful golden hair. For like, Madam, must give way to like. And woe to those for whom nuisance arrives in their world!"

Thus the sexton ranted. and he threw his right arm forward as if he were one of those giant signal masts on which a lantern hung which was meant to illuminate the world. The hostess, however, remained silent, and kept sewing.

Then a wild yapping was audible from the yard. You could distinctly hear the rattling and clinking of a chain, and now two brown hunting dogs rushed diagonally across the yard to the entrance.

"Here comes Mr Heinrich," the sexton reported.

And the little woman, who had long since recognised the heavy, ringing steps of her son, sighed a little to herself, and added, "Yes, now we will hear. The boy has been gone the entire night, and that cannot mean anything good."

But if the mistress of Werrahn had guessed in what way her son had completed his journey home, then the quietly stirring concern over her boy would have captured her entire heart.

But how had Heinrich Kalsow arrived home?

***

A reddish yellow day was already dawning over the dilapidated brick walls which shut the town off from the sea when the young farmer strode out along that ruined edifice, through the low buttressed gate of the old fortification, and into the countryside. Up on the ledges and capitals of the grey ruins, a flock of white seagulls crouched, huddled close together. They cried sharply and strangely through the billowing morning mist. And the further the wanderer got with his ringing steps, the stranger and more inexplicably the confused calls of the storm birds followed him. But for the man pondering to himself, the voices in his own chest resounded with much more mysterious and puzzling things, sometimes exulting, sometimes anxiously falling into a dull silence.

But no — but no. He, Heinrich Kalsow, could cherish a great joy. Indeed there behind him, in the walled town, there lay a dead woman. That woman on whom he had hung since earliest youth with timid awe. The wife of a colonel. Dear heaven, how unbelievably distinguished this title had sounded to the little fellow. And was it really thinkable, did it not exceed every probability, that the daughter of this fine, proud lady, that this wonderfully beautiful, glorious creature had placed her hand in his in the midst of the stress and hardship, to then nestle her limbs trembling and shaking against those of her childhood friend as if she wanted to never leave him anymore. Certainly, quite certainly, he could only apprehend the idea of this silent devotion thus. She was so incomprehensible, that shimmering golden creature who constantly dallied like a teasing fairy through the awkward boy's dreams, she had placed her fate without bucking into the mighty work-worn fists of her childhood companion. Why and how, the ever more powerfully striding fellow was unable to account for it. It was so. It was quite definitely so. And even if no audible word had fallen between them, or any cool and sober arrangement had been made, the bond which must outlast a life full of happiness and bliss was concluded, the ring which bound two souls in faith and respectability, he had forged it himself.

The young farmer raised his head high, and looked over the flat, calm land. How precious to think with unspoilt mood of this plain spreading out infinitely. And what he perceived there, he felt to be almost like his own fate. Over the stubble fields, a milk-white, seething mist, which the quietly drawing wind aired a little only occasionally. Yes, his youth had past. In darkness and apprehension. But quite beyond, over the brown arable land, was the vehemently seething disc not climbing up red-hot there? Quite certainly, the future sparkled for him. That distant land of joy on whose borders he had tapped until now, into whose inviting open country he will march now with his firm, pithy steps. Certainly, the last word had not been given. The absolutely certain and ledger-like word, such as his mother loved. But that was not needed at all either, a comforting voice in his inner being contradicted this doubt. Such businesslike behaviour could not be desired from the young being in all the distress of the moment. No, what remained raised above all objections of the mind was finally that powerfully erupting emotion which had driven the abandoned girl into his arms, that elemental, seething passion which still roared now in all his, the strong man's, veins. It seemingly shook him so that his gait lost its constancy. No, that was genuine, that alone formed the lasting thing.

And thus he rolled on, his feet submerged in the mist, his head though held up to the blazing flames of the morning sun.

***

A fearful silence arose when Heinrich Kalsow had imparted to the mistress of Werrahn the passing of her childhood friend. The old lady sat unmoving in the yellow wicker chair before her sewing table, and looked rigidly at the white floor. The son also lingered silently before her, and if both the brown hunting dogs had not weaved about the young farmer snuffling and sniffing, and if the sexton Vierarm had not expressed in a strange, jarring twang his sympathy for the woman who had passed away, the trepidation in the large broad room would have become almost overwhelming. The returned man followed with suspense every movement of the old woman.

Would his mother now surely shed a tear over her lost childhood friend? He almost wished it. For he had never seen the gaunt old woman cry or even show a more vigorous emotion. Only, as tensely as he waited, the facial features of his mother did not change in any way this time either. She instead kept her brown eyes riveted for a long time and thoughtfully on the floor until she finally raised her head to emit slowly and with consideration, "Again one less loving soul. Well then, we will all be called away and make place for you younger ones. That is God's will. And now, my boy, did you buy the winter seed?"

The son, who towered powerfully and sturdily before her in his turned up boots, shook off his thoughts, all the dreams and hopes which wanted to whir back to the town like white doves to circle the beloved blond head there. How would he be able to make clear to his mother and put behind him this greatest of occurrences in his life? If she were now to lose that cool restraint opposite this outsized happiness which filled him completely, that cool restraint which he had constantly so admired in her with business matters?

"Did you buy the winter seed?", his mother, Lotte, repeated anew, as if the news of death were now dealt with once and for all.

"Yes, mother — yes — that is dealt with."

"With whom?"

"With the merchant Kirstein, mother, I met him at the market."

"So, so." The mistress of Werrahn began playing with her pencil. "So with the Jew? Did you also see the stock list beforehand, Heinrich?"

"Yes, mother, everything was done. And the man treated me quite properly."

"And how much was it?", his mother inquired further, as she adjusted her glasses, and drew a little blue notebook out of the drawer of her sewing table.

"I have for the present bought for 800 marks."

"Good. Clover seed as well?"

"Yes, mother. And then I also ordered a sample of his superphosphate."

"Well, yes," the old woman puckered her lips a little, "you are for these artificial means. See, my dear sexton, that is how the youth think today. And now just let me note the expenditure."

With that she carefully wetted her pencil, and began awkwardly accounting with her little scribbly letters in the blue notebook.

Heinrich, however, looked at the sexton, who made no arrangements at all to conclude his visit. And when now a sharp, cosy aroma arose down the hall from the adjoining kitchen, indicating clearly a braising goose, the young farmer saw with unease how the gaunt, clerical gentleman sat down full of cheerful expectation on the green rep sofa, directly under a small plaster statue of the saviour who was spreading out his hands of bless-ing over the world. And hence sexton Vierarm himself presumably considered his place and his hope for some lovely roast as absolutely endorsed by heaven.

Then Heinrich Kalsow shook his short-cropped blond head with displeasure. The man must go, for he hindered him from the discussion which should now follow.

"Mother," he rose. "I want to ask you something."

The little woman did not look up, but continued her writing.

"So?" she responded. "Do it, my boy. You want surely to inquire about how our ill white mare is going?"

"Yes, that too, mother. Of course."

And when mother Lotte, still immersed in her work, had assured him that she had placed with her own hands a chamomile compress over the suffering horse's aching hoof, he began anew, stuttering and hesitantly, as he slung his arm a little about the back of the old lady's chair.

"Understood, mother, chamomile is good. But see, I wanted in particular to tell you something in secret. Something just between us, since it only concerns the both of us, mother. Will you?"

The powerful voice had brought this unmistakeable wish up so distinctly as well that the sexton still did not comprehend the tender request.

"And some garlic belongs with it," it passed through the man's mind at this moment approvingly.

Then all the blessed mist of the future which curled already so pleasantly and teasingly to his nose, was shooed away by the cool words from mother Kalsow of Werrahn.

"You want to speak with me alone, Heinrich?"

"Yes, mother, don't take it wrongly, but it is needed."

The Girl Who Lost Her Way

The old woman turned a little to the sexton and pushed her glasses back on her forehead anew. "Then it is no use, my dear sexton. You see how it goes here. And you surely remember what we were speaking about. Now it comes. I will be delighted to see you here another time."

"Oh, but that is a pity," the sexton sighed, whereby he slowly rose like as if he had all the time in the world. "But family discussions happen of course. You are surely having roast goose today?", he added, still lost in dream, when he had already grasped the ancient woolen top hat which formed his pride. "Yes, Mrs Lotte Kalsow of Werrahn, roast goose is a gift from God. In particular, when it receives a little bit of garlic, as the Jewish folk tend to apply to it so admirably. Otherwise I am not so much, as you well know, in favour of the offspring of Abraham. But in roasting geese, we can learn from them. And now farewell, Mrs Lotte Kalsow of Werrahn. And ponder in a serious spirit what I have told you about the golden blond demon. For I am a connoisseur of people, and see human matters in their development. God, how beautiful that roast goose smells! Good morning, Mrs Lotte."

After these words, he put the enormous cylinder on his tousled head, and when, after an awkward bow, he strode with his spindly legs in stiff dignity across the yard, he looked as if a giant brown-scarred beech trunk, from which all the branches had been carefully hacked off beforehand for this attempt, had come upon the idea of taking a little stroll. At the entrance, however, sexton Vierarm hesitated once more, sniffed with a last effort, and murmured to himself, enraged, "I owe this golden blond demon the beautiful roast goose which escaped me. There we have it. Did I not say it? All adversity comes from women."

***

The hour had finally approached in which the giant Heinrich Kalsow wanted to speak with his mother about his fate. And he began that as follows. He was still standing before her, but now he bent his broad-shouldered figure a bit down to the little woman, and at the same time twiddled bashfully with the horn buttons of his grey fleece jacket.

"Mother," he began with controlled voice, and yet in trembling self-consciousness. "It was a bad night. That you cannot imagine at all."

The old woman, who, for the first time during the en-tire conversation, let her hands, on which the blue veins ran in so many branches, rest unoccupied in her lap, moved her head a little in reflection.

"Yes, my boy," she informed him, "you have not yet seen many people die. Someone who has seen his entire family pass away, like I have, and who has in addition stood here in the village by so many beds of suffering, also becomes accustomed to it. And habit, my boy, eventually dulls against everything. Certainly, youth may not believe it," she added, more for herself.

The young farmer, however, breathed deeply, and seemed to want to shake off his memory. Then it poured forth from his innermost being, "I will in any case never forget it, mother. Now the Colonel's wife lies there, so still and calm, as if she were only resting. But as long as she still had breath, then —".

"What, my boy?"

"Mother, I don't know at all actually whether I may share it with you. For it seems to me as if it had been a secret which the distinguished old lady emitted from her lips only in her fear of death. You know, mother, it was almost as if she had to absolutely entrust this last thing to someone."

"Was nobody else with her then?", mother Lotte inquired as if not comprehending, and moved her glasses imperceptibly.

"No, mother, only Hertha and I."

"So just you two alone. So, so." The old woman gazed for a moment inquiringly into the face of her son, in which she saw an agitation foreign to her trembling. And then she asked directly as if the young man had not just then uttered a serious misgiving, "So, what did the Colonel's wife say at the end? Make it quick!"

Then her son told her. He hid nothing. All the tormenting heartache by which the dying woman was tortured, her nameless fear of poverty, as well as the horror of being overtaken by hardship, even the half incomprehensible sighs of the woman passing away, he had preserved everything in his faithful memory. And in deep, genuine sympathy, he sought, as his own heart pounded mightily, to awaken the concern or perhaps even the cooperation of his listener. But mother Kalsow hardly stirred, and although she had listened in great suspense, she now grasped her pencil anew as if she intended to transcribe the facts she had just then heard into numbers.

"Yes," she nodded, as she sought to look over at the awkward man who only with effort hid the trembling of his powerful limbs. "Yes, my boy, that I well imagine. My friend Mathilde did not economise quite so well. She never needed too much for herself. But for her husband. For her handsome husband. How that should happen with so many women who think then that the world is governed with that bit of love. Oh, it is not so at all."

"But mother," Heinrich suddenly intervened in haste and excitement. "You were yourself such a good wife to our father."

"No, let that be," mother Kalsow interrupted. "That I won't admit to you. You know that the children are not allowed any view over that. That I am not fond of. And now tell me, what will become now of little Hertha? Is she moving to her sister, Professor Rogge's wife? Or —".

Now the decision must be made. If he did not obtain the courage now to make clear to the strict mistress of Werrahn the complete facts, on which there was nothing to be done, then — this he knew from experience — the moment would be missed irretrievably. A thousand matters of the day would lead the little woman now here, now there, the daily grind of work would hinder her from lending him a willing ear so soon again. Thus it must happen now. And finally — he also had a will for it. And if he had also almost never brought it up with his mother before today, the man on whose shoulders the main burden of the work rested, the son, who did not rest all summer and winter long to increase the maternal possessions, stood firm on one thing, the wish of his own heart, there he must remain master, there only one opinion counted, and that was his own. All the young people in the country thought so. It had pushed itself between young and old like a new law. And the awkward man straightened up, and was resolved to obey this wise command.

"Mother," he stated, and his voice suddenly sounded loud and pithy through the room. "Hertha will not be moving to her sister's."

"No?", the old woman then asked, without stirring. "Where then?"

Here was the moment. The moment stood before the doubting man like a dark figure raising a black club against him. Higher and higher. Now fell the blow. And he ducked instinctively.

"Mother," he burst out hoarsely, as his hand began stroking the back of the wicker chair insistently and hastily without thinking. "I told her that she should, that it conformed with your own wish —".

"What did you tell her?"

"That she — that she —". And now the giant tried, like a little child who is begging, to grasp his mother's hand. "That she would be welcome in our house. I told her that. And look, mother," he continued with overflowing goodness, "here with us it is not at all so bad. What does one more head here at Werrahn amount to, right? And mother, see, if you should perhaps believe nevertheless, which would though be really quite improper, that you would have more costs to budget through the increase, see mother, you should not notice it in the slightest." He straightened up, expanded his chest, and now breathed fresh and easy, and as if with relief. "For mother," he laughed with full throat, "look at me now, can I not work ten fellows into the ground? And I promise you that I will honestly do that, for I rejoice now in Hertha's staying with us. Yes, that is it, I rejoice. And now mother, don't make such a serious face at me, for it was you yourself who came upon the idea. No, dear mother, tell me rather that I have acted rightly, and that it is a pleasure for you."

Only in Werrahn, hasty answers were never provided to rushed questions. So it also happened now. The old woman leant still and erect in her wicker chair, and while her left hand was still being held by her son, her right, holding the pencil, stroked the mahogany table top of the sewing table a few times as if dusting. Then Mrs Lotte even blew a bit of dust from the shiny surface.

"That's right, mother," Heinrich Kalsow stuttered, a little concerned already by the unexpected silence. "It is good with you, and I have acted properly."

"Properly?" The old woman raised her strangely narrow countenance slowly, and in her calm eyes there was no agreement to be read.

"Yes, my son," she began with serious restraint, and it was noticed how she considered every single word. "I have surely thought of this plan in passing, but I did not know at the time, Heinrich, that you would be so utterly rash in constituting such wishes. That does not conform at all to your usual ways. And hence, my boy, I would like once more to have explained why you were so hasty just in this instance?"

But instead of providing an answer, Heinrich just opened wide his large grey eyes with their thick blond bushy brows, and at the same time, he balled his fists in astonishment. What? Hasty? Yes, dammit, his old lady must finally notice that? Why did she ask about that first? Did this well-considered hesitation not look entirely as if the calculating old lady wanted to oppose the wishes which stormed more and more wildly through his breast, as madly and chasing as when the spring storm was whipping and shaking the poplars by the stream, did it not seem as if the mistress of the house wanted to oppose this ardent desire at the outset with an insurmountable barrier? What did he still have there to explain in full? And with a stubbornness which you would never have trusted this loyal face of youth to possess, he suddenly pushed his firm bull-neck forward, and threw back dully and drily just like the way he was perhaps accustomed to ordering his labourers at ploughing, "Mother, what use is explaining in full here? I want the little girl to move in with us. I want it. And so, good."

Hear, hear! Such a tone had never arisen in front of mother Lotte in Werrahn. The blue wallpaper on the walls seemingly leapt back in fright, and the old lady reclined in her wicker chair as erectly and stiffly as if someone had spoken to her in a foreign language. Then the slender blue-veined hand instinctively rose to her wizened breast while the fingers moved trembling.

It went still. Until the old woman breathed deeply and audibly.

"You want it thus?" she said quite gently, and at the same time, a practised ear would hardly have been able to perceive any inner agitation in the speaker. "Yes, yes, you don't want everything in life. Over that, much can be said. But, so that you know it straightaway, Heinrich, I will explain to you at this moment that my wish does not agree with your own. Quiet, I already heard it, you want it! You will be master here at Werrahn after me, and you are actually already so now. And every man must take responsibility for his actions. That you will be very much in need of. And now, my boy, I won't order you to do anything, I won't advise you to do anything, now do what you cannot leave off doing."

The tender little figure rose, and she went with quick short steps to the tiled stove to bend down shivering over the firebox. But as she bent, she turned her sharp head under the white bonnet back to her son once more, who had that day shown himself her master for the first time.

"Good, good," she emitted, and this time something like rising fury from the fire blazed in her even voice. "Do it then as you wish. But with one proviso that you already know, you must not come to me later. With complaints. They have never been willingly listened to at Werrahn. They have been absent from us here for some time. And now, my boy, look for your sister Anna in the cow stalls at once. See if she isn't finished yet. For the three girls have been milking since six o'clock already, and I need them now in the farmstead for doing the laundry. Go!"

Only, why does the young farmer not follow the so clearly stated admonition? Why does he remain standing rapt and struggling with himself in the doorway, from where he sends uneasily questioning looks to the woman who has turned away? Might he not for the first time in his life be bearing the feeling of his own responsibility? Did he also consider these slender, weak shoulders of mother Lotte to be more suited for bearing the burdens of life than his own which strove so mightily and broadly? He rubbed the grey duffel material of his jacket with both fists until he finally stuttered in clearly erupting anxiety, "Mother, I have something else. The most important thing."

"No, no, no more for today, it is enough."

"Yes, but mother, you must know it straightaway —"

"No," the old woman cut him off, as she warmed her hands before the hissing fire. And this time, she seemed not to want to tolerate any dissent. "Enough, my boy, enough. Perhaps I know everything already. Perhaps even not. Go please. Go! It'll all turn out okay. In life everything comes soon enough."

Then the son let his raised arms sink down to his sides in discouragement, bowed his head between the doorposts as if he intended to stride through under a yoke, and paced out the floor with his ringing steps. Mrs Lotte Kalsow of Werrahn, however, bent lower and lower so that the reflection of the flames played on her withered face, and you could no longer understand what she was murmuring to herself. Only one phrase stood out, "Young folk — young folk."

However, that was just the favoured expression at Werrahn.

3

Jochen Tobis stood in the cemetery. He was planting snowdrops on a freshly buried grave. And under this mound, his old patroness, the wife of Colonel Boddin, had been slumbering for eight days. Bright and luminous, as if from transparent blue glass, the cloudless winter sky stretched over the graveyard. Across the strung-out expanse, the fields of people rose in uneasy, craggy lines. It looked quite wondrous. Here one such last resting place towered high on its projection of earth, there again another slumbered deep down in the furrow so that it seemed wondrous and rapt. In red, turbid splendour, here and there man-high, blood-red bushes of berries rose, as well as infrequent exotic willow shrubs which had assumed in this gentle early winter a sumptuous violet colouring. Enormous bouquets of violets similarly ran rampant over the simple, white and black crosses. Jochen Tobis, however, propped himself on his spade, wrapped his right hand in his green apron, and looked raptly at the country road winding past, which, following the course of the narrow stream, led into the town. Far in the distance, behind the last fields, the sea rested black, iron, and unmoving.

Over the country road, however, a solitary couple strolling along were now approaching. Both dressed in black. The man in a dark overcoat billowing down and with a slouch hat, which he wore a bit tilted forward on the black hair of his head. His dark eyes were also searching the ground as if he dwelt far away from his companion or could not find the solution to an inner discord. The girl at his side, in contrast, was small and delicate, while a long black veil flowed down from her bright head. Certainly never had the clothing of sorrow and despair lent so much enticing and coquettish charm to a girl's figure.

"How prettily she places her feet," the white-haired gardener ruminated, having become aware long before of the presence of the living in this solitude. "Look, fairly dancing, one — two — hopsa, and then again one — two — hopsa. She seemingly twitches and itches in her limbs. Hello, Mademoiselle," he interrupted him-self, and drew his old soldier's cap from his ragged white hair. "I was just here now. And with the favour-able weather, the things here will take root beautifully. With us here outside, all such things become certain and definite. Will you not come in, and visit mother for a bit?"

The couple, who were now looking over the low brick wall running uphill in wavy lines, looked at each other doubtfully.

"Will we go in, Oskar?", Hertha finally asked her companion. And yet it was as if, despite her readiness, a quite shudder shook in the girl's voice before this place.

No wonder! Everything presented itself to the viewer as dilapidated and restless. The gloomy, melancholy charm, the furtive, wistful, divine peace which stretched about this field containing the rubble of human exist-ence, all this the sparkling eyes of the girl were unable to perceive.

Not yet.

She has surely not yet struck root enough, Jochen Tobis would have adjudged. Only, at the moment, the old man also passed his invitation on more insistently to the girl's companion.

"Professor," he suggested, "as I hear it, you are a very clever gentleman. And the son of my sister, who has an ironing facility — very fine laundry, Professor, you can rest easy there with your shirts — her son August tells me often that you tell the boys what happened with man and the folk in olden times. You tell them old stories. But see, Professor, I can do that too. I am in fact able to report to you the entire fate of every mound here. And completely right to the end, Professor. It lies therein. That is the main thing. And if you would set down here a little on the grave which I am planting here, and I will help you out a little, pay attention, then it will be for you a little as if your dear mother-in-law, Colonel Boddin's wife, had not gone away at all, but rather as if she were wanting to tell you from beginning to end her own long story. And it is very instructive. Even for a learned man. Will you now not come closer?"

Here the old man stretched out his hand invitingly with the bunch of snowdrops, and acted as if he had seized the most favourable opportunity for requesting genial company. But to the uncommunicative man with the dry pursed lips and the slender and yet broad shouldered figure, which he carried somewhat hunched forward as if its possessor were constantly seeking something on the ground, to him the invitation of Jochen Tobis seemed to sound absolutely natural. With a vigorous, jerking movement, he threw back his coat and tossed his sharply defined narrow face to the side a little, which he constantly did when he made a decision, to finally utter with a sombre, imperious voice, "Come, Hertha, we will enter."

Only, the little one hesitated, and threw a long lingering, timid look over at the fresh mound of earth.

"Oskar, I think only — I want —".

"You don't want to then?", the Professor suggested curtly, whereby he threw his head about again to the other side. "Then we won't. But decide, in any case. No ambiguity."

"Yes, you see," the charming figurine stuttered, and she pressed her arm under his as if in fright. "It sounds so unloving, Oskar, that mound of earth over there is something strange to me. Something unattractive which distorts my image of my mother. I simply don't like to see such things. You will perhaps find it very mean of me, won't you?"

Her companion threw a half-glance at her, and then shrugged his broad shoulders curtly. Then he set off in motion immediately so that his companion was forced to continue.

"Mean or not," he uttered definitely at the same time, and in his voice that dogged severity came through again which he was so seldom able to shed, "it does not come down to that. The principle thing remains that you don't tell yourself any lies. That, everyone owes to themselves."

And as his steps again strode out more powerfully, and his sombre eyes peered about on the country road anew for something lost, he said raptly to himself, "That is the key principle of all education — — godforsaken philistines! And that is why they dismissed me too!"

"Yes, for it is no different," Jochen Tobis murmured, holding his cap in hand in astonishment as he gazed after both of them walking away in the distance. "For it is no different. For we must still wait a bit for the visit. But it remains funny anyway, Mrs Boddin," he turned to the half-planted mound on which the snowdrops were already stretched protectively. "There you now have a little daughter, and she wants to have nothing more to do with you. Have you perhaps not quite educated her properly? Or does our life today no longer stand quite so decently? What has actually happened to thankfulness? The people out there have degraded so many things. That too, Mrs Boddin? That too? This is remarkable to me."

He pushed the spade into the soft earth, sat down on the grave, and after he had pulled out a crust of bread, he began having his early meal amidst his resting friends.

***

A sharp, regular hoofbeat arose a few moments later behind the two pleasure walkers striding next to each other into the town. And immediately after, between the bare poplars of the main road, through which the wind hummed softly, the white uniforms of two cuirassier officers appeared riding alongside each other in a race. The steel helmets flashed in the morning sun, and from the shiny breast buttons dazzling sparkles shot forth. The long sabres clattered loudly and noisily against the flying flanks of the snorting animals. In unopposed haste, they stormed forwards, the young reddened faces bent forward and directed straight ahead as if it were all about carrying an exultant news of victory through the grey buttressed gate of the old Pomeranian fortress. And yet they brought only the ancient tidings of joyful youth which wants to wrestle mindlessly with life.

"Hey, hey, forwards, Falada!"

"Move your legs, Milord! Do you hear, old boy? A bit of music in the bones!" Thus the powerful voices shouted laughing and unconcerned over the country road, and at once the elegant English hooves of the steeds thundered, striving anew.

Piercing whinnying merged into it.

The Professor suddenly paused, and threw his coat about so that it fluttered in the morning air. Then he thrust at his slouch hat curtly and contemptuously.

"Aha," he said with displeasure, and stuck both his hands in his trouser pockets as if in conscious bourgeois defiance. "The braided gentlemen are craving it once again. Step to the side, little one, so that they don't ride over you at all."

"Would you really be sorry about that, Oskar?" she tossed tossed out once more half unthinkingly, for her soul already looked forward to the martial image.

Instead of an answer, the Professor just pulled his companion to the side so that she staggered. Only, the little one neither felt the ungentle movement, nor had she taken the trouble at all to address the meaning of his action.

"Just look, look, Oskar," she called out instead with interest, and into her voice that light shaking glided again which worked so charmingly on all men. "How well the foremost of the two cuirassiers sits in his saddle. He barely holds the reins in his hands — now he takes the turn! Just look, how sharply he turns his horse! Do you perhaps know the gentleman?"

Her brother-in-law possessed just then time to throw at her with a short irritated laugh, "Admittedly I know him. It is the young Count Hohensee of Wildhagen."

"What? The son of the neighbour of mother Lotte Kalsow at Werrahn?"

The Professor raked at his black goatee, and intended just then to remark disparagingly to his sister-in-law that he had had the honour of educating the young aristocrat during his school days in the common ideas about the command and course of history, only his response had already been engulfed by the thundering gallop of the horses. At the same pitch, it roared now dull and thudding — bam, bam — bam, bam. And quick as thought, like a white cloud driven along by the storm, both the rushing horses would certainly have blown past the pair, when — at the last moment — the blond creature, so deeply veiled in black clothes of mourning, could not resist a flashing, completely compelling inspiration over which she could not give any sort of account, no, she could not withstand it any longer. What drove her to this pertness, she did not apprehend. Yes, her cool mind was marvelling in the next moment, when the incident had already completely concluded, at her own act with an unbelieving smile.

But yet it had happened.

Right before her, in the yellow dust of the country road, her little leather handbag suddenly lay. It had slid down so quickly and imperceptibly that not even the Professor waiting next to her could have determined whether the little bag had been thrown or had fallen down unintentionally.

Very deft, really extraordinarily skilful.

And see, all her further calculations also met the light of reality with lightning speed.

"Hey, hey! Stop, Milord! Obey my boy!"

The reins of the gleaming black horse are pulled at vigorously, the animal climbs up a little, but, straight afterwards, the figure of a tall white rider springs rattling from the saddle.

"Here, most gracious," a laughing voice speaks as the little bag is presented carefully by the two fingers of a cuirassier's glove. "I hope that this precious leather object got away without any damage. I have the honour!"

With that the rider sets his tall gleaming boot in the stirrup again, and in the next moment, he is surely already racing away. Only, now something insignificant must hinder the separation. Right at the moment when he wants to swing up, something distant and ridiculously small, which nonetheless guides all human fate, then compels the young aristocrat so that all of a sudden a quite especially delicate woman's boot must attract his attention. A small, narrow, patent leather shoe.

"By God!"

Young Count Fritz von Hohensee is a connoisseur of women. Of all his regimental comrades, he is noted for it. And he himself just smiles when it is contested.

"By God!"

He must look up, and nothing further happens than that two pairs of eyes read one another in astonishment, yes, almost in shock, for a short while.

The encounter only lasts for a moment scurrying past, then something is stammered, the pairs of eyes separate nonchalantly, and, shortly afterwards, the clattering of the steed announces that a wordless tale has been broken off in the midst of its telling. Entirely at an end? Jochen Tobis knows better. He knows the end. And the chronicle reports further.

***

The silence which, after this insignificant occurrence, arises between the two walkers was not interrupted anymore. They did not stride next to each other anymore, but an interval held them apart.

There was probably no intention in it. Only when they were striding through the low arch of the town gate, and the ringing of their steps echoed from the bare walls, did Hertha lift her blond head to express something incidental. And yet her brother-in-law noted with tart disapproval how much the soul of the girl still fluttered about those frivolous and inane things.

"Oskar, I think I did not even thank the young officer once for his courtesy. And yet at the same time, it was actually a breakneck stunt which he dared for me, don't you think?"

The Professor wrinkled his brow, and stroked his goatee with one of his fitful movements.

"Certainly," he replied, and at the same time, he shook his coat as if he must fend something alien, something irksome to him away from his entire being. "That you should not have forgotten to do. Just think, what a want of breeding, and how will the dear Miss be judged in the mess! But now leave off the chatter," he interrupted, whereby he pulled out his watch. "Your sister Agnes will have gotten up in the meantime, and you know she does not like waiting. For me myself, however, the so-called work nears once again. Threshing rubbish notes in the town library. — I no longer have anything else to do."

"Do you not give any lessons at the High School anymore, Oskar? Is it really true — —?"

"True, true. You hear of course that they have had me dismissed. Because of religious misinstruction. A second Socrates. Or at least suspended. Do you understand what that means?"

"Oskar, did you not then like giving instruction to those dumb brats? Does some inner need not exist for you?"

"Like? Hm!" The man threw a side glance at her, and began inquiring into and reading the narrow, luminous countenance. He sought again. "Like?", it finally came out once more. And an inner fervour spoke along with it in secret. "If they just let me. If I just once were permitted to teach as I wanted, then — —. But let us leave that. Enough," he concluded, pulling together his coat with hasty fingers as if he were thereby able to enshroud his innermost being again. "Here our ways separate."

They had arrived at the small, sloping market, surrounded by pointed-gabled houses, from where a crooked side lane curved to the town library.

Then it occurred to the little, incurious creature as a good last thing, that she must show some pleasantry to the parting man. She thought about it as a moment scurried past.

"I have already often asked you to show me your collection of pictures and sketches," she started finally with quick resolve. "Why do you refuse me so persistently?"

"Hm." The man murmured something, tossed his head to the left and right, and wrinkled his furrowed brow. "What do you know about it?" he began finally, not quite amiably. "Has Agnes told you something?"

She offered her hand in parting, which the Professor, whose gaze again strayed about restlessly between the bumpy cobblestones, did not notice.

"Do you not remember?" she replied, "how you recently locked your pictures away in your chest really bashfully when I accidentally entered your study? Are the images so dangerous then?"

At the same time, she twisted her blossoming lips into a smile. But her flighty being irritated the man in the overcoat.

"Dangerous? I want to give you good advice, Hertha, leave off the coquetry with such — well yes, with such serious things. And hide? You are right. There are even men who guard the last thing they possess, their only treasure, with mean avarice. I perhaps count myself amongst such misers too. They are nasty fellows! And now I must go."

They offered each other their hands, and soon the man had vanished around that corner which had to deprive the girl of his sight.

Would he surely turn back once more?

Hertha stood on the steps which led up to the house of her brother-in-law, and waited. She waited almost yearningly for a friendly greeting. She had until now been so much accustomed to such sunny blossomings of life. And now even deprived of the smallest attentiveness? Only, his steps rang out more and more distantly. And now the sea wind swished over the open square, and it made the girl's long black veil flutter like a large black bird which wanted to claw itself firmly into her blond hair.

Then she lowered her head, and climbed up the few steps with heavy, aggrieved thoughts which seemed to take her heart in calloused fists.

It was now her home. A desolate, rough, comfortless place. And the little golden blond dreamt yet of fairy tale castles and cheering subjects!

"Wait!"

***

The afternoon had sunk down gently and greying. From the sea, a blackish mist climbed up, billowed over the town walls, and now lay heavy and impenetrable on the roofs of the small town like gun smoke after a massive battle.

On this afternoon, Hertha stood by the window of the Professor's residence and looked over at the hulking town hall in the middle of the market. It had been erected from enormous grey stones back during the time of the Dukes of Pomerania, and in front on the round bell tower which had an awkward red cap pressed deep over its head, there you could still see the embrasures from which Slavic Pomeranians had tossed stony greetings on the heads of pillaging Poles and wild Swedes. Now an iron hurricane lantern hung down from a considerable height, endeavouring pitifully with its single little flame to penetrate through the thick mist. Only with little joy. It looked as if a piece of rotting wood somewhere from a dark cellar were twitching back and forth in dull light.

Comfortless desolation and a leaden silence was surrounding the deserted square. But even in the broad, humble room at whose window the girl was still leaning, silence reigned. A simple, white, ceiling light poured its cosy light down on a table covered with a beautiful green rep cover on which all sorts of magazines lay strewn, but the other young, thin woman, who had seated herself on the sofa to read, seemed to linger with her thoughts somewhere else entirely than with these portfolios. In her simple black dress, she had in fact pressed herself into a corner of the sofa, whereby she had not forgotten to push a cushion carefully behind her back. Now she was plying soundlessly at some needlework, while she kept her tired eyes directed distractedly at the white painted ceiling. This pressing silence may have already reigned for some time between the sisters when the seated woman finally began with a thin, almost lamenting voice, "Now it has already long since struck six, and Oskar is still there next door teaching both his private students. My God, and today he takes on yet another. Where shall it all lead? He will in the end not spare any time anymore for his home and children, since he now must earn so much more. Of myself, I don't want to speak at all. Were you saying something, sister?"

Then Hertha was torn roughly from her meditations. She turned, and the bright light met full and gleaming on her beautiful, narrow little face which resembled so little that of her sister.

"Yes, it even involves a poor, but very talented boy," she responded, "whom Oskar teaches entirely for free. Don't begrudge him the joy, Agnes, of having found a worthy place for his knowledge."

And as her sister now inquired, somewhat put off, as to where Hertha had learnt all this, the girl added confidently and definitely that she had accompanied her brother-in-law on his morning walk that day.

"Accompanied?"

A shadow passed over the suffering countenance of the crocheting woman. Then she pursed her narrow lips so that a distinctly distressed concern was painted on her features.

"You were with him?"

"Yes, Agnes."

"But dear God, our livelihood is already a difficult one anyhow. Why does Oskar constantly need to impose new burdens? Yes, if he had only led home a wealthy woman," she added with quiet self-incrimination.

When the Professor's wife uttered this, those blue sparks which always appeared when her interest or her curiosity was more strongly excited began to ignite in the flashing eyes of her sister. She immediately pushed a chair to the table, bent forward, and as she propped her blond head in both hands, she remarked quickly, and yet unobtrusively, "Why actually did Oskar marry you?"

"Me? The way you ask it too," the Professor's wife responded, piqued, whereby her breast sought arduously to fill with breath. "He was just very fond of me then. At the time, I was also not so faded as now. And then —", here she leafed about nervously in the issues from the portfolio so that the strings swirled and rustled between her fingers, — "the poor man was also deceived."

"Deceived?" The listener's breath died away from her mouth in suspense. "How? Quick, tell me!"

"Why should I rake it all up once more," the older woman parried reluctantly, and at the same time, she bent back in her cushions as though lost. "You know that our father, in order to be able to indulge his many artistic leanings — oh, how superfluous they were for conventional life — you know that he contracted a debt burden which gilded our family for a vanishing moment with the appearance of wealth."

"And you think, Oskar, a man like him, could have had in mind —?"

The Professor's wife sighed.

"What do you know about my man? No, no, I don't believe that at all. I just sometimes cannot subdue my thoughts and keep them in order properly anymore. In any case," here she muffled her voice, and in her entire tone crept something extremely anxious and timid, "cannot Oskar hear us too? He is only next door in his study?"

Hertha nodded. Her brother-in-law sat separated from them only by a baize door, and was talking loudly to his students. You could distinctly hear him scraping his feet from time to time, and discern how the two high school students recited all sorts of Latin fragments to him.

While the two women were still conversing, a strangely acrid smell had arisen in the broad room. The scent must have been gradually penetrating through the keyhole and cracks in the door. But now you could sense most definitely that fish or some sort of smoked food was being roasted on the stove in the adjoining kitchen. Even in the Professor's study, the air seemed to have filled with that marinating cloud. At least the sisters heard how there were a few coughs within, and then an irritated exclamation came from there.

The Professor's wife placed her needlework to the side, clasped her hands, and after she had despondently turned her head with its ash blond, lacklustre hair from one side to the other, she lamented to herself with her weary intonation, "Dear God, I don't know now at all anymore how I shall make it up to him. Especially now, when we have such worries about our existence. Before, freshly roasted herring formed precisely his favourite dish. And you can believe me, it did not come easy to obtain this meal of fish now in winter. But I don't know how it happens. Since a few days ago, the being of my husband has scared me still more than before. Don't you notice, he acts still much rougher and more taciturnly than usual. And at the same time, always the sparing, pitying thing for me, when he approaches me sometimes to stroke my hair. Believe me, Hertha," she added somewhat more expressively, as she directed her shadowed eyes more sharply at her delicate sister, "it does not come easy for a married woman. Something has probably come between us," she continued more calmly. "He probably compares me even. How shall I make it through?"

The grieved woman had spoken her words quietly and passionlessly as if she had read those sentences from the volumes of the magazine portfolio. But Hertha started. Her eyes turned dark, her sharp teeth clenched together.

Where was it leading? It implied an accusation. Was not a hate-filled repudiation hidden behind that barely understandable murmur? The girl quickly rose from the table to place her hand on the seated woman's shoulder. And strangely, now she also noticed how the arm of the beset woman winced in shock under her touch. With a sharp tone, she began, "Are you calling me something alien, disturbing?"

"You?"

The courage seemed to abandon the questioned woman again. Oh, she had never possessed the resilience for struggle and conflict. And now she should wrestle with her own sister, with the last thing remaining from the idolised mother who had passed away?

"Don't ask such a weighty thing," she stammered. "How can you even? I quite certainly did not mean you at all. And then —," here she stuffed the cushion nervously somewhat more firmly behind her back, and gathered herself for a last effort — "and then — also no danger would threaten me from you anyway. You would not do anything to hurt me, would you?"

There it seemed to the battle-ready little one though as if a humid, sick hand suddenly wound itself clasping about her neck. She was barely capable of even repeating it, "Hurt? How should I interpret that? Agnes, what are you aiming at actually with all your suggestions? Tell me — tell me immediately," she demanded more vigorously, as a quickly escaping redness sprang over her pale countenance. "I don't like such secrecy. You are not perhaps distrusting your honest husband?"

The attacked woman wrung her hands, and so great was the superiority of the little one over the broken-down nature of the older sister, that the despair-shaken woman suddenly collapsed as if hit by a fist. She pressed her head between her arms bedded on the table, and straight afterwards, a hefty, spasmodic sobbing shrilled through the broad room.

"I — I don't know at all what I should say or think. I am just frightened. I am namelessly frightened, Hertha. Through all the time of my marriage, I have been seeking for a key which will unlock the being of my husband. But it does not want to be opened. Does not perhaps even want to give or offer me anything. Oh, it is pathetic, Hertha!"

Once more, the beautiful blond's heart faltered in her chest. The hammer in there did not want to beat for a moment longer. Her sister was afraid? Of her? Of her? Thus it beat and jerked through her mind, and she did not know whether the voices of darkness should cry out in triumph or should be afraid. Only, at the next moment, an end was being readied for all these doubts.

Already a few minutes ago, you could have heard how, there in the adjoining room, both the students were taking their leave. Yes, even now you could still hear their joyfully liberated skipping down the stairs. Straight afterwards, the baize door was slowly opened, and the Professor stepped over to the women. When Hertha looked up, she noticed how her brother-in-law was wearing an old green jacket which he had once used on a mountain journey long in the past. From his firmly closed lips hung a short tobacco pipe like those soldiers use on their marches. A pleasant, sweet tobacco scent immediately merged on his entrance with the acrid clouds which were still penetrating through from the kitchen.

"What are you up to?", the Professor began, without properly looking at the two women, placed his hands behind his back, and strode up and down the room.

His wife pulled herself together.

"We have been reading a little in the magazine portfolio, Oskar."

"So." The man threw his head back and forth, and placed himself by the window.

Bleary, misty night, as is common in towns on the coast, was already pushing thickly and starlessly against it.

"Hertha was reading too?", he asked after a while, turned away.

"No, I wasn't," the little one countered, compelled by something to put herself into a contrast with her sister.

With that the conversation was finished for some time. The Professor again took up his wandering. But then he sniffed about the air with raised nose as if the penetrating smell of fish were bothering him ever anew. Certainly a complaint, or even just a remark did not force itself over his lips. Instead he stepped as though without designs over to his wife, and stroked her shimmerless hair a few times.

"Things good?" he asked.

"Yes, thank you, Oskar, very good."

"And the little one."

When the woman felt reminded of her offspring, no amiable smile passed over her features like mothers commonly tend to display. Rather she was startled, and brought her hands confusedly to both temples.

"You are right, Oskar," she stammered. And it sounded quite as if she wanted to beg in apology over a neglected duty. "I must see to him. And then I would like to see to the evening supper as well. There is fried herring," she added somewhat more hopefully. "That's good with you, dear Oskar, isn't it?"

"Very good, very. Thank you."

The man stuffed new tobacco in his pipe, and after Hertha had helpfully passed over to him a match, he took it from her hand without thanking her, puffed a few times, and placed himself again in his place by the window. The propensity for conversation seemed to be lacking in him. For a moment, it remained still between the three. Then the suffering woman began with a last attempt, "Will you perhaps come with me to see the children lying in their beds?" Now she smiled nevertheless, and it sounded as if she could show both of them a hidden treasure visible only to her. "Will you, Oskar?"

The Professor turned to her, "Yes, certainly," he agreed.

He calmly took the pipe from his mouth, and was just intending to follow with his head bowed, his eyes again searching the ground erratically, when the intentions of the couple were suddenly and unexpectedly broken. Hertha straightened up. Her little delicate figure stretched, and as she also bedded her hands behind her back, she strode quickly behind the table so that she now stood in her close-fitting, black dress between the couple.

"You wanted to show me your pictures, Oskar," she demanded, abruptly insistent and commanding, as if it were a redemptive task to steer the tall man next to her away from the pressing monotony of this house and his family.

"Did I?" The Professor threw his head around in astonishment, and his look glided from the floor on which it was usually straying up to his sister-in-law slowly and doubtfully as if he could barely recall his promise. "My pictures?", he repeated. At the same time, he shrugged his shoulders a little dismissively. "You mean the few sheets, colour prints, and photographic images which I compiled arduously and for a few groschen. Why do you want to see them?"

Then Hertha whipped her foot lightly.

"Because it interests me to get to know that which you consider worthy of fuss and collection," she responded overbearingly. For it was irritating to the spoilt girl when a man did not comply immediately with one of her wishes.

But the Professor stood for a while, and stared in front of himself. Then he strode, shrugging his shoulders, to the door which he pushed open with a curt movement of his hand.

"Come," he commanded in his hard, abrupt way.

"Oh, that is good," the girl responded delightedly.

Did they both, finding themselves together, not see how the woman left behind made a quick movement as if she wished to plunge after and follow the man striding away? Did they not perceive the deep, rattling breath which struggled from the labouring breast for a moment? It was too distinct for the delicate little blond, whose ears were even in sleep able to catch the tiniest noise, to have been able to ignore. By the door of the study, she suddenly faltered. Then she hurried back, and stroked the plain hair of the older woman sympathetically, almost tenderly. The girl felt more and more distinctly what an unexpressed torment must be enclosed in the suffering woman's breast, and this knowledge made a strange cleavage spring up from her thoughts. It was so ridiculous, what her sister feared from her. She, the beautiful, proud creature who dreamt of life as if of a subjugated province, she who saw herself moving in a carriage drawn by eight horses into a marble palace, escorted on left and right by young riders in white uniforms just like one she had seen that morning, she, the cool, rational Hertha who was so very much conscious of her innate power over men, that she should begin her life course with an absurd love affair with her brother-in-law? A suspended school teacher? Inconceivable! She threw an astonished look from her calculating blue eyes at the waiting, awkward man, and really did not know whether she should comfort the suffering woman next to her with a few kind words, or whether she should toss some defiant words at her from between her clenched teeth.

It was definite, Agnes was far too insignificant and foolish a person. Without a doubt. And suddenly exhaling powerfully and turning fully to her brother-in-law, she said calmly and not as if doubt had bored into her just then, "Now come, I am ready."

But the woman whom she wanted to leave sent a quick, hopeful look at her husband. But when she read no encouragement from his features, she again let her head sink onto her breast apathetically.

"Yes, yes, Hertha," she burst out as if apologising. "There remains to me too little time for such intellectual pleasures. I must put our children to bed, and then I would like to look into the kitchen once more."

And when the tall door had long since closed behind both of those who wanted to draw hand in hand into the sunlit fields of higher humanity, the woman stood there listening still, no longer possessing the time for the finer joys of life, clasped the table top, and stretched her neck forward as if she wanted to catch, decipher, and interpret every word which was spoken in there behind the green baize.

4

"May I sit in your armchair at the desk?" Hertha asked.

The Professor, standing in the middle of the room, first drew a few puffs from his short pipe, lost in thought. After that he plucked here and there at his green jacket like someone who is not able to achieve clarity over a decision. He finally threw his dark head from one side to the other again.

"Not in my chair," he decided in the end, "there is another here."

With his foot, he then pushed a round wicker chair to the side of the large, flat piece of furniture which, because it was covered with green leather, had acquired for this spartanly simple furniture the name of a desk. The room also looked bare and sober otherwise as the girl now looked around. On the desk, a simple lamp made of cheap metal was burning, sending out its shimmer to modest, spruce bookcases which were placed disorderly, large and small, against the walls. The maps and star charts hung down over them, and, from a corner, the beautiful, colourfully tinted copy of the Venus de Milo towered down from a column. But anyone who stepped closer into the shadows of the corner would notice that this decorative piece had been made from plaster. Carpet was completely lacking in the room. So it happened that the steps of the man restlessly strolling back and forth echoed loud and hard.

But why did the powerful man in his green mountain jacket nurse such a timidity over the possibility that the delicate blond creature might nestle even for only a few minutes in his chair? Why did he send a hasty glance at the seated girl during his wandering, wherein did he not notice how the girl followed him under her lowered golden blond eyelashes? She was also thinking about the refusal. And a distant notion betrayed to her that the uncommunicative man must feel a sort of fear of her there. That allowed her to breath out a few times loftily and satisfied. For this knowledge did her good.

The academic wandered back and forth for a while yet. But then he shook himself, and with a jerking movement, as if he wanted to throw off a burdensome thought which had become too heavy for him, he bent down unexpectedly to the large wall closet whose lowest drawer contained a number of sheets and pictures. Carelessly and awkwardly, he threw them then on the table before the girl. It echoed in the bare room from the violence of the toss for a moment.

"Here you have my so-called treasures," he growled at the same time. "Pfennig pictures, as you see. They are the possessions of beauty which I carried into my life, and even this my gentlemen inquisitors would like to snuffle after most of all. And now you can laugh about it, Mademoiselle, if it suits you."

Only, Hertha did not smile. A fine ability to comprehend betrayed to her though that the taciturn man had delivered to her at this moment the one thing which he himself possessed in his innermost soul, that last asset which he had doubtlessly guarded from the looks of all others with anxious collector's joy.

"Does Agnes know about these pictures?" she inquired inconspicuously, as she sought to give her voice a quite indifferent ring.

"Agnes?" The man shrugged his shoulders, and again let his eyes skim about the floor for lost property. Then he strode curtly and defiantly to before the window, and gazed over to the jutting Pomeranian tower. "She does not know," he responded abruptly. "For what purpose? It is not worthwhile."

The girl had meanwhile unconsciously spread out before herself one of the colourful sheets. A white, naked figure gleamed towards her. It was the Titian Venus slumbering in her divine grove. So humanly complete, and hence so divinely elevated. And around her, a hushed world was resting peacefully, an image of inner harmony.

Hertha stared down into this landscape. And a certain concern began painting itself in her features. Her heart beat louder against the tight black dress, and she could not explain why. Slowly and timidly, she unfastened her light blue eyes from the object of her gaze to then let it rest fleetingly on the man who was still turned away from her. At the same moment, however, as if he had felt her strange look, the Professor also turned. Then he grasped suddenly at the pictures, and gathered up the entire series hastily and without any courtesy.

"Why are you doing that?", Hertha started, believing she heard ever louder beats through her entire being.

"Me?"

The man shrugged his shoulders, and again tossed his head heftily towards his right shoulder. His dark countenance was blanched, it seemed as if he were striving with all his strength to conquer a pressing unease. Then he rumbled curtly, "What use at all are these — well yes — these unnecessary humid lessons? I don't trust you. I don't know whether, in looking at such a treasure, you are free of the impure thoughts like today's youth unfortunately cherish. So, I wanted to say that to you."

And at the same time, he again threw a half timid, half admiring look at the little one, and it ran like a distant shiver over her back. Ridiculous! She remained quite calmly with feet crossed and head lowered on the little wicker chair, and the shimmer of the lamp glittered placidly on the golden tips of her hair. And yet — such desolate thoughts had not tormented him for years. Really, he would not have wondered in the least if this firm, youthfully fresh body had suddenly unveiled itself to him in just as naked a splendour as depicted in the picture which he now tossed back in the drawer again with furious passion. And something compelled him anew to affront her.

"Enough, enough, I know quite well where all your thoughts are heading. The danger which threatens our fatherland exists in that precisely. And this danger, it comes from the women. A misunderstood philosopher has caused all the mischief, and he now works away creating mischief in the minds of the female youth who don't understand how to think. I know quite well that writers and thinkers in recent times have unfortunately steered all the thoughts of German girls and young women to the instinctive urges. And as a result of this stray teaching, young women now believe they are fulfilling a high and sublime mission, they think they are serving a freer, a more divine approach to life when they laugh at the traditional one to indulge in bold enjoyment of a pleasure unfettered and exultant, by which they must cripple an entire national tradition. For the mirror image of a folk is always depicted by its women, not the men."

A smile wanted to twitch about Hertha's lips, but Oskar Rogge balled his fist as if he wanted to strike down every opposition, and he continued more grumpily, "Silence! When Rome's matrons adorned themselves and dressed in see-through bitty garments, only then did the world empire inwardly disintegrate and collapse. The worst thing of all, however, exists unfortunately in that a mob of menial fellows has helped just you unfettered female creatures to an overvaluation of the opinion of contemporaries, which makes a self-reconsideration by women and girls almost impossible. What complete foolishness won't they talk the female sex into believing! Oh yes, the demonic woman has been invented! And tales are told daily of the strange secret, of the inextricable puzzle within the feminine nature which even the wisest do not want to unveil. Don't laugh, you are also acting it out finally. From every teenager, a sphinx has been gradually construed. Where in all the world, I ask — I, the Professor Oskar Rogge, a farmer's son who, thank God, strides with tough boots through the streets, where in all the world has a rational man with open eyes even once encountered the demonic woman in the light of day? Where? What sphinx has ever given the puzzle up to a healthy man? No, one thing is certain, before Germany's women and girls are not dislodged from this maze of alien pretentiousness, before they do not learn again that it stands for their half of existence to become mothers in loyalty and concern for the folk, before they have not felt inwardly that those men of the folk are capable of achieving the highest which is stimulated and spurred on by the most glorious and faithful women, for that long the German maiden must walk astray."

"The German maiden?", Hertha repeated. Her sparkling bright eyes adhered wide-eyed and avid to the countenance of her brother-in-law, whose dark face had filled more and more with passion and suppressed fury.

"Leave it, leave it," he fended as he moved his shoulders vigorously, "it is something long faded away."

And with that he kicked roughly against the lower drawer of the closet. But how strange! How was it even possible that the spurned girl felt all these rough movements, yes, even the kick against the creaking wood, like a strange, confused sign of affection?

It was roaring in the ears of the little one. The storm wind of something in the future blustered about her head. Almighty, powerful Lord in heaven, why did her thoughts plunge in confusion, why did she have to close her eyes in cosy numbness as if she wanted not only to hide from herself, but also from the gnawing realisation, which laughed and mocked quite distantly in some hidden chamber, that all this hate-filled rejection which the struggling man threw in her face wildly and grimly, signified for her some sort of rare, never-heard-before homage? That was nonsense, was doubtless vague and unhealthy feelings; and yet over — over.

She was no longer thinking, she did not distinguish anything anymore, the passionately shaking, hard voice of the strange man had gagged every opposition. Insensible and lost in herself, she slowly let herself glide down onto the room's simple black leather sofa. And as if she only felt through a distant veil how the dispenser of all these new things which had condensed in her to a dull music stood next to her, how his hands grasped her shoulders, and began to shake them as if he wanted to make understood to her some last thing painfully and insistently. She trembled so violently that it appeared quite natural to her for a moment that he was holding her upright with this movement so that she could spin the strange dream further with closed eyes and quivering lips.

"Listen to one last thing," she heard through the turbid cloud of his sharp words which were hitting her heart and brain incessantly alongside a contradictory sense of well-being. "You are one of those straying. You signify such a danger because you fancy yourself to be one of those false queens who think they can transform and subdue with their little bit of squalid charm. And hence I am warning you, girl. I am warning you, do you hear? Turn back, and take a look at yourself while time still remains for you."

He shook her more and more vigorously at the same time, his fists grasped her flesh more and more roughly, and she ceded herself to him more and more placidly, and without any opposition. Thus a thunderstorm goes over a still meadow enclosed by forest, and buries it under storm and ice.

But what was that? Did not a sharp voice shrill through her shadowy darkness? And did not another answer straightaway, well-known to the dreamer in her stammering disjointedness, and yet rising up as if from thick, long forgotten night? She still did not want to open her eyes. Only at a vigorous movement of her companion did she notice that he must also have felt this disturbance.

"Agnes," the Professor burst out, starting with an unexpected jolt.

At the same time, he tossed the creature with whom he was struggling aside as if he were afraid of soiling his hands.

And the girl, returning from distant expanses, stammered as if in astonished recollection, "Heinrich Kalsow."

And then she opened her eyes, and as the little blond lay still reclining, the eyes of both individuals strayed together, and met for the first time. Strange, in the next moment, at the first step on the flat lands of the earth, the close presence of the strange man filled her full of unease. Something threatening infused her eyes, and her little fists balled as she now threw her arms forward as if she had to defend herself from something hostile.

"But no," she reproved him, and a cloud of displeasure passed burning out over her brow. "What do you want from me? What is all this about?"

And then they both listened again to the voices in the adjoining room.

"So, Mrs Rogge, Hertha is here?"

"As I told you, here — here with me — or rather in there, with my husband."

"In there. Aha! I see well, that is good. There she is certainly learning all sorts of beautiful things which are in the rare books, right?"

"For sure — I assume so. Quite definitely."

"And how is it with Miss Boddin otherwise? We have not heard from her for eight days now, Mrs Rogge. And then my mother suggested — that is, actually I come alone to inquire — I mean, you must look around for once. For you see, every minute I always believe that the door at our place at Werrahn must open, and Miss Hertha with her beautiful blond hair could enter. She promised us in fact. That is, I must assume thus. But if she is here with you, then certainly —".

"Go in, Mr Kalsow. Yes, yes, just go in. You need not be shy. It is perhaps good if the pair are interrupted. I mean, they have already expected too much of each other. And anyway — anyway, supper! The clock is already heading for eight — perhaps you will give us the pleasure — —. Don't fear, open the door and go in."

And then the hinges of the portal really creaked, and, with a deep, somewhat awkward bow, in stepped a tall, broad-shouldered figure, about which an old Frankish frock coat flapped which you could see would not have been used often by its owner. It had strange creases, and its wearer at first stroked the short-cropped stubble of his skull a few times uncertainly before, as if asking for forgiveness, he began with his powerful and yet boyishly stammering voice, "Good evening, dear Hertha — Miss Boddin —", he corrected himself, "and a beautiful good evening to you too, Professor. It is certainly not right of me that I disturb you, for —", here the young farmer

laughed almost ashamedly. "You have certainly explained something elevated and learned to your sister-
in-law which the likes of us don't understand at all. And
here I fear actually — and if the Professor's wife had not
suggested —". He looked around ingenuously at the lady
of the house, who still lingered with neck bent forward
in the doorway as if she did not dare enter. But all his
demurring and apologising were in the next moment as
if forgotten and swept away. For Hertha sprang to him,
and with an impulsive joy like she had never shown him
before, the little blond creature, who appeared so tiny
next to the towering man, grasped both his hands,
shook them, squeezed them, yes, you could even have
thought she wanted to press her cheeks caressingly
against his work-worn fingers.

Oh this broad, good-natured countenance of the
young farmer, radiating with veneration and devotion, it
raised her into the dancing night of her vague feelings
like the wide, laughing, good-natured moon which
pushes through thick darkness to contrast clouds,
forests, streets, and villages from one another in its mild
light.

She could see again, she again distinguished good
and evil, and her entire heart exulted for a moment towards the awkward fellow. With astonishment, both her
companions observed how she danced and leapt about
the bemused visitor, how she clapped her hands, to finally pluck teasingly here and there at his unbecoming
coat in the complete admiration of the rapt.

"Oh, you are here, Heinrich Kalsow — you are here."

And then she was laughing brightly and freely again
in-between, and yet did it not sound to the ears of the
innocent man, who saw himself feted so enthusiastic-
ally, as if he had caught from somewhere a distant,
indefinable sob.

From where did it originate? Why did his calm mood so abruptly fall into such an anxious seething?

With large, serious, and startled eyes, he stared at her. Then he grasped her hand almost protectively, but drew his own back in the next moment embarrassed.

"Hertha, dear, how is it going for you here?", it erupted from him, whereby he forgot in his confusion that his soul had called her 'dear' in front of witnesses.

She paused for a moment to brush down quickly and hastily her elegant, black dress. Then she sent a proud dark look over to her brother-in-law, who remained standing with legs apart in the middle of the room, unconcernedly sending massive blue clouds into the air from his pipe.

"There you just stand, you ugly, brooding man," the rescued girl thought, pursing her mouth. "There you stand and worry your life with such sombre, squalid things. I want to rejoice. And praise God, there are still people who want to help me do so. Praise God, praise God!"

And without answering the farmer's earnest question, which seemed to surge forth more and more importantly from his good-natured eyes, she turned his figure in her haste and excitement with both hands several times about its axis until the man, infected by her delight, finally broke out himself into a loud, contented laughter. It sounded fresh and unhurried through the space.

"Oh you, you dear little one, that I surely notice now. A blind man feels it with his stick that it is going well for you here. And I rejoice over that of course. But look," he continued stuttering, and it seemed as if he wanted to wrestle out something serious, "you had promised me though — on that night, I mean, when we stood at the window — that — you know of course — and hence I have actually come here to ask you whether you perhaps won't —".

Only, it remained his fate simply that all his incoherent questions should never reach their conclusion. For Hertha had long since pressed him down onto the black gleaming leather sofa, and now she protested constantly that he must of course stay for supper, and how pleasant his company would surely also be for the Professor and her sister. She entirely dispensed with the fact that the lady of the house had a short time before complained about the pressing burden of the housekeeping. No, she turned instead animatedly from one to the other, constantly asked and inquiring, "Right, Oskar, she should stay? Do you know what, sister, I will accompany you into the kitchen. You don't guess at all in fact that I can play the little housewife too. I must only know for whom. Right, you will take me along?"

And before the suffering woman, who perceived with true relief the blatant joy of her sister, could decide on some answer, the excited girl had already drawn the compliant sister with her, and the men remaining behind heard soon after her cheerful chirping, laughing, and calling from the nearby kitchen. Clattering of plates and tinkling of glasses blended together.

"Yes," Heinrich Kalsow suggested, feeling the need to steer the silent host somehow away from his thoughts, "yes," he began, "I can well think, Professor — as well as I understand it — having such a small, blond, joyful being in the house, that must surely have the effect of a robin redbreast in a bare room when it begins turning cold and winterly outside. Don't you think so too?"

The Professor lifted his head, looked at his tall opposite as if he did not rightly comprehend from where this figure had emerged so suddenly, and nodded fleetingly. After that, he resumed his wandering through the simple, half empty room without noticing in what self-consciousness his odd, taciturn being placed his visitor.

"He is surely thinking about his school lectures," Heinrich Kalsow consoled himself, following the Professor's path in astonishment with head turning to and fro. But the next moment, he lapsed into his own dreams as he examined the tall, colourful shelves of books with unhurried pleasure, books which he assumed Hertha read daily and understood.

And when the name "Schiller" lit up for him on one of the shelves of book spines in gold print, it occurred to him with joy how during wintertime with mother Lotte in Werrahn in the large blue, living room amidst the old cosy ceiling lamps, the sexton Vierarm had read aloud William Tell with his pathetically jarring voice. Oh, those were really beautiful and elevated hours. Certainly, mother Lotte had not been okay with the murder of the bailiff, and had expressed the view that "the authorities must be respected. The matter does not please me. But continue please."

"Alright," the dreamer spun onwards, and smiled to himself. "If the blond thing with her sweet voice which always trembles so gently will only read from Schiller in Werrahn, then — yes, then everyone will certainly listen attentively, and it will be as if a fine music passes through the house. And mother Lotte likes listening to music."

"You are thus a childhood friend of my sister-in-law?", the Professor suddenly intervened in these smiling images, having unexpectedly broken off his path before the seated man. Now he threw his head with a jerk towards his shoulder. "Didn't she live for some time on your farm?", he continued, and at the same time, took the pipe from his mouth.

The questioned man nodded animatedly, and struck himself on the knee smugly.

"Yes, Professor, yes," he responded unhesitatingly. "She was with us when she was a little girl, and I can tell you, we have never forgotten the time. There was no tree on which she did not sit, and no horse which she had not pulled out of the stables. The little thing was like a golden spinning top which leapt in the sun. Do you understand?"

"So, so."

The Professor threw a sharp glance at the seated man as if he were marvelling at where this awkward man could have pulled such a comparison. Then he said roughly and dismissively, whilst he tore at his black, stubbly beard without thinking, "You are quite right. And such a being requires at once a firm hand, good man. She will definitely need it. And in our land, the hands which can hold the reins are becoming rare."

"How do you mean, Professor?", Heinrich Kalsow stammered, not comprehending at all why a distant fear suddenly beset him. It seemed to him as if the words of the scholar also contained a strict admonition for him.

But why?

He passed his finger indecisively along his somewhat too high collar as if he must in this way create air and freedom.

"How do you mean, Professor?"

"Me?"

The scholar broke free, strode to his desk, and began tapping his pipe there.

"Nothing at all," he then emitted indifferently. "Don't think any further about it, my dear man. I don't believe that you personally could address this conviction some-how."

And then a blond head suddenly leant through the doorway. It again turned bright in the room, and the gentlemen were invited to the table.

***

It was only a simple evening meal which was now taken by the four people, of whom each hid a secret from the other in their soul. An acrid smell streamed sharply and insistently from the brown fried herring, and on the large table, the few plates appeared tiny and lost. And yet — at least at the beginning, for the meal ended gloomily — a certain good mood did not let itself be shooed away by the feasters.

Hertha chattered and talked away. She possessed a jesting word and an obligingly helping hand for everyone. And when she constructed a framework of fish bones, clothed it cutely with slices of potato, and crowned it in the end with a drolly formed head of bread, all the good-natured farmer's qualms, excited in him by the strange intimations of the Professor, fluttered away. He could again devote himself to a loud and ringing mirth.

"Just look," he cried, pointing to the little monster, as he bared all his teeth with delight. "Doesn't it look almost like our good sexton Vierarm when he holds the collection bag at the church door? Just so. Yes, Hertha," he continued, enraptured by his own mirth, and as he forgot all caution, "you will now soon be seeing all the old acquaintances in Werrahn again."

The words had been spoken.

Then the girl hesitated for the first time.

"See again?", she repeated, short of breath.

The fork clattered lightly from her hand. All eyes were directed in that moment at the blanched girl.

"And they will make settling down easy for you. That you can believe," Heinrich Kalsow continued speaking, somewhat slower and more insistently. His mien became more earnest, his blue boyish eyes more rigid, and he had the feeling that now perhaps an exchange could follow which was more arduous than any he had ever concluded.

If only the Professor had not spoken at this decisive moment. Why did the grumpy fellow have to also open his mouth right now? It really happened at the wrong time.

"You intend to move to Werrahn?", he tossed out indifferently, although the scholar was unable to unfasten his eyes for the moment from the empty plate.

It remained silent for a while. You could hear nothing but the audible breathing of Mrs Agnes, as well as a gentle scraping since the farmer was moving back and forth on his chair uncomfortably.

How would she probably answer? And why was the damned fellow unable to look anyone in the face?

But the little blond sat stiffly erect, she did not eat, she did not drink, but rather gazed rigidly at the grumpy, black-haired man who did not dignify her with a single glance. Then the host indifferently placed a new fish before himself, and continued his questioning without excitement, yes, even incuriously.

"You have never given us before today any indication of this resolve. Of course, we will in no way oppose your wish. Of course not. But do you consider then," he turned calmly to his wife, who most of all wanted to seek to tear away every word from his lips, "do you consider such a change, dear Agnes, so shortly after the sad event which your sister has only just experienced, to be expedient and fitting? What do you think about it?"

Oh, when the poor thing felt herself asked so quietly and earnestly by her husband, whenever she was commanded to utter an opinion by the man so formidable to her, then her opposition was overcome at the outset.

"Oskar, I actually believe," she stuttered, and at the same time, she sent a glance across to Heinrich Kalsow imploring help, for a mad hope whispered to her that here sat her only confederate, "oh, Oskar, look, I actually believe — —. But of course, if you think," she corrected herself, as she ducked fearfully, "then it would please me of course, if Hertha remained with us for quite a while."

And as she emitted this with heavy tongue, she was then compelled by an overpowering force to have to reach across the table to the little blond her withered hand on which the blue veins ran so wearily.

"You will of course stay, sister, as long as you want. As long as you want," she repeated, swallowing, and quick tears climbed up into her extinguished eyes. "Or have you decided otherwise perhaps, Hertha?", she stammered quickly in an imploring way afterwards.

Now the Professor also raised his countenance, and see, the entreaty of the upset woman must have reached him. Dismissively and not very amicably, he jerked his head towards his shoulder anew. All eyes remained riveted in breathless inquiry on the narrow countenance of the little one.

"You are of course free to choose," the Professor judged with his rough voice. "It does not fall to any of us to want to influence your path and your fate somehow. To none of us. And if you have decided to live in another circle, in God's name. Quite clearly, in God's name. The question only remains for us, as your relatives, as to how you will stay active at Werrahn. Has something already been determined in that regard, Mr Kalsow?"

The young farmer straightened up to inform in a clear, open, manly way. But at the same moment, that accursed inner dithering befell him. Yes, for all the world, had something actually been determined then? Had he not neglected in the last resort to make some binding arrangements as clear and contractual as those provided by mother Lotte in all matters? The devil, yes, he should not have actually forgotten that.

He straightened up, pulled his coat tighter about himself, and as he looked at little Hertha with a yearning intent, disjointed, self-conscious words slipped from him, "Stay active? Yes, look, Professor, Hertha and I, we had reached an agreement actually on the sad night — that is — not actually reached an agreement, but we had sketched it out only that it need not behove your sister-in-law to need to take up any occupation with us in Werrahn, at least not immediately. My mother and sister will see to that, and above all things, I will too. For you see —", here he stretched and turned seeking help to the suffering woman who sought to slurp up each of his words like a vivifying elixir, "you see, Hertha shall move in with us as —". He lowered his good-natured eyes to the table top and, lightly trembling, his hands turned the plate in circles. "As my — well yes, Hertha, we had come to an agreement —", he stammered, demanding confirmation.

Again silence hung over the small flock.

A few, short minutes. And yet they pressed down like black clouds which make everything unrecognisable, men and fields.

Heinrich started. In complete numbness, entirely unbelieving, he had to shake his head. But dear God, that could not be an evil trick which was played on him there. It was never ever the little Hertha though who had leant so trustingly and seeking protection on his shoulder that night. It had happened though. That at least he had not imagined to himself. Or had he? Or had he? Mother Lotte thought indeed that her son had often been walking around as though in a dream recently. Could he perhaps have imagined all sorts of things? That would be truly frightful. And a damp warmth hit his forehead. Quite certainly, the being who now so airily, almost heedlessly, gave an indifferent answer to the most difficult question of his existence, this blond, lithe creature, had never in his life been seen by him before. Never, that he might have sworn. He pinched his fingers to convince himself that he really sat in a circle of living people, and then considered once more in his sluggish thoughts what he had just heard. Did it not sound like the following, "Yes, but dearest, best Heinrich, thank you heartily for your invitation. And I don't refuse you either, quite certainly not, that you must not believe. But what is hoped on such nights and put in prospect, you see, that is not all to be taken literally. You do see that, don't you? Incidentally, I will come to Werrahn. Later, in a few days. That will be okay with you though, won't it?"

And then Heinrich Kalsow sat, murmured something, and at the same time, he heard a man put forth with his own and yet cracking voice that he would of course take much pleasure over her visit. And his mother too. Of course, mother Lotte as well. And then they conversed over this and that.

The strange man who spoke with Heinrich Kalsow's voice explained that a new piano was being acquired for the large, blue living room — that is — actually he was buying it himself, for he had thought that for a dexterous, practised hand which could scurry back and forth so quickly — he did not mean anyone specific — that for such delicate fingers, the old upright had become too tuneless. Yes, those were insignificant things which interested no one. And the large black cow which mother Lotte fed herself, it had given birth to a calf black as night. As black as had never ever been seen in Werrahn. But on its forehead, the newborn bore a white cross. However, sexton Vierarm had prophesied over this strange occurrence that it would bring an unbelievable fortune to the house. And now everyone waited on that. Certainly, he, Heinrich Kalsow, had assumed that this fortune — hm, yes — —. And he also thanked them many times for the supper. But now — the company would surely see — now he must go home, for he had left his horse with the German House tavern's hostler.

Then the strange man who accidentally carries the name Heinrich Kalsow is standing on a landing of the front stairs. Hertha illuminates him with a small kitchen lamp whose brass panes she holds before her face so that her features lie in shadow, whereas the parting man must close his eyes before the blinding beams. He hesitantly offers her his right hand.

Will she surely grasp it?

But she places her fingers gently and ingenuously in his own. Then the man suddenly lets go of the offered fingers as if molten lead has been poured into his hand. And in dull growling, like that of a kicked dog, it burst out of him, "Hertha — little one — you must not resent me, but look — I would never have believed it of you!"

"What do you mean, Heinrich?"

Only, the man cannot explain it. Ponderously and creaking, he descends the stairs, and when he is riding across the heath in the pathless night, stride by stride, he raises his head and stares up at a lonely star which sometimes sparkles like a will-o'-the-wisp, and other times vanishes into a dark chamber. And the man directs the eternal question of humanity at the indifferent star, "What is truth now actually? What should be relied on? It was promised to me! It was though —".

But the star, the blue star — it is Venus — locked itself in its black chamber and does not return. The night wind wreathes about the horse's feet. A large sombre snake slipping through the heather.

"It was promised to me though —!"

5

It tolled from the Pomeranian tower. Eleven strikes hummed wearily and drowsily through the thick black mist which hung over the market square at night. The old tower clock just then had the coughs, and it could not tolerate the damp night wind at all. But it was able to adduce a good reason for it. For when you considered that the old mechanism was actually an enchanted gift, which Duke Bogislaw IV, known as a terrible sorcerer, had nailed firmly under the red bell tower to mock the citizens so that it should chase those citizens from their beds and the governing councillors from under their nightcaps every night with its ghostly voice, then it was correspondingly excused.

And there were ghostly things under the red bell tower. Every child in the venerable fortified town knew that. When the moon in particular danced back and forth in the black sea of clouds, when the drowning stars grasped at it in terrible flashing fear as if for a silvery buoy, precisely on those cheerful nights, the enchanted clock began its peculiar handiwork which could certainly not be imitated by any other marker of hours.

The old lady had really extremely whimsical caprices. She did not call out the hours, she was too hoarse for that. No, she gave birth to them. Really living little monsters, barely the size of a shoe, with grimacing faces, and humped backs and fronts, who all wore on their head an iron red cap. That was the legacy of their father, the weathered Pomeranian tower. But according to the wishes of the ducal sorcerer, these monstrosities were assigned, hampering and hindering, bewildering and deceitful, to intervene in the life of the good town.

***

The old clock coughed. Eleven times. The moon pushed against the large red cap so that silvery blood flowed down on it. And see there, there the wicked rascals were being born. All around the upper ledge of the bell tower, there they crouched in a ring with dangling, stunted legs, clattered with their wooden clogs, held on with their hands so they did not fall, and the eleven monstrosities made such a clamour that the dishevelled peregrine falcon, which had nested since time immemorial in a hatch of the town hall, whirled down screeching and squawking into the great assembly hall to strike there fiercely with its beak against the moonlit picture of Duke Bogislaw IV. It hacked at the duke's eyes. It knew its man.

"Look — look", shouted the most hunchbacked of the monsters, who had a tufted wart as large as a radish sprouting on his nose. "Down there, behind the window, there a lamp is still burning. What an ugly, blind metal lamp. I am fond of such lamps."

"Look," whined the second, whose mouth reached from one side of the little red cap to the other. And in his maw grew just a single tusk. "The lamp does not illuminate him. It flickers utterly fearful thoughts into the dogged schoolmaster's brain. That is good. I want to creep into the wick, and blow a little. Whee!"

Then the other ten raged and whisked about, "Is right, is right, young one. Over there in the house, there we can now keep our hour. There it is so wide. And our mother, and the painted duke in the hall, they will have their joy. Come young ones, who is to be the first?"

And with that, they scuffed, slipped, and clambered like giant dark-grey bugs down the crumbling walls, and rushed squealing and miaowing over the bumpy cobbles of the market. A stray black poodle which was sitting before the house hid its head, and began whimpering.

Whee — whee — whee.

The mob is in, the twelfth hour can begin.

***

"I am Oskar Rogge."

Thus something pricks and whispers in the brain of the solitary man who still crouches before his desk at this late evening hour to stare, with arms propped up, there into the already drearily burning light of the cheap lamp. And the wick hums so peculiarly. It lisps and giggles. And sometimes it peers forth like a tiny, red cap furtively out of the yellow flame.

Whee — whee — whee.

On the man's neck, invisible, foot-wide hammers pound. But woe, they hit all the nerves which lead into the brain. They know how to find these paths with aching certainty. And it rustles on his chest and on his clothes as if he were being pulled and torn at, so that he springs up to begin something unheard of. And how oddly, how quite strange and fearfully the humble white door creaks and cracks, the door which leads into the hallway at whose end the strange girl slumbers — this strange, white girl — —.

Hopefully she lies surely in deepest rest, and guesses nothing of the eerie, tantalising scurrying and wafting which swirls through the house and the blood of the waking as if slowly cooked under a hot desert wind.

"But no, but no," the Professor defends himself, and strokes his neck. Then he looks again with straining into the lamp.

"I am Oskar Rogge, a schoolmaster who has been suspended, and who must soon surely be chased away. Yes, that I am, and yet am not again either. Strange that people in a sense can watch themselves when they take action and walk, when they enjoy and thirst, when they burgeon, and when they die. The one half of humanity burns constantly in the fire, a blast furnace which is heated by feverish fervours, the other half freezes in eternal ice, and behind walls of snow and glaciers, hard as glass, they shut themselves off contemptuously against the neighbouring land of fire.

And yet one soul.

How unbelievable, how quite inconceivable, and the struggling man presses both balled fists to his temples as if he wants to catch and scrunch all the raging thoughts between his fists. But around him, it continues to hammer infuriatingly. Even the bell above the lamp tinkles and rings.

"Strange, quite inconceivable. I love my profession, would like to give my heart's blood to these bright-eyed boys to drink so that they can see as I do, so that they can feel as I do, so that they can fancy as I do that dead heroes and gods sit and walk next to them. I love my profession, this precious gazing into the past and future. And yet — oh, that is ghastly! How my heart rejoices secretly and boyishly over this constrained freedom, it staggers like a drunk, because I shall now soon be a miscreant, chased from the straight road of the phil- istines. And because this miscreant will be able to live and ramble properly in the way of vagabonds. Agnes — — what is that? Is something not shuffling there in the next room? Just like the cheap stiff garments of a woman rustle when she wants to give her steps wings? Is she creeping once more through the bare dark room next door to eavesdrop on me?"

He springs up vehemently, and kicks the door back. Only, nothing stirs in the blackness, and it is only the white floor which creaks and sags so strangely and irrit- atingly.

And again the man throws himself into the hard armchair, and the hammering of the smiths clinks louder and more vociferously.

"Certainly, I am with Agnes. Did I not give her my name which was respected until then? Was she not fed, clothed, and sheltered by me until today? Indubitably. Be calm, quite calm, it will also remain so in the future. But — pit-a-pat — pit-a-pat, over there, there it blazes about the altar of beauty, and should I not worship what seemed adorable beyond all measure to more beautiful peoples, more glorious races? Poor intimidated soul, fly across, return in unconcerned flight to your warm homeland. It is so close, so tangibly close. The breath of the slumbering demi-goddess — Leda, Helen — Ariadne wafts across. She has come alive quite like the naked ones, the ones dancing in beauty, in your poor home. A gift of the gods. An exultant poem of the immortals."

As if wrenched up by countless, tiny hands, the man springs up. His chest quivers, his eyes spray fire when they are directed at the humble white portal. Soon the wood must burn, and the path will be free.

"Gift of the gods," it calls and teases around him as he paces out the room with his great powerful strides. "Poem of the immortals!"

Pit-a-pat — pit-a-pat.

"What does it bother me that her heart does not beat in goodness? Why do I feel fury because her mind secretly lurks on that which signifies her life's fulfillment? Thus burns and blazes the entire youth of today. Are you appointed to quench the blaze? Fool! Bungling moralist! Burn and blaze with it!

> Ring out, drum, in sacred praise!
> Oh take, you gods, the ornament of days,
> Oh take the youth in flames to you!"[*]

---

[*] From J.W. Goethe's "Der Gott und die Bajadere: Indische Legende".

The Girl Who Lost Her Way

The door has sprung open, the humble, white door. Did he open it? Was it a wind gust which pushed it open? There it moves on its hinges, it giggles as if with hoarse, mocking voices, "Look!"

"Look, our hour is here. We have let it turn sour, but look, the house is burning. Now come, come next door! We want to crawl into her bed. We want to kiss her heart with our burning mouths. We want to tousle and rustle in her blond hair until the flames ignite even there. And then we will be finished, for then it will be midnight!"

***

She cannot sleep. And she cannot wake. From time to time, the moon chases a pale silvery wave over the bed, but straight afterwards, the night tosses black masses of sand after it, and all is again dark and fearful.

She cannot sleep. And she cannot wake. In a twilight state, she hangs between heaven and earth, and from the gate of dreams, wicked night creatures fly toward the wavering girl. Sometimes she opens her blue eyes, and then she thinks she notices how eleven red drops of blood are slowly circling over her bed. Or are they strange, tiny red caps? The girl sinking back deeply is unable to distinguish that anymore.

How heavily she breathes! Something is burning over her. Truly, these red points must be venomous fires which want to consume her.

Help! Under the covers!

Oh, that provides freedom. You can scoop some air. And she is also alone.

And again the moonlight floods over the white limbs, again the night grumpily throws its black cloth around the exposed girl.

Strange, strange!

Werrahn? Does it signify a place of refuge? Is it a prison?

"Heinrich, Heinrich, don't look at me so. I don't need to give you my word. I don't want to imprison myself yet. I don't like the calm. I need the unease. And hope, and thousands of possibilities. And thousands of possibilities wave to me, don't they? What am I doing in this house? I don't know. You should not ask me. Caprice perhaps. And I will soon relent. But not yet now."

Not now?

Oh this fear, this heavy iron plate which suddenly presses down on the soft breast, directly now when it wants to rise up, no, when it must rise to peer at the dark figure which towers close before her pillows.

But that is Agnes!

"Agnes, for the grace of God! What are you doing here? Why are you staring with such loathing at my limbs? Help me, help me, I want to cover myself, I am freezing. I want to go too, if you wish it. I will obey everything, just don't do anything to me, do you hear?"

And then?

It no longer a dream. No, painful reality. Her hair, her wonderfully rich blond hair is being pulled by a bony hand. Once, twice.

Mercy! The tortured girl emits a loud cry. But in the room, it all remains empty, and with an unintelligible sigh, she hides her aching head in the pillow. Then she presses her hands to her quivering breast, and wild tears fall from her eyes.

Thus she sobs half the night. From pain? From fury? She does not know. But the bright drops pour incessantly.

***

But it was no night spectre which had lingered in the little one's room. And Oskar Rogge had not been deceived either when he fancied he caught the rustling of stiff garments in the next room.

In this night, there was eavesdropping at all the doors.

The poor, hounded wife was really creeping through the dark rooms, squinting for hours with aching eyes through the keyhole to catch every movement of her husband. And then she dragged herself anew through the narrow hallway to where the young one, the blond, the most hated one was enjoying her hospitality. But cautiously, inaudibly, on tip-toe so that nothing of her unholy doings would be felt. Oh, if she had met Oskar here, who thought her to be long since sleeping with the children, she would not have known how she could have explained her actions to him. But for the first time in her troublesome and burdened existence, such a responsibility seemed incidental to her. She knew she barely surmised what she was doing. But she felt one thing quite clearly. She was constantly hearing thousands of quiet muttering voices which whispered in her ear, which spoke in the air around her to mumble to her from everywhere, from here and there, "Watch out. Now it is happening. Be suspicious, watch every gesture. Connect every word. For see, you are the weak one. But the strong, the healthy, they are clustering to one another. And now the hour has come. Now it is where it will strike over them."

No, she does not want to be edged out. She wants to defend herself. She will do something ghastly. If she only knew what. And she implores the night, the ghastly night before which she shudders, to supply her with one thought, one terrible plan. Only, nothing arises in her poor martyred brain, nothing comes to life.

Then the last thing nears.

In furious and yet powerless thirst for revenge, she has just clawed and raked in the girl's light blond glory.

Oh, that was good! But the next moment, she has fled. It drives her back again, she must spy at what the other one who comprises her property is beginning. For the holy laws of marriage stand recorded thus in her poor martyred brain.

The man belongs to the wife. He is not free.

He is her king, but he belongs to her.

She spies through the keyhole at what the crowned man who yet bears her fetters has devised against her. Will he carry out the monstrous thing? Will he really gather together out of all the heavens the courage which is required to smash this clasping, iron band?

Tormented by shaking fear, but at the same time also with burning, gnawing curiosity, the poor woman squints through the little, light-filled opening. And then — then the appalling thing springs toward her.

The door has flown open. The small white connecting door.

Did he open it? Or was the way opened for him by invisible forces? Is sin itself cheering him on? Is he driven by it to commit this enticing madness?

She wants to scream. But she is too clever for that. By no means, no screaming! That would betray her. But the bony hand gropes somewhere. Wildly in circles about itself. She is searching. She strays. She misses her objective. She wants to snare a bundle of matches. And then fire in the apartment. Flames, fumes, smoke, and horror!

Or retribution?

Could she not run to the old rector? To the rector with the peruke who sits anyway in judgment on the disciplined?

And would it not be priceless to scream on the way? Loudly scare the sleepers from their rest? With the alarming cry of lament which must actively collect all weary, hounded, trusting women like her, "Wake up —

be appalled! My property which must think like I do, which must feel like I do, which must desire like I do, be appalled, it has received a will of its own, and seeks to turn against me. Get up. Collect yourselves. Protect me and you!"

She is standing on the street. She staggers across the market square as if flames were leaping from her house and the arsonist must flee. She has thrown a blanket around herself. But she does not feel it. Her fingers rake and grasp about in it, but she has no feeling for her own movements anymore. How warm the night is. Or damp? Or icy? And to where does the way lead her? Where is she being chased? Indeed, Agnes, to the old rector with the peruke? It is night. Do you want to ring him out, the old man, from his peaceful slumber? And how will you endure the eyes which are appalled at the married woman who delivers her husband to the judge?

Onward — onward. But just away from the house out of which the flames are blazing.

And there — praise God, there she has already entered a side lane. An angular little alley, so narrow and crooked that the gables of the houses opposite each other almost touch. Like successive black standards, the darkness hangs down here heavy and rigid. It is as if the hurrying woman must constantly beat back one black sheet after another if she intends to force her way forwards.

But listen! The sea wind which whistles up through the corner does not blow its signal in vain.

It greets her. It announces her. It reports the straying woman to its mistress, there below the violent, busily raging sea which lurks below the steep way behind the beach boulders.

And now the nearing woman notices how individual streaks of light are washed back and forth by the flooding blackness.

Back and forth, up, down, sparkling diamonds, appearances and deception, with which an ugly Moorish woman adorns her bosom to stash them away again.

Agnes, now speak, you tormented woman. Why do you throw your gaunt hands shuddering before your countenance as you loom up on one of the large beach boulders? Does it not widen the heart when you see this living expanse rolling away to eternity, which lives and breathes in the night? Are your senses not becoming brighter now the element is spitting its ice-cold breath about your burning temples? Are you doubting still that the vastness was set to it from the original beginning so that it would embrace the little, the tired, those unable to live, and rock them to sleep?

And your deed would not be deemed great and self-less. You would go in, quietly, without lament. You will disappear, carried away from the investigations, object of a loving memory, just like once happened to the heroes and demi-gods who were taken just as tracelessly from the earth. Have you not often heard your husband lecture about that, the husband who now cuddles with the delicate one, the white one, the blond?

Do it! Down there, on the last edge of the reachable, a silver streak flickers in bare, mother-of-pearl coloured brilliance. Believe it, that is the bridge over which the blessed stroll into the field of their hopes. Into dreamless nothing or into blossoming gardens of stars where thousands of suns light your steps, and the aether quivers with choirs of angels.

Don't you hear them? They are already singing for your reception.

Only, the hounded woman has no eyes for the enormous bed in which she should slumber. That infinite expanse which roars across to her so admonishingly, it just tortures and oppresses her daunted heart. And her ears shudder when the whinnying sound drones against her boulder, "Do it, do it!"

No, no, I must not, I don't want to. What an ugly sight if my little one saw me rocking here in the sunlight. Ugh, why such an ugly impression? And then — I'm freezing. I can't climb down from this stone either. Why should I smash my limbs? That is not the right thing to do. Quite certainly, I won't find it here. But just let me, let me. I know a place already where I can stretch myself out. There, my pale countenance turned to the sun, they will find me then in the morning light. It is good thus. It is beautiful thus. Not here. There.

And the desperate woman arduously fumbles her way down from the wet boulder.

***

Right next to the churchyard wall, there it shines behind a pair of opaque glass panes. For shortly before midnight, Jochen Tobis is performing there in his greenhouse a mysterious action. He sets splendidly upsprouting, red bushy azaleas in larger pots. And this business must play out right before the witching hour, for otherwise it does not get the right consecration according to ancient gardening lore. Thus he stands with rolled up sleeves, and with glasses on his fleshless hooknose, and hums a jaunty song as he plies away:

> Shall I be dying then?
> I'm still so young, young, young —*

Finally, however, he finishes up with both his question and his work. The red bushes stand planted about on the uppermost shelves. And hence it is time that Jochen Tobis also gathers his lantern to stroll with it leisurely, wheezing and murmuring, out of the miser-

---

* From Friedrich de la Motte Fouqué's *Der Sängerkrieg auf der Wartburg: Ein Dichterspiel.*

able shack. The place slowly submerges into darkness behind him. From behind the opaque panes, it no longer shines over the field. And only the lantern sways along the fence like an enormous glow worm fumbling its way in the darkness over the planks.

Must I be dying already?

I'm still so young, young, young —

"Thunderbolts," the old man suddenly falters, and holds his lantern away from himself.

What does that mean? That would be strange though. Why in all the world is a veiled figure looking stiffly and motionlessly over the fence here?

"One thing is clear indeed, they will not do anything to me here, for planting the graves, that is actually a business which in all respects signifies no business at all. It is an obituary. Evil men don't bother such people. And a ghost? I have certainly already met one twice. Should it be time again already? Looks like one."

With that he sits down on the next grave without any fuss because his old feet are failing the service to some extent, and he clamps the lantern between his knees.

"You want surely to recover a little out here?", he asks over the fence.

The figure is startled. Then a weak, barely comprehensible female voice responds, trembling with fear and shock, "I saw — I saw lights burning here. And hence I thought — —".

"Eh, of course," the gardener softens his tone. And his mouth, surrounded by countless wrinkles, chews and moves as if it must actively agree. "Of course, that is understandable. Lights and a churchyard, it is a bit ghastly, isn't it?"

And when the black shadow does not answer, Jochen Tobis decides to continue talking whatever happens, for a conversation seems necessary to him for his own safety. People who speak, he thinks, become mild-mannered. Perhaps he will also succeed with a right gruesome legend in scaring off the shadow or ghost from the entrance to his cemetery.

"If only these damned things did not consist of pure air, and could waft quite easily over the fence to climb down on my neck from there. Bad, bad."

And so he crouched on the grave, held the lantern firmly clamped between his knees, and talked eagerly to the black figure, "What I wanted to say, if the lights here in the churchyard begin to burn, yes, that is a peculiar matter. And most people don't know the story. But I can still remember it well from the years of my childhood. Who still thinks now of my predecessor here in my work, Jochen Knapp? Jochen Knapp was a fellow, almost two metres tall. And he did not even need shovels for the graves. He dealt with it all using his hands. They were like two washtubs though. He was a steady fellow. When he walked across the churchyard, it thundered among the graves so that the dead were woken by it, and they could not sleep. Yes, like that he was. Are you still listening?"

The shadow murmured something from out there, and held on tightly to the slats of the fence. Jochen Tobis, however, warmed himself with his lantern, and continued speaking in haste and fear, "Here, where I have my hothouse, there behind the wall, there lived Jochen Knapp. And the remarkable thing happened to him there in the year 1842. It had in particular already occurred to him that there was on the night of Good Friday frequently a knocking on the green shutters of his window. What could that be? Once he thought that it was surely merely the mocking wind. But in the second year, then he noticed that a hand was pounding on the wood, and it seemed to him as if he heard coughing. In the third year, however, he decided to stay awake, and hence lay dressed on his bed. And look, shortly after midnight, the wood was really knocked on by a heavy hand, and a voice called out with a really foreign pronunciation, 'Open up, Jochen Knapp'. At these words, my predecessor pulled his lantern to himself — here, it is still the same one which I now use — and stepped across the threshold of his house. Had he not had the lantern, he would surely have not been able to distinguish anything, it was so dark and pitch-black all around. The easterly stormed ice-cold over the churchyard's trees, and bent them back and forth until they creaked. Sand was thrown up from the graves and whirled about in the air. Before the house, however, stood a man like Jochen Knapp had never seen before. He wore a black tricorn above his pasty pale face, just like the pall bearers wear these days when they want to bury first class. About his shoulders flapped a black velvet cloak, and his legs were stuck in quite wide pants, black stockings, and buckled shoes. About his neck, however, the man had hung a golden medallion. It flashed and sparkled in the moonlight. And on his left side, he wore a short thick dagger. "Light my way to the chapel," the stranger commanded in his foreign voice. And remarkably, Jochen Knapp, who would have preferred to have run away, he became, when he looked into the pasty face, so weak and powerless that he raised the lantern up with a deep sigh, and walked ahead of the stranger. Oh, what a fright this path was for Jochen Knapp. Wherever he looked, everywhere the cemetery was full of life and people. On all the walks, countless black figures pushed their way, locked and pressed tightly together, all of who looked like the man who had woken my predecessor. Utterly black cloaks and black tricorns. And at the same time, not a word spoken all around. But Jochen Knapp noted well that the closer he came to the chapel, the thicker and more numerous the crowds of men around him became, and the faster they seemed to thrust forwards as if time were short for them. Now they stood before the chapel. Heaven help, everything brightly lit. The door wide open. And inside all filled up to the altar by the black-clothed crowds, who stood head to head as far as the furthest corner. When Jochen Knapp enters, a pair on the last bench move to the side, and make a place for him. Then Jochen Knapp sits down among the strangers, and holds his breath in heart-clenching fear. What does he see, what does he hear there? Remarkably, behind the altar on which two enormous wax candles are burning, as is not at all usual in this region, there stand three an-cient, white-haired men with billowing silver beards. The one on the right has a large white book before him-self, and the one on the left has a similar one in black. And as often as the tallest of them now, who is in the middle, calls out a name, just as often the one to the right draws a thick strike with a quill pen over a page of the white book, and straight afterwards, the one on the left writes the name in the black folio. And always when such a foreign name occurs, then one of the audience rises, crosses himself, and goes out of the hall. To where, that Jochen Knapp does not know. But see, gradually the names become more distinct and recog-nisable. And as Jochen Knapp now thinks to himself, it occurs to him that he heard many of these names here in the town in his youth. And the people who now rise also have on quite sensible, black coats, and durable caps on their heads. That is strange though. And the longer it lasts, the better known and more familiar are those called up, and gradually Jochen Knapp realises that the people walking past him had only died ten or twenty years before. But it always continues. Young and old. The man before the white book strikes out one after the other, and the man before the black book quietly inscribes them again. Then Jochen Knapp becomes eerily apprehensive. And just as he wants to creep quietly out the door, the entire assembly suddenly turned around to him. What is it? "Jochen Knapp," the man in the middle calls. My predecessor was not able to tell us anymore. When he again came to, he lay where my hothouse now stands, and his lantern had just snuffed out. But you can believe me, the people whom he heard called up on that night of Good Friday, they were all taken away in the same sequence by dear God. And the last was Jochen Knapp himself. He was two metres tall, and had hands like wash tubs. God bless him."

The wizened gardener told such a legend. Fitfully, and interrupted by frequent coughing. But as he now blinked up from the lantern which gave him warmth and light — goodness — no, it was based really in truth. The shadow had vanished. It had surely climbed up into the night, and was now snoring in the dark grey clouds which sailed about the moon like hulking ships.

"No," Jochen Tobis determined, as he cautiously leant over the red brick wall once more, "it hasn't sat down here either. Look, my story was probably too powerful for it. Yes, a peculiar power lies in the old stories. But now home, and into bed," he goaded himself, whereby he set off on his way, tottering and doddering. "At sunrise tomorrow, I must water the repotted azaleas in the hothouse. For otherwise they won't strike root. And it comes down to the roots. Good night," he wished quietly to himself, as he nodded familiarly to the last graves.

The iron gate clattered behind him. And the old man slowly shuffled out onto the main road.

But yet!

Jochen Tobis possesses only weak eyes, and the enormous glasses which he wears over his fleshless nose were obtained from the annual fair and do not make his eyes any brighter.

Down there in the narrow ditch, next to the red brick wall, does not something stir there? When a stray moonbeam flashes down from its black cloud, it then encounters a snow-white countenance. The eyes are closed, the mouth is speaking madly. But the green, venomous fire of fever is burning on the sick brow.

See — see!

The little bedroom! In it lies a bed showered in moonlight, and on that the white, bare limbs of a girl. Ugh! Ugh, she wants to strike. She wants to scratch bloody scores into the white satin. But the monstrous breeze and whirlwind tears her on. A market square. Dead still lanes. And down there, the sea which surges and advances against her, which swills and rises until it fills her ears with roaring water, until she hears it gurgling through all her nerves, "Do it, do it! Don't you notice, now he is tearing her from her bed. Now they are cuddling together. How long will you yet wait?" And then the flood breaks in too, and tears her away. She does not let herself be deceived. There are numerous black figures rushing across the churchyard, and taking her into their midst. Away to the chapel.

"You cannot walk, Agnes? Come, we will carry you. You must hear it, your name, as if droned with trombone blasts from the lips of the white-bearded old man there behind the altar. But your heart is bad, your mind is diffident. Are you not lurking for when both the others — so hated by you — are also named?"

And there — there! What luck. There it sounds with the blasts of trumpets, "Oskar Rogge — Hertha Boddin — Agnes Rogge."

And then the enchanted clock of the town hall strikes the hour.

One o'clock.

***

"Hertha — Hertha."

Thus the Professor cried shrilly and with desperate power, and at the same time, he struck his right hand as if senseless against the wood of the door which he was easily capable of opening.

Listen!

From inside there is a dull call, half joy, half horror. Then it goes quiet again, and everything stiffens into a tense listening. The next moment, however, the agitated man, who has not found his wife anywhere in the house, who considers himself inscribed with the mark of Cain, and who is too weak, and anyway too exhausted and encumbered to bear this burden as well, has in the next moment left the threshold of sin far behind. With bare head, he roams about on the deserted, night-filled streets. Sometimes here, sometimes there. He rattles every locked door as if the woman he seeks, the mother of his children, the woman of his bourgeois honour must infallibly emerge there.

Nothing.

And he rushes onward. Down to the sea.

Now, oh, now he first comprehends that peace and certainty form the bed and pillows on which he alone is able to slumber.

Dear God, sole God in heaven, how may creatures who arduously pay your tribute, who look forward to lunch and supper, and for which the reading of the town paper signifies a morsel, how may such beings peer at the stars on which the naked gods stroll?

Ridiculous. Sinfully ridiculous.

If only he finds Agnes again, his peace, his uniformity, his bourgeois honour. Oh, only this last thing.

Thus he wanders about the lanes for the entire night. But when the houses open in the morning, and the well-dressed and clean people step out, the broken man flees timidly and appalled back into his empty house.

The dawn of the day penetrates into the bare spaces weakly. And the haunted man hides away, as if blinded by the weary light, behind the furthest corner of the large cupboard in which his files and pictures are stored, those beggarly pfennig sheets. Oh, just not to be reminded of them. If Agnes were now to step through the door, he would hand over to her all the stuff so that she could light the stove fire with it to prepare a cup of good, hot, enlivening coffee over it. How beneficial such a drink would be now. And how he misses it. How pricked and tormented he is by the memory of how his wife for years set before him such a refreshment at the strike of seven. Now nobody thinks of him. For the young creature, the little blond — away, away, banish every thought of her, of this egotistical, pleasure-seeking creature, the image of today's youth. The healthy fresh maiden surely lies motionless stretched out on her pillows. That goes without saying.

It is becoming lighter and lighter. Just today, it is a radiantly sunny day. And now someone will find Agnes somewhere. And he sees with his wide-open eyes how the people stand around the outstretched woman, how they whisper, ask each other, and provide themselves with muttering answers. And each word stabs at his bourgeois honour, and tears it into pieces.

Then there is a knock at the tall, baize-covered door. A gentle, delicate hand.

Is it her? Should he really be reprieved once more?

The strong man, the farmer's son, felt so powerless that he was unable to rise anymore from his corner. His lips just stammered quietly, "Come in."

6

"Now, Director — will you be so kind as to lead. Please, most courteous of you, now."

"Burr — curr — what circumstances. Matters of etiquette. Well, for my sake. Burr — curr."

Before the green baize door by which this short ceremony was concluded, two remarkable little men were standing. They appeared to have climbed into this life out of a picture book from the early nineteenth century to pay the senior teacher Professor Oskar Rogge an important visit.

Yes, it was the old grumbly, thoroughly upright Director Jarling of the high school St Catherine's. He it was, with his unshapely, heavy, creased brown frock coat like those you only find still in cute silhouettes, he it was with his brown peruke which sat somewhat askew on his left ear, and with his crookedly bowed countenance riven by thousands of wrinkles, which he could never raise properly to look his opposite straight in the eye. But that had a quite special reason.

The poor little old man!

In his prospering youth when his limbs were not yet wilted and withered, he had — so the rumour passed through St Catherine's — shot his own brother on a hunt by accident. And since then he eschewed in a deeply drilled incrimination from freely raising his head towards his fellow man. But this thoroughly upright disposition hid his own fear and uncertainty behind a fierce rumbling tone. Yes, his students even related that he frequently appeared in the classroom in his agitation with a strange seven-tailed knout, and performed every strange figure possible with it amidst thunder and lightning.

Burr — curr.

There dear God had meant well with the old man in that he delivered to him for his representative and Deputy Rector the gentlest, most good-natured, finest, and quietest creature that had somehow entered the world of pedagogues. Precisely a companion piece. For the little, well-dressed, distinguished bachelor in the grey, immaculate, silk-lined frock coat, with white vest and yellow silk gloves, the mathematician Professor Sutry, wore a likewise fine and delicate peruke on his white-scrubbed head. Only, although it was definite that he possessed several such artificial hairpieces for variation, yes, that he even affected a quite special one for each day of the week, ordered exactly by number, it was on the other hand completely accounted for and palpable that Professor Sutry favoured with his hair adornment, in a quite special delight over colours, the green hue. From the light silvery green of poplars, this remarkable symphony of colours ascended right up to the deep mermaid green of the mountain lakes. Apart from that, it was considered difficult to wrest the little man from the battalion of algebraic letters which he commanded like a general, and whenever life put an urgent question to him, he was only grievously and reproachfully able to yield a parrying 'now — now'.

Both these gentlemen appeared at the earliest hour of morning, as the enchanted clock on the Pomeranian tower was just announcing quarter to eight, on an important mission to the study of the senior teacher Professor Oskar Rogge, who cowered, hunched up, shivering, and with bleak mind behind the large cupboard.

Outside, the day was brightening with ever more purity and light, and the clarity of the cool glassy blue sky increased the ungovernably feverish fear of the man in the corner to an open unease.

What did he care for it all?

Both the musty perukes were certainly creeping to him, around him — the suspended one — amongst even countless — items — and burr — curr to announce that the blessed provincial school council have chased him completely from his office because of stray teachings. A corrupter of youth. He could drink the cup of poison. Burning hot and warm. Just like Agnes had been accustomed to provide a hot drink at this hour. Oh, how he missed the refreshment. And still more the hand which offered it.

And as both the old gentlemen made themselves comfortable at an unconscious hand gesture of his on the simple wicker chairs, his disturbed disposition again screamed for the firm ground of the bourgeois life which had splintered under his feet. Plummeted rattling into the void. And he now stood by the abyss, stared down, and from the eternal darkness, the dead countenance of Agnes shone up to him.

No, no, he must not teach. He, who had denied the highest, the most glorious treasure of the educator, kindness.

Noble is the man, helpful and kind.[*]

And for whom was it all?

For a light skirted, half-naked mermaid who could only laugh, giggle, and mock, and boast running up with white limbs.

Almighty God! Help, help!

He could only imagine her naked and untameable.

Help! Help!

The struggling man instinctively turned his head, and listened. From the room beyond the hallway, he

---

[*] From J.W. Goethe's "Das Göttliche".

thought he heard rustling and splashing. The sound made his heart falter, squeezed his fists together.

Almighty one, give me back what I have lost.

Noble is the man, helpful and kind.

"Burr — curr," Director Jarling rose in his chair, fondled ruff of grey mariner's beard which surrounded his wrinkled face, and twisted his head so askew that it seemed as if his small, pig's eyes wanted to attempt to peer over the back of their possessor.

But at the same time, the gentle Professor, Professor Sutry, tapped him softly and circling on the knee, and added soothingly and introductorily, "Yes certainly — just now."

"Burr — curr," the Director grumbled. "Dear colleague, coming accursedly early. But held it to be our duty. Not delaying any longer."

"Yes now — now."

Then Oskar Rogge awoke. He felt that the next moment would bring information about his fate. But see, suddenly he did not wish himself luck or relief anymore. What use in all the world to him now was calm, order, and certain tenure? Since he had become a man without peace, since all his thoughts were chasing about like wild bloodhounds in the lanes of the town, seeking, seeking. With his right hand, he performed a contradictory movement, breathed out heavily and rattling, and then emitted rashly and in cutting haste, "Let it be though, my gentlemen. Let it be. I already know everything. I will go my way. But not now, I have in particular —".

With these words, he wanted to spring up, for the unfortunate man thought to hear an inconspicuous noise penetrating up from the street. Director Jarling, however, twisted his mouth grouchily. Then he pushed the restless man back in his seat dully and heavily with his broad paw.

"Lively temperament, dear colleague. Burr — curr."

"Now — now."

"You will perhaps have to restrict something. Men in employment, even the intellectuals, must unfortunately curb their temperament. As beautiful as it is in itself. Glorious even. Otherwise easy to run into corners. Burr. What did I want to say, Sutry?"

With these words, the old grouch pulled at a button of his finely dressed Deputy Rector's grey frock coat, which was not accepted benevolently by the painfully clean man at all. Only, it belonged to the duties of the ordered and clear mathematician to continue the interrupted speech for his Director in such miscarried instances. Hence he raised his forefinger, and after he had likewise tapped Oskar Rogge on the knee as a preliminary, he spoke with his fine rasping voice, "My dear colleague, we have in fact — just now — yesterday evening had a consultation on your matter with the high school inspector."

"With the —?", The Professor sprang up so that both the other men were appalled. Everything rattled about him.

"Did you not hear anything?", he cried, as his look strayed flickering and burning to the windowpanes. "It seemed to me though as if from the street —".

For a moment, the three listened, only, everything remained still.

"Burr," the Director chided, and spat unconcerned on the floor. "Sit down, dear colleague, listen. But very important."

"Now — now."

"The high school inspector was to begin with very outraged. Cost great effort to bring him around."

"To bring him around?", the Professor stammered, these words suddenly opening a new door on life for him. "Bring him around? How do you mean, Director?"

"Will hear right away. But please, don't always interrupt me. Very unpleasant. Right, Sutry?"

"Yes, certainly," the Deputy Rector confirmed, as he again raised the white finger with the signet ring. "Logical train of thought is then hardly possible. Now — not entirely factual."

"Tell me, my gentlemen," Oskar Rogge, feeling tortured by doubled forces, called to both the old men now without thinking, "tell me finally what you know. You surely note that life is pushing me to and throw. I can not describe to you at the moment how heavily and painfully. Hence, tell me — tell me!"

Astonished, and a little anxious, both the perukes looked at one another over this outburst which was so unexpected by them. But then the mathematician, Deputy Rector Sutry, as the cooler man of facts, took the word first, "Now now — excuse me, dear colleague, that I'll recapitulate in brief. You gave your students during a lesson a not quite — now now, shall we say — not quite popular view over the essence of the Gospels. You called, my dear colleague, if I am correctly informed, this surest document of our faith — simply now — a wonderful poem which the was comparable with the most beautiful and most popular of our great Goethe. You added admittedly — now now — that such poetry of the world need not stand up to historical critical examination at all because it merely addresses the feelings. And you drew the conclusion, since all primal religion originated from art, that the enormous and overwhelming artistic worth of the New Testament would be a better guide into the light for devoted faith than all knowledge, than all history. Very nice — now now —", the mathematician added, lost in thought, whereby his exacting nature completely forgot that he was lingering here as as a superior and strict judge.

"Are you mad, Sutry?", he was immediately guided by his director, who had pushed his peruke impatiently from one ear to the other, back onto the prescribed path. "Nice? — Burr — curr. It does not stand for discussion here. The main thing is that we both, Sutry and I, have vouched for it with the high school inspector that your entire omissions, dear Rogge — remain nicely calm, best colleague, nicely calm — that your entire omissions themselves only display the poetic texture of a literary temper. Burr — curr. A release, so to speak, of the imagination from the secret treasure chest to which the entry does not stand open for the dumb youths. And for our surety, and because you are as it were a steady fellow, and since we also have had enough public scandal over this, everything shall remain with your superiors. I just have to give you a private telling off. And that is happening herewith. Because of the office. Burr — curr."

That was the bourgeois life. The great road lay simple and smooth again before Oskar Rogge. Not sunshine, but yet a steady blue sky arched over it, and the overwhelmed man, whose heart hesitated and fell silent in his body, he saw mobs of his students striding across the broad lane, bare-headed, and with shining eyes. And he felt how the youth spread their arms out yearningly to him, the teacher, who had gifted them more than the usual, than the stifled and locked away.

How did it just happen that he nevertheless remained motionless and firmly entranced in his chair? Why could he not exult? Why did it on the contrary force him to shrug his shoulders coldly and without passion, as if he intended to push away from himself the so ardently desired bounty of life?

Only, before he was able to yet decide, there was a dull knocking at the door.

Once — twice.

What did that signify? Was his overtired and slack imagination leading him to believe in phantoms, or was it really the old gardener Jochen Tobis who stuck his ragged, white head through the crack in the door to nod to him meaningfully, "Oh, for a word, Professor."

And then he had also already left the two concerned perukes. With a leap, with a single leap, he stood on the other side of the baize door, and there — there — in the midst of the light of day, there sat Agnes, his lost wife, on the simple sofa of the large room, and smiled towards him numbly, and without any visible signs of excitement.

And strange. No cry of recognition. No word of joy. No poignant apology. Nothing of all that happened. But when Oskar Rogge sat again before his superiors in the next minute with a simple, roughly composed apology, both the old men noticed that something had been released in the soul of the man. That here dwelt a man reclaimed by bourgeois life.

It still frequently sounded within, "now — now", and "burr — curr". But in the end, Director Jarling of St Catherine's placed his hand on his senior teacher's shoulder, and so earnest was the moment that a miracle happened. The wrinkled, deeply bowed head rose, the small timid eyes pricked the listening man directly in the face.

"Listen, Rogge. Now get dressed, and go to the senior class today. I believe the boys are scared for you. But a word of advice, my dear friend, pick yourself up on the way. What you proposed there, that I have considered from the beginning to be the reaching, to be the longing for the beautiful, the prohibited, and the unreachable which slumbers as hope and desire in every man's breast. But, dear Rogge, the inheritance of labouring men exists in that they all have this wondrous thing to lock away in the big sturdy wooden chest of modesty and forswearing. Only a few geniuses open them once every hundred years. And even then it is still questionable whether they have fetched out with the hidden treasures beneficent and advantageous things. Don't take offence, dear Rogge. And now adieu. Burr — curr."

Thus the Director spoke.

Oskar Rogge, however, had won back his bourgeois life. He bowed his head deeply, and since he stood directly before the cupboard in which he hid his artistic treasures, he kicked with his heavy boot dully and thudding against the drawer. That was his wooden chest.

And from the next room, something was still muttering and humming, the splashing and scurrying of the naked mermaid for whom there was henceforth no space anymore in this house.

BOOK TWO

1

Sexton Vierarm at Werrahn had received the visit of the devil on the 1st of December.

The exalted guest had climbed down the chimney, had then crept through the sexton's square, tobacco-scented, bachelor's room, not without having stirred the leather bell pull which hung down from the middle of the ceiling onto the sexton's mahogany table. For the religious man dealt with his Sunday tolling business from here. In the end, however, his hellish highness sat himself at the foot of the bed which stood in the small white painted alcove, pushed his claws under the red and white checked bedcovers, and pinched the sleeper's big toe.

"Ow," the man thus woken cried, "Ow, ow over the damned gout."

"You are a muttonhead," Master Lucifer responded, brought his tail forward, and struck his admirer with it powerfully on the nose. "Do you think that I would give up with such trifles around Christmas? Look, if I want to torment you, then I could have it easier. Then I would, for example, have spat in the middle of your forehead, and then you would have dreamt the most revolting things. Let us assume that you would have seen yourself, for example, as you were sitting in mother

Lotte's dining room, but with firmly bound arms and legs. Around you though, there would have been the reddest and fattest hams hanging, you know, so juicy. And liver sausage with large pieces of fat. And smoked goose. And smoked eel. And look, and then you would have not been able to move, and would from all that have only drawn in the wonderful smell."

"Stop!", the sexton cried, the sweat of fear dripping from his forehead. "I cannot bear that."

"You are a muttonhead, and you remain a muttonhead," the prince of hell insisted, and at the same time, he pinched the sexton on the other toe. "Do you think that I trouble myself to leave my warm subterranean room for the sake of such trifles when we are now also all thinking of Christmas? No idea. No, but I have thought something up. I have thought something up," he repeated. And at the same time, he rubbed together his ragged claws so that the red sparks sprayed forth as if under a blacksmith's hammer. "I want in fact to pack you all in white cotton wool. So high and firm that you will lie in it like the tin soldiers in a toy box. Pay attention, tomorrow I will already be starting on it. But when you believe that I am all finished with it, then you will be steeply enveloped. In this toy box, in fact, I will send you then a little kobold who shall torment and nag you so that you will always be wanting to spring out of the box in fear and unease. But he-he! The white cotton wool will hold you fast, you will not be able to go. And that will be my Christmas pleasure then."

"Woe over the nuisance," sexton Vierarm wailed, already feeling ensnared and sunken irretrievably in an enormous box of cotton wool. "Father, Son and Holy Ghost, free us from the hellish spirit."

"Oh what! If you come to me with such phrases," the visitor responded, shaking his head, "then you are becoming too stupid for an amicable trade with me.

Consider that, Master Vierarm. And now for a little farewell drink, cheers!"

With that the evil one reached under the bed, drew out a well-filled bottle of red cherry brandy, which the religious man tended to hide in this always dark dungeon, spat three times powerfully on the neck of the bottle, and the next moment, he had drunk perhaps half the contents.

"Stop, stop, my cherry," the sexton then cried as if possessed.

"Shut your mouth," the black fellow took his leave. "It is a quite miserable brew. But soon I will bring you for once a bottle of my own. Burnt ten times in purgatory. Fine, I tell you. And now turn around and think of the white cotton wool and the kobold. So. Adieu!"

And when sexton Vierarm stuck his wavy grey head out the window the next morning, he noted with horrified estrangement that the prophesy of his friend had already arrived. The sexton's house was already packed in. Everywhere, on the main road as well as on the distantly stretching fields, foot-high, white, glistening snow lay. The poplars on both sides of the house stretched out monstrous white arms and fingers, and the crows swirling croaking around the bare treetops carried white flakes on their wings.

"And how it snows," sexton Vierarm murmured as he now raised his black eyebrows enormously high and thoughtfully. "This wild bustle is not natural snow at all. It is a phenomenon. I don't want to speak about it, but I have my own ideas. And the kobold? Hm — how was it with them? Now, I will in any case warn my good friends. And first I will go to mother Lotte at Werrahn."

***

The farmyard at Werrahn was enclosed by the high, thick, white rampart as if by a glistening wall. Indeed mother Lotte had the entrance shoveled and cleared every morning, but it was not much use. And when Heinrich Kalsow, her son, who now strode along the lonely country road many times on the long, workless days to peer as if by chance at the distant snowed-in town from which something should be hurrying towards the country man — what? That he did not know exactly; perhaps spring, or happiness, or deliverance from the fearful silence which weighed on him — but when he returned in the twilight hours, then the entrance was already snowed in again, and the giant then had to free the way with mighty thrusts.

Thus it gradually became ever stiller and more silent at the farmstead, and the people were more than ever reliant on themselves.

It was one of these still winter's evenings. Outside, the snow was trickling in unrelenting, turbid flakes, and the white silence seemingly hummed over the farmstead and the entire district.

There sat Mrs Lotte Kalsow of Werrahn on her green rep sofa in the wide blue room, and held from time to time a small sheet of gold and silver tinsel before the light to convince herself as to whether the merchant in the town had not perhaps also delivered some of the previous year's for the gilding of the nuts. For the lady of the house of Werrahn prepared golden and silver nuts for the Christmas tree. And she was pursuing this business with that unshakeable earnestness which distinguished her with any undertaking. At the window sill meanwhile, her son Heinrich sat in the large armchair, smoked from his short tobacco pipe, and looked attentively out into the dark, unrecognisable, driving snow as if this whirling, mad, soundless confusion were a mysterious script which he must by all means decipher.

The tobacco clouds drew blue and fine towards the flickering light of the lamp, and in the massive stove in the corner, a cheerful fire crackled and hissed, which mother Lotte loved above all else. This sound of bursting pieces of spruce was dearer to her than any theatrical show, yes, it reached up in its melody almost to a beautiful piece of music.

It remained still for a long time between the two.

But finally the lady of the house pushed the large round glasses up onto her forehead, looked a few times inquiringly over at her averted companion, and finally shook her sharp little head dismissively. She moved her neck so energetically that the white muslin bonnet with the black velvet ribbons swayed alarmingly on her tiny head of hair.

"I am already eighty now," she said, and rattled the nuts.

"Yes, mother," the young farmer responded indifferently, without changing his position.

The old woman scraped a little more momentously with the white porcelain plate.

"Anna could help us a little too," she continued, shaking her head. "What is she up to now then?"

The son pulled himself together, and drummed lightly on the panes of the window which had just begun to ice up.

"Oh, mother," he tossed out softly and indifferently. And at the same time, he again sent a more powerful draught from his pipe. "Anna is over with the girls in the farmhouse, and having the laundry tumbled and pulled together."

"Hm."

The old woman pondered for a moment. But then she began eagerly working again at her Christmas decorations. The golden tinsel rustled under her busy fingers.

"Tell me one thing, my boy," she began as if by chance, whereby she rattled in the most emphatic way with the nuts in the small canvas sack. "What sort of horseman was that who spoke with your sister over the wall of snow this afternoon in the half gloom? Did you observe him too, Heinrich?"

Her son nodded.

"Well, who was it then?"

"Oh!" Heinrich straightened up in his chair, and hid his hands comfortably in his pockets. "Mother, you know him too, it was the young Count from over in Wildhagen."

"So, so. The Count."

The little woman worked more avidly, and her nuts rattled incessantly. Finally she said calmly to herself, "Young Hohensee must have important business to make here in the vicinity. Don't you think so too, Heinrich? I've noticed him recently so frequently before our farm. I think he is resident there in the town with the soldiers? And there it should actually be stricter."

"Eh, mother, he surely finds himself on holiday for a few weeks out here at his parents'. And here he is surely exercising his horse a bit."

Mrs Lotte bowed her head lower, and seemingly sank into her work.

"He does not exercise it exactly," she opined with her calm voice. "Not exercising when it stands still for half an hour by the wall. In any case, a beautiful bay, long-legged. The old Count understands something about farming. With him you can make business. He is one from the old mould, isn't he?"

After this discussion, mother and son fell silent anew. And both listened to the cheerful stove fire.

Puff, puff — it crackled from the green stove. And the red light trickled cheerfully over the white floor.

"Strange," the lady of the house thought, and plucked a little at her glasses. "The boy has become far too monosyllabic to me in the last few days. In winter it might pass, but it must be driven out of him by spring. We will make do. He will gradually get over it. He is a man indeed. And my son. And the best for such a thing simply remains family and work."

"Do you feel hungry, my boy?", she interrupted herself, for she carried the desire to draw the taciturn man closer to herself. And when the farmer, more to show a favour to his mother, had casually nodded, she instructed him to call his sister in so that the table could be laid. "And afterwards," she added, "we will listen to a bit of music again. Pity that sexton Vierarm is not visiting us this evening with his violin. The man is a great artist though."

But see, sexton Vierarm stood then in federation with uncanny and occult powers. Hardly had the name been mentioned than there was an earnest and solemn knocking on the door, which was scrubbed so white that it seemingly radiated. Mrs Lotte listened attentively. Then she pushed her glasses onto her forehead.

"Come in."

Nothing stirred. Instead the white wood was pounded mightier and more admonishingly, as the holy inquisitor tended usually to observe on dark occasions.

"Come in," the lady of the house at Werrahn repeated anew, as her face brightened in understanding. "It is the sexton," she added then, nodding her head. "He has such an especially spiritual way of announcing himself. Come in!"

And really, there the familiar tall figure was already bowing in the white doorway, not appearing at all so spindly today because he wore an old fivefold embroidered cloak which had been passed on from olden times to this frivolous generation. But just that fivefold black cape imparts its owner a quite striking solemnity and dignity in the eyes of the old lady. And whenever that item of clothing hung well-protected on the antiquated birch stand in the corner, mother Lotte could not resist skimming past the place as if by accident to caress the worn gleaming material once fleetingly with her hand.

"Stay tough!"

That was the house maxim at Werrahn. And the em‐broidered cloak had in fact followed this command through its entire life and acts.

"Stay tough!"

"Blessed good evening, my dears," the sexton bowed, and looked down helplessly at his thick, snow-covered five-folder. "How is the well-disposed health?"

And after he learnt that it went tolerably for the old lady as well as her entire house, the visitor drew forth from under his voluminously folded cloak a heavy violin case which could have very well been used as a small child's coffin during the time of an epidemic. Then he placed it very carefully onto the armchair by the win‐dow. This receptacle was in fact treated by the religious man with maternal care, and it was an established cus‐tom that the thus protected, precious object was only permitted to rest on a cushion.

"So."

"Sit yourself down, sexton Vierarm."

"Yes, Madam. I will be so free."

And after the cloak had found its place on the birch stand, mother Lotte strolled diagonally across the room, and tapped benevolently, almost pityingly on the five folds.

"Terribly bad weather, my dear sexton," she said sympathetically.

But the tall visitor shook his grey wavy head, and passed his hand lunging and dragging through his mighty mane.

"Bad weather? Mrs Lotte Kalsow of Werrahn," he re‐peated. "It is not actually bad weather. Not natural and proper. You must not believe that I have appeared only because of the music, or perhaps even because of the supper. Although I will give you the honour, if you amicably and kindly allow, of taking a modest place at your table. Not for that reason. God forbid. But, Mrs Lotte Kalsow of Werrahn, I have recently had apparitions, visions so to speak, which I consider myself duty-bound to interpret for my neighbouring humanity so that they can orient themselves to the coming terrible event. Hm," — the speaker interrupted himself and raised his nose sniffing. "But what I wanted to say. How lovely it smells here of roast. Of things which God confers on a blessed house. Is this perhaps also only a deplorable feigning, or should it really —?"

"No," mother Lotte confirmed with a delicate smile. "On two days of the week, there is at Werrahn also something warm for the evening. And you have struck the day, my dear sexton."

Amidst such preparations, the visitor was coerced to his vested place on the green rep sofa. And after he had placed his long legs quite improbably so that he could neither inconvenience the lady of the house with them, nor damage the polished table legs with his nail-studded boots — for such an injury was capable of strongly endangering the disposition of Mrs Lotte — in short, once he had brought himself into a harmless state, the religious man began with great lust to preach about those apparitions for which he was pardoned or damned. Something of the apocalypse of Saint John the evangelist streamed like a black stream amidst his words.

Meanwhile, Heinrich Kalsow had left the blue room at the request of his mother. He was meant to fetch his sister. And so both the old friends, the residue of a good, solid, religious time, found themselves alone. Mother Lotte counted her golden and silver nuts on the porcelain plate, carefully so that, God-willing, not a single one was missed. The sexton, however, placed his red handkerchief on the headrest of the sofa, for it was known to him that the lady of the house would protest against the possible greasing of the furniture, leant his head back, and rolled his sermon out booming and deep.

"I have seen him, Mrs Lotte Kalsow of Werrahn."

"Whom, my dear sexton?"

"Him, whom I do not want to name. With good reason, Mrs Lotte. With good reason. But through him, a warning flowed to me. We shall be packed in white cotton wool. Well? I ask you, are we not? Snow two feet high. That is the fulfillment. And secondly, a kobold shall be sent to us so that it distracts, confuses, torments, frightens, and leads us into darkness. Woe over the creature which the night spews out. Even if they also be light and blond natured. I have pondered for a long time and arduously, Mrs Lotte Kalsow —", here he placed his hand on his forehead to prove how difficult this labour came to him. "I have martyred my brain over what sort of kobold could surely have been meant. For you know, Mrs Lotte Kalsow of Werrahn, according to holy writ, there are ten thousand different evil spirits. And it is difficult to find one's way among them. Finally, though —", he straightened up, and moved quite close to his attentive listener. "Finally, though," he whispered insistently, "I came upon the idea that it could perhaps concern a human kobold. You know, dear friend, such a one as was expected here a few weeks ago. With silk skirts and see-through stockings where the white sinful flesh peers out from the silk mesh."

"Enough," mother Lotte said, and struck lightly on the table. "Why do you describe it so at length?"

Only, the religious curiosity of the visitor was only half stilled. He caught the slender blue-veined hand of the lady of the house in his massive paw, clasped it, and moved still nearer, as far as the sidearm of the sofa permitted anyhow.

"You have drawn me into your confidence a bit, Mrs Lotte Kalsow of Werrahn," he continued his attempt. "And you know, I am like a grave. The grave of Moses on Mount Sinai cannot be more untraceable and reticent. Thus tell me then — I ask purely for the sake of spiritual comfort and friendly encouragement — has our Mr Heinrich struck the idea of the distinguished visit from his head a bit already?"

"Yes," the little old woman tossed back curtly and tartly.

It irritated her that she should have been forced to relinquish the innermost secrets of her house. She would also have never ever reported anything of the secret sorrow of one of her own.

"We are over that, sexton Vierarm. Tell me rather something from the district. You get around everywhere."

And as if she were locking something quite especially important in herself, she sent a quick side glance over her guest, adjusted her glasses, and looked rigidly at him with her grey, bright eyes sparkling behind the lenses, which a mortal could only escape with difficulty.

"Have you not recently," she inquired firmly and erectly, "been at the castle at Wildhagen?"

There the serious prophet's mien of the religious man smoothed itself out, and a placid complacency played over his features.

"At the Count's castle," he replied, nodding his head, and yet full of pervasive pride over his distinguished acquaintance. "Yes, my dear friend, with Count Hohensee and his noble wife. In fact, that is a house like one finds in books. A noble and a pious house. And what a woman she is, her most serene highness the Countess, she had

Georg Engel

us fetched again, my pastor and myself, for family prayers. Properly in one of the Count's carriages with four
horses. For the high-born lady knows what behoves the
clergy. And my pastor preached profoundly and for a
long time as he always does. And I then had to play on
the house organ, and should also have sung as well,
which I couldn't, however, owing to hoarseness. And finally, there was then a Sunday meal like our Lord and
saviour could not have found better for the wedding at
Canaan. For her most serene highness is also a tasteful
woman. Think, Mr Lotte Kalsow of Werrahn — your
own kitchen in honour — but there, there was —", the
teller smacked his lips in blissful recollection. "Carp
with Polish sauce. Prepared in the Jewish way, Mrs
Lotte. That is the most excellent of all. And then there
was wild pig, with which she had used proper Burgundy. And then, Mrs Lotte, a plum pudding which was
really burning with blue and green flames. But my pastor, he just blew on them, and see then, the fire died
away. But it was also tasty beyond all measure. Yes, you
see, this was a house which all the great and mighty of
the earth should take as an exemplary model."

In full feeling for all this bliss, the sexton stretched
back again, crossed his hands over the wretched bend of
his body, and as he narrowed his eyes raptly, his lips
murmured half unconsciously, "Lovely, these smells are
lovely," whereby he meant surely the aroma which
streamed out amiably and inviting from mother Lotte's
kitchen.

The lady of the house, however, was not of a mind to
be distracted from her main topic. She had in the meantime taken a large white tablecloth from a massive
cupboard, and was now spreading it over the round mahogany table. But in the middle of this work, she threw
out half indifferently, "Did the young Count take part in
the family prayers, my dear sexton?"

The religious man nodded.

"What do you think, Mrs Lotte," he responded. "For such pious work, everyone in Wildhagen who has legs is commandeered. From the lowest pig boy right up to her serene highness the Countess herself. Yes, young Mr Fritz also took part in it. And he looked so stately in his white uniform that he could have been bowing any minute before our most majestic Emperor. And after the lunch, he even gifted me a long heavy cigar. A sophisticated one with a red band like those they smoke in the distinguished officer's mess there in the town. With that, I seemingly became noble and aristocratic. And you cannot think at all what delightful tales the young Count is able to tell. Sometimes about the military, about his Colonel and about excellent and distinguished horses. And other times again about music and dance, which he especially loves. Why not? The youth, if they otherwise stroll so piously, need not always place one step before the other. For my sake, they can also dance if they just don't entertain sinfully covetous ideas at the same time, and if it also does not make them dizzy. And that it surely won't with the young Count, who can endure such things. And then he related things about Berlin where he had been assigned for a long time. And you should just have heard, Mrs Lotte — how he talked there about the court. With all the baronesses and countesses and courtiers and emperors and queens. Such things as I so like to hear. You obtain an idea of how far the human race can advance in its brilliance. And see, such a young count is also just born to it that the entire world belongs to him. Dear God wants it thus. Don't you think so too, Mrs Lotte?"

The lady of the house stood still, took off her glasses, and stuck them awkwardly into a leather case.

"Certainly," she agreed. "So long as it involves baronesses and countesses, the entire world may, as far as I'm concerned, belong to him. That does not concern me at all. But tell me please, sexton Vierarm, have you not perhaps noticed in the young gentleman that he — hm," she interrupted herself, and plucked here and there at the tablecloth until she had to lower her head further as if by chance, — "have you not perhaps also noticed that it must not just always be baronesses and countesses with the young gentleman?"

"How do you mean, Mrs Lotte?"

"I mean that he contents himself and gets along in his amicability and condescension also with quite common town girls at times? I am not thinking of anything specific. Have you perhaps noticed such a thing?"

"Me?"

The sexton abruptly leapt up, and his wide fiery eyes opened as large and vast as if proper biblical manna were raining down from both the beams in mother Lotte's blue room.

"What are you saying! Not to be believed, Mrs Lotte. Should it happen here perhaps? Have you perceived something of the like?"

"No," the old woman cut him off coolly, whereby she began folding the serviettes intricately and with practised hand. "I asked you only by chance. Out of a curiosity, understand, with which such old women as myself are frequently plagued. But other than that, I possess no special reason."

"Look, that does not matter at all. That does not really matter at all, Mrs Lotte. Leave it all to me. I will watch out. You know my pastor desires that I keep tabs over the goings-on in the parish. Sweet — sweet, town girls? Eh, that would be, yes! And then such a highborn count? But what do I always say? The devil walks about the countryside, roaring like a hungry lion."

"May be so," the lady of the house cut him off, shrugging her shoulders. "But since you are just speaking of hunger, here come Anna and Heinrich. And now we will eat our supper without hurry. And for the flaming plum pudding, my dear sexton, you will get some grated green cheese from me. Herbed cheese, prepared by Anna herself."

"Good too," the sexton replied, exhaling. "Everything has its time, wise Solomon said."

And with that the inhabitants of Werrahn sat down at the table.

***

A pleasant, sweet music had long been flooding through the blue room. Mother Lotte's daughter Anna was sitting at the new piano and playing Mozart's minuet. For Mrs Lotte did not want to know anything about the modern musical arts. Because they made her head dizzy, as she said. By the side of the piano, sexton Vierarm had taken up his post, and when he stroked his bow long and drawn out over the strings, then his figure bent in the most remarkable contortions so that it sometimes looked as if he had lost something on the floor, or as if he were aiming to strike at disturbing flies in the air. Occasionally he also scratched apprehensively. Then mother Lotte coughed quietly in warning, "Hem — hem."

But all in all, the guest divested himself of his task quite decently. And the lady of the house of Werrahn was more and more attached to the belief that she was hosting a great artist.

Solemn and grave, measured and old-fashioned, the minuet drew through the space.

Heinrich sat in his armchair by the window. But strangely, as unconditionally as he also tried, he was unable to listen attentively. Soon he had to stare through the iced-up window at the driving snow which fought itself more and more wildly outside, and it seemed as if the fine flakes had faces which nodded and whispered to him, "Come, come. We hide a secret. Search — search. Don't you hear, it rings and tolls. That is luck!"

The next moment, his gaze again flew over the tall, slender and yet powerful figure of his sister, who touched the keys with so devoted and yet so cheerful a expression.

"Truly, a strong, a self-assured woman," the pondering man thought. "How brightly she can laugh. How confidently and expectantly she can command her subordinates; without excitement and noise, everything comes to its proper place through her. And if she is once distracted, if she is fond of someone, and chats with him, like today over the wall with the young Count — oh, he has already been here more often, I have certainly noticed that — how confidently and without danger she handles it all. Barely a meaningless interruption which the next moment she does not think of anymore. Listen, now she is singing. Really, that is even a voice which sounds healthy and fresh. And me? — I should also though —! I am yet a man, and have my work. And yet! Can it be possible that the memory of such a small being holds me fast, and torments and alarms me? That it prowls about me, and does not let me rest? I must — — I would like —".

Only, the giant was unable to reach the end of this mental labour. Pulled up by an unconscious helplessness, he rose slowly, and since nobody was paying attention to him at that moment, he opened the door without a noise, and in the next moment, he was already in the quiet yard.

Snow, thick soft snow crunched under his feet when he paused for a few seconds. The delicate notes of the minuet penetrated through the iced-up windows, behind which the blue wallpaper of the illuminated room shimmered cosily. Here outside, however, coldness reigned. From the roofs of the farm buildings, arm-thick icicles hung down, knobbly and firm. And the smoke which struck from the low chimney was pressed down by the masses of snow and played like a burning red cloud over the roof ridge. Heinrich pulled a soft cap from his side pocket, covered his head, which was already lightly soaked by flakes, and strode in his wide-lunging gait out of the yard. The country road stretched out unrecognisably before him. Only the snow at his feet glimmered with an indefinite pallid light. Thus he walked along. And again he strode the path which led to the town. Ever anew. And with every milestone he passed, it seemed to him as if he were getting nearer to his own, that which belonged to him, and which he must obtain if the power were not to be slowly stolen from him which normally filled his entire being. Left and right, the fields had to spread out. But in the thick whirling snow, he was unable to catch sight of them. His gaze only penetrated a few metres. Then everything was a grey dim driving, a living curtain which was pushed and shaken by a powerful fist. And what boundless calm lay over the silent land. Yes, he felt it. The stillness came creeping along, took his arm, and bedded its white head on his chest so that his breath almost stood still.

Strange, earlier he had hardly known feelings like that, at least he had not noticed them.

Now he paused, and stretched.

What was the point of this aimless wandering? Did he perhaps want to get away along this miles long stretch to wander through the gates of the sleeping town finally exhausted and shivering with cold? And then? Should he wake the townsmen with the cry, "Give her back to me! Give her to me! I am an oaf from the coun-tryside who seeks after one who laughed at me, who broke her word to me, whom I am too bad for?!"

Shaking his head, he sat down on an iron chain which was stretched between two way stones before a ditch, and looked up at the heavens. Up there between the impenetrable white bee swarms which passed skittishly and snappily in mad balls against each other, there it twitched back and forth as if by a stray redness. Usually the farmer knew this phenomenon of winter well, but today he stared up in astonishment, and was taken aback. The next moment admittedly, his thoughts had again scurried through the gates of the town, and now they chased restlessly and disturbed around the little blond person.

There he saw her before himself again, how she had leant the slender head with the blond hair on his shoulder that night. Oh, every little hair formed a golden glittering shackle which was slung binding around his soul. And then again a different image. How she had sat chatting and smiling at the table in the Professor's house. And her gaze had wandered weighing and appraising from the uncommunicative man of the house over to him, the guest, the intruder. Always back and forth. But then — then had come the inconceivable moment when she pretended not to know anymore about her promise, about her covenant which was given in the face of death quietly and sacredly. Or could such a thing really be forgotten?

In the midst of the wild driving snow, the awkward man struck his forehead so that the iron chain rattled under him. From his burdened chest, his breath climbed in great white clouds. Then he shook his head in desperate astonishment. Both of these images, the little one in the blue dress, and that in the black, they were two different people. The one denied the other. Was there such a thing? Was that often to be found with women? Or did only this one possess that one uncanny art? Oh God, she had actually lied. And what did he disdain so strongly on this earth but an untruth? He would have rather taken a mangy dog in his arms than offer his hand to a liar.

Cling — a-ling — cling — a-ling — cling — a-ling.

The solitary man paused. A sled so late? He pulled out his watch, and tried to read the dial despite the darkness. It was already going close on nine.

Cling — a-ling — —.

Now, a sled was probably gliding past there, which was trying to reach the neighbouring Count's estate for an evening get-together. Perhaps it was young cheerful officers from the garrison who were guiding their vehicle themselves. The bells were shrilling so brightly and silvery. And startled from his brooding, the young farmer looked straining down the white road. Now the whinnying of horses snorting loudly through the night could already be heard. Praise God, through that the eerie spell of silence had been broken. Life was approaching again. And Heinrich pulled himself together, dusted the snow from his clothes, and scolded himself for having dreamt off for such a long time here aimlessly. What must his own people think of him? Mother Lotte, his sister, and even the sexton Vierarm? No, no, all this brooding did not help him at all. He owed the house at Werrahn to chase it away from there.

"Stay tough."

When he thought of mother Lotte's favourite saying, he had to smile.

The sled flew past. In front, wrapped up in a fur, the coachman. Behind, turned up and bound, formless things. It must be chests and boxes.

Strange!

But there in the middle? What does that signify?

Heinrich leapt up furiously. No, no, he did not want to be overwhelmed in any case by his imagination again. But then! Look though! The figure in the dark coat — is it not of black velvet? — she seems so small, so pliant, so delicate. And is she not now holding her hand before her eyes as if she wanted to fend off the flakes which hindered her from peering out after him?

"Heinrich!"

"Stop — burr —!"

The steeds stamped, the sled stopped.

Then it was suddenly so bright about the staring man, as if the ball of the sun had plunged to his feet through the middle of the snowy night, and everything were ablaze in a supernatural, glaring fire.

"Hertha! For all the world! Hertha! Is it possible? You yourself? No, no, it is all surely not true at all. Where are you coming from? What are you wanting here? Are you coming to us? Or do you perhaps want to go on further? You aren't thinking of it at all, are you?"

"I want to come to you. To you. To you, and to your mother. And you, Heinrich, have surely been sitting here awaiting me?"

"Me? I have — yes, I have been waiting here for you. Dear little one, every day I have been coming out here to wait for you. Do you believe that?"

"I believe everything of you."

And then suddenly both the soft velvet sleeves were slung about the steer-like neck of the man. The little figure leant out, and the blond head under the black beret embedded itself again in that place where it had once lingered on that night of death.

"Hertha, dear little Hertha, what are you doing? It is me, Heinrich Kalsow."

"Praise God that it is you. Oh, you do not know, Heinrich, you do not know what is driving me. You cannot guess how much I need from you. Advice and help. For everything which my mother saw in her last dreams has been fulfilled. Stay quite calm. I want to tell you."

But the man, before whose ears it is whooshing and roaring, who hears choirs roaring thundering over the fields, and who is in a mood as if giant fists were casting him up high into the winter sky, he defends himself, he shakes his head. He does not want to hear or perceive anything. Just home. Home with her. He must hide the infinitely valuable treasure. He must not give her away to the country road.

He sits next to her. He holds the reins instead of the sleepy coachman, and the quick steeds swish with wide lunging strides to Werrahn. They are not heard. No hoofbeat is audible. It is as if the vehicle and people are gliding over clouds.

To Werrahn. To Mother Lotte. To Werrahn.

***

But when the sled had arrived in the yard, Heinrich Kalsow hesitated. For the first time, depressing and difficult thoughts occurred to the farmer, who had been educated by his mother for the practical things of the world. The measured and yet delicate notes of the minuet were still penetrating out from within the blue room whose lights shimmered through the frost work on the window. And it passed vanishingly quick through the mind of the son of the house that his placid home would be at the moment less prepared for anything than for the little blond visitor whom he just now had wanted to introduce by the hand radiantly with joy. Only, the doubt was already intercepted by the fresh voice of the girl, and Heinrich had also immediately overcome all obstacles as if by magic.

She sprang out of the sled, and shook herself.

"You are making music inside, Heinrich?" she asked with cheerful surprise, as she gently touched his arm. "That I take it for a good sign."

And as she now caught the German melody of the old Frankish dance, she could not contain herself, from spraying her skirts a little in the middle of the night and in the deep snow, and performing a deep minuet bow to the dumbfounded farmer.

"See. So my gentleman!"

The movement was so fine and delicate, so undreamt of in its entire surroundings, that the man watching began laughing all over.

Yes, that was quite certain, with this radiant blond creature came joy. What he absolutely needed to ask still was why she had been silent so long, and for what reason she appeared only now at nighttime? Certainly, mother Lotte would deal with everything in order. With both hands, he grasped the dancer's lovely arms. And then the confession forced itself haltingly from his quivering lips, "Oh, how beautiful it is, Hertha, that you have finally come."

"Yes, it was time," the guest replied as if her appearance were quite in order, yes, as if it formed something long expected.

And yet, as if under a spell and held fast, neither of them turned their steps to the house, but rather as if affecting to wait for the unloading of the luggage, instead an inner timidity held them back from entering this peaceful, snow-covered farmhouse.

A ringing sled could not arrive unnoticed in the evening hour at the farmstead. Mother Lotte had long since caught the sound, and charged her daughter Anna with looking up the strange disturbance.

For a moment, Hertha jerked back at the hand of her guide when she perceived the tall, well-proportioned figure looming in the dark hallway.

"It is my sister," Heinrich whispered encouragingly to the apprehensive girl.

But from within, a clear, reasoned voice sounded, "Heinrich, who are you bringing us so late?"

Then the entering girl, the artful girl, felt that all her strength, all her bewitching life spirit must be called up in help so as to force an entrance once and for all into this house which was already throwing an obstruction against her at the portal.

"It is me, dear Miss Kalsow. Me, Hertha Boddin."

And whilst a gentle exclamation of surprise was heard from the other side, the girl springing in had already grasped both the hands of Heinrich's sister, who almost towered over her by a full head, and now squeezed the surprised girl's fingers with such warmth and such a friendly look that the tall simple girl was already at the first approach unable to resist a certain reverent heartiness.

Just look even. It was a distinguished young lady. The daughter of a colonel, who now slung her arm so trustingly in that of the daughter of the house. How could she deprive herself of such condescension? And straight afterwards, the clever and practical Anna learnt through a quick side glance over to her brother what an inner joy the tall awkward man seemed to feel in the closely nestled girls' figures. That decided it. This knowledge robbed her even of the contemplation of how the little gaunt woman there in the blue room would surely judge the intruder, the delicate blond guest.

And now questions and answers passed quickly back and forth.

"Dear gracious Miss, what a beautiful surprise you have given us in wanting to visit us for a while. And I may surely also have your luggage brought in straightaway? Hey, where then are Jochen and Krischan? They must help."

"But tell me, will I not also be a nuisance to you?", Hertha whispered bashfully, as she lowered her blond

head self-consciously under its black beret. "I am following your invitation though. Only, since I am really
coming for a few weeks — oh, I would have confided in
you about it, dear, dear Anna — right, I may call you
that? — I would have confided so much to you —".

"Not now, not now," the daughter of the house objected, touched. "We have so much space here. And if it
were okay with you, then I will have your things immediately brought up to the loft room next to where I
sleep. I think you won't feel so lonesome then. Now just
come, dear gracious Miss," she added somewhat apprehensively. "I can already hear our mother walking up
and down before the door in there. And she is certainly
already curious about whom we are keeping out here for
so long."

When the name of mother Lotte occurred, the little
blond felt a painful stab again. Always the mother! In
what dependency both the people next to her are held
by the old woman. For her own late mother had lived so
entirely differently with her. And yet — and yet! The reluctant girl had to force herself, it worked though to find
a home, a refuge, without the others noticing anything
of her distress.

No, that must not be. She had planned for these
country people to have to always see her visit as a gift.

"Yes, come," Heinrich also wrested her now from her
anxious thoughts, "mother will get impatient otherwise."

The humble white door was opened.

And there the small gaunt woman really stood
already close to the threshold as if she had been listening straining there for the past minutes. She also
seemed not to be surprised at all, although her hand
was only stretched out to the arrival with difficulty and
hesitantly. But yet — her crooked nose thrust somewhat

more pointedly than usual, as she now rasped meaningfully, "Good evening, dear Miss."

She offered her welcome, whereby she wiped her
hand back and forth on her black dress.

"You did not give advance notice. Otherwise we
would have certainly waited with the supper." And
pointing to a tall figure who had climbed onto the window sill, and had thus assumed a somewhat wizened
and towering aspect, she added in introduction, "This is
our friend, the sexton Vierarm. You may perhaps
already know of him from earlier, dear Miss."

"Entirely on my side," Mr Vierarm tossed in without
waiting.

Hertha, however, trooped up to the little woman, and
quite suddenly she dropped her luminous blue eyes up
close to the observing eyes of Mrs Lotte, but then she
abruptly slung both arms heftily about the chest and
neck of the astonished woman. She kissed the old woman directly on the mouth.

"Why don't you call me Hertha, like before, mother
Lotte?", she cried trustingly and insistently. "My mother
talked to me so often about her best, childhood friend.
Hence," she added with strong resolve, "surely why you
offered me, dear good mother, a place in your house for
a few weeks, to set me up to some extent from the blow
which affected me. Right, that is how I may understand
it?"

"Hem — hem."

The mistress of the house cleared her throat, half
turned to the sexton, who was performing a rocking
movement in the air with his violin bow, and then let
one of her weighing, balancing looks sweep over the
little figure. But the devoted expression in the expressive blue girlish eyes became more and more eloquent
and imploring, until mother Lotte could no longer withstand it. And she would have also hesitated just now,

and given some elusive answer, if she had not also met eyes with her son at that moment.

He still remained under the modest white entrance, had his fists clenched together, and now looked questioning and doubting from the little blond to his mother, and again from the mistress of the house to the arrival. Then it poured haltingly and cautiously from the mother's lips, "If it pleases you out here with us, dear Hertha, and if our entire life and activity does not appear too foreign to you, then it shall delight me to see you with us for some time. We will yet discuss your prospects and plans, for you have surely already brought together your thoughts over the future. That a person must do. And now, Anna, take the girl's coat and beret, and make sure that our guest receives something that will hold her body and soul together. For you may surely be properly frozen through, my child," she added sympathetically.

And when Hertha had asked that the company should not be disturbed through her presence in their musical pleasures to which they had been paying homage up to then, an apprehensive smile slid over the prophet's countenance of the sexton.

"No," he said, as he climbed down from the sill, and waved the violin bow in the air. "Not this. My art, I mean, my manual skill on the violin surely suffices for Werrahn. But for such an educated Miss, it may not be easy grazing for the ears. What do you say to that?"

Then Hertha felt with the sure instinct for all the utilities of life which characterised her that is was advisable to conquer this man too, if her own time of rest in the house she had just entered should prosper.

The unrest, the doubt, the uncertainty, they raged and shouted behind her.

And so vehemently was she assailed again by these pursuers tormenting her, that she sprang up, secretly burning, to catch and correct the opinion of this tall man who would otherwise have remained so heartily in-different to her.

And see there, she was immediately able to let her fresh, welling laugh ring out, and while she assured in a quite naturally appearing cheerfulness that her musical knowledge was only quite superficial because she only felt joy and love in couplets and operetta melodies which were too light and meaningless, she had already sat down at the piano. And now one of those tingling ballads passed through the blue room, falling so to the ear, so capricious and charming, that the old beams straightened in astonishment, for such zest for life had not yet rushed through this space often. And then she hummed between her red lips, which quivered and twitched at the same time, the lightheaded tingling text. Her hands flew, her little body rocked back and forth gracefully.

Who could have been annoyed with her there? Even the lady of the house at Werrahn, who stood there at first astonished, almost stunned, was gradually caught by the skipping melody and the recital full of the joys of life. And when mother Lotte looked almost a little curi-ously at her companions, she perceived that the other three were also intoxicated by the same magic.

"Just look, look," mother Lotte thought, and shook her head a little apprehensively. "There the tall cur-mudgeon, the sexton, now stands, who may not suffer her, yes, who even calls the pretty blond girl a kobold. There he stands at the window, and swings his violin bow with all his weight as if he must be conducting a band. And how funnily he raises his leg from time to time. No, that would really be laughable. And now just my two. Heinrich and Anna. No, really there attention must be paid. My daughter, at base though my cool, sober image, she has even clustered behind the seat of the strange girl, and strokes her fine, silky blond hair quite gently and tenderly so that the girl barely notices it. She is giving of herself so quickly? That is strange though. But Heinrich now? How he stands askance from the instrument, pressed tight in the corner so that he does not even need to turn his eyes from the singer. And how he stares at her. How the big dumb boy smiles. Pay attention, pay attention, mother Lotte! Here it is about guarding and fending off. But not now, rather slowly and gradually."

And as if she wanted to violently break by a quick word the spell which held everyone caught, the old woman threw in-between clearly with her cool and hard voice, "Since when have you been playing again, my child? Does it not disturb you in your mourning?"

These words should not have fallen. The music immediately stopped. The white quick hands fell like rotten wood in the lap of the little one, and the miens of the three listeners darkened and straightened up reproachfully towards the mistress of the house.

Hertha, however, sat for a moment motionlessly. Then she slowly led her fingers to her temples, pressed them as if she had to bring herself to her senses, but then fluttered up, pushed her chair back, and took the astonished little woman in her arms again. She brought her blond head so close to the shoulder of mother Lotte so that the old woman could see only indistinctly and blurred her red imploring mouth.

"Oh, Aunt Kalsow," she asked. "You see how it goes with me. You are quite right when you scold me. Just do that. Do it properly. For you see, I cannot even defend myself against this sort of music, I composed myself so seriously too. But it shall not occur again, auntie. That I promise you. And you aren't angry with me now, are you?"

Then the little woman was defeated for the second time by this humble remorse. And the lady of the house of Werrahn felt so confused that even she ignored in the first moment of surprise how her blond guest addressed her familiarly in her flattering submissiveness. But from then on, she did not feel it anymore.

They sat once more at the table, for the new arrival's sake, as she had had such a long sled journey through the cold and snow behind her. And again mother Lotte of Werrahn wondered exceedingly over the sexton even troubling to converse with the alien kobold.

At first he began explaining to her the extremely peculiar arrangement of his violin case, in which things were housed which did not usually appear in similar receptacles. For example, a peeled potato which should be capable of holding the moisture conditions of the famous receptacle constantly at the same level. In addition, however, a dry frog's leg which stood in some mysterious relationship with the electricity or tension of the strings. In conclusion, however, he showed her a piece of rosin which he maintained was drawn from the shop of the same merchant from which the great demon Paganini had obtained through trade a similar piece on his passage through Stettin a long time ago.

"And now it makes my strings daemonic, dear Miss," he explained earnestly. "For the daemonic, that you can believe me, is generally as essential in life as in art. All people who are a bit different have something of the daemonic. Whether they be blond now or dark-haired. But first you must eat, eat, you need not stop because of my insignificant conversation. But if I may fetch you sometime for a walk, or if you yourself sometime with Mrs Lotte, or with Anna, or perhaps also with — — hem — with Mr Heinrich should have the honour in my modesty, then I will tell you more about the demons around us. For it is necessary that the women folk also know something of it."

Towards ten o'clock, the sexton said his farewells.

And when Anna grasped the candle to light the steps to her room ahead of the blond guest, mother Lotte stretched her hand towards the girl with her slow measuredness to then utter a little hesitantly, "Sleep well, dear child. And tomorrow we will discuss this and that together. Then you will tell me about your plans, and why you have journeyed so unexpectedly from the town. That surely has a reason, doesn't it? But now just go sleep. Good night."

"Good night."

Anna accompanied the arrival upstairs. But when the daughter of the house wanted to open the door to the mansard room behind the large brown balcony, she suddenly felt her hand held back. The figure of the strange girl nestled quite close to her own. And to her great surprise, Heinrich's sister felt how a pair of soft arms were slung firmly and yet quivering about her chest and hips.

"Anna," a quiet voice asked in her ear. "Be a little fond of me. Try to. Please, please, just a little. I need it so."

And without waiting for the answer, the candle was taken out of the hand of the astonished girl, and the stranger who wanted to become at home in this house had vanished behind the mansard door.

Outside the blustering gale howled about the house, and Anna climbed down the white-washed steps of the stairs in thought.

But something wondrous then happened. In the dark shadows of the floor, the tall figure of her brother loomed. And as the descending woman now tried to stride past him, her hand was grasped hastily and abruptly. He squeezed it tightly. As if he had something to thank his dear sister for from the bottom of his heart. But nothing was said between the two siblings.

They parted wordlessly.

And soon the accustomed calm and certainty again lay over the home at Werrahn. But outside the flakes tumbled, and the white bee swarms passed humming about the house.

***

A quarter of an hour later, Hertha lies in her bed. It is a great massive piece of furniture in which her delicate figure almost loses itself. A proper farmer's bed which is meant for giants. But this time, the girl does not stroke down the covers, for she is chilled. She distinctly hears the snow pecking against the windows as if a hungry bird desires entry. Then she lifts her head, and gazes for a moment startled through the angled window casement of her mansard room up at the dark chasing clouds from which the millions of white points are being shaken down.

Oh, how uncomfortable the effect of this silence is.

And as the sleepless girl looks around in the narrow, light blue painted room, in which only a few light spruce pieces of furniture serve for comfort, she is carried back by her scared-up thoughts to that house which she only abandoned hours before.

Abandoned?

She throws herself about, and presses her hands against her breast. Her heart hammers loudly and furiously behind her soft silky skin.

Abandoned?

Chased away! It was indicated with cool sober words how her longer sojourn could have resulted in misinterpretations. Because the circumstances of a teacher do not permit bearing the concern for another's existence. Yes, even how the insertion of a stranger must impart an inner unrest into the intimate life of the two spouses who are dependent upon one another.

Inner unrest!

The taciturn incommunicative man had really strewn about such half ridiculous words. Oh, he was even just a bald, famished philistine like the many others over which he so often held court. It had occurred to the little one though as if finally a badly dissembled horror had discouraged him from looking her in the face, or even touching her hand. And as she tossed about in the thick heavy pillows, the knowledge trickled over her that, despite all that, this man must be one of those over whom her power was bestowed. Yes, yes, it swished an idea into her, stronger and ever stronger, such a sovereign power like that which that schoolmaster had spoken of in his fury, such a power was housed in her, strove for activation and victory, and it would amount to her fate to use this bewitching force. Oh, how well this consciousness did her in all her sorrow and in the midst of her threatening abandonment.

Perhaps though — perhaps though! Perhaps there was yet a way up. This solid, respectable house of Werrahn perhaps signified only the first step on the ladder which led up to the sunny path.

And as her skin shivered with the chill, she clenched her little fists together, and stretched her limbs defiantly as if she had already seized the rungs of that invisible ladder, and now intended climbing up the rocking ladder despite storm and thunder.

Up — up!

She closes her eyes. And she puts her little foot ever firmer on the rungs, and climbs up!

2

Early in the morning, six o'clock on the dot, Anna heard something scurrying and rustling in the next room. She started, and pondered. The darkness still floated before the windows, and the inexorable dusting of the flakes could be guessed at more than recognised. Still half-conscious, the beautiful tall woman stretched, and brushed from her forehead a strand of the full brown flood of hair which trickled wildly and gaily about her head. Then a first timid thought announced itself to the awakening woman.

What did that signify next door? Had mother Lotte already climbed up the stairs perhaps? The old lady was certainly the first early riser in her house. But now in wintertime? Impossible! Indeed mother Lotte certainly already stood, with her old blue dressing gown on, down below in the kitchen with a burning candle stump, and was preparing the morning drink for the others whom she did not begrudge another half an hour of rest. But to penetrate up here at this hour? The old woman did not do that.

But before the daughter of the house could account further for it, or even contemplate her neighbour, it seemed to her as if the door were shortly opened. Straight afterwards, a shadow scurried through the darkness, and as she straightened up with a gentle exclamation, there her little blond neighbour was sitting, already fully clothed, by her on the edge of the bed where she took Heinrich's sister in her arms without further ado. According to the custom of girls, she kissed the surprised woman furiously and passionately on the mouth and cheeks.

"Yes, but dear Miss —".

"Quiet, quiet, I was just a little scared there next door."

"But why have you risen so early?", Anna objected.

"Oh, only because I thought that mother Lotte would perhaps set store by it. That does not matter. I terribly like to do it. But may I not be a little helpful to you now, dear Anna?"

And before the girl addressed really knew what was happening to her, she felt how the stormy blond was brushing her full brown hair admiringly with both hands.

"God, what a splendour," she heard Hertha call out in honest enthusiasm. "It is the most beautiful hair you can imagine. Makart brown, it's called. You know, after the great painter. And you hide it so? Please, please, will you allow me though, Anna, to do it up for you once? It must be curled. And luckily I brought an instrument for that with me. I will be right back with you."

Again something rustled through the room. Next door there was a vigorous rummaging here and there, and as the strong country girl got out of her bed with a leap so as not to be completely surprised, the little blond was already with her again. And now she had brought a burning little candle with her. The light was glittering on the golden tips of her hair and weaving a luminous shimmer about her.

The two offered a peculiar picture. Half in the light and half in the shadows. The smaller one in the close-fitting becoming dress of mourning which she seemed only to have chosen so that the bright white of her narrow face and the sparkling splendour of her hair could be contrasted even better by the sombre colour. And the other, tall and towering, in white shirt which did not hide her growth, and with bare arms and feet.

"I want to get dressed," Anna cried in shock.

But as much as she begged, the little one, who seemed completely carried away by her wish, pulled the balking woman down onto a chair and grasped her hair caressingly. And after a tiny spirit burner had been lit on the bedside table, she began her beautifying work amidst all sorts of exclamations of joy.

"How glorious! How splendid! No, if you could see yourself, dearest, loveliest Anna. Stay still, I will fetch a mirror, and you can look in it."

And then she stood again behind the silenced woman and curled the beautiful hair and crimped it, and then intertwined it in a half grecian knot.

Really, the wholesome strong, country girl offered a glorious sight. And the little one felt so enchanted by her work that, still remaining behind the chair, she embraced Heinrich's sister with intensified joy to kiss her stormily on the neck.

"Oh, now a count must come at the very least," she cried, and clapped her hands. "For less than that, I will not show my work at all."

"A count?", the admired woman repeated.

A fine redness instinctively scurried across Anna's features, and quickly vanished again.

"That is all silly stuff. And what will mother Lotte," she added a little fearfully, "say to this new getup? But now quickly into your clothes."

She hurriedly got into her stockings and skirts, but could not prevent, despite a vigorous defence, the little blond guest from attending to her with a perfectly stormy devotion. First she was buttoning up her bodice, then she was smoothing out her skirt, yes, she even carried over her boots, and endeavoured to facilitate Heinrich's sister's putting them on.

"But it's not working. It really does 'not' work," Anna stuttered bashfully, not being able to explain to herself at all this readiness to serve.

Only, all objections were suppressed again and again by a cheerful smile or by new caresses.

Mother Lotte was not yet in the large blue living room which was now peering into the uncomfortable dawn, when both the girls came down the stairs. The old lady stood rather at the red brick stove in the kitchen, over which an enormous angular chimney hood rose. Kettles and kitchen equipment hung on iron hooks all around the flue. But how the mistress of the house paused when the two friends now entered.

"What's that?", she burst out just entirely taken aback.

Then she set her glasses on her nose. And as she held a milk pot in her hand, she gazed at her so advantage-ously altered daughter with ever larger eyes. But no word escaped her. Only the small narrow goshawk's head rocked back and forth a few times apprehensively, after which she turned again to her stove top without having heeded the morning greeting of the pair.

"See after the maids," she just threw to her daughter.

Then Anna left the redbrick room quickly and almost in flight.

The guest, however, and the mistress of the house re-mained alone. But what had begun up there in the girl's room repeated itself here too. Little Hertha seemed to understand the old lady's silence well. For in the next moment, she stepped up to her with a light step, and stroked the arm of the old woman familiarly as she moved back and forth so busily.

"Mother," she wished quietly, "good morning."

"Good morning, my child," the old woman replied in-differently.

But the blond was not to be shooed away so easily from there. Without waiting for another word, she ran quivering to a corner, where the receptacle for the small chopped pieces of spruce was tucked, and now she carried a load of these pieces of wood over so that mother Lotte had to turn around.

"What is that about?" the old woman inquired hoarsely.

"Nothing at all, mother. The fire is not burning properly. Don't you notice?"

"What? And you want to help me with it?"

The old woman pushed her glasses up onto her forehead. And when she now had to see how the guest first pushed a straw mat before the stove door to be able to kneel down on it cleanly, and how the little spry fingers now placed the pieces of pine one after the other in the fuming opening, without twisting her mouth at the haze streaming out, mother Lotte shrugged her shoulders, and, without saying anything further, began rattling with the iron rings of the stove.

"What does it mean?", she thought secretly at the same time. "What does the little one want? Keep watch!"

Meanwhile Hertha had finished her work. Now she rose, stepped back a little, and attentively dusted herself off.

"That is alright," mother Lotte judged. "There can be no objection to that."

But the next moment, it went through the limbs of the little woman like a jolt.

"You need more water, mother," the blond namely determined behind her suddenly, having meanwhile looked into the water butt. "The container is empty. I will fetch it for you."

"What? How? Where?"

The old woman held tightly onto the iron bar of the stove, and turned around. Had she heard right? Really and truly, Hertha had grasped the water bucket, and was, without waiting for a response, hurrying out to the yard into the dawn, snow, and cold. The thing did not even know where to find the pump.

Remarkable! Remarkable. It did not all agree with the picture which mother Lotte had painted of her guest. Where did the falsehood start here, and where did a genuine and true being begin?

"That is difficult, that is indeed very difficult to distinguish," mother Lotte murmured, and still held tightly onto the iron bar. "It's not easy at all to take. Here I must open my eyes. But I also must not be unjust. God forbid, my own pleasure does not play a role here. But it means paying attention here mightily."

With that she set a kettle on the stove, and waited.

***

At the well, many of the loveliest idylls of the human race have played out. The shepherd Jacob saw his Rachel there, and served her. And at a well in the white sands, the Saviour met the Samaritan woman —

When the little one with the wooden bucket stepped out, a cutting wind was whistling across the yard. It was blowing the flakes diagonally in front of her. It was still so dark that Heinrich, who was clearing the stables with the groom Riek, had his companion bring along a stable lantern. The light flickered uncertainly and twitching through the dim panes.

"Someone is coming there," the fat, short-winded Riek reported, freezing.

And straight afterwards, both men saw how a delicate little person flew through the middle of the driving snow to the thickly snowed over wooden pipe of the pump, which took up its place quite in the middle of the yard. In her right hand, the wooden bucket hung down, and with her left, she gathered her dress simply and cheerfully.

"Look," fatty Riek said, and grinned.

The bucket was put down, and the lever began to move.

Then Heinrich was with a spring by the side of the little one.

"Hertha," he stuttered, and then correcting himself, "dear Miss —".

He stretched his hand out, and stared now at the bucket and now at the visible feet of the little one, which had sunk in the thick snow, as if he could not make out the entire affair under any circumstances. But from the other side, a fresh unconcerned laugh rang out to him. The breath of the blond climbed up like a white spring cloud before him.

"Morning, Heinrich," she wished, and at the same time, she offered him her slender hand, still warm and glowing with life despite the cold. "Do you want to help me?"

"Yes, but why then —?", Heinrich stammered and shook his head so that the snow fell from his black fur cap. "You don't want though perhaps to —?"

But the little one was already pressing the iron, thickly frozen bar into his hand.

"Quick, Heinrich," she exhorted. "Don't hinder me. Mother expects me within, for she needs the water. And now quick, one — two — three."

She held the bucket strongly under the outlet pipe, and the young farmer also showed himself to be so un-able to shake off his astonishment that he could not object. With a powerful unburdening movement, as if he had to show his entire strength to her, he worked the lever. And then the clear, icy water shot into the bucket.

"Huh," Hertha cried. "That is fresh."

Then she took her load, stretched her left arm out horizontally as she had frequently seen the maids do, and now she began hauling the full bucket across the yard. But Heinrich did not want to tolerate that by any means. He grasped likewise for the handle of the container, and thus they both strode now as good comrades to the hall of the house. But it seemed almost as if the little one entertained misgivings about chatting all too much and all too audibly with her awkward companion.

"Turn around, Heinrich," she warned, when they had reached the door.

"Yes, but —".

"Sh — sh — quite quiet. And now leave me."

"Yes, but, Miss Hertha," he asked quite bashfully. "Will you not at least come out later once more so that I can show you our farm?"

"What do you have then?", Hertha tossed back, still in a hurry.

"Well, pigs, cows," and more hopefully, he added, "Naturally also horses, a breed of our own. We even have two foals," he added invitingly.

"Foals? Eh! Yes, that will work. If mother Lotte allows it, I will spring out to you for a look afterwards. But only for a quite short while, right?"

"Yes, yes. As you wish. It's alright with me," Heinrich stammered.

And then he saw how the little one again stretched out her left arm to carry her container alone and without help from now on through the hall. She just turned her head quite fleetingly once more back over her shoulder to the man she was leaving behind. And see there, she smiled, and nodded good-naturedly to him. The man left behind, however, grasped his ragged grey jacket, and jiggled the material back and forth.

"How she places her feet as she does it," he pondered. "Two such dear little things. When you see all that. Oh, when you must see all that!"

And when he wandered shortly afterwards with his farm manager through the cow stalls, the teasing shuffle of those pretty boots which he had heard before clattering over the red bricks of the entrance still rang in his ears.

Clipp — clapp.

"Oh, that is pretty," he murmured.

"Do you mean the red cow?", his companion asked with a sideways glance.

"No, I was just thinking," the farmer corrected himself, and then he jiggled the fleece of his jacket about again as if to free it.

***

In the blue room, there was also a surprise.

When mother Lotte appeared at the breakfast table where she was accustomed to having her morning coffee alone with her daughter, for her son tended at this time to already be tending to his business, she found the large round table laid more invitingly than ever before.

Where did that come from?

The blue and white striped serviettes made from the coarsest linen, which had been woven by a forbear of the mistress of the house herself, these little cloths suddenly stood in the form of swans on the table. And even the fresh country butter which usually spent its existence in an unshapely lump on the plate, even it had assumed as if by magic the shape of the imperial eagle. It all looked so appetising that both mother Lotte and Anna stood quite surprised at the entrance after they had appeared at the door. But then Heinrich's sister clapped her hands delightedly, and hurried promptly to the little one who was still busily making the last preparations at the table as if she had undertaken something quite obvious and commonplace.

"Lord," she said in shock, as she was now grasped by the hand stormily by her friend.

"Is something not right perhaps?"

"No, not at all! How charming you know how to make things, dear Miss. Really, everything becomes so distinguished and nice in your hands."

Now mother Lotte also stepped up to the table, and took a close look at the work. But she too bowed her head finally in agreement, and as she turned the plate of swans around in a circle, she uttered approvingly, "Very pretty. Really. It looks properly tasteful. And if you possess sufficient time for such a thing, then you can take pleasure in it."

But Hertha blushed, and looked as happy as if she had not taken in the quiet reservation in the old woman's approval. And yet the most inconspicuous of glances which mother Lotte let sweep over her guest during breakfast, as soon as she thought herself unobserved, also did not escape her. No, the little one chatted and talked on instead, unconcerned and in a good mood, and it did not take at all long until it appeared that the arrival also possessed an unusually cheerful ability to imitate the weaknesses and small peculiarities of her fellow man. And when she had placed herself on the window sill to suddenly perform a movement as if someone were striking at imagined flies in the air with a violin bow amidst all sorts of bodily contortions, even mother Lotte was unable to suppress a quickly fleeting grin over this well-done imitation of the sexton Vierarm. She indeed added straight afterwards, "Now, now! He is in any case a very loyal and steady man. Without inner falseness. And you must judge men accordingly."

"Certainly," Hertha responded, as she climbed down from the sill, and began clearing away the cups. "He also pleases me extraordinarily."

With that, this submission was also dealt with.

When she returned from the kitchen after some time, there sat mother Lotte unengaged on the green rep sofa. She seemed to have prepared herself for a discussion with the little one. But Hertha turned her head a few times, and peered out into the yard.

The grey dawn had faded away there, and the flakes were falling whiter and ever brighter.

"Are you looking for something there, my child?", mother Lotte inquired.

"Me? Not exactly."

"Well, there would be nothing there. Do you want perhaps to see the work spaces sometime? I consider it quite sensible for people to be clear about their surroundings. Did you perhaps have such an intention?"

Then the little one nodded ingenuously.

"If you'd permit it, mother Lotte —", she responded respectfully.

"Permit?" The old lady rocked her head, and looked at her earnestly. "I have nothing here at all to permit you. How would I come to that? You are yet my guest, dear child. So just jump out."

Then Hertha quickly set the becoming fur beret on her blond hair, and hurriedly put on her elegant velvet coat, which made her appear even more slender than usual. Only, the old woman held her back once more.

"Don't take it wrong," she interposed. "Do you not possess any other clothing for such walks? I mean any more ordinary clothes? For out here, such fine things will suffer, won't they?"

At this question, a hot, sincere glow rose on Hertha's face. She was ashamed of her poverty, and looked at the floor. But at the same moment, the mistress of the house continued more kindly than she had ever spoken with the little one, "Okay. That doesn't matter. Then we will send for a warm wool jacket from the town like those which are needed out here."

And when Hertha tried to raise her hands in resistance and shock, the old woman added determinedly, "Just let it be. It doesn't matter. Such things will surely find their use here later. And now just go and have everything shown to you by my son."

So the old woman knew that already too. Yes, mother Lotte heard the grass growing, even when it was germinating hidden under a covering of snow in winter.

"A clever woman," Hertha thought as she now strode delicately across the yard. "You have to either admire her or hate her from the heart. Or both at the same time. Who knows?"

***

Meanwhile Heinrich was standing in the open doorway to the stables. Actually he should have long since left the yard, for he wanted to single-handedly lead a pair of horses for shodding to the village smithy, because there they were using a new English method which he intended to use with the animals for the first time. But nevertheless, he had lingered and hesitated. For the first time, his labourers experienced the spectacle of their master leaning unoccupied on the post of the open stable door to stare lost in thought away over the snow to the entrance of the house.

He waited. He remained patient, and kept waiting.

Truly, he would not have moved away if the clock back there in the village had not also gradually shown the midday hour.

And then — then finally he saw the unfamiliar figure stepping forth from the house. The young farmer started, and pulled his jacket together. No, how delicate and distinguished she looked again. He had already often seen the young aristocratic women of the district as they travelled to the neighbouring count's castle, but could anyone perhaps measure up to this one here?

And did he dare raise his wishes to her? Was he capable of reminding her of a given and forgotten promise? A promise which was given only in the hour of the deepest misfortune? No, he told himself at this moment, he must never again come back to that. That was a direct injustice to the little one. And he was certainly the last to want to exercise such an ugly compulsion. If he only knew why she would have hurried out to Werrahn now despite all that. And what strangely good words had she whispered in his ear the previous evening from the sled? What had she spoken? Did he not know anymore? And now, when the little figure was approaching in her fine velvet coat, his head was humming again, he was again feeling that half joyful feeling as if a thick cloud were lifting him up.

Now she stood before him.

"Now then, Heinrich," she asked him, and stretched her hand quickly towards him. "Will you now acquaint me with your favourite things? Yes?"

"If you will be so good," the young farmer stammered in confusion, since his eyes were unable to detach themselves from the close-fitting black velvet coat which appeared to him to be the epitome of everything precious and select. "If you will be so good?"

"Yes, of course. And now just step along."

She gathered her dress a little as she now stepped over the threshold of the horse stables. Her companion, however, lowered his eyes. For every movement by her, every turn, the light rustle of her dress, her barely audible breathing, even the step of her feet, everything tautened the innocent man, everything infused him with thoughts and feelings which shooed away every clarity from him. He heard something quite distinctly swishing about himself and over his head. That was his happiness swinging a silk flag. It could be nothing else.

Now they strode through the stables. He showed her first the plough and workhorses and felt quite concerned when the little one, with a serious and expert demeanour, brought his attention to the animals' particular flaws and defects.

"See, Heinrich," she cried, bent down, and pointed with her hand. "The long-legged mare here has a tumorous back hock."

Heinrich nodded.

"Correct," he replied, quite overjoyed by her knowledge.

"But why do you not have it burnt out with copper?", Hertha continued, and looked up at him curiously from below. Her blue eyes were lit up even more than usual.

"From where do you know all that?" Heinrich asked, seemingly reverent towards her.

But the little one informed him with a smile that the Colonel, her late father, had owned a pair of his own horses. Yes, he had even lifted her often as a small girl onto one of his steeds to teach her the various gaits. Then Heinrich raised his round short-cropped head, and such a surprising thought seemed to grasp the ponderous man that he had to instinctively press close by her side.

Only, she remained standing unchanged. She just let one of her short laughing looks sweep up to him anew.

"Dear Miss," he stuttered, secretly struck to the depths of his soul by her gaze. "Could you then — I mean — would you be fond — or would you take a chance on going for a ride sometime."

And when a strange sparkling sputtering shot into her light-blue luminous eyes, he continued more delightedly and persuasively, "You must know we in fact have a ladies saddle here. I gifted it once to my sister Anna for Christmas. But certainly then —", here he faltered.

"But then?", Hertha drove him on interestedly, whereby she tapped his chest with her finger.

The young farmer fetched a deep breath, and tried to remain calm.

"But you see, then —", he stuttered, "our mother did not want to know anything about it. But with you, it is a different matter," he added more boldly. "And if you wish, then we will both try it sometime."

"Both of us?"

"See now," the blond thought. "He is yet a dear boy. To give me pleasure, he will even dare to do something which the old woman has prohibited."

But she openly shook her fine narrow head energetically.

"That won't work," she suggested definitely.

"Why, you don't want to accompany me?"

He had clasped his hands tidily, and his massive figure ducked as if something had fallen on his neck. Then Hertha touched his chest again.

"Be sensible, dear Heinrich," she consoled him. "I must certainly not undertake such a thing here during the first few days. But we will wait. It will yet happen. And then we will both be very delighted, won't we?"

With that, she offered him her little hand again, and now Heinrich enclosed and squeezed the offered fingers so that the little one would have liked most of all to cry out. After that, they strode further along the individual stalls. Right at the end, in a closed box, they found the mare with her foal. There it leapt happily about in the narrow space. And when they both approached, it pushed its slender head demandingly through the slats, and snuffled at the hands of its visitors, for it was accustomed to being gifted bread and sugar. And really,

Heinrich fetched a few pieces of sugar from the pocket of his fleece jacket. Only, Hertha placed herself in his path.

"Me, me," she begged stormily.

And when she had now slung her arm caressingly around the neck of the young animal, and placed one piece after another of the sweet on its tongue, Heinrich thought anew that he was hearing the swishing and fluttering which constantly pursued him. His happiness swung its silk flag rustling more and more.

"The little animal has never seemed so pretty to me before," the enchanted man thought. "Funny, funny. She needs only touch something, and immediately it becomes as beautiful as it has never been before. I think if she tried once to offer me her hand properly and for a long time, I would also look different to how I do now."

At this moment, he saw how the girl made a light tap on the nostrils of the foal, since it was becoming more pushy. And turning to her companion, she burst out hastily, "Tell me please, Heinrich, is the little thing already christened? Does it have a name?"

"No, that hasn't been done yet," the tall man responded, whereby he pushed his black fur cap back and forth. "But I have it," he continued quite excitedly and taken by his own idea. "It is quite clear. The animal must be called Hertha. May I do that?"

Now the little blond also clapped her hands, sprang at her companion with delight, and stroked his arm flatteringly and full of joy.

Oh, he felt so well and warm as a result, as if he were standing in the sun, and swallows chirped about her, and summery spider threads nestled drawing softly against his cheeks.

"Yes, Heinrich," she cried, "do that. It shall be named after me. And you will always treat the little animal well, won't you, and not let anything bad happen to it?"

"What are you thinking?" he responded falteringly and yet full of bliss. "But if you wanted — that is, if you would permit me — I don't even know whether I may allow you —".

"Well, what then? Thunderbolts, Heinrich, is it something so bad then?"

"If you — I just mean — oh God, look, I want to ask whether you would perhaps like to accept the little animal from me. I mean — whether I may make a present of it to you so that it is entirely your own and —".

And then something happened which he would never ever have allowed himself to dream. In the half-light of the stables, in which the daylight only broke in through the high-placed window covered in cobwebs, the little one rushed up to him. She slung both arms around the erect, motionless man, and nestled close to him like a child spoilt with rich gifts. Without a word flowing over her lightly quivering lips, her eyes spoke alone. Those remarkably bright eyes displaying the colouring of the glassy blue northern sky. They enticed, they coaxed, they promised, and the red lips smiled so peculiarly as well until the awkward man fancied in his confusion that he no longer felt the ground safely under his feet. With his rough trembling hands, he pushed the girl back.

"I have to go now," he murmured, without rightly knowing what he was saying. "The horses are to be shod. By the smith, Fielitz. I must really go now."

He opened the door uncertainly, and threw it far back as if the intention of letting the daylight flood in as brightly as possible was driving him. Then he drew two of the previously determined horses from their stalls. The little one, however, laughed at him ingenuously, "Won't you take me with you, Heinrich?" she inquired.

As these words rang out, he already stood out on the cobblestones of the yard, and now looked at her over the back of one of the horses uncertainly.

"To the smithy?", he suggested in disbelief.

"Certainly. I would like so much to see it with you once."

And at the same time, she was catching the reins of the animal, and was about to lead it out through the door to the man when the young farmer, however, took the halter gently but decisively from her hand.

"Don't take it wrongly," he asked considerately. "I would prefer to lead the animals alone though."

And when the little one, now already on the country road, asked why he was begrudging her the innocent pleasure, the tall man turned his head bashfully to the side, and threw out in his disjointed way that the people out there were not rightly accustomed to such things. They would perhaps make their comments about the distinguished young lady in the velvet jacket who pulled a horse along behind her. And that he would not like to endure.

"Funny people," Hertha thought when she now strode next to him. "It is not so simple though."

But soon the little incident was forgotten.

They went along on the white country road in the sparsely falling flakes which were adorning her dress with silvery stars, and both animals often whinnied loudly and joyfully into the silent landscape. And here, in the fresh cold air which widened the chest and cleared the eyes, here next to the man who was so abso-lutely devoted to her, the little creature was suddenly again struck by that elation of reigning, of which she had been warned, and which she could not do without.

Onward — onward. Just dare!

Had the dumb awkward man not refused one of her wishes? Unheard of! For that she must now show him straightaway how mighty she was. And she playfully grasped for the reins of the slender brown stallion which minced along next to her.

"Oh, Hertha," Heinrich asked in shock.

Only, the elegant young lady in the black velvet jacket just nodded to him ingenuously, and then she began running out with the animal in a trot.

"That is not proper — that is really not proper," Heinrich stammered.

But look how she runs along in her fluttering clothes, her golden hair tousled and sprayed by the wind, and how her silvery laugh now rings out, there the image was so beautiful, so captivating that all bitterness vanished from the man gazing after her, and a gently approving smile began playing about his lips.

"She is just still half child," he thought forgivingly.

They arrived thus at the smithy. In the open front space, the smith Fielitz was already waiting with his assistants. The horses were handed over, and soon the sparks began spraying about the anvil in the dark workshop. The open hearth twitched and hissed. And straight afterwards, the ringing lusty heaving of the hammers rang out over the country road.

Heinrich himself held with his massive hands the hooves to be shod. Hertha again realised, lingering curiously close by him, what enormous power must slumber in the muscular arms of the young farmer.

Clap — clap, the hammers boomed.

Heinrich did not stir. Then a distantly tormenting idea crept up on the watcher. What would happen if this sleeping giant straightened up for once? It would have to be terrifying if he ever became conscious of his shackled powers. Could this power not also occasionally turn against her, she who yet played with him, for whom it offered some fun to tempt his dull spirit and then push it away again?

And as if she wanted to calm herself down, she tapped the bowed giant soothingly on his broad back.

***

The shoeing had just come to an end, and the horses had just been handed over to one of the smith's assistants who would lead them back to the Werrahn estate, when a vigorous barking arose in the open vestibule. A conspicuously large black poodle simultaneously shot past, rolled around a few times growling and panting through the snow, and finally threw itself back in front of the young farmer as it began barking furiously. The dog appeared obviously to be in an absolutely hostile and distrustful mood.

"Get," Heinrich cried, as the girl adroitly tossed a piece of coal at the yapper.

The dog recoiled, but the next moment, it continued its leaps even more furiously. Its black eyes flashed and sparkled at the same time.

"Hey," a solemn voice suddenly rasped, unexpectedly becoming audible behind the young couple. "Throwing and 'get' are no use at all here. Eh. For this is no common dog. You can believe me that. I have already put it to the test."

With these words, sexton Vierarm, for it was him, shook the five folds of his black cloak slowly, rocked his iron-grey head reflectively under his misshapen top hat, which could quite well have been used as the funnel of a threshing machine, and then stretched out his hand simply and meaningfully to the young pair.

"Good morning, Mr Heinrich; good morning, dear young lady," he wished them. "Sweet, sweet, already feeling fresh? Yes, the weather is well suited to such little casual walks. No, no, I don't say anything against it. I was suggesting. But now just think how it goes with me. There I sit this morning in my room — in my study," he corrects himself, "and am reading the uplifting book about the cathedral building in Strasbourg. There the bricklayers in fact worked with soft cheese and hock instead of with mortar. Just think. It was such a noble build. And a barrel of Liebfraumilch wine was carried to the first sexton of that cathedral in his office on the first night for bribing the devil, a barrel as high as a fully-fledged hay wagon. Yes, they were still good and appreciable times then. But look. As I now read about these gratifying events with scientific interest, something scratched at my door. 'Quiet,' I say. But does it surely calm down? No, it scratches still worse. And indeed with an uncanny power as if one of the lions from Daniel's lion pit — you will think surely of the touching story — wants to come in to me. 'Well, then thus in God's name,' I say, stand up, and look through the crack in the door. But what do you surely think now? There sits this stray dog outside, this strange unnatural poodle, and shows its tongue to me. I was frightened. For I had never seen such a red tongue before. Mr Heinrich and Miss Hertha, I swear to you, the glowing iron of the smith Fielitz is nothing in comparison. And from its throat something was steaming. That I observed exactly. I thus said, 'Take yourself away.' For you must talk to such animals in this way. I have in particular once seen Faust by Wolfgang Goethe acted in town, and it was also done there in that way. But does the uncanny animal mean well? No, it does not. I think then a piece of wood should be thrown at it. And that I then did with all my strength, see, like this!"

Here the sexton bent to the side, threw his body back with the five collars, and made a hefty throwing motion with his hand. At the same moment, however, the poodle ran at him with a furious barking, and snapped at his fingers.

"Almighty," the sexton cried. "There you have it. The beast did exactly like that. Merely with the difference that it caught the piece of wood in an incomprehensible way in its snout and placed it politely, yes, even with a fake bow, at my feet. And when I threw the door shut before its nose, what do you think happened then? Do you think perhaps that the black emissary went away? Eh, it did not occur to it. There you don't know it well. No, it suddenly jumped in the open window with a leap that made my hair stand on end. And then it immediately crept under my bed — excuse me, Miss, but it was really so — to fetch out something which I usually tend to ferret away there. But what that is," the religious man cut off with a quick hand gesture. "That has nothing to do with the matter."

"Well, and now it runs after you?", Hertha laughed heartily as she poked the young farmer in the side.

Only, the sexton's sharp eyes must have spied this movement.

"Don't laugh, dear Miss," he reproved her, and twisted his beardless, wrinkled countenance grouchily. I simply have the fate of being plagued much from this side. And I will not be free of it again so soon. But if you perhaps want to convince yourself of it? In the hall of my house, there lies a piece of wood. Then you can convince yourself of it with your own eyes."

"Ah yes, sexton," the little blond agreed in the brightest enthusiasm. "I think a household like your own to be terribly interesting. Right, Heinrich, you must not overlook it?"

And after Heinrich had also declared with a good-natured smile his consent, the sexton nodded flattered, set his top hat more firmly on his forehead, and pointed with his stick towards the end of the village.

"It is only a few steps," he indicated. "Do you see the green cottage there with the snowed-over stork's nest on the roof? I live there. I attach extraordinary value to a stork's nest in fact," he added instructively. "It has a quite special and liberating power."

They strode out boldly as a group of three, and the little one pressed so close to the clergyman, and she blinked so often and admiringly up into his serious prophet's countenance that sexton Vierarm's cautious disposition gradually melted.

"You are a very bold thing, dear Miss," he ascertained with measured acclaim. "Mrs Lotte Kalsow of Werrahn can surely be pleased by that. Isn't that right, Mr Heinrich?"

"Certainly, that she can," Heinrich answered from the other side.

The sexton puckered his scrubby forehead.

The spectre from the first night of December occurred to him once more, and that he was actually strolling with a kobold across the land.

But as he now squinted down at the small child-like figure, and at the same time suddenly felt his own astonishment that she had pushed her hand in his own like a small girl, as if it were that she were wanting to entrust herself completely to his fatherly care, his kind-heartedness and complacency seethed over in his temperamental soul.

"Not a trace," he vocalised his thoughts. "You are something very nice!"

And again his neighbour said loudly and delightedly, "Right? Yes, I want to think that."

Even the uncanny dog sprang up at the blond, and snuffled tenderly about her black velvet coat.

"Hm," sexton Vierarm murmured. "That will appear very alarming to me again though."

Thus they came to the church. There a new idea crept up on the man with the five collars. The yellow iron-studded oak door which was inserted into the rectangular brick tower, did it not stand open? How would it be if he tested once whether this little blond creature next to him also possessed a Christian and religious disposition? For he knew how to prove that. For that he already possessed his methods.

And, without further ado, he strode with his long legs to the door, pushed it back, and asked both his companions to enter. It was indeed only a small church, he suggested, but the Countess had just a few years ago at her own cost had it freshly painted, adorned with a wonderful wooden panelling, and decorated with the most beautiful stained glass windows.

"And the main thing is," he added, "the high-born woman has just a short time ago in fact endowed a new organ. It came directly from Cologne, and has a sound like only a few in the land. And since I have a day labourer at hand who could tread the bellows, so —".

Hardly had the words fallen than Hertha also sprang before him, raised up on her toes, and now she stroked coaxingly and caressingly his chest which lay hidden under the five snowed collars.

"That you must not let us overlook, dear, dear sexton," she begged. "You shall play the organ so wonderfully. And there is no instrument which I would like to hear anywhere near as much. Right, Heinrich, we will sit together, and listen quite still and devoutly."

The sexton was won over.

"Well, then come," he commanded.

A narrow dark nave received them. But from above, an unearthly light flooded through the colourful panes of glass and strewed blue and red wreaths onto the choir benches and lower down onto the white flagstones. The steps of the three walkers echoed loudly in the empty space.

At a signal from their guide, Hertha and Heinrich settled down on a bench close by the pulpit which clambered up a white round column. The sexton, however, placed his hand to his lips as if he wanted to advise silence and devotion to the two once more. Then he distanced himself with his long strides. The ringing sound fell silent, and it remained entirely still for a while in the dim dark space.

But what was that?

At first a quiet drawing and breathing, as if a crowd of children were starting to sing with quite fine little voices. And then — it roared and thundered. In the strong echo, the waves of notes broke on the bare walls and washed back ebbing again. And now the old song of resistance and praise of the northern faith thundered through the church, ruled by strong fists:

A mighty fortress is our God.

Yes, sexton Vierarm was a master of the organ. The powerful notes which he enticed from this instrument which had been built in Cologne to call to penance and edification up here on the coast of the sea, those mighty, soul shaking sounds, they were his axes and his cudgels which he swung against the evil enemy and the powers of darkness. Ever again! Ever onward! Until the horned one fled whimpering from there with smashed skull, and angels' heads pushed through the starry heaven of the roof above him to sing silvery and pure their songs of forgiveness.

Where lay the secret thoughts of the blond, all too earthly creature who had come to experience an hour of exhilaration or delight?

At first she had quietly offered her hand to her neighbour as if she were afraid of remaining alone in the emptiness. Now she withdrew her fingers from him with a hard abrupt jerk. Her light blue eyes opened and stared up to where all the storm and stress was ranting down from. She was still defending herself. For a short span of time, she tried to move closer to the awkward man to once more exchange a mocking look with him. But just look, look! How serious and pale his countenance dawns towards her in the half darkness. He had lowered his head, and folded his hands. Then it also passed through her soul. A icy shock flew over her as if she did not belong here. A shiver ran down her back. The thundering voices roared constantly around her, "Look at yourself! Be true! Humble yourself! Have you not just rattled at the posts of a bourgeois house, and was it because of you that it did not collapse? How you rested naked and exposed, and full of overwhelming desire on your bed? And whom were you expecting? Confess though, whom? Was the door locked? Did you not rather keep yourself ready to dance along in that mad witch's whirl which you call the dance of life? And now? Turn the strangely glittering eyes with which you charm your admirer, turn them inwards. Why have you trooped in here? Do you not intend to break the power of the old venerable woman, to take possession of her treasure, her house, and her children? The humility which you feign, the readiness to help which you show, do they originate from a pure, a compulsive need? Or is all that not false, insincere, bogus? Woe if there were now an eye which penetrated all that, which also recognised you as you are. How will you justify yourself? Woe! Woe!"

My God, my God! She had come into this village church, playful and frivolous, so that she would be thrown into bonds here? So that her will, which wanted to dominate, would be worn down and sink to its knees? Never ever! Why right now? Why right today?

Buck it, spring up, and defend yourself!

And again the battle rolled over her head. She perceived quite distinctly with her inner ear how the demons which the exorcist threw his battleaxe against raged and roared. And with a deep sigh, she sank back, and closed her eyes.

Praise God, praise God! What a gloriously forgiving angel song. Now it had happened, the evil was conquered, and the announcement of forgiveness also came to her.

"Hertha, for God's sake, what's wrong?"

"I, I — let me be."

"No, you're crying, you're sobbing. Are you not well?"

Then she threw both hands before her eyes, pulled together her last strength, and remained sitting upright.

And what happened then, she only felt blearily and as if through a white swarm of flakes. A stillness occurred. A terribly menacing stillness. Then ringing steps. A white snowy landscape surrounded her. And suddenly she could no longer contain herself. With a vigorous movement, she tore her hand away from her companion, who had been holding it firmly to support her, and she rushed from there at a furious run towards the house at Werrahn.

To be alone, alone. To show her tears to nobody.

She was a foolish, far too easily shaken child.

"Yes," sexton Vierarm said, and placed his artist's hand heavily and weightily on the shoulder of the astonished farmer who was gazing stunned after the woman hastening away. "She has a soft and Christian disposition, Mr Heinrich. Pay attention, we will set her right yet. And with the poodle there, I will also come to terms, you shall see."

3

"So," the old Count Karl Anton von Hohensee said, and contentedly slapped his full torso, which stood out round and neat from his light blue trousers. "So, my boy," he said to the young cuirassier Lieutenant who sat opposite him with open tunic and smoking a cigarette at the coffee table in the light panelled, tiny breakfast room. "Our smoked ham really tastes better and better. Our housekeeper Westphal is in fact a true artist in this area. Immaculate. Truly, the old woman runs the smokehouse excellently. Do you want another piece?"

"No thank you, papa."

"Good, then I'll take it. It's no misfortune either. Well, what did I want to say," he recalled during his contented chewing, "damned brat, I must by and by hold with you a little keeping of the accounts."

"Do you really consider that unavoidably necessary, old man?" the young officer responded, as he bared his small, well-kept teeth into a smile.

And as he drew out from his trouser pocket a golden case, he passed the little precious object over to old Count Karl Anton, and offered the contents with an obliging bow.

"Well, old man, then strengthen yourself first please. Finest Goldmark. Jewish-Turkish tobacco. Is decisively milder when you have sucked yourself full of it. Beautiful — and now kick off."

"Silly boy," the estate owner contradicted, but drew a cigarette from the case anyway, lit it, and then leant back puffing and blowing.

"This time you are not winning through with your devilry, my little son, don't fancy that. It is not so simple, my dear. And if you want to protest much here and play the grandee, then we will buckle your sabre belt a bit tighter, understand? And now pay attention. You have in fact been nastily snitched on here."

"To you, papa?"

"Yes of course, to me too. But that would not be saying so much, for I am unfortunately a much too tenderly feeling and understanding sire. Unfortunately, dear God. No, but what is much worse, to mama. And it is a grace of God, boy, that she has not yet brought your morning devotion to an end, otherwise she would set about your body terribly, my son. But it does no harm if we also have some serious words with one another."

"No," the Lieutenant said casually, and without great excitement. "No, we won't."

And at the same time, he poured himself a glass of port, and held the golden brown drink with pleasure to the light so that the sparse beams of the morning son had to reflect in it.

"Cheers, old man. We won't speak a serious word with one another; I in fact concede everything. Although I don't know at all beforehand what mama has forked up again. But that does not matter. I confess myself guilty at the outset. And do you know something, father? In the meantime, I would like to exercise the English stallion a bit. The animal is otherwise becoming a bit dull in the legs to my mind, and you know I have registered for the Stettin race."

"What, again already?", the old gentleman cried, slapped the county newspaper which he was reading onto the table, sprang up, and wandered wheezing and puffing across the parquet floor, which was only covered by a pair of modest Persian carpets.

"Who is holding the unnecessary thing against you then?"

"Oh, merely a few weak prospects. Fritz Basedow on Atlantic."

"Aha, the lazy boy. That's surely the Pasewalk cuirassier? Also such a little fruit for living off. Well, and who else?"

"Cavalry Captain von Schwengen on Cleopatra."

"I see, the gambler from the Hanoverian Uhlans. Well, there again a right handsome company has come together. Tell me, can little Elten from the Potsdamers also not be far away? Take care, brat, the old man won't pay for it anymore. There's a nasty fuss. And the Colonel of the Guards Regiment is not to be jested with either. So, and since we are here together now, I want to declare to you point-blank that from today on I am no longer in a position to —".

What a shame! The old gentleman, who did this title much wrong, for he was a man who had not yet left his fifties, and with his small corpulent figure, which everyone testified to being of abounding strength, gave the impression of a brisk, unshaken health; what a shame, Karl Anton had just set himself in a pose of respect which he usually only rarely used opposite his boy. With legs set apart, each stuck in a turned up boot, he stood before him and rubbed his red nose now irritably, a distinct sign that he was not averse to a pleasant little binge where the sparkling wine of the French flowed. Assuming of course that his strict wife, Mrs Anne-Marie Luise, born the daughter of Baron von Pötteritz, had turned her back. Lise, as Karl Anton called her informally, felt such gluttony to be directed against every penance and tended to stroll about alas almost constantly in a Good Friday mood.

"Well then, boy, now open your ears properly for once."

But what a shame. The manly run-up would not make the leap. For at the door, there was a hard, if also respectful, knock, and when Karl Anton, seeing himself interrupted, cried out furiously, "Well, in the names of three devils, come in!", then the superintendent Hartmann also stood before both the gentlemen, dressed in green fleece jacket and tall farmer's boots, to bow fleetingly before his chief. He stroked the short blond full beard which surrounded his tanned face, and placed without further ado a large heap of letters and papers on the table.

"Milk accounts, Count."

"Wonderful."

"And here is the bill for the new machine hall at the brickworks."

"What, what? That already? Hartmann, you surely have had too much cherry brandy? Or do you believe the ducats —"

At this point, Karl Anton unfortunately swallowed the beautiful allegory, and since he saw that his administrator was not yet making any move to withdraw, he again pulled recklessly at the red protrusion on his face as if it had offended him grossly.

"Still something? Ah, I note it already," he snorted, whereby an new fit of coughing almost laid him on his back again. "You are not escaping your damned dementedness. You want to drive me all the way into bankruptcy. It goes to splendidly for us country people. And the expenses for our dear family are becoming ever tinier."

Here a glance shot from the flashing blue eyes over to the son who just then tapped Superintendent Hartmann informally on the shoulder to also offer him now his cigarettes from the golden case.

"Well, Hartmann," he commanded, "now don't play the modest man. I buy in bulk. I can light up my entire squadron."

And with that he dropped a handful into the other man's fleece jacket.

"Thank you, Count."

"Well, thunderbolts," Karl Anton now snorted. "Do you want now perhaps to have the estate? Does your hailed-on, horrid discovery still haunt you?"

The Superintendent nodded, very satisfied, like someone who has guessed something correctly. —

"Yes, Count. It is real marl which we have found un-der the wheat field."

Now the noble estate owner let himself fall into a rocking chair, and rocked back and forth in silent fury so that his short legs were swung dangerously close to the Superintendent.

"And you truly believe, you mad prick, that I will let go of about 200 acres of the best wheat fields because of that? Hartmann, don't take this badly, you must be drunk."

The official, however, was accustomed to such good opinions on the side of his chief. Laid-back, he shrugged his shoulders, and at the same time, he was already bringing out a brown bag from his pocket, which he now placed on the table without any particular haste.

"Here, Count, you have the test of the chemical laboratory at Greifswald. And here the analysis. The gentlemen write that it is the best, high-grade marl like is only found in such perfection on the Ural-Baltic ridge, a fertiliser and catalyst of the first rank. I estimate the annual yield for us at a minimum of 30–40,000 marks. And for the five acres which unfortunately seems to lie without this precious content, I have already found a buyer."

"So, have you?", Karl Anton growled, as he stopped rocking, and rubbed his nose avidly. "Who is it then, if I may ask?"

"It is our neighbour Kalsow. The old lady sent us her son who manages the business in her name. And if you permit, Count, I will call the young man in right away, for he is waiting outside here in the hallway."

At this announcement, the Count rocked up from his comfortable situation, sprang onto both feet, and tramped back and forth before his inferior, trapped between fury and satisfaction.

"Have him brought in straightaway," he grumbled. "It's really quite nice. All goes as if greased. Well, now tell me please, when will you put me under guardianship?"

And as he poked the Superintendent in the side, he continued in a quite business-like way, "Well then, Hartmann, what are we demanding for the five acres? Such rounding off is a meal for the old lady over there. It must not be knocked off cheaply. So we reckon 3,000 marks."

"Too high, Count."

"2,500."

"Can't be done, Count."

"Then a heart-breaking 2,300. Not a pfennig less. I will not negotiate. And now let the man in please."

And when the Superintendent had gone out for a moment to lead the visitor in, the old gentleman wandered up and down with his hands behind his back, tossing grim looks over at his son who seemed to follow this entire business with overt satisfaction.

"Don't laugh," he growled. "You have unfortunately not a shimmer of it now. You possess not the vaguest idea of it. Well, and this Mr Kalsow by the way," he added, snapping for air. "There we would have it. That is precisely the valid point. We will yet discuss that, my dear boy."

"So?" the Lieutenant said unmoved. "Not me, papa. Incidentally, I must tell you the girl is a splendid apparition. A little number, father. You should see her."

"What?" the old man cried, unable for the moment to suppress his laughter. "Hold your snout, brat. I would sincerely not like to tolerate such familiarities. Heavens, if your mother knew."

"Well, she knows," the Lieutenant said calmly, and lit a new cigarette. "Her clerical chief spy, sexton Vierarm, may have informed her of my new discovery already. Come in!", he interrupted eagerly, for there was a knock at the door.

"Come in!", Karl Anton roared after him, not allowing such business-like affairs to be taken from his grasp.

"Mr Kalsow," the old Count began cordially after Heinrich, who had appeared in his inevitable, creased frock coat, had bowed formally and a little awkwardly before both the aristocrats. "Mr Kalsow," Karl Anton heralded with the greatest obligingness, although he had just been raging so vehemently, and at the same time, he shook both the guest's hands powerfully. "I am extraordinarily pleased to see you at my place. You are the most proficient farmer in the entire district here, from which we can only learn. Yes, only learn," he cried suddenly over to his son, who bowed obligingly and elegantly to this call, as if his father had shown him a special honour. "Yes, only learn. What is your dear mother up to? Also a vigorous lady with whom I had the honour to dance in earlier years at many a country ball. Well, that she will surely have given up in the meantime. We are not getting any younger unfortunately. And now sit down please, Mr Kalsow, please. And what I wanted to tell you was that the five acres will cost 3,000 marks."

The Superintendent cleared his throat, the officer laughed, and Heinrich Kalsow shook his short-cropped head negatively. After that, a quick bidding followed. And after it had come down to that price which the noble estate owner had earlier fixed with his Superintendent, they were in agreement.

"Beautiful," Karl Anton coughed, and slapped his round torso contentedly. "It has been given away far too cheaply. Once again shorn outrageously. No pure affair of charity. But now the wine. We will open a bottle of red to it, eh Mr Kalsow? Hartmann, you will give us the pleasure too."

And without paying attention to Heinrich's embarrassed defence, which comprised something stuttered about great honour, the noble estate owner rang the bell. The wine was brought by the waiting servant, and the four gentlemen encamped around the breakfast table which was still laid. The glasses clinked together loudly and joyfully. The officer told neat and cheerful stories, and the old Count tapped each of his guests familiarly on the knee. But if the young owner of Werrahn had been more worldly wise, then he would have had to have noticed that Karl Anton was moving closer and closer to him, and seemed to have something special planned with him. For suddenly he placed his arm unobtrusively around the shoulders of the young man, and whispered in his ear, "You have a right cosy household, as I learn from the pastor and our sexton Vierarm to my joy. Well? Is that right?"

"Yes, thank God, Count."

"And you possess a sister, don't you? She is meant to be a magnificent woman."

The officer looked up at the ceiling, and set little smoke rings climbing into the air. The old man, however, squinted at his guest craftily, tapped him on the knee anew, and finally whispered to him mysteriously,

"Take care, young friend. Take good care. Such flowers tempt butterflies and whippersnappers. You must nip them in the bud at once. Understand?"

But before the warned man could get his head around it properly, the cuirassier had already sprung up, and was holding his glass out to him.

"Papa is right," he cried cheerfully. "We will toast the beauty in our district, so neglected in this respect. Cheers, cheers, cheers! My dear Mr Kalsow, your dear mother and your beautiful sister!"

"A quite godforsaken brat," the old Count sighed, sinking into himself.

But then he tipped the contents of his glass devoutly down.

**

The farmer's sled remained before the ramp of Castle Wildhagen. Both browns whinnied loudly when Heinrich stepped out, after the concluded business, with the young Count who appeared even more imposing than usual with his fur trimmed, grey coat collar. He had pushed the white cap with the red stripes a little daringly onto his right ear, and between his lips, he held as ever the cheerfully glimmering cigarette.

The parting man wanted then to make a measured bow in farewell. Fritz Hohensee, however, murmured something like "poppycock", and pushed his arm familiarly under that of his companion. And again Heinrich brought forth something vague which sounded like an excuse or like a timid defence. Meanwhile, the young officer, however, had set his black, spurred patent leather boot on the runner of the sled, and now plucked at a button of his overcoat before the decamping man. Then he inquired with great interest whether Heinrich was not feeding up a solid everyday riding horse at Werrahn. But it must be a black horse, for in his squadron, the comrades all rode on black horses, and it must have a strong lower back, in a word, "not to end up dead", for with his last nag, he had been deceived by the Jewish horse dealer. And when Heinrich answered him that such a stallion was in his possession, and the Count could some time give him the honour, or he, Heinrich, if it were permitted, would gladly even send the animal to Wildhagen for approval, Fritz Hohensee played inattentively with the black honour sword which he was carrying under his left arm, and as his cheerful blue eyes sparkled, he suddenly called out, slapping the other man ringing on the shoulder, "Man, you know something? Take me with you. I have time. Such a reprobate holidaymaker does not know where to start anyway, and I will look at your black treasure straightaway myself."

There was no objecting to it. But when they were now both sitting next to each other in the narrow sled under a blanket, and Heinrich had grasped the reins of the vehicle, the farmer then had to turn his head often as if instinctively to the young officer.

Strange, strange. Just what had the old Count up there meant with his incomprehensible words? Was it a warning? And about whom? Not perhaps about his own son though? God forbid. That would be unnatural. And his passenger also did not look in any way thus. On the contrary. His fresh face full of the joy of life shone next to him and seemingly radiated with cheerfulness, wit, and good health. And how amiably, how simply and not in the least patronisingly the aristocrat talked with him. No, that was actually a splendid fellow.

And when the officer offered the sled driver a cigarette now from his golden case, and pushed the thing, when Heinrich tried to decline, without fuss between his lips, the last qualms of the harmless man had flown away. Quite surely, the old Count must have meant something else.

But what surely?

"Listen please, Mr Heinrich," the man next to him suddenly tore him from his brooding. "Do you know something new? You have actually become a damned proud gentleman."

"Me? Oh, Count."

"No, no, you can believe me," Fritz Hohensee continued, and tapped the other man instructively and reassuringly on the shoulder. "I know that you are notorious as a model fellow for the entire district. My old man has loved to rub that in my face. But if you have also come so damned far, you need not actually forget that we both walked together into the sexton Vierarm's school here as little trouser wearers. Do you remember still? A B: ab, B A: ba. Damn his method! And later we were also comrades at the high school in town. Mathematics with Professor Sutry: $a^2 + 2ab + b^2$. And the tangent and the hypotenuse. Well, that was a lovely country. Just — just — extremely ignorant," he then impersonated.

"Truly," Heinrich replied suddenly, gripped by the memory. "The old gentleman was actually unforgettable."

The officer laughed brightly.

"Wasn't he?", he continued. "If I were to dream it today, then I would fall from my bed in fright. Well, and see, you seem to have entirely forgotten this comradeship. For otherwise you would never ever be able to act so foreign and measured towards me."

"Oh, Count," Heinrich stuttered, not grasping at all why the young aristocrat was showing so much kindness and condescension towards him, the insignificant man. "You cannot possibly be serious."

But Fritz Hohensee, who seemed unable to bear this evasion and fending off for long, seized his arm with his white-gloved fingers, and shook it back and forth as if he wanted to bring an obdurate man to his senses.

"But man," he cried quite astonished. "Do you not want to, or can you not? Do you think then that it does not signify a truly refreshing drink for me to know next to me again such a decent, unsophisticated friend of my youth? A man without all the fumes and frills, without fancy dress and ceremonies, as is unfortunately common now in the wide world? You are frankly a break from it. And what is nicest of all, you seem to have no inkling of it."

"No, Count, I really have none," Heinrich stuttered, instinctively letting the reins fall, and no longer paying attention to his horses.

With his left hand, his companion now took the reins from his hand, but he stuck his right towards him openly and with compelling friendliness.

"Well, man, then give me your paw for the time being. I will not desire more from your hand. But if it would be possible for you, and if I should not be boring you, then do me the single pleasure, Heinrich Kalsow, and accept it with grace. As a good old friend with whom you don't make a fuss. To whom you even speak an honest word sometimes, and whom you occasionally permit to pour out his silly heart accordingly when it has pushed itself into a corner a bit. The last would even be a medicine for me frankly. Fifteen drops daily. Well, now don't pull such a serious and thoughtful face, Heinrich Kalsow, but say, 'Fritz Hohensee, you are right'."

Then the charm which radiated from this young man who was gifted with so much freshness and joy for life also mastered the cautious disposition of mother Lotte's son and monopolised it. Hesitantly indeed, but with flaring deep joy, Heinrich clasped the slender, fine hand in the white-suede glove. He held it cautiously, enclosed it in his massive paw as if he were frightened that its pressure could turn out to be too powerful and painful. But it poured from his innermost soul as he now brought forth the assurance of his friendship haltingly and abruptly, "Yes, yes, Count, if you really want that — I mean — if I am not too lowly to you for it, with a thousand joys. I only fear that you will not find with me what you are seeking. For that surely needs a quite educated and sophisticated man. But if it merely comes down to a loyal attitude, yes, Count, that I surely trust in myself. Of that there is no mistake."

And the young aristocrat suddenly also let the reins fall onto the blanket, took the other hand, and now by the four hands in the slowly gliding sled, a bond of friendship was sealed which was sought by both sides for the moment, and was intended perfectly honestly.

For the moment.

But the moment is the king of minutes. It harnesses them, it saddles them, they fly along with it, sometimes as a gleaming white horse, sometimes as a deep black horse, but at every road junction, they break apart silently under the rider.

Do not trust the moment.

***

Mother Lotte sat by the window sill of the blue room and calculated, wet the pencil, and wrote in her account book. Both her young girls, however, stood not far from her, and endeavoured on behalf of the mistress of the house to wrap up a ball of grey wool skeins, for the lady of the house tended to make winter stockings from this colour for her entire neighbourhood. And when her daughter had once objected to these shapeless pieces of embroidery, mother Lotte had then overruled such rebelliousness against her taste with a vigorous shake of the head, and accompanied it with her favourite expression, "Young folk, young folk!"

It was quite quiet in the room. Even Hertha's cheerful laughter, to which they had already become accustomed, was missing today.

Strange.

Without Heinrich's mother or his sister having really noticed, the blond guest had become ever quieter and more thoughtful since the day of the church visit. Not that her readiness to be of service or her friendly being had suffered under it. Oh no. Only more obviously, without appearance or imposture, the little one now offered a helping hand everywhere, calmly, definitely, and noiselessly, where it was needed, and quite as if mother Lotte served as example for her. Thus she had at times been surprised by the lady of the house as the girl swept out the room unbidden. Yes, when she was once too late in appearing for the common lunch, she was surprised then by Anna as she tailored and mended the clothes of the daughter of the house as well as her own in her little mansard room. And what her hands touched also blossomed seemingly new and colourful under them.

"You should not expect so much of yourself, my child," mother Lotte had even said once.

But secretly the old woman rejoiced over this transformation, and it was one of her most difficult inner qualms, whether she should devote herself now to the little one wholeheartedly and maternally or not. Certainly, experience still advised her to wait and not act prematurely. For you could not know. Such little, spoilt princesses had moods from time to time, and you must actually test them still more strictly. And see there, such an opportunity should also occur to the tottery old lady.

One evening, sexton Vierarm had just sought out the convivial home at Werrahn to perform for mother Lotte the newest hellish trick of his poodle, and there occurred unforeseen and quite suddenly that incident which was so unpleasant and frightening for mother Lotte.

"I call this black beast in fact 'Sus', Madam," the sexton had just said. "Sus means, as my pastor explained to me, pig in the distinguished and old Latin tongue. And I call my poodle thus because our Lord and Saviour, as you well know, exorcised the screaming spirits of the possessed from a herd of pigs. And now I want to insult the dog indirectly by it, and indicate to it that I see through well where it comes from. But look. Sus is the most scientific dog I have ever seen. When I just take my top hat off — see, thus — then it grasps it by the brim and carries it to the nearest chair. But he does the most satanic thing when I play the violin. For the hellish creature can tolerate that least of all. Pay attention. I merely draw a few strokes — thus — and immediately Sus dances on both hind legs like a dancer at a farmer's wedding. Have you perceived such a thing from a proper poodle, Madam?"

Mrs Lotte Kalsow, who was likewise most edified by Sus's performance, probably wanted to stand up just then to throw it a piece of ham as a reward. At this moment, however, the old lady tottered back and forth, and she had to hold fast to the back of her chair for a while, otherwise she would have fallen.

"Mother Lotte," you could hear little Hertha call at the same moment, and her voice sounded strangely anxious and afraid. "Why are you looking so red? For God's sake, is something wrong with you?"

But strong Anna had already embraced the old woman with both arms, and Heinrich had rushed out as if mad to drive to the country doctor, Dr Abraham, who practised in the next village. And when the old general practitioner appeared after an hour at the bed of the mistress of the house, who lay with glowing head on her pillows, murmuring incomprehensible fancies to herself, the bald-headed practitioner first sedately took a pinch of snuff, to then whisper sympathetically and mysteriously in the ears of the relatives, each individually, "St Anthony's fire, my boy, St Anthony's fire, my daughter. You provide ice regularly and take this powder here which I brought with me. But the principal thing remains to watch over her day and night. For such old vigorous ladies who acquire St Anthony's fire for themselves can make fools of us if possible, and we would rather not suffer that."

And now it happened, what the ill woman would never have believed if she had not experienced it herself. After the first four nights, the strong Anna, though accustomed to the strains, had in fact already fallen off, and had to almost be taken to bed by force. And by the bed of suffering from now on, Heinrich and the little blond guest, who had once been described by sexton Vierarm as an especially nasty kobold, remained, silent and alone. Sometimes, when the old lady awoke from her confused dreams, she then felt with pleasure how the slender, cool hand of the little one lay comforting and refreshing on her burning skin. And if the suffering woman then groaned something to herself in her incomprehensible whispering tone, the little one then knew immediately that the time was approaching to trickle a few drops of the beneficially cooling lemonade over the dry, cracked lips of the feverish woman. Whenever the old woman opened her eyes, she always saw the blond head of the little one who sometimes smiled at her melancholically, and other times stroked her grey, turbid bush of hair encouragingly.

"Good, good," the ill woman then murmured.

And then came the day when that sorrow befell the old general practitioner Abraham which he secretly cursed so often.

Mother Lotte had one beautiful morning come to her senses, and was again free of fever. Yes, she even forbade further visits by her general practitioner most resolutely, for each of these visits cost after all, as she could already calculate, two marks. And that was truly not a small amount.

And when the general practitioner went away on his rattly carriage drawn by a miserable nag, Heinrich had bound a pig to the carriage in the joy of his heart, as this often happened to the doctor with thankful farmers. And the old medic was Jewish, and could make no use of this donation. He often looked back over the edge of the carriage on the way home at the trotting and grunting bristly animal which in addition forced him to travel at a slow pace.

But mother Lotte was well. Though she did express a special thank you towards her nurse. But something unusual occurred nevertheless when the old lady appeared again in the blue room for the first time, where her own children already awaited her at the covered coffee table. She in fact offered each of them her hand individually. But she pulled little Hertha up, stroked her beautiful blond hair once gently, and said casually, "Now dear you can sleep properly again, my daughter. And in the next eight days, Anna will bring you coffee in bed at eight o'clock in the morning. For such youth needs its slumber."

And then she tapped her once more casually on the cheek, and concluded her contemplation with the very benevolently spoken words, "Young folk, young folk."

Yes, the lady of the house of Werrahn, she who was so difficult to influence, mother Lotte, had called the little, blond, artful bird 'dear' for the first time. And anyone who did not comprehend that as a sign did not understand the character of that old lady who was accustomed to ruling.

The Girl Who Lost Her Way

***

Mother Lotte sat by the window sill of the blue room, calculated, wet her pencil, and wrote in her account book. Both her young girls, however, stood not far from her, and endeavoured to wrap a ball up from the grey woolen skeins. This was happening in such a way that the little blond spooled the large, grey ball, while the daughter of the house swayed the woolen ply back and forth with her widespread hands to ease the work of her friend. And the silence which arose between the three women would certainly have lasted a long time yet if bright bells had not tinkled suddenly before the entrance.

"Heinrich," the old lady announced without lifting her head from her calculations.

At the same moment, however, both the others paused.

What did this vigorous movement by Anna signify? Why did she let her raised hands fall so abruptly to support herself, bent far forward, on the back of her mother's chair, from where she stared out at the yard, forgetting herself and breathing loudly.

"Who is this officer then?", Hertha threw out quite unsuspectingly. "Are we perhaps receiving a visit today, mother Lotte?"

"Yes, God knows," the old lady responded in a long drawn out tone, whereby she reluctantly set her white bonnet right. "It will probably be such a thing."

Then her glance sought the countenance of her daughter, who remained unchanged in her place. Straight afterwards, however, the old lady put her pencil to her mouth, and began calculating again unconcerned.

"The gentlemen are going into the stables," she suggested indifferently. "Why not? Heinrich wants perhaps to sell one of our two riding horses. And if it is well paid for, then —".

She tapped her pencil on the table, and threw out over her shoulder, "Anna, the wool is falling from your hand. Raise it up, my daughter, and then you can keep winding it."

And rightly. So accustomed was everybody on the property to obeying the instructions of the lady of the house that the tall strong girl immediately shook something from herself to then seemingly quite unaffectedly take up her occupation again. In long swinging movements, the grey strands of wool were again led back and forth. Yes, not once did the girl dare to change her position, for she still remained with her back to the window.

Thus half an hour had again elapsed in deep silence when the three women noticed anew how the stable door opened and a lad led into the yard a tall, unbridled, black stallion which was now to show all its paces before the two gentlemen following it. Soon the observers inside saw how the noble animal stormed around in circles with its guide in a wild gallop, and straight afterwards you could perceive how the black horse, steaming and snorting, set its graceful feet in a slower tempo.

Both girls had long since forgotten their peaceful occupation without the old lady being able to hinder it. With large, astonished eyes, both little heads watched the spectacle, nestled close together and bent far forward. But the strange officer must have also discovered the inhabitants of the blue room, for he suddenly exchanged a quick word with his companion to then straightaway turn fully to the window, and lead his hand to his cap, obligingly saluting.

A pity. Only mother Lotte from her window sill was in a position to respond to this greeting. And she did it with a stiff-backed measuredness as if she were firmly forged to the back of her chair, and could only give a few signs of human civility with her sharp, narrow goshawk's head. And as she bowed her white tulle bonnet almost imperceptibly, she growled a little gratified to herself, "Look, even that too. How nice. But I don't think it belongs to the business. And now he might soon actually be finished having a look."

Only, even this wish of the old lady would not be fulfilled. The lady of the house had to shake her head with more and more astonishment. Lord in heaven, what was all that about? Why did the distinguished visitor not finally say goodbye to her Heinrich, for they seemed to have reached an agreement? In contrast. Oh, that was really strong. Was the aristocrat not pointing quite openly to the room now? And was it really possible that her boy, her big, dumb boy, was performing an inviting gesture as if he wanted to answer the other man, "Count, please enter. My family will take a great honour from it"? Truly a scandal. The lady of the house read all the words off the awkward young farmer's face quite clearly. But she just said out loud, "Now it's becoming a bright day," rose, stepped away from the window sill, and strolled once through the room so that the innocent porcelain vases on the mahogany commode clinked and rattled.

"There is something wonderful about modesty," she determined during her wandering.

And when she perceived the blanched countenance of her daughter quite fleetingly in skimming past, and how the fingers of the otherwise so strong girl wavered about on her dress in restless movements, she burst out, perfectly irritated, "Devilry!"

It was the same word which the old Count Karl Anton had already found appropriate to use for the present case. Only little Hertha was not touched by this secret family discord. Her right foot placed strongly by the window, she stood there, distractedly let a strand of her golden hair glide through her fingers, and the thought swirled incessantly through her head, "Where have you seen this man once before? Is it not the same man who —".

Only, she did not get any further, for the door was already being opened, and amidst several awkward bows by the young farmer, who obviously sought to screen by this politeness the estranging silence of his family, the martial guest entered the blue room.

For the first time.

Above on the ceiling, both the wooden giants cracked loudly and menacingly. In their way, they shook their heads, and mother Lotte, who had learnt to understand the language of both over many long years, heard quite distinctly how they asked each other reproachfully and grumpily, "And the lady of Werrahn suffers that? She says yes and amen to that? Young folk — young folk."

And then there was a jerk again, and it rang out furiously, "Bad — bad."

***

Fritz Hohensee wanted of course only to kiss respectfully the hands of the ladies, and above all and quite especially that of the lady of the house.

Yes, such a cavalier. Even mother Lotte, who wished the Count's visit, complete with the sold horse, would go to the devil, was incapable of bringing her disposition clearly to his consciousness as she heard the young, fresh officer chatting in such perfect gentility and harmlessness. And how the elegant young gentleman knew to place everything which somehow belonged to Werrahn in a dazzling light.

Thunderbolts! What a stately stallion he had just bought. His comrades in the accursed, desolate nest back there would simply be flabbergasted. And what now concerned Mr Heinrich even, it simply offered an undreamt-of pleasure to conclude a business with such a noble and steadfast seller. Apropos, his papa, who could undoubtedly only be most satisfied over this addition to his stables, would send over the money the next morning through a groom. Or stop! Of course. If it were permitted, then he, Fritz Hohensee would offer himself the great pleasure of bringing over the sum personally on that very stallion. For the animal would of course feel a desire to go to Werrahn. — Here a gentle bow followed before the three ladies. — And since he was just a good-natured fellow, he could not oppose such a heart's wish from the creature. And when Heinrich, who could not explain the aloofness of the three ladies at all, had asked in a half imploring tone whether the Count would not want after the sharp sled trip to take part in the family's modest breakfast, his new friend fell into a proper rapture. But naturally, what a question, if the gracious lady permits it, of course. And you don't need to have the least concern over the menu, because he had already heard from sexton Vierarm of repeated meals which offered wonderful country bread at Werrahn. And if he were not wrong, then he thought he had heard that Miss Kalsow was herself the creator of this artwork. It was too nice that he might for once personally taste such a delicacy. He had already had the pleasure, was actually an old acquaintance, for the gracious Miss had allowed him when he rode past to exchange a few words with her over the yard wall. And she could not at all fathom what joy it gave him, growing lonely out here, to be offered such a little ingratiating discourse. And now the other young lady. Lord, her hair recalls directly the world of folk tales, because only fairies were described with such adornment on their heads. Meanwhile, what he wanted to note was that he must have also already seen the gracious little one somewhere. Perhaps in the town. And after Hertha mentioned that she was a daughter of Colonel Boddin, Fritz Hohensee sprang to his feet with a jerk, clicked his heels together so that his silver spurs rang out, and cried in extreme delight, "But certainly, my most gracious Miss, Colonel Boddin of the Fusiliers. A quite distinguished gentleman. His picture hangs in the mess. And if the remark is allowed, the similarity appears to me also to be unmistakeable."

Again a bow, the silver spurs clinked anew, and yet it offered mother Lotte a true satisfaction because the little blond placed her hand so hesitantly and reservedly in the officer's offered right hand.

"Really, really, that is to be praised. My own silly girl, who stares at men like a wonder of the sea, could take an example and model from that."

And when the little one now backed away completely to the lady of the house, pressing her slender little body close to the old lady, and also slinging her arm familiarly and tightly under mother Lotte's, the old woman felt with a certain envy how the little blond creature, who had changed so much to her advantage, intended to participate in the convivial reception of this young aristocrat only as an indifferent observer. The cuirassier too, thus also directing only a few occasional words to Hertha, seemed to possess a mind and eyes only for the daughter of the house. Amidst hearty laughter from Heinrich, who surely did not feel anymore the tense situation and the secret irritation of his mother, the guest began helping the beautiful and stately Anna with the buttering of the bread so coveted by him, and it really presented a wondrous picture as the young officer in his becoming, blue tunic held the enormous round slices of country bread to take in their aroma at a respectful distance, but yet with blissful notions. And after the guest had now experienced entirely by accident that Anna was treasured in this narrow country circle because of her alto voice, he started, electrified, and began to beg from heaven to earth for her to give him a sample of her ability.

"Please, please, dear Miss, without false modesty. Come. After the precious sample of country bread, a quite small bite of music. I will accompany you, and pay attention, I, the hapless musician, will, carried away by your mastery, become a Liszt, a Hans von Bülow. Well, you will note how I play."

He sat, lifted the piano lid, and when the beautiful, tall girl, now pale, now red, could not decide in her heart's anguish on a specific song, the cuirassier commanded with an exuberant laugh that she should sing "Watch on the Rhine".

"What, what?", Heinrich stuttered.

But Fritz Hohensee insisted on his idea. He was already beginning to stir the keys, and see, what nobody would have believed, a wild, disorderly, truly artistic ingenuity unfolded here. In wonderful, mad, tumbling chords and fugues, he varied the hymn so gloriously and masterfully that Anna had to fall in with glowing cheeks. And now it rang out louder and ever louder like a remarkable, never heard before torrent; the waves, foam, stones, and debris roaring in unending falling into the valley:

> Dear Fatherland, you may be calm,
> Kept firm and true, the watch by the Rhine.

The performance of them both sounded so carried away, so woven together, that even Heinrich had to join in with his powerful bear's voice, and soon the entire room echoed and thundered with this fathomlessly mad and yet deeply churning music. Only mother Lotte fingers nervously the mahogany top of the round table. But woe, even her sharp, grey eyes were distracted by the strange thing which was being performed here. Otherwise she would have certainly noticed how little Hertha stood next to her with hands that clawed into the back of the sofa, and with eyes which like a stormily moved sky sometimes dimmed and sometimes flashed in bright lightning.

> Dear Fatherland, you may be calm,
> Kept firm and true, the watch by the Rhine.

"Quite beautiful," mother Lotte judged. "But it is not healthy. Enough."

4

The inheritance of humanity also materialised in the country circles of Werrahn. Time strolled along like a sower who strews unworried in the furrows of the present, and if the day ripens anew, then he will return as reaper to harvest it. The hours, however, sprinkle over it like raindrops.

"Yes, that is really so," sexton Vierarm murmured, for a miracle had just happened to him again.

He sat leisurely in the sexton's room in his deeply upholstered armchair before the round table onto which the leather bell rope hung down so harmlessly, and now he sang with devoted pleasure and beautiful, bright emphasis that song which he had already performed today in the church with such force that even a pair of deaf, knitting women on the last bench had nodded contentedly with their bare heads and said, "Yes, the sexton Vierarm, he has it in the chest."

From his wide open mouth, however, it sounded as follows:

> The one is king, Emmanuel prevails,
> Tremble, enemies, and pray for flight.
> Zion however, be ever glad,
> Refresh your hearts with heavenly fruit.[*]

Be it now that the pious content of this song had exercised a special impression on the disposition of the poodle Sus, or that it happened in consequence of a perfidious, hellish calculation, in any case, the door opened with the last verse, and in waggled the black assistant, the emissary of unearthly powers, to place before the feet of his master a just sprouted, green birch sprig which the animal had carried in its snout up to then.

"Look," sexton Vierarm said quite aghast, as he picked up the scented little branch, and examined it from all sides. "It is Ascension Day, and Sus brings the first greenery into my house. I must ponder straight-away whether that has any significance. But the glory of truth. The sprig smells really heart refreshingly of fresh mash, and it is a glorious and pleasant day today. Come, Sus, drink your milk."

And then he began once more anew:

> The one is king, Emmanuel prevails,
> Tremble, enemies, and pray for flight!

At the same time, he pulled on the bell rope at ordered and measured intervals so that it tolled far out over the greening meadows and sprouting fields, bimm — bumm, bimm — bumm.

> Zion however, be ever glad,
> Refresh your hearts with heavenly fruit.

***

---

[*] J.L.K. Allendorf's hymn "Einer ist König, Immanual sieget".

"Yes, it is glorious weather," old Count Karl Anton also suggested, riding through his fields with his son at a comfortable gait, and patted his gentle white horse caressingly on the neck at the same time. "Well, always slow, Marianne."

Meanwhile, turning to his white-coated companion, he suddenly jiggled his red nose reluctantly, and growled unamused, "The devil knows how it happens, my boy, but it seems extremely funny to me, since when actually have you discovered such a family attachment? Your dear mama, our Anne-Marie-Luise, had in fact hardly begun her first song of devotion this morning — well, yes, I have nothing against it, and am also already accustomed to it — when I hear you galloping on this black Werrahn horse into the yard. Tell me one thing, boy, you surely love me?"

"Of course," the officer then replied with a somewhat embarrassed smile, whereby he stroked his fashionable, English beard. "When one possesses such a distinguished father."

"Yes," the old man said. "Has something to it." — He struck his turned-up boot with his riding crop. "Do you want to also reveal to me now perhaps where you were wanting to ride to when I just caught you here at the fork in the road? Well, out with it."

"Oh, papa, nothing special at all lies behind it. I just wanted to enjoy the glorious day a bit."

"So," the old gentleman responded, suddenly being very serious, and held the other's bridle firmly so that the black horse of the officer had to stop abruptly. "Then I will share something with you here very briefly, my dear boy. If you intend to fool around, I won't cover for you, understood? Not with my good name. I am absolutely of the view that in our present day everyone must earn his own name. There is nothing to inherit there. Do you hear?"

"Yes, but papa — I don't know at all actually —".

"Well, then, all the better. And now, my sweet boy, a few more quite incidental questions. Where are you heading actually? What is actually becoming of you? When you took every lesson possible for studying foreign languages, what did I do then? I forked out, and said 'wonderful' to it. For I thought that it was perhaps directed at a diplomatic career. After a short time, you knew like a prodigy how to make yourself understood in the most impossible dialects of the Lord, then you all of a sudden decided on a career as an officer. Excellent. All your ancestors were. Your uncle Berthold even became a commander. And you? Eh, I have seen for a long time already by your face that the gaiter service bores you."

"Bores? But, dear papa, from what do you deduce that?"

"Do me the single pleasure, lad, and let me finish speaking. I can at least ask that for my dear money. So, what now? Farmer? Son, that is also no profession where the fat harvests grow thus into the hand. The job needs to be damned well understood in our times. And in business, there you must be able to handsomely deceive the various gentlemen of Abraham and Cain. Well, and do you know how to do that? Until now, I have only noticed that you entertain quite different relations with gentlemen of that sort. So, now perhaps music? For I hear that they already call you 'Richard Wagner' in the garrison."

"Listen please, old man, now you come, however, really to quite eccentric stories," the Lieutenant defended himself, blushing, and pushed his white cap vigorously onto his ears. "It only concerns a regiment's name."

"Quite rightly," the old man persisted, and again tapped his Marianne tenderly on the neck. "And I was called Shell-Anton, because in 1870 such an accursed hussy whistled directly between my legs. Well, yes, with this accursed lounging about in peace, you know nothing about that. But now tell me please, brat, but please, a bit seriously, have you come to any thoughts about your future?"

There Fritz Hohensee straightened up more boldly. His ingratiating countenance, which shimmered as white and red as a precious apple, again began to radiate that brilliance which everyone who neared him, and especially poor Anna at Werrahn, was entranced by. With his riding crop, he struck the air vigorously a few times before he called out into the blue day proudly and as if free from all worries, "So, old man, because you have now disposed happily of your moral sermon, let me tell you that I just want to spend the few years which remain to me in the garrison as pleasantly and happily as my youth requires. For see, father, I really don't take it all so amusingly. My nature just needs merriment and savouring; well, in a word, I must dispatch by all means with the most beautiful things there are in the world, with glorious women, with a freshly sought out danger, with art and poetry, in short, with all the storm and fizz, before I can become here at our Wildhagen such an upright noble businessman as you are now."

"What, brat, you want also to —".

"No, let it be," the Lieutenant reassured him, and suddenly pulled at the reins of his black horse, which had been constantly scraping impatiently with its hooves, so that the noble animal now rose up high and had to be released by the estate owner. "A few such litres of your blood certainly also flows in me. And what usually lumbers about in my veins, old man, sometimes seethes and boils in such a way that I would like to race from sorrow and misery at the wall with my head. I prefer not to explain that at all, for you would not comprehend it with your conventional German mind."

"Boy, I would like most of all to box your ears," Karl Anton suddenly cried. "These damned times have corrupted you beautifully."

The cuirassier guided his horse for a step away from the gentle white horse of the old man, looked very seriously over at him, yes, you could even notice how harsh creases furrowed around the young man's mouth and temples. Then he stretched out his hand to the old Count with a quick movement.

"So, father, now give me peace," he concluded with a darker voice than usual, which seemed to allow no contradiction. "You know I can only tolerate a certain degree. And now let me go my own way in peace."

"Yes, yes. Go to the devil," Karl Anton roared, his face turning a burgundy colour. But he suddenly added quite unexpectedly, as he almost folded his hands beseechingly, "Boy, boy, don't cause me any sorrow. Take God into your heart, you hear?"

But the son just waved to him with a half, somewhat bashful smile, then he rushed at a full gallop down the country road. The hooves of his steed clopped with short, sonorous beats, and, from both sides of the road, the wind strew white cherry blossom down on the man racing along. It was as if a giant, white snowflake was being driven through the midst of spring.

"No, no," Karl Anton murmured to himself depressed, as he looked down quietly at his greening fields. "He in heaven will not begrudge me that. Such a dear, handsome boy. And my only one. No, not that, that I cannot believe."

***

At the same time, little Hertha found herself in the most hidden and secret corner which could be traced in Werrahn.

On the edge of a sparse oak grove, in whose midst an almost circular, small meadow had thrust itself, the mill stream flowed past broad and deep with bright, cheerful water, and right in this place had burrowed a large, sandy bed. On the other side, the water was bounded by a row of sturdy poplars which swayed back and forth in the gentle spring wind, and from trunk to trunk stretched fresh, slender, voluble willow brush, under whose roof of leaves a flock of colourful goldfinches twittered up and down, for close by the forest there was a thistle colony which this folk favoured. Here at the stillest place, mother Lotte had had erected over the waterfall a square tent frame supported by sheet ropes so that the residents of Werrahn could rinse off their troubles and burdens after work in the crystalline natural basin. On the present Ascension Day meanwhile, the place lay deserted. Only the first yellow brimstone butterflies, which were wanting to prematurely greet the spring wandering through the land, fluttered about the hundreds of golden daisies with which the meadow had already been adorned; the flock of colourful goldfinches swished here and there, and through the sun-reflecting water, a gang of tiny sticklebacks scurried occasionally, being drilled by a larger little fish. Over on the other side of the poplars, an aged stork strutted alone, nodded its head reverently, and listened casually to the croaking of the frogs as well as the monotonous humming and chirping of the grasshoppers. Over the fields and forest and meadows, however, a transparent, reflective net of sunlight was stretched.

Then a hurried, light step approached along the edge of the stream. In light summer garb, with uncovered head so that her golden hair, struck by the rays of the sun, sparkled like a thick wreath of those daisies, little Hertha strode along. Sometimes she looked down at her yellow little boots which secured her narrow feet so firmly, other times she airily waved her large, yellow straw hat which she wore slung over her arm in Friederike's way on a blue silk ribbon[*]. When she had reached the meadow in the oak grove, the blond lingered for a moment, shaded her eyes with her right hand, bent forward, and looked delightedly at the cloud of drifting butterflies which struggled with each other for the privilege of love and life. Suddenly the little one exulted loudly, but the next moment, she was shocked by her own outburst.

Lord, she was not accustomed to that anymore at all. If it had been heard by one of the people with whom she now constantly dwelt, and who observed, assessed, and tested her.

Strange — strange — she sat down by the edge of the stream, and gazed down at the silvery surface quickly whirling past, which reflected her narrow head in trembling, quickly smeared lines; for such a very long and indescribable time, the little one had now already suppressed under the constant observation her innermost tendencies, plans, and hobbies — and now? Now it seemed to her almost as if that active life which had usually stretched her limbs, had slowly and peacefully passed away. Yes, even peacefully. Really, most strange. How could she have usually crouched here so inactively in the grass, one hand propped behind the other, just so, half reclined, to look with still, innocent interest between the poplars out into the fields to where the stork undertook its dignified morning stroll?

Now it bowed and hacked with its red beak in a wide, glistening puddle of water which had remained behind from the last inundation.

"He has probably caught a little frog," Hertha thought, and again she had to wonder that her once so

---

[*]   A reference to J.W. Goethe's description of his first meeting with
      Friederike Brion, the inspiration for much of his early poetry.

drifting, so inconstant temperament had let itself be caught and comforted in such unworldly observations.

She cosily stretched her slender little body back still further, and began raptly plucking out a welter of grass stalks in her vicinity. Her thoughts just crept onward wearily lost in dreaming.

But oh, how pleasantly mild this calm, which was formerly so hated by her, lay about her soul and body. It was as if an old, soft, wrinkled old woman's hand were constantly stroking her hot breast and pounding heart; it was as if this were mother Lotte's hand. In deep, trembling complacency, the little one embedded both arms under her head so that the light played blindingly about her forehead, then stretched, and shut her eyes. And as green and brown beetles hummed around her, it seemed to her in her drowsy state as if fine, unearthly voices were lisping in her ear, "See, you sweet, little blond, this contentedness, this passing away of all the wildness and recklessness, surely in that exists in the end your happiness. It looks quite different to what you pictured before. It isn't a torrent rushing down, but a long forgotten, slumbering pool, surrounded by a thick wall of humming willow brush. Yes, a still pool only known to a few. And look — look — look — but remain calm, little one, remain calm — how long will it last until you will link to the one who commands over all this peace here, who can make it permanent and fixed for you; link to him, the tall, kind, honest giant who folds his mighty fists to pray to you as if to a divinity?

"Heinrich? — oh — oh —". She sighs and stirs in the grass. But the humming little voice rocks her again.

"Stay still, sweet little one, stay still, we crickets will sing to you of happiness. Have you noticed yourself what a consuming venom is imparted to human bodies by passion, the wild, unshackled passion, that murderous and yearning passion? How it disfigures even the most beautiful? Look up at Heinrich's sister Anna. Has she not grown taller and more gloriously than you? A mature, summerly woman? And take note — take note, little one. Have you not discerned for a long time in the calm, seemingly so unshaken woman a veil over the eyes like that which only arises from poorly suppressed tears? And the haste and the unrest and the deep sighs which sometimes come through to you from the next room at night. — How do you explain the wild stammering, the rushed talk from tormenting dreams? And then, little one, oh, you are clever, you have long since observed the hide-and-seek which both these two, the handsome blond, boyish Count and that woman yearning for devotion, play before the others. How often has a smile passed over your features when the tall, secretive girl affects to her mother some compelling errand which must lead her here and there in the district or into the town. Have you not seen them both at the time of the spring storms stepping out of a district tavern? You indeed turned your head, you clever little one, and struck off down a field path. But since then you know what is left for you to think and believe, don't you? Is it so? — Is it so?"

In ever narrower circles, the beetle folk hum and fly about the sprawled blond head. The rays of the sun are caught in the enormous mesh of a cobweb spanning between two lime trees, and the drops of dew which hang there in the invisible chambers glisten and throw back the flooding light in a sparkling way. Like emeralds coming to life, iridescent green flies stand almost motionless in the air before suddenly flashing away.

But there — what is that?

The little one sits up quite abruptly, brushes her hand across her forehead, and looks confusedly about herself as if she could not think for a moment. What is that though? The letter? That strange, tiny letter which she received today in an unfamiliar hand, and which invites her so curtly and definitely to a rendezvous there out at the farm building below the old burnt down windmill? Right — right. She eagerly passes her hand under her bib and fetches out from there the crackling note. How definite and demanding these few words sound. There is no doubt, she knows quite exactly, those lines originate from the nobleman who has actually never paid proper attention to her, and who now intends perhaps to use her as an intermediary, as a messenger of love. Haha! The foolish, frivolous wretch. Now he is certainly creeping about the burnt-out wooden ruins, whilst she whom he seeks keeps herself hidden at the opposite end of the Werrahn property to tear up his invitation into a hundred little shreds over the gently rolling stream.

Look, how they swim away. They whirl about, they circle one another, and vanish. No, no, no break from the peace. The gentle, unthinking calm flatters her so benevolently, makes all her limbs so wonderfully soft and supple.

And as the little one gazes after the white shreds, the wish to also check the coolness of the waters then wins power over her. Yes, it is true, everything invites such a secret, rippling bathing.

With a quick resolve, she springs up, sticks away again the letter's envelope, which still remains; she is already striding over the small board which leads into the space stretched with canvas; and the next moment her fingers are stripping and undoing her light items of clothing. Now she stands resplendent there in full sunlight, and stretches. Only the onrushing water is able to eavesdrop on the white figure, and the green tops of the lime trees which peer over the open wall strew buds down over her. A lengthening and stretching. And then something white and glistening shoots back and forth on the surface, sinks and resurfaces again, scraps with the foam, and scurries behind the flickering rays of the sun. The living emeralds which accompanied her, however, still shot and flashed above her, and they threw strangely green shadows over her wet, silky skin.

***

Across the willow brush which curled its leaves to and fro in the gentle breeze between the poplars, sometimes green, sometimes silvery white, a black horse's head appeared. Its nostrils widened when the animal sensed the water nearby, and it tossed the foam away like white flakes so that it looked as if freshly fallen snow was being driven down the stream.

But there was something else to listen to there. Over there in the enclosed meadow, did not a brightly clothed young lady sit there, on whose blond hair it glistened as if from dewdrops, and who — thunderbolts, it was really so — endeavoured to pull a pair of enchanting black stockings onto her bare feet?

God — Fritz Hohensee forgot every caution, pushed the willow branches to the side, and bent himself down low to be able to send a full, thirsting glance at the charming picture unexpectedly gifted to him. God — how it sparkled and flashed. She was sitting there like one of the scurrying dryads, like those the accursed fellows, those modern painters, now created, and which they enveloped only for fun and for prudish eyes with all sorts of soft scraps of clothing. The one over there must have just climbed out of the water. No thinking any longer. "Wait, you witch, now I will seize you. You shall pay me, you fresh, blond caper."

A hefty squeeze of his leg, the slender steed bounced back two steps, both forelegs tautened angularly and tightly towards the rear as if the noble animal intended bucking with all its might against what would follow. A shudder passed over the trembling limbs and then — — —.

Almighty!

From the other side a scream. The blond fairy fell back in the green scene as if a lightning bolt had struck through the sunny haze before her. Is that possible?

It flies over the stream, black and white, indistinguishable, an uncanny mass. And now something is whinnying loudly and insistently before the sprawled girl, a pair of flashing blue eyes clasp her as if they wanted to singe through her innocent white dress, and a cheerful voice blares exultantly in her ear, nothing but the one phrase, "Prisoner of war!"

The thick wall of oaks echoes these words. Then a dull jump, and the white-coated officer with the gleaming patent leather riding boots stands before her, the horse's reins casually enclosed in his fist. Then Hertha also jumps up from her sprawled position. Her first movement is applied to her white skirt. She seeks to cover her bareness. Then she fixes a pert, defiant smile to her lips, although her heart skips and trembles in fear and unease.

"Good morning, Lieutenant," she begins as ingenuously as is possible for her.

But from the other side, it resounds in an absolutely different key. The quivering of expectation, of victory, of possession already penetrates the voice of the rider whose cheeks are overflowing with the brownish floods of spring.

"Good morning, little madam. Here we would be then."

"Yes, I see that."

"Good, then permit me surely. Right, it is allowed?"

The Count throws himself down close next to the girl. The meadow shakes for a moment from the dull fall, and the little one's heart rises into her throat.

'What does it mean? What will happen?', it storms through her disturbed mind. With both hands, she grasps firmly backwards into the grass, and aims to hold herself upright. For God's sake, not to let herself be driven away from the peace which has surrounded her so sweetly, so incipiently. The gift of mother Lotte. No, defending herself against it. Here it is about defending herself. Bucking against the reaching over of a wild youth which she fancied to personify in herself shortly before.

Remain firm, throw her hands forward, and chase away the importunate man.

But as the young officer now flashed his eyes at her with such a shrewd expression, and placed his hand for a moment lightly on her own, she was incapable of pulling herself together for something decisive. She just quietly lisped to herself, "Don't."

"Yes," the Lieutenant began straightaway, "we are thus rebuffed. I just come in fact from the old Werrahn mill where I looked at the charred beams so devoutly, as if I were a salaried fire brigade commander. Please, why did you not come, little Miss?"

"Me?"

So damped down was her nature already by the acquiescent taciturnity, which she had practised for mother Lotte's sake for so long, that she could only be dully astonished over the almost artless insolence of the aristocrat.

"I don't know at all what you mean," she continued without thinking, and yet her dark eyebrows were already knitting together somewhat more closely.

Then again a light, suppressed cry of shock. Had that really happened? Had she actually felt the fingers of this man on her neck and breast? With a bold grasp, the rider had taken possession of the shreds of paper which still peered forth from her bib. Now he held the crumpled envelope towards her.

"You should have come though," he began anew, and it seemed as if he did not know at all what words he was using, his gaze constantly encompassed the little, quivering figure of the blond so admiringly and in homage.

Drops of water beaded continuously from her hair, and she held the white skirt stretched tautly and tightly about her bare feet which the officer had glanced at only fleetingly and almost with awe.

"You should have come," he repeated once more uncertainly, as he grasped for her hand anew.

She hastily drew her fingers from him.

"What actually do you wish from me, Count Hohensee?", she cried suddenly, remembering herself, and in her voice there came through quite unconsciously again that enticing quivering and swaying which had already evaporated here at Werrahn. "I did not know that we both had something to agree on with each other which my friend must not hear, right?"

"Yes," the officer murmured, tore handfuls of grass from around himself, and strew them in her lap. "I did not actually know either."

"Or do you perhaps want to explain to me," the little one now straightened up in full fury, whereby she could in fact render no account over why she was lashed by such a passionate excitement, "do you perhaps want to explain to me why Anna Kalsow goes about in tears? So tell me then!", she added more fiercely and reddening. "Don't dodge it. I have long wanted to throw it in your face. Are you not actually ashamed at all? Does your sense of honour not forbid that you, an officer, a great man of the country forces himself against the expressed will of the mistress of the house into this harmless family for no other reason than to agitate a trusting, good and beautiful creature, even perhaps to infatuate her?

Does a man act like that whom we are also only accustomed to call upright in the common sense? So lift your face. Look at me please, if you are capable of it."

Her breast trembled, her entire body flew, but she fell back suddenly as if numbed. Instead of an answer, the white-coated man with a wild grasp had clasped a hard, sinewy arm about her so that she had to fall back unresisting. And now she felt, as she thought thunder-claps were shaking the earth, yes, that the drops of water on her hair were hissing like molten lead over her eyes to annihilate all view, all perception, now she felt half paralysed in horror, and yet with a simultaneous contradictory relief, as a man's head buried itself in her lap, and that straight afterwards her feet were covered by mad kisses.

And see, the sun was going down, it was becoming night about her. She lay acquiescing, felt tears pressing through her eyelashes, and thought the last hour of her existence had begun. And the last hour swelled with sweetness, and the white death lay next to her and kissed her.

Then one of the living green precious stones shot humming through her weakness. With a superhuman effort, she jerked up, grasped at her half undone, flowing hair, and spoke quite naturally, without deceit or affectation, just lost and lamenting, "Yes, but — good God!"

The Count had sprung up, had grasped the reins of his horse, and it looked as though he wanted to swing into his saddle to flee before this helplessness. If this had happened, the misery would never have uncovered the roof of the house at Werrahn to gaze on the desolation through the empty beams. But a quick breath from the little one, for which she could do nothing which she had not intended, held the rider back, and shackled him again to the place of aggression. With his back leaning against the horse, he began spraying accusations and re-proaches against her as if this little blond creature with whom he had exchanged barely a hundred words had confused his existence, present and future.

It sounded thus, "Why does Anna go around in tears? Why do you ask me that, you wonderful little thing? You know right well that the stronger one always behaves properly. And who is surely the stronger in the house at Werrahn? Who? Why do you always remain silent? This silence which speaks so enticingly? Why do you always distance yourself, and draw towards yourself with entwining cords? You know all that quite well. One only needs to gaze into your eyes to realise that you anticipated all that. And then, what does a mistake bother me when I emerge from it? We young people are here so that we can steal the crown from the moment. Believe me, in that exists the greatest pleasure. It is in a way the new, precious religion of youth. And you, you glorious, wild creature, you don't deceive me, you think just the same."

It swirled in Hertha's ears. The rustling of trees, the lisping ripples of the water, the humming of the beetles, the painful gasping which rose up in her own breast, it all danced about her like a mad music. She heard the tinkling of little bells, tolling bells, dance tunes, and in-between thundered quite distantly the organ of sexton Vierarm. She wanted to straighten up, but her oppressor hindered it, as he was pushing up close to her with his horse so that she had to remain lying on bare knees before him. Her remarkably bright eyes raised to him, like a recalcitrant prayer, she had to listen to him continue.

How strange. He bent down lower to her, and while his fists were balled as if she had done something serious to him, that hot stammering broken by an inner passion continued, "Intrusion? Who has intruded here?

You have done. You, the distinguished young lady, the member of our elevated circle, you have as it were smuggled yourself in here. Yes, yes, so it is."

He shook at her clasped hands. "Then answer me though, if you possess the courage to. Why are you bewitching this good, honest boy, this Heinrich who would never have dared direct his glance to you without your encouragement, why are you befogging his poor, ponderous head? But, but, you shall answer me," he raged on hoarsely. "It is all deceit, clowning, but never ever an inner whiff of truth. Yes, I hear that you, the fine, little, silken creature, are already considered in the district to be his bride. I ask you, why do you do nothing to tear up such a web of lies? You must do that though. You must realise though that you must do that, don't you?"

The officer shook and pulled so strongly at her hands that he tore her without thinking up from her kneeling position. Only as much time still remained to the little one to prop herself with both hands numb and faint against his chest, and as she murmured to herself with fading senses, "I thought you were his friend. How does it concern you, how I decide over my future? How can a friend behave so badly towards the other?", and as this all slipped out from her without inner sympathy, the slender body shuddered again as if under blows, for following the strong movement, the excited man had pulled her to himself, and closed her mouth now with seething, drunken kisses.

"And I won't suffer it, it shall not be, it must not —", she heard yet as a hissing by her ear, and then again this silent, horrific, all-dissolving struggle until it suddenly became infinitely still about her.

Remarkable — oh how strangely remarkable.

She lay there outstretched with wide spread arms in the fresh grass. The mad gallop of the steed rang out from a distance, and when she opened her eyes, she then saw through the green wall of poplars, quite far away on the country road, a white point appearing and disappearing and becoming smaller and tinier. But she could not retain this picture either. Without any thought, fully apathetic, as if in ruptured contentedness, an angel who had just been thrust by a black fist from the heaven of light, she lay with closed eyes. Above her, the battle of the beetles hummed on, and a little elder bush which clustered with reddish blue crown under the oaks shook its leaves down over her sympathetically.

The water rushed onward, the wind continued. Spring rode on a sun-horse far off over the fields, and the abandoned creature lay and watched how her tears glistened in the morning rays over the grass.

***

"Quite certainly, now we will find her," Heinrich said, who had been searching about with his sister Anna already for hours, spying in the fields and hedges, and in ever increasing, only arduously suppressed fear, for the little one had, for the first time since she had dwelt at Werrahn, missed the midday hour so that even in mother Lotte a poorly concealed concern had arisen.

"She will come. Of course, she will come — who knows, young folk, young folk," the old lady said to herself. And yet the mistress of the house noticed in the restless movement which grasped her entire being what close sympathy already attached her to her delicate guest. Where would she be then, such a prudent little thing who restrains herself so much? Perhaps fallen asleep over a book in an elder bush. For the little one was reading a lot recently. That was not something bad, for she only read good books.

"It would perhaps be right though," mother Lotte asked her children finally, "if you would keep a lookout for her. It is certainly only an oversight. For the little one usually keeps to punctuality and does not want to make us worried. So go — go quick!"

Before the stream, Heinrich faltered. With a spasmodic movement, he grasped the hand of the tall girl accompanying him, and pulled her closer to himself.

"See, Anna, see there!", he tried to gasp, pointing across the willow brush. Only, his sister did not hear him. Half turned to the side, her hand, to protect against the rays of the sun, placed over her large, rigid eyes which burned dark in a white countenance, she remained erect next to her brother, and her look sank into the distance, to where between the poplars of the country road something white and shadowy like a luminous bird skipped from branch to branch. Her eyes gradually turned black. Then a dim red glow shot over her as far as the roots of her full, dark brown hair, and now — now the strong woman swayed as if she had misstepped in the furrows of the field, and grasped in passing for the arm of her companion. But he noticed nothing. As if he were completely alone in this world of shoots and germination, he pushed his steer-like head forward, the sweat of fear broke from his forehead, and as he pushed back the willow bushes to peer over there towards the outstretched figure, uncertain and with veiled eyes, it then slid half senselessly from his lips chilled as if in fever.

"Not dead — merciful God — Lord in heaven, only sleeping! Right, Anna, only sleeping?"

And suddenly the man's clenched chest suddenly widened, and a scream blared out of it so that the oak walls shook. And as if hit by a bullet, the little one jerked up, back into reality. With mad eyes, both hands pressed to her forehead, she stared over at her waker, the one who freed her from paralysis, the spell, and the lost, tormenting feeling. As if she were arising from a ditch of stinging nettles.

"Hertha! Hertha!"

"Heinrich!"

With a powerful leap, the giant sprang over the stream, tumbled towards her, almost thrown to the ground by his own weight, and lifted her up, tenderly and yet fiercely like a child rejoicing over a doll found again.

"Dear little one, it's nothing though?", he stammered as his awkward fingers stroked her, fumbling and examining. "What happened? For God's sake, what fears we have had."

The blond then thought to herself. And like in that night when the scythe of death whistled before her ears, she suddenly threw herself, unworried about the observer, at the chest of the awkward, swaying fellow, buried her head there as if she wanted to hear and see nothing more, and stammered constantly only the mad, drunken words, "Praise God, oh praise God!"

And as it were as if she fancied herself followed, she turned her head once more to the side to throw a timid, appalled look at the country road. "Don't, don't," she murmured at the same time. But the farmer was not letting her from his arms anymore. As if in a fever, he carried the white, trembling burden, who threw herself about back and forth on his chest, back over the stream, and he did not once notice that her bare feet dangled down, and it was as if the silky little hairs on them flickered in the midday sun. Only in front of his sister, on the other side of the willow brush, did he carefully set down the salvaged girl, as cautiously and hesitantly as if the blond was made from glass, and she could possibly be carried away in a leap.

"She is here, Anna, there you have her." And a broad smile released all the tension from his good-natured features. "Haha, just think, she had dozed off, had bathed, and had then fallen asleep. That is sweet, eh?"

No answer. His sister just stretched out her hand, and, without bending down to the found girl, she burst out curtly and dismissively, "Where are your stockings and shoes?"

Heinrich was startled. And when he saw that the little one also hesitated, he sprang back without speaking once more over the stream to emerge straight afterwards with the missing pieces in the glow of the sun again.

"Help her, Anna," he asked, turning away. "Truly, she must have forgotten everything around herself."

Only, again the girl addressed did not stir. The eyes of both girls just found each other for a moment. And what the little one could recognise in this single, dark glance from the daughter of the house at Werrahn must have been so frightening that she assembled her clothing in wild haste, and now sprang up to cling to the arm of the country girl. Only, the tall girl stepped back as if unwittingly.

"Let it be," she said clenched. "Mother has already been expecting you for a long time."

"Yes, to mother, to mother," Heinrich also cried, not having the slightest idea of the silent struggle of the two.

And in his effervescent joy, he grasped the little one's hand, and pulled her away stormily with himself. Her skirts fluttered, and meanwhile her half scared, half relieved laugh rang out again and again, "Quick, Heinrich — to mother Lotte — home — to Werrahn."

But when they had already reached the yard, and behind the window of the blue room, the waiting, grey head of the lady of the house had appeared, what happened then?

Nothing further. Only what Hertha had feared in her innermost, tormenting foreboding happened. On the threshold to the red hallway, Heinrich's sister, who had walked wordless behind the two until then, bent down close to the little one's ear, and whispered to her, "This afternoon in the garden. I have to talk with you. Do you hear? Don't forget. I have to talk with you."

***

The sun threw slanted rays over the yard at Werrahn, bright shadow carpets already lay over the white dry cobblestones when Hertha stole quite gently away from mother Lotte's side. As now happened more often to the old lady since her illness, she had nodded off in the midst of speaking, sitting on the green rep sofa. The little one slowly loosened her fingers from the blue-veined hand of the old woman whom she was still stroking familiarly, and slipped out on tiptoes. The low, white door creaked a little as it was closed by the little one carefully and with held breath. Then — a short hesitation in the dark, red hallway. Once more, the rebellious reluctance stirred in the blond. Was it not actually cowardly, was it not cringing, did it not resemble the silent and degrading obedience of a servant that the word of such a simple country girl sat so firmly, so steadfastly in her heart? If she now tried to defy it? If she did not stride to where she was ordered? For she felt with distinct aversion that the so imperatively uttered wish of the daughter of the house amounted to a command, "I have to talk with you!"

Could the suspicious girl perhaps have spied something that morning? But no — she threw that far behind herself. And again she grasped at her temples behind which the blood faltered and hammered. She had been abandoned by all the world, a helpless, exposed creature. And what had happened then finally about her and with her? A loose, lightheaded escapade over whose boldness she would perhaps have been amused formerly. And now? Why did it lie like lead in her feet? Why could she not banish the painful, shaking vision as if fate itself had placed its hand against her neck and pushed it now before her?

Yes, it consisted of that, of that alone.

She was unable to give an account, to contemplate, to find a way, neither to the right nor the left. Her blazing, sharp understanding had drained away from her as if by a miracle, and she felt nothing but this pounding and jostling, this horrid grasping by a hand which jostled her even now without contradiction and went step by step with herself. She resisted, leant mulishly back — it was no use. The fist in her neck struck her forwards, the back door of the house opened, the sedate light of the late afternoon streamed towards her, and she saw herself striding reluctantly and compelled along the narrow path of the country garden. Widely laid vegetable plots stretched out to both sides. Gooseberry hedges and currant bushes, from which the fruit already glistened green and unripe, bordered her path; green beclouded cherry trees greeted her in a disorderly and wild way from the midst of the beds; and colourful walls of blue and white lilacs fenced off the entire, strung-out arrangement from the surrounding fields in which the evening song of the crickets was already wavering.

And see, the little one did not perhaps appear too early, but she was already awaited. Before an arbour, which was planted for various seasons so that now wild grape vines, a large leaved bean stalk, as well as reddish blue elder intertwined in each other, before the dark dim entrance of this peaceful place, the tall figure of the daughter of the house already towered, looking away. She sometimes plucked quickly and vigorously about the vine leaves, other times she bent down to pluck a few velvety blue irises which grew in a bed at her feet, and twined them heedlessly into a bouquet. But even as the little one's step was already crunching over the garden's gravel, Anna did not turn around to the approaching girl, as if she could not bear her sight, or as if she intended to wait until the last moment to stand eye to eye with the nearing girl. Now the little one had reached Heinrich's sister.

"Here I am, Anna."

The girl addressed straightened up ponderously. Her taut, ample limbs seemed to need time to stretch themselves fully to their dominating height. Then she answered bashfully, as she still plucked about uncertainly at the leaves of the arbour, "It's okay. I wanted — I wanted —".

And since no sound was able to form in her parched throat, she turned back and forth helplessly and awkwardly to suddenly press the little bunch of flowers into the hand of her blond guest entirely contradictorily.

"There, take it Hertha."

"Yes, quite okay, quite okay," the little one murmured, being completely flustered by this unexpected gift.

And when she wanted to thank her, she began stroking lightly and consolingly the beautiful, full arm of the other girl. Then the country girl started, threw her head back proudly, and shook as if a caterpillar had touched her blossoming skin.

"Leave that," she demanded, "I don't need it."

And then she forced the surprised little one, who still carried the blue flowers in her hand, imperiously and with a strong movement into the arbour. It all happened so overwhelmingly, and at the same time a little crudely and rustically, that Hertha slid onto the narrow bench of the arbour timidly and with bated breath to look up with anxiously clasped hands at the girl towering so powerfully over her.

"Have you something against me?" she stuttered in fear.

And again her heart almost surged into her throat and took away her breath. Only the girl standing before her cut everything off with a sharp gesture of her hand.

"Don't," she said with a hard and rough voice which did not usually appertain to her at all, "the key thing remains that you were with him today, or were you not?"

"With him? Whom do you mean?"

"Don't lie — don't lie! If you are looking for excuses, then I need not ask any further because then I know everything anyway. What did he want from you? Why did you meet in such a hidden place? And why were you lying like a corpse on the green lawn when he had barely ridden away? And why did I know nothing about this rendezvous? And for what reason did you hide it from me now? Have you something to hide? — Hertha, tell me. See, it is not curiosity, I must learn that, so infinitely much depends upon it. Such a dreadful thing as you cannot fathom at all."

And then something happened which this arbour had certainly never seen before. With a whimper as though arising from a freshly broken heart, the tall strong girl sank, as if hit by a cudgel, to her knees, and hid her head in the little one's lap with a shaking convulsion. The strong, work-accustomed hands groped at the seated girl's body at the same time as if she were searching for a hold which she would never be able to find on this earth. And again it swelled up choking from the sorrow-raked depths, "Hertha, I cannot tell you — you must understand me thus too. I must — I must learn from you this moment whether I — dear God in heaven — my mother — whether I — —".

"Dearest, kind Anna, what then, what do you want?"

When the broken-down girl had caught the childish voice of the girl seated before her, she looked up haggardly, shook her head slowly and in astonishment, and laboriously pulled her proud figure up. Then she stepped to the entrance of the arbour, looked out at the blurring pale evening glow which already hung heavy and seeping on the flowers and fruit trees. After that she brushed her hair from her forehead, and as she ordered her dress mechanically with her hand, she said quite calmly to herself as if it applied to the most common of things, "From your answer, I will see whether I may continue to live."

"How, what?"

It was starting to horrify the little one. Her own poisoned memories, fear of herself, cutting terror of the future and the paralysing horror, as if the pale face of the girl standing before her, which dawned yet greener and more decayed through the shadows of the leaves, already belonged to a dead woman, it all rippled through her with a mad, overwhelming fear. She sprang up jerkily, pressed herself against Heinrich's sister and attempted to grasp her limp hand. A devouring, gnawing consciousness of guilt lead her at the same time, she wanted to console, to comfort, to provide the most certain promises for the future. And yet, how strange! When she stroked the skin of the other girl, a nasty aversion overcame the agitated girl. For a second, it shot repellently and disturbingly through her churned up mind that next to her stood a woman who must have obtained something precious, who had seen the perihelion, had climbed a peak from which it was perhaps worthwhile to plunge into the abyss to then rest somewhere as smashed up as she had lain that morning in the green meadow.

Then the voice of the country girl rang out anew. And this time it sounded sharp, imperious, and determined from her bloodless lips, as if she had a right to extort any answer from the beggarly guest, from the tenant who solicited her daily bread, "Now tell me! I will not tolerate this proud silence any longer. You are no better than I am either, don't imagine it; and if you do not confess willingly — you, I can force you! Do not wait for that! What have you to tell me?"

The poor girl should not have demanded so rustically and overbearingly. Before this unaccustomed tone which affronted her, stabbed her, the spirit of deception all of a sudden rose up in the little one, the supple one, that spirit which had kept hidden for so long under mother Lotte's warning hand. She crept seemingly sycophantically under the arm of the other girl, and as she embraced the proud body of the raging one with both hands, she began drawing up with delight a glittering canvas, treacherously mixed from falsehood and fact. Why this county girl needed to force herself into affairs which had elapsed quite harmlessly, but which had bequeathed only fine vibrations to an artistically formed soul, from whose secret needs this "poor in spirit" girl could not possess any idea at all. Thus deceiving only prettily, white-washing, and harmlessly colouring so that this state of peace was secured at all events in the bustle and hazards of life. She chattered, she prattled, she dabbed with her delicate finger on the arm and breast of the listening girl to explain everything more clearly to her until she finally succeeded in getting Anna to exhale deeply.

"So, he only met you by accident?"

"How else? You heard, he did not dismount once from his horse, but chatted with me about something insignificant over the willow bushes."

"On the other side of the stream?"

"Quite right, he remained on the other side."

"And Hertha, you can swear that to me? Can you — forgive me for pressing you so — affirm that to me on the memory of your late mother?"

A light drawing of breath, the little one placed her hand on her heart. But then she responded humbly and determinedly, as she nodded her head defiantly like a little child, "Yes, that I can."

Then a deep, limb loosening groan broke from the tormented girl's breast. Without any concern, she spread her arms, drew the blond to herself and more carried than led the surprised girl back into the arbour. And here, sitting on the bench, she placed her load in her lap, drew her to her stormy breast, and caressed the little one like a mother caresses her child. Confused words forming a confession followed again, which filled the little one with abhorrence and envy. But gradually the steadfast, work accustomed Anna became calmer. Her mind was lead back to the present, and the blond who still rested sycophantically in her arms already heard clear, sober, and reasoned sentences.

"And tomorrow then, I will go to the old Count at Wildhagen."

Then Hertha thought she had not heard correctly. She pulled at the other's clothes in shock, as if she wished to deter the girl from her decision. "For God's sake, you really want to dare that?"

"Why not? Why don't you think that I should under-take it?" the other asked distrustfully.

And again it became high time to soothe the hard-ship of these large, rigid eyes.

"But yes, but yes," the little one relented, "it is surely right. I'm just frightened."

But the practical daughter of the house was not let-ting anything divert her anymore. Clarity, everything screamed in her. She must obtain clarity. And hence she pressed the huddled girl closer to herself, rocked her in her strong arms, and then whispered quite insistently into her ears, "Hertha, and how is it with you and Hein-rich? I am not deceiving myself there, am I? You cannot have acted out such things? It is the last thing I desire of you. Tell me, you sweet, blond dear, just one more thing, just this one. You will stay here with us, we all love you so, you will become Heinrich's wife, won't you? That is your intention, your wish, you are agreed? Speak though!"

Did Anna not notice that a tremor passed over the supple body which she rocked in her arms, and how the little one's limbs suddenly became heavy and motionless? No, she guessed at nothing. She only perceived how gleaming drops shot into the light blue, shimmering child-like eyes. And the harmless girl did not understand that these were tears of fear and rage.

And yet! What a bashful, anxious silence which did not want to end. Like a strange, unfamiliar power, that tormenting hesitation streamed from the little one and made her slight body appear very heavy. The honest country girl could not bear that. Why did her friend, before whom she had thrown herself down, whom she had begged to like a religious icon, and whose head and breast she constantly covered with passionate kisses, why did the strange, defiant creature press her pretty, red lips together none the less, as if she wanted to restrain and close off the smallest word, the most inaudible sound from the eagerly listening girl? Why? No, that she could not bear any longer. She still held the crying girl in her strong arms. Now she suddenly lifted her fist as if she wanted to reach back to strike. The black shadow of her hand rested in the middle of Hertha's countenance.

"Have you deceived and hoodwinked us all?", she suddenly cried out with a raw and wild voice. "Hey, then something has happened. I don't know at all whether I am really fond of you, or would not better slap you in the face. Take care, something has happened!"

Her fist sways up higher, the shadow becomes smaller. Then Hertha opens her damp eyes, she looks at the hand ready to strike above her, and all of a sudden, everything around her and in her transforms. Fear, it is an invading, breaking-down fear which makes her cry out softly; the horror of being pushed about, the deep desire for the still, cradling peace which she has enjoyed for so long in this corner oblivious to the world.

"Take care," something gurgles once more in extreme, choking menace.

And then it breaks and pours out unresistingly and overflowing from the little one. She straightens up, she strokes the cheeks of Heinrich's sister with her soft hands, she slings her arms about her neck, she kisses her on her dry lips. And in rushing haste, she strews mild words about herself and her oppressor for comfort and appeasement.

"No, no, what are you thinking, I have not deceived you, I want to stay with you, I like staying with you. And if your brother finds pleasure in me, then he shall have nothing to rue. Quite certainly not. And now don't hit me, Anna, don't threaten me, and be fond of me again. Will you?"

The half-disc of the moon climbs up the blue wall of the heavens fluffily like a little cloud. The evening wind rustles over the branches and carries the sweet scent of the nearby meadows with it. Do you hear, both of you, how it shoots up from the evening mists of the fields in sharp flight? Do you understand the long drawn out wavering and twittering? That is the lark who flies against the field swallow in the competition of the twilight hours. On its black wings, it carries up the last red shimmer. All around in the beds, roses and carnations are closing and offering once more a cloud of scent so that it undulates heavily and sweetly across the ground. That is the peace of Werrahn. And you have invoked it.

***

The Girl Who Lost Her Way

The peace of Werrahn takes effect preciously, and anyone who lets himself be robbed of it is a fool.

The simple supper of the country residents has already been enjoyed, and since mother Lotte has already sought out her bed, and Anna sits in her room to write with hasty fever before a flickering candle a letter which she has already frequently torn up and begun anew again and again — she will surely scarcely end it — Hertha, who yearns for calm, stands at the back fence of the garden where thickly clustered pink hawthorn bushes bend down heavy and weighty towards the adjacent meadow. She has stroked back the sleeves of her white dress a little so that the fresh cool air can skim over them better, leans with them on the edge of the fence, and now she squints with head propped in her hands through the branches of the red scrub, which has darkened in the twilight of evening, out to the nearby sleeping meadow. The thousand-voiced chirping of the grasshoppers is swelling ever more insistently and monotonously. But meanwhile, slow, heavy axe blows become audible. Close by the little one in fact, Heinrich Kalsow pauses and bangs into place with the axe a wheel hoop which has loosened during a trip on the bad cobbles of the country road. The iron rings droning and dull. And his work could certainly have finished long ago if the farmer did not often keep watch for the little one, whom the moonlight has thrown a silver cloak over, and did not anyhow think himself unobserved as well.

"That there can be such a glorious thing in the world," the rapt brooder thinks as he lets the axe fall for a moment. "Look, the golden crown on her head. And all about her slender limbs it's so white — God forgive me the sin — as if she were naked. But you can't think that at all. And how graciously she keeps company here.

Oh, if she just wanted what I want. If that were possible. If that could be given to me."

Again he makes a sharp blow against the iron, red sparks spray up, and from the yard, the rolling barking of the great dane who, already untied, occupies its guard duties.

"Woof — grr — woof."

But through the barking, the little one is flushed up from her thoughts. She turns back and encompasses with her eyes, from which the reflection of the moonlight now flashes silvery, the domestic work of her companion curiously and thoughtfully at the same time.

"How well he keeps everything in a good state," it went through her mind which was weary from thinking. "He governs like a faithful servant for the people who have entrusted themselves to him, without coveting the least for himself. And how dependable and straight his word is. Really, he stands there as if he had the peace of Werrahn held firmly in his giant fists. And yet — and yet — whether you can really be so content, whether you can forget everything which you formerly — —?"

In her pondering, the little one was reaching for a branch which swayed full and bushy over her head. But obviously, she is much too small. Indeed she stretches on her toes, only, her outstretched fingers are just unable to reach the first blossoms.

Praise God, that would be an opportunity. With a leap, with a single leap so that he would almost have run over her, Heinrich stands at her side. A powerful grasp, the tree rustles, shakes, strews its blossom down over her, and then the farmer stretches with an awkward, bashful movement a branch towards her, which is not much smaller than the girl herself.

"Here, Hertha, if you want to have it."

"Of course. Hand it here, thank you."

She takes the branch in her hand, tears off a few twigs, and as she takes a single red flower in her mouth, she nestles others in her blond hair and also sticks a pair of blossoms before her breast.

"Look, is it not pretty?"

Then it again happens about the tall, hulking fellow. The bright moonlit night, the chirping of the grasshoppers, and above all this weaving, enchanting magic which emanates from the little one, it all numbs the unspoilt man. He feels that he must say something now, yes, that perhaps the question of his fate is moving closer. And yet he is only able to stare incessantly in persistent admiration at the dark blossom which glides back and forth gently between the girl's lips.

"That small mouth," he thinks, completely moved. But then he decides on something difficult. He is still holding the axe in his hands, and as the moonlight awakes a bluish glow on the blade, he stares down at the wooden handle of his tool and suddenly asks something which seems so significant to him that he undertakes to only murmur it.

"Tell me please, Hertha, you have been dwelling here now for a long time already."

"Yes," she responds, taken aback.

"Have you never been scared at our place? It is so lonely here."

"Oh no," she snaps her fingers nonchalantly, and looks out into the meadows where the grass gleams and sparkles with the dewdrops and moonlight. "It is beautiful at your place," she continued half unthinking.

How well the words act on him. He imagines it is quite similar, it must surely be quite similar, to as if the little hand were gliding caressingly over someone cheeks there. And the strong man feels so rapt over this picture, the thought surrounds him so flatteringly, that he almost continues acting as if in a dream. He turns the axe back and forth awkwardly, and asks with lowered voice, "Would you like to stay with us for a long time yet, Hertha? Would you endure that?"

"Yes, why not? If I do not fall as a burden on you?"

"Oh, of that — of that there can be no thought," he would like to stammer, "you are not a burden to us, you — you —".

Only, his chest stretches again so mightily, something so sticky and heavy climbs into his throat that he only brings out a wheezing breath.

And then something emerges, a horror of the night like only the black spirits of the depths which the sexton Vierarm scented everywhere can have thought up.

Why did the great dane, who had been guarding the house at Werrahn as of recently, rush in a few breathless leaps through the yard gate into the garden? The slender, powerful animal does not bark, there is no sign of fury to be seen, and yet it has its sharp jaws bared so that its teeth flash in the blurred soft light.

"Heinrich!", Hertha cried flinching, for the dog, who may be balking at the large branch which she carries in her hand, is hunching its back strangely.

And then — a cry of fright! And everything which now follows races past as though in flight. With a hellish growl, the excited beast sets for a spring. It shoots up, the little one tumbles.

"Heinrich, Heinrich — take pity!"

How? For the great mercy of God, the little creature who had just spoken with him like a bride, is being mauled? The lovely figure will lie on the ground, torn apart, unrecognisable, a formless mass? And a beast shall drink the dear juice of life? Then that shoots up which brewed deepest in this dull, unwitting nature. They have often later feared it at Werrahn. But at the time, it was climbing into the world for the first time.

What a strange struggle. Man and beast against each other. A bellowing, a biting, brightly reflecting the silvery gleam of the moon which is rising up in the twitching axe, a soft, dull smacking, streams of blood which hiss sparking and spraying in circles like red fire. And then a long, relieved cry.

No, the blond does not know herself anymore. As he stands there thus, the dull man, the bloody axe in his right hand, his eyes wide open in shock, and at his feet the slain attacker, still twitching and fuming, something then overcomes her, before which there is no escaping, against which she is unable to defend herself, which carries her away like a red wave.

She seeks help, she seeks protection. Is it horror which tears her forward, admiration, or strayed terror?

With an indescribable sound, the slender figure, shaking in all her limbs, throws herself at the man's chest.

He does not want to believe it. Mad, drunk, uncomprehending, he fumbles over the soft, round shoulders. But then — a blinding awakening. The gentle flickering of the night stars radiates in his face in supernatural flames. And with a powerful bellowing like can only pour forth from the chest of a giant longing for blessedness, he stretched his arms, threw them together clasping around the little one, and through the night booms the one jubilant word, repeating ever anew, "Mine — mine!"

They are the betrothed of Werrahn; but at their feet, the spirits of the depths are licking the forgotten blood.

BOOK THREE

1

Do you know what the words "yes" and "no" mean? Assuredly, you do not know. They are such short, harmless syllables, but their actual value, their sanctifying or crushing character, you do not know.

Sexton Vierarm worked them out once. He also in fact composes sermons, secretly of course, when his pastor is not looking. At nighttime, as soon as he sits before the kerosene lamp at the round mahogany table over which the bell rope hangs down so cosily, then he puts his religious views down onto great yellow sheets. And openly confessed, they create a much more profound, picturesque, and mysterious impression than those of his superior. And it remains an eternal pity that he hides them in his bread cupboard.

Over "yes" and "no", however, he has expressed himself on the yellow paper as follows in his Isaiah-style:

Look, between both these words there lies in fact everything in the world. They are the whole. The "yes", however, my dear devout people, my good community in Christ, is a white dove. It feeds on the pea seeds from your hand if you hold them out to it. It sits, should you sleep, up on your bedstead, fans cool air over you with its wings, and skims over your soul. Assuming that the latter is not already with the devil. So mild is this dove. The "no", meanwhile, is a black rat with red eyes. Thus of the quite rare sort. This beast springs, when you go walking in unease or contemplation, at your trouser leg, runs up it, and gnaws at your heart. It hurts simply hellishly. And should the beast see the white dove sitting over your head at night, then it hops on its neck, and sucks out its blood. Dear community in Christ, you will have noticed long ago that all rats descend from Satan. It is his favourite beast, he breeds them the way we humans keep rabbits. And hence the "yes" stems from dear God, but the "no" from the devil incarnate.

Sexton Vierarm knew what he was on about it. "Yes" and "no" are the two ropes on which the earth hangs.

***

"Why can't Hertha sleep?" Heinrich's sister often asks herself in her room during the restless spring nights which now follow. "She throws herself about, whispers, she sobs frequently, she gets up, and toddles about in bare feet. She is surely feeling uneasy the way brides feel?"

Oh, the foolishness!

Anna does not guess at how the little one spends these hot nights next door in the humid room.

The blond lies now almost always exposed, uncovered on her pillows, for she is consumed by a mad, ungovernable yearning to caress her own, beautiful, smooth body with soft, delicate hand as if she were feeling sympathy with her slender limbs which shall now soon be given away for the pleasure and enjoyment of another.

"Is that possible? Will that ever happen?", the errant girl then stammers about the other one into the bright flicker of the moon which dances green and trembling through the narrow room. Shadows sway up and down in it. That is the shade of the lime tree's leaves, whose branches rustle dully before her window.

"Oh," the white dove whispers over her head. "He is so good."

"Oh, so good," the restless girl whispers.

"So honourable."

"Ridiculous, what use is being honourable? But me? Look at me; I languish so! Look at my body. Is it not smooth as a satin ribbon? And my limbs, do they not curve as if they wanted to embrace someone, to enmesh insolubly with the coming man?"

Then the big, black rat is also running over her, and gnawing at her heart.

"Beautiful, little, blond, glorious one."

"Oh really, you are good to me, do you really think that I am prettier than the others?"

"You're the most beautiful in the entire land. Your limbs gleam like drops of water in the sun. Just like the dew shimmered that time when the Count lay next to you. Do you still think of him?"

"Oh, I surely think — leave me, I don't want to think of it." —

"Does a bride dream like that?" the dove admonishes meanwhile, and beats her wings. "Consider that well. — And your Heinrich, is he not nice?"

Then Hertha rolled over so that the dove fluttered to the side and the green shadows danced on her bed.

"Nice — nice — what a dumb word, I don't know, you have to laugh about it." And she beats her breast lightly so that it gives off a bright note. But straight afterwards, she wails in pain, and turns her countenance to the wall. It is digging over her heart, it is boring into her like a ravenous animal. And the tantalising, whistling voice as well, which creeps into her ear, though she buries her head deep in the pillows.

"You, you most beautiful of all, he yearns for you, the handsome, white boy in his sparkling uniform. A Count — do you hear? — Countess. You are born for the heights. And he is rich. Think, when you will drive through the capital; coaches, horses, liveried servants, all the shining silver, and the clothes of soft silk, and the box in the theatre when the thousand electric lights are glowing. The King himself will pull out his glasses to observe you. 'By God, a beauty!' And to obtain all this, what do you need?"

"What? — what? — tell me!"

"See, your arm, how full it is, how round. You just bend it, and the most insensitive man will sigh. Do you believe me?"

"Yes, yes — — but — oh, I don't know."

A leap, the struggling girl has left her bed, and just as she is, naked, exposed, feverishly hot and freezing, she runs to the window and presses her forehead against the cold panes.

But down there?

She sees the yard paved with pale silvery stones, and there, right under her, there stands Heinrich and stares up at her. She has often surprised him at it as he has kept watch over her until the crack of dawn. Now he places his hand over his eyes, for the giant figure is swaying.

Why? — Why? Can he have seen her? And he is not angry with her?

And shaken by sorrow and misery, she sinks to her knees before her bed, and grabs and pulls at the coarse farmer's linen until the material crackles and begins to tear.

***

But she is not always so full of bristling and defiance. When the yellow morning sun plays in the white curtains, then the blaze of thought dies out, the everyday treads with certain feet and itself takes the astonished girl by the hand and leads her out to her fiancé.

There he sits on one of the charred beams of the mill which he intends to reconstruct, holds his short-cropped, blond head lowered deep over his chest, and his hulking forefinger occasionally strokes back and forth on the wood as if the ponderous fellow intends to devise a ground plan. At his feet, the wild, endless heath spreads out. Red, yellow, brown, and blue, it billows in confusion when the spring breeze passes over the damp flowers. And it also wavers in the air in all the colours, for butterflies tumble closely pressed over the damp leaves, and the humming and buzzing of swarming bees billows from everywhere.

Does that disturb the giant?

He cannot calculate any further, his large finger crooks, then his entire hand rises to shade the man's eyes, and finally the enormous figure shakes itself because a shudder thrusts through the powerful man in the midst of the gentle air.

"My God," he murmurs. "Last night — an end — soon an end."

Then a little hand places itself on his shoulder, he turns ponderously, and recognises — her, she for whom his senses scream. Then he emits a mad cheer, so wild, so roaring that the little one would have flown in horror if he had not already seized her with his fists and embraced her.

Oh, these violent gallantries, they constantly cause her a mortifying pain, they break some fine sounding string in her every time, until she becomes an empty, soundless instrument. And yet — and yet, something compels her to devote herself dully and patiently to these enormous, plunging tendernesses.

"Good morning, my sweetie," he exulted.

"Good morning, Heinrich."

"Do you not want to give me your dear, little hand too?"

"Yes, here."

And when she sensed his rough, demanding kiss on her fingers, she closed her eyes so that she did not see the blossoming heath anymore, leant on the knee of the seated man, and waited for what else he would decide about her. But then it also happened. He raised her chin up, and now he kisses her on the lips, drunken, delighted, senseless, and at the same time in the feeling of honestly acquired possession, like the farmer who has finally cut a well from an arid earthen shaft and now scoops the clear water, more and ever more, at the same time murmuring in lusty joy, "Wait, now I have you."

"Oh, leave off, Heinrich."

"No, that I may now do — and you have really come to me, my dear child; did you not follow me on foot?"

"Me?"

She looks at him in astonishment, but then she nods in confirmation. Why should she not offer him joy? "Certainly," she replied, "I wanted to meet you."

Yes, it is easy to fill the giant with bliss. This little concession makes his ingenuous countenance, which until now was always overshadowed by a soft touch of worry, light up, his coarse mouth opens into a ringing, liberating laugh. The next moment, the little one feels herself embraced anew by his massive arms so that now only her head with its luminous, blond hair remains free. But this time, she seeks to wrench herself away, but what is the strength of a little sparrow against such a clasp?

"Don't struggle, my dear," Heinrich stammers —
"now it is at the point finally; yesterday, in fact, I spoke
with my mother. She also thinks that there is no point
anymore in waiting a long time. So the wedding will be
in six weeks, and in eight days our engagement shall be
celebrated publicly. Well, isn't that beautiful?"

"In eight days?", the little one repeated choking.

"Yes, and it shall be merry here with us. That you can
believe. All our good friends and neighbours are invited.
The pastor and sexton Vierarm, and the doctor Abraham, and your relatives, Professor Rogge and his wife,
who must not miss it under any circumstances. A cousin
of my mother is also coming, Uncle Ludwig Wippermann. The rich uncle of our family. Yes, and you know,
little one, whom I want to ask to give us the honour?"

"No, whom?", Hertha asked in reply, as she attempted to move a little in his clasping arms.

The giant began stroking her cheek with his massive
right hand, and spoke further full of joy.

"Think, I met in fact yesterday by our boundary the
young Count Fritz Hohensee. You will not believe at all
how friendly he behaved towards me. And then —".

"You did not tell him perhaps about our engagement?", the blond suddenly cried out quite loudly, and
propped both arms against the chest of the seated man
as if she must absolutely free herself to be able to finally
scoop a single deep breath. "You didn't —?"

"But," the farmer interrupted gently. "Why not? That
I did."

"And he? — What did the Count say about it?"

"God, what should he say? He rejoiced."

"Rejoiced?"

"Little one, why are you looking at me all of a sudden
so wide-eyed? I have not done anything wrong, have I?
See, it will now soon appear in the paper, and then
everyone, everyone in the entire district will know what

a great, enormous fortune has fallen into my lap. And I can tell you, the Count realises it too."

"Why? Say it then — what did he do?", the little one burst out, and see there, with a smooth twist, she had abruptly escaped so that the seated giant must now gaze quite astounded at the girl who has slipped away. His large blue eyes rounded in admiration.

"How adroit you are," he determines finally with an approving smile. "Like an eel."

Then Hertha stamped her foot, "Alright," she urged impatiently, "but what did the Count think? — Why don't you ever finish anything?"

"Yes," Heinrich continued his recollection somewhat more reflectively, for he had to think about what circumstance could make the little one so excited that she even stamped her foot. He rocked his head. Yes, yes, if mother Lotte had observed it. It did not behove an engaged girl at all actually. But, oh God — he folded his hands, again overwhelmed — how wondrously cute it had looked despite all that. "Yes, Hertha," he continued sedately, "when I told Fritz Hohensee in advance about my happiness, he stood there at first quite rigidly."

Then the little one performed a quick movement. "And then?", she threw tartly at him.

The farmer stroked his short-cropped hair, and nodded his head a few times as if all the words from the conversation with the Count were gradually streaming back. "Yes, and when I told him then that our engagement was set for eight days, then, Hertha, then he looked for a long time down to the green oat field, and then he finally uttered something which I did not really understand at all at the time, and today actually even less."

"And what was that?", the little one inquired, quickly approaching, and at the same time, she stroked the knee of the seated man with her hand as if the ponderous fellow could thereby be brought more easily to talk, "quick, what did he say?"

"Yes, he seized my hand, and suggested quite seriously, 'My dear Mr Heinrich, in eight days, your engaged girl, your beautiful engaged girl, will then know thus through which door she has to go'. — I wanted to inquire of him again 'Through which door?', when he explained his sombre words already himself, however, 'See, dear Heinrich,' he tossed out, 'we men go our entire life long from one door into the other. At the moment, I am myself on the point of opening a new one, for I am moving very soon to the war academy in Berlin. But beforehand, dear friend, even exactly in eight days, I am taking a long desired holiday which I intend to spend in Tyrol and in Switzerland.' And as the young gentleman squeezed my hand quite powerfully, he also added, 'The likes of us also have something which must be knocked out of their head.'"

"He said that?", the blond pressed with short breath meanwhile, ceding herself now without clear consideration to the embracing arms of the giant. "Aren't you mistaken?"

The giant shook his head, and tenderly caressed her arms. Gently and tenderly, he obviously feared breaking the little rococo figurine in the white, wafting dress. "Yes," he confirmed decidedly, "it was exactly like that. Word for word. But do you know too, little one," he added sedately, and his hand pressed more heavily, "that I entertain a suspicion?"

"A suspicion? — You?"

Then it emerged, something indefinite flashed over the blond hair. With a timid, suppressed cry, she rose on tiptoe, slung both arms around the neck of her fiancé, and as she bent the surprised, swaying man down to her, she whispered with her red, trembling lips which came closer and closer to the hulking fellow, like two whirring red beetles, "What do you mean, dear, good man? — What sort of a suspicion? — Get away, it is nothing."

"But, but," he wanted to apologise, but the enchantment took his senses from him; both the red beetles he had caught were already sucking at his soul. "You beautiful sweetie, do you not understand then? I mean only my sister and the Count. Have you not long since also noticed it?"

When Hertha heard this sentence, the tension gave way. Her bright eyes opened wide. Without her really intending, her raised arms fell down, and then — with a jerk, she escaped the dazed man to finally put forth coolly and reflectively, "Yes, so — you need not alarm yourself over that."

"Right? — Right?", Heinrich stuttered, "it is nothing serious? But I consider it good though that he gets out of sight. Better is better. For nothing can come of it on my day."

"Yes, but, what does that concern us?"

"Certainly — certainly — of course, you are right — not us. For us, my white, silver lamb, deliverance comes happily in eight days. Ah — a proper release. If only it weren't so far. I don't even know anymore what is out, nor in. I saw though today — —".

"What, Heinrich, what?"

"I mean — I think — you could not sleep anymore either. You were lacking rest, right? Last night —".

"Heinrich — for God's sake — were you perhaps standing last night — —?"

"Yes, little one, in the yard. And then — don't be angry with me — I did not even know — —".

An impassioned cry screamed out. It is as if it were drawn forth from the heath, for all around it becomes deathly still for a minute. The butterflies linger with outstretched wings, the bees are no longer humming, even the wind falls silent and stops.

"Hertha — what's wrong? — Forgive me dearest child! — Lord, why do you not answer me? Why are you running away from me? Hertha — Hertha!"

Too late.

A white shadow travels over the heath. The trampled flowers crunch under her feet, the bright skirts waft and flutter — she whirls away from there as if on white wings.

The giant springs down from his seat, "Hertha — Hertha — forgive me," he wants to shout.

Then a laugh rises on the heath. The bees are humming again, the butterflies are fluttering, even the westerly wind toddles along, it blows the pollen before itself for future fertilisation and giggles at the same time, "Love? — Look, I blow it before me. — Love? It is without sense or laws. Seek after the higher things. Seek — seek!"

***

From this hour, Hertha did not know what to do anymore. The words of the young Count hummed and sang constantly around her, "In eight days, the door will stand open."

Which door?

What did he mean with the sombre words? For he had undoubtedly sent this prophecy to her, only to her, secretly sent by the other man whom she was engaged to. Was the stranger perhaps suggesting that she could reject the secure repose to deliver herself fleeing to the uncertain, to the waves of chance, to what was possible? Ridiculous that he could think of such a thing. The short-sighted fool in love with life! She was too clever for that. But that he could express such a thing at all? Did he think he possessed a power over her? Oh, there he was deceiving himself, she loathed being bossed, she wanted to govern herself and grasp at the reins in another life.

Ridiculous.

But she was sick of all the deliberation. Her cheeks were blanched, and her feet did not step anymore with the same spring as before.

"She walks like such a little wagtail," mother Lotte had adjudged only recently.

June was already being inscribed now. It was one of those hot summer days which draws like a white sand man through the land. Every speck of dust flashes and flickers so that the eyes of the day labourers in the fields have to close, blinded under glowing red foreheads. And where the figure of its luminous finger stretches out, there the waves of grain die away. The grass folds up, and like a feverish breath, hotly gasped frisson fumes over the searing expanse.

"Come, Anna," the lady of the house at Werrahn said to her daughter on this morning. "Heinrich has harnessed the carriage, we will travel into the town to complete the trousseau."

"And Hertha?", the commanded girl objected distrustfully, "should she remain here alone?"

Mother Lotte sent one of her sharp looks out, then moved her narrow goshawk's head in assessment, and her answer sounded indifferently, "Why not? If she shall later some day do as she wants here? Why not today already? I entertain no distrust towards my children. That they may demand. By the way, she complained of headaches, and then I sent her to the sexton Vierarm. He shall simply place his fingers on her forehead, for he maintains that he possesses a magnetic power. Perhaps it will be of benefit. — Come."

Both women went from the yard.

Meanwhile, the blond was striding in the opposite direction to the humble house of her friend. For really, the exorcist, prophet, and magnetiser had become a passionate admirer of the delicate young lady from the rococo period. Indeed, the religious warrior himself had not foretold this affinity, but he had quite gradually nevertheless obtained a zealous affection for this fine, and as he believed, chosen tool of Satan, and he considered it directly to be a blessing conferred on him by the Lord to drive out the evil and lurking spirits from the little one.

"So, it rages in the head there?", he inquired with boundlessly reflective mien, when the little one now stood opposite him in his cosy studio, and he knitted his black eyebrows majestically deep under the whirl of his iron grey tufts. "Hm, I know well why it is, you are already daunted, and would now like out."

"Yes," the little one responded as she opened her bright, radiant eyes to the man whom nothing escaped so easily. "Dear papa Vierarm, I have migraines."

"Eh, my daughter," the sexton caressed her, having meanwhile placed his hand on the little one's head. "So, migraines, you think? — Eh, that is just one of the false names under which 'He' — you know well whom I mean — creeps through the land. But I am on to him. I know his life habits. I recently read in a book that one calls it occultism. Yes, I am such an occultist, but a sharp one. And you say mother Lotte sent you to me alone for this sake from Werrahn?"

The little one nodded.

"Now, that's sensible. The woman has brains. Has the mind of four men. But now come closer please — we want now to set about 'His' emissaries with the nippers. Hold still."

He placed his gaunt, fleshless hand on her forehead, murmured something, and his rolling prophet's eyes blazed in such a convinced, smoking fervour into her own that the little one went weak. She began trembling, her thoughts waned, and in her darkening condition then, the drilling pains had suddenly vanished. Instinctively, she had to smile.

"Now I have 'Him' here in my hands," sexton Vierarm abruptly spoke with powerfully triumphant voice through her dreams. "I feel 'Him' quite clearly. 'He' is physically tickling in my fingertips. But now he is imprisoned. See, so." With that, he sprang hurriedly to the table, pushed his hands quickly under the cover of the large Bible and cried out, breathing deeply from his chest, "Obey!"

At the same moment, the poodle Sus, which had followed the conjuration up to then from under the table with squinting eyes, raised a painfully disturbed whimpering.

Sexton Vierarm nodded with satisfaction.

"Do you see?", he said, and patted his patient lightly on the cheek. "You can notice the success of that. Sus does not like to endure it when I act so terribly with one of 'His family'. But now 'He' is banished, well?"

Then Hertha clapped her hands ringing in delight over the wondrous old man. For the moment, she could think of nothing else but this strange incident. But then she was again beset by a heavy weariness unfamiliar to her. Seeking help, she looked at the massive sofa in the sexton's room.

The religious fighter, however, lapsed into embarrassment. In the struggle with the prince of hell, he had surely given a good account; meanwhile, to keep a blond maiden with such sinfully blue eyes sleeping in his clean bachelor's home seemed monstrous to him.

He stammered, began to deliberate, scratched indecisively at his wavy tufts, and looked for excuses. Finally he said bashfully, no, that would not be right here. Besides — he breathed out, yes, that was a good idea — besides, he had also been summoned by the pastor, must leave, and lock up his residence. But that does no harm either. The unnatural thing must be driven through nature. "And then look, girl, fourteen days ago, I first cut my hay, it smelt splendid, and before the hay loft over there leans a broad ladder. A prince's castle can have no more beautiful or comfortable a set of stairs. Spring up there, and before I return, the last trace of your pains will also have passed away. Well?"

Then Hertha clapped her hands for the second time. This old Bible basher was yet the only one in the entire district who constantly complied with her addiction to extraordinary events. For that he must be rewarded. She spread her arms wide, rushed amidst a bright cheer at the surprised man, clambered up the rigid man, and the next moment, a hot kiss was burning in the midst of the smooth-shaven face of the old Isaiah. He stood motionless, and snorted like a mulish horse. But when he saw the little blond straight afterwards spring with a few nimble skips across the yard, and scurry shadowy quick up the ladder, he looked around in boundless disconcert at his poodle, which just then was wiping its snout contentedly with its paw.

The sexton smacked his lips, "This has never happened to me before, friend Sus," he established finally. "Such a thing is thus called a kiss? Hm, I must say, all in all a right pleasant feeling, even if it should originate from hell. Come, Sus, the pastor need not learn anything of it, I will assume it on the discretion of my office."

He grasped his stick, and gentleman and poodle went from there.

**

At the same time, old Count Karl Anton was sitting in the half-round sunroom of his wife, the Countess Anne-Marie Luise, and had drawn his right leg high over his other, and was now cleaning away solicitously at his turned up boot as if the dull lack of lustre in the leather did not give him any peace. And whenever he, out of breath, raised his red, sun-burnt countenance, he wondered anew at how the overly slender woman with the fine intellectual features and the gentle brown eyes, which did not seem to belong under the prematurely white and wavy hair at all; as said, he wondered ever anew at how his Anne-Marie Luise could so calmly and confidently embroider a precious cloth there on the window seat of the half-round sunroom, while he was over here seemingly pinched by his inner unease. He drew the other leg up, propped it anew, and at the same time, he let his eyes, seeking help, sweep along the circular walls. Everywhere, green and blue Gobelin's, which Anne-Marie had brought into the marriage with her, hung down, and they showed depictions of stories of passion in glaring colour.

Karl Anton sighed heavily, but suddenly he spat into the middle of the room as if to free himself, and burst out with the words, "Ugh, the devil!"

The Countess twitched a little with her large, lowered eyes, but did not raise her head from the silk embroidery in her lap.

"Did you say something, Anton?"

"No, Anne-Marie, I just spat."

"Hm," a sideways glance now wandered under the lowered eyelashes over to the man of the house, which was meant to express to him a gentle rebuke over his behaviour in this half-holy space. Anne-Marie did not in fact speak much, and yet those around her knew to interpret each of her looks like a detailed speech. Hence the Count also struck his boot impatiently, and became clearer. He had been longing for this discussion for weeks. He must not push it out any longer.

"Tell me, child, what actually are you working on with that black velvet? It looks like a wine decanter."

"It is becoming an altar cloth, Anton."

"So — so." The estate owner passed his hand over his nose, then he brushed it over his close-lying, parted grey hair. "So — so. Well, then let me tell you something, Anne-mouse. We have already done so much for the dear Lord. Now he could — God forgive me the sin — pay us back for once."

Before this quite unaccustomed attack against her holiest ideas, the fine, white-haired woman let her work fall abruptly, and quickly raised her head. Her large brown eyes first rested for a long time on the agitated man who now moved back and forth nervously and scraping on his chair. After this long pause, however, it seemed as if the mistress of the castle had already divined everything.

"Anton," she began, as she raised her hand gently towards him. "What are you concealing from me? Express yourself."

The estate owner spread his legs, bent forward, and looked emphatically at the stone floor. He avoided at this moment meeting the large eyes of the mistress of the castle. But then he shook his fist at the floor, and burst out half in fury, "Poppycock, me, and to hide something from you. You have known already for a long time everything better than I do, Anne-Marie. You possess merely the damned fashion of remaining silent. But I cannot endure it. To me it is again like on the evening before Gravelotte where such a damned scared foreboding also went through the squadron that the heart of even the most dashing youth slipped into his trousers. Anne-mouse, let's both not deceive ourselves for God's sake. It is never ever going to work out well with our little rogue."

As the father had more groaned than spoken this, the pious woman winced again in the sunroom, and she slowly pressed her raised hand against her breast.

"Anton," she wanted to reply calmly, but her voice trembled so that she had to start again several times. "If you have nothing tangible, then do not unfairly accuse our Fritz either. Is he not our kindhearted, dear, only boy?"

The Count seized the arm of his chair, and shook at it. "Yes, kindhearted, but corrupt, Anne-Marie, — corrupted to the bone by these new ideas which stamp our youth directly as a danger to the entire fatherland. The goal is missing for them, Anne-mouse, an idea like we possessed. What do they consider to be the highest thing today? Profligate living, believe me, they are proud of that, and our boy is already stuck to the neck in the muck!"

"Anton!"

"No, no, mouse, be calm, I am not doing your darling any injustice. God knows, I would have my right hand hacked off for the brat, but the way he is going with his life makes us — no, don't look at me like that, child, otherwise I'll lose the courage to speak — I tell you, he is disgracing us. Disgracing our old esteemed name, and drawing us into the profligacy with him. I am ashamed to ride across our boundary."

"Almighty God — what? What did you say then?"

Before the penetrating fear and vehemence of his words, which were so utterly foreign to her usually fearless husband, the mistress of the castle had risen, and now she stepped behind the chair of the estate owner to there let her hand glide down onto his shoulder. Through the simple black frock coat which Karl Anton always put on before taking himself to see his wife, the rough man felt how his wife's fine fingers quivered. An increasing coldness seemed to stream out from them. And yet he passed his hand mechanically, as if by a previously conceived resolve, into his breast pocket, and now he brought forth with his fleshy hand hesitantly and falteringly a crumpled letter.

"Here, Anne-mouse, but stay calm, here you have the mess."

"Is that a woman's hand?"

"Certainly, what else?" He threw another look at the strong characters. "Well yes, it could also have been written by a man," he admitted. "Our country girls write thus nowadays."

The Countess's fingers tautened still more firmly about the shoulder of the seated man, and something empty and absent penetrated into her voice. She surely only continued the conversation at all because she meant to rescue herself from her thoughts through the sound of her words.

"And who is the writer?" she inquired softly.

"Who?" Now the noble estate owner struck the arm of his chair heftily, and as his countenance became covered up over his stiff neck with a coppery redness, he burst out erupting, "Who? Who do you think, Anne-Marie? You can't be deceived. Not you. Yes, it is from the daughter of our neighbour Kalsow. The girl is asking me for an interview. Do you understand what that means?"

The tall figure of the woman imperceptibly sank down somewhat lower.

"Poor Anton," she emitted softly.

"That I return to you. Poor Anne-mouse!"

A pause occurred, the Countess stood motionless.

"And now?", the pious woman asked mutely, and at the same time, she looked out the window past which the golden sunlight was flying. "How will you direct this for the best, Anton? For it must be directed for the best, mustn't it?"

And all of a sudden, she threw her hands before her face, and sobbed quietly. What was that? Before this breakdown of the cool, passionless woman, whom the Count saw for the first time during their long marriage in confessed sorrow, Karl Anton lost all self-control. He sprang thudding onto both feet, shoved his hands under the tails of his fluttering frock coat, and strode like a prisoner who would like to break out, again and again around the walls of the half-round room. And thus as he measured out the space, he carelessly brushed his hand down the green and blue Gobelin, or he also threw an uncertain look from his grey and raggedly browed eyes at his wife. But suddenly, he came to a sharp halt. He stood directly under the taking down of Christ.

"Anna, would you reconcile yourself to it?"

From the other side came only a quiet breathing, but then she spoke abjectly and yet clearly, "Yes, Anton, I would also take on the heaviest burden. For through us, no witting injustice may occur. That would be like a mocking of your and my previous life."

The distinguished lady had spoken so calmly and yet full of genuine pious humility, that her listener re-mained for a moment fully in the spell of this overwhelming, anguish-filled soul which was truly ex-pressing in that moment the sense of its entire existence. Straight afterwards, however, the man struck the Gobelin in full dogged fury.

"Anton, for God's sake!"

"Damn, the rogue has even brought us to this."

"That is not true. It cannot be true."

"But, Anne-mouse, have I lied to you in all my days? You would merely have needed to look out the window just now, then you would have been able to see your pure little fruit already creeping about on other paths in plainclothes. On other paths. You can make a verse out of that. But now come, mother", he continued forcibly relenting, since he noticed that his Anne-Marie was fumbling about as if she were spying out a seat — "now both us old ones want to sit down together, and see whether we can yet perhaps cut a sole that fits for this boot. Anyway, you must contribute to what I should say to the girl when I see her face-to-face, for look, Anne-Marie, I am truly lacking the courage. Yes, yes, that is it, nothing more than the quite usual, simple courage."

***

"This godforsaken girl."

The strong Turkish tobacco does not drive away the pulsating, breath-taking unease either. The slender young man in his well-fitting grey casual suit, the soft felt hat pressed boldly and creased on his forehead, who is lurking in the meadow behind the sexton's property, throws constantly one burnt-out husk after another into the dry grass, and then stamps out the fire impatiently with his foot.

He lurks.

He steals up like a lynx which wants to break into the hen house. See how he leans his supple body forward from time to time spying, to straight afterwards, like a swaying willow branch, snap back again quickly. This devilish woman must have enough of the old sexton sometime. He has seen her wander in, and she will hopefully not take an hour of devotion in there. No, she does not look like that. Hopefully she is not pious. That he can at the moment want least of all. No resistance, no restraints, no, for all the saints, if it shall end well, a willing sacrifice, a discharge of this white seething fervour which already runs boiling and brewing through all the lanes and paths of his brain. Or — that would be terrible — or should the little withered Renkenbach be proved correct? The only one of his comrades with whom he sometimes conversed in the mess because he entertained an interest in the works of military science which the terribly serious, pitiful man writes about the Boer war which he took part in. Should he be proved right? What did the inconspicuous fellow in the shabby, creased tunic say when he recently sat opposite him behind the big Manila cigar in the club chair, in whose hollow the gaunt body of the other almost vanished?

"Hohensee, your womanising signifies no experience. It does not exalt us, it demeans. It is un-German, unclean, and in the end also unmanly. Even just because it brings us down further towards the animals. And believe me, woman in her majority these days signifies unfortunately the most finely organised amongst the animals. What you are doing there — don't take me wrong — it is no triumph of manhood, but rather no more and no less than a selling and squandering of your humanity."

The feeble, crawling voice of the weary looking, worked-up man had brought forth all that without any passion. Each word after a puff from the Manila. But it had struck home. Fritz Hohensee, the handsome, elegant cuirassier who appeared opposite the comrade with the ugly furrowed forehead like the King's riding horse next to the knacker's cart nag, suddenly had burning heat shooting up under his forelocks. He had wavered for a moment. Should he perhaps reveal himself to this quiet, dreamy brooder in the tunic, beg him for advice on how he could free himself from that tormenting situation with Anna Kalsow without hurting the poor, dishonoured girl, but also without taking on the last, the quite impossible duty? For that, that he could not do. No, that the girl too, if she thought rationally, must not possibly desire. Not just because of the difference in class; not just that, that could perhaps be vaulted over, he was indeed a modern man — certainly, what would the elders, Karl Anton and Anne-Marie Luise say to it? For them, the battle in the Teutoburg forest was fought only yesterday. Ugh, the devil, what a miserable affair! But — but, yes, that remained the principal thing — he did not love this simple, actually accursedly boring country girl at all, he was lacking the "passion passing with the power of the storm, which breaks down every obstacle until it purifies itself in the sating of its eternal hunger according to a law of necessity". Ah, nonsense, he knew quite well, they were utterly absurd phrases which he had gleaned together from new writings announcing salvation. Actually right pathetic. But so comfortable, so protective against all reproaches which might be raised perhaps against a swaying man from a pious upbringing. Should he perhaps stand there alone as a fasting man, as a distressed tanner whilst all around him the entire world relieves itself secretly and openly out of joyous habits and customs with violence and boldness from that which just suits it? No, as long as you are young, you must swim with the times. Certainly, the opposite would have directly been a rout, a cowardice. And what remained the principal thing, now, right now, brawled in him, it overflowed before chest-binding, limb-tautening longing. No, this time it was fury, rage, because this beautiful, smooth, elfenly supple creature which belonged in his sphere should be taken by a dumb, lumbering farmer. With this girl, he meant it seriously, oh so terribly holy and dutifully. And her? She laughed at him, the luminous blond head seemed to despise him and push him away. Oh, that must be changed, barely four days remained to him yet, then, then this hated rustic engagement would be celebrated with rejoicers and many barrels of beer and champagne, while the servants danced in the barn. What tastelessness! You must rescue this silky, smooth little creature

from it straightaway. And then, itself only four days remained to him, then he would move to Berlin for the
war academy, and straight afterwards, he would take his
holiday trip. Strange how that all coincided as if some
systematic predestination ruled over it.

But stop — stop! Thunderbolts, now pay attention!

During his strained thinking, he had dispensed with
the target of his observation, now, — what scurried
there, in the narrow gap between the sexton's house and
the stabling, up the ladder to the hayloft? She will not
have? No, you never see such a thing, the varmint truly
flies up the rungs, snap, in, you see the hay scatter, and
now the dormer window slowly creaks. Thunderbolts,
yes, the girl is constantly doing something which can
straightaway twist one's head. How taut and supple her
fine limbs curved when she clambered up there? And
how her white skirts whirled, no, it was quite certain,
here the fortune which he could only find embodied in a
woman was finally waving to him. To seek fortune, you
only ever lived in the world for that.

And then!

He had hardly suppressed a bright cheer when the
sexton finally strutted solemnly with his dog down the
country road. Nobody had noticed the observer.

And he crept quietly and furtively closer.

***

Oh, how cosy and fresh the hay smells. How deeply
you sink in it, as if you were vanishing entirely from this
world into an abyss of meadow smells. The stalks prick
and tickle the skin so pleasantly, and, really, the old sexton proved right, something intoxicating pours from the
dry grass so that every thought hums along colourfully
in confusion like green flies shooting here and there.

The little one stretches, — hear how her cushion
rustles, then she tosses herself about, draws her arm un-

der her head, and, straight afterwards, her cheeks redden like those of a slumbering child.

Quite alone.

That is the last pleasant feeling which befalls her darkening consciousness.

"Quite alone — without Heinrich and all the others — oh good, very good."

The meadowy abyss closes over her, and she glides ever more gently into the green shallows.

"Quite alone."

Strange — her dream is surely only deceiving her — the further she is carried down, the more distinctly she hears how something toddles towards her out of the dark hollow. Step by step, quietly, creeping, clambering. And now — is something not pounding close by her ears? Are waves of air not penetrating suddenly through her green protective walls? All of a sudden, she is completely awake. On all fours, like a frightened animal, she creeps to the dormer window. Her dress has become so displaced and out of order that she slides along on bare knees over the hay.

See there — see there — before the half-open hatch, a creased, skewed felt hat emerges, and under it — as if she could not have guessed — the well-known, tanned and pert, youthful countenance with the commanding, flashing eyes.

Yet a step higher, already the brazen man looms up to his neck before her. But she has ducked so low that she almost lies on her chest, and only her hands encircle in desperation the uppermost ends of the ladder.

Her heart races that someone can look stormily and feverishly at her slender neck. Oh, and yet — horrific, shameful to think it — it is such a pleasant, cosy feeling to be pursued like such a wild animal which shall now soon be struck dead. Oh, dead, dead by these bold hands, if that were possible!

Now the gesture of silence is performed by the man toddling up. He moved his finger to his mouth in warning. The little one, however, squirms like a snake somewhat closer, and her hands shake the ends of the ladder.

"Don't, Miss, you see, I must speak with you for a moment."

"No, no — I will call for the sexton."

"Sexton Vierarm is not at home."

"Then I will throw the ladder down."

"That I don't believe. Hertha, do you really want to break my arms and legs?"

"Yes, that I want — that I must — when no other choice remains for me — take care!"

"Dear, sweet little one, only for a single moment. You don't know how fond I am of you!"

With that, he bent as if he wanted to take the last leap. Then it roared in the ears of the abandoned girl. Certainly, she does not know anymore what she is doing. Something mutters to her that she will do a good deed to the man there whose whispering infatuates her if she now scuttles him. Oh, it must amount to an unheard-of pleasure to now see his blood flow, down there, in a round, still pool. And then — and then — with both hands, she pushed the ladder back with all her might.

What happened then, she no longer apprehended. How should she even? Her eyes are blinded, her feelings blunted. Half mad, bent over, clinging to herself, she notices yet that something heavy tumbles through the air. A dull fall below, a slam, a stifled cry of pain, and then she throws herself with her face in the hay and grasps spasmodically with both hands at the long stalks. In this short minute, she dreams, sees images of an eternity.

Marriage.

The Girl Who Lost Her Way

She is striding with the enticing man whom she just killed, and who now lies soundlessly below on the cobblestones with broken neck, to the altar. The organ roars, just like it thundered that time, but she herself dances to the sounds, arm in arm with the Count, a wild, unfettered dance, and he kisses her at the same time on her avid mouth so that her lips hurt.

Strange that the dead can still dance, and that their arm trembles so warm and alive. How soft and cosily it is slung about her body, and how firmly and confidently she is drawn up.

Then a jerk, a mad rubbing of the eyes, and a slack relenting.

No, she is not amazed anymore that the young, criminal man whom she finds still more supple and distinguished in his grey casual suit, no, it does not amaze her anymore that he crouches next to her on one of the hay bales, and she does not bristle either, when he now slowly and carefully lifts her onto his knee. Now it is all the same, she can close her eyes, lean her head with its blond hair calmly against his shoulder, and be kissed until her breath runs out. Why not? It is all unreal. If this moment has not yet brought death, then it will certainly come straightaway. She is just emptying the last drops of the poison chalice, and then everything will break apart, and the blissful end will be there.

"Hertha, I am so terribly fond of you. Do you know that?"

She nods so that her silky hair flicks about his chin. Why not, now the end is unavoidable, why still lie?

And again she nods.

"And I may hope, may I, that you are also not entirely fed up with me? Well?"

There she opens her blue eyes once more, nestles closer to him, and smiles suggestively.

Oh holy, blessed end, now near — lay a poisonous red flower over my countenance and let me suffocate. Come, dear, friendly sleep, why are you hesitating? You are expected. So hotly, so avidly.

Only, the end does not let itself be beckoned. In the hay loft too, the "yes" and "no" dominate, which sexton Vierarm described in such an Old Testament way. Behind the white limestone wall, something scurries. A rat sweeps with its soft, splatting feet across the smooth floor, and at the same moment, the oppressor whispers something in the awakening girl's ear. It sounds almost like something real, like something from this world which awakens reason and calculation? And then with an abrupt cry, she comes back to life.

"Leave me, don't touch me any further."

"Little, dear, sweet blond, it is not possible that you want to ruin yourself for eternity in four days. That they won't. That you cannot, something stronger than you forbids you from doing that."

Then she brushed her dress down, and moved away from him. The expected end is not coming then?

Strange, at that the empty, sunny day now looks in the dormer window again, and hence the girl peers over to her companion, suspiciously, inquiringly, for she expects now reasons from him, a new law which could perhaps explain or justify her action, the action which he demands, her tearing away from everything. Every word is suddenly weighed by her.

And he?

In his shaking fervour, all those sentences occur to him which he himself chanted off, which made him certain because they rang out everywhere in the world.

"Sweet child, give me your hand."

"No."

"A single finger."

"Not now."

"Good, then listen, you must not sell yourself because you will injure the first, the holiest, the most natural duty to yourself."

"What does that consist of?"

"Of what? Heavens yes, how can you even ask? I am no scholar, but every child knows now that everything else is subordinated to our own personality."

"Everything? Even gratitude?"

"Ridiculous — little one, don't speak like a pastor. Anyone who worries today about gratitude, whistles at it when our own interest, our feelings of comfort are at stake."

"And where do we seek our feelings of comfort?" stutters Hertha, to whom his words, yes, even his feverishly sparkling eyes seem at this minute loathsome, and who feels more and more unresistingly beset by a paralysing dizziness. "Where — shall — we — seek our — feelings of comfort?"

Each syllable tumbles over her lips.

"Well, child, now you are going all out. You are not bad at examining."

With that he sinks down casually from his hay bale so that he now crouches down beneath her, right next to her little feet whose black stockings peer out uncovered from her half-open yellow, ankle boots. Then the excited girl wants to draw back the yellow things, but the young man has already stretched out his hand, and is holding the foot firmly. For a moment, nothing fills the semi-dark, summery sultry loft but a short, groaning breathing which is emitted by both the solitary individuals jointly and rhythmically. But then thick, glittering tears shoot into the little one's eyes; gnawing, tormenting fury makes them pour forth, inner shame over being incapable of defending herself, because she is not, like other honourable girls, protected from such attacks as it were by a high, holy wall.

Oh, and that too!

Blanching, half paralysed, while her lips quiver fever-ishly, she must endure how her feet are kissed; hot, wild, idolatrously worshipping, and she knows only the one thing, if she is not held in this dizzying second by her reason, by something level-headed, then the floor will slip away from her, then she will again submerge with numbed, unresisting senses into the green shal-lows. And then the stigma is there, and the soiled end.

Whether that would be so bad? How might that surely be?

No, no, speaking, asking, distracting, tearing open the heavy lids, and keeping an eye on the day, for God's sake, above all just the bright day which steals bluishly through the ajar window, above all not losing it from her sight.

And then finally, praise God, she is able to tear her foot away so that the man lying before her is thrown up ungently. And her voice shrills raw and alien, for she asks, only in order to bring something up, "Answer me finally. Where shall we seek our feelings of comfort?"

"We?" He looks around confused and seeks to master himself. Actually he would like to laugh that he should act in such a situation instructively. "Ah yes, we modern people, you see, you sweet little creature, we shall not just stupidly and timidly resist our inner storms and urges. For we thereby kill off the most holy and most tremendous thing which is demanded by an independ-ent nature. Hm, yes, you see, you notice, we also cannot at all, we are, amidst the great blowing storm which only sometimes shakes people over-powerfully, incap-able of it without hypocrisy. You feel that this minute, child, like me, don't you? That you must feel, you dear, little, blond, luminous thing? Will you still marry your farmer?"

This time he clasps her feet, and rears up kneeling himself. These passionately infused eyes move ever closer to her, her blood hammers together ever closer and more furiously, it is a last struggle only before the sun plunges from the sky and night will roll over the earth.

And then — whirling about, rushing, wing swishing, a troop of white doves pass in through the window. See there! Sexton Vierarm's powerful image comes to life. Just five to six white, innocent birds who want to peck a few grains from the barn floor, but what a remarkably sharp, fear awakening, flurrying noise.

Both the pale faces stare distracted. But then an abruptly arising guile gains power over the entire being of the little one. Before her oppressor is able to make himself clear, he sees how she leans her blond, tousled head on the wood of the dormer window to peer out straining. Then an impatient signal.

"Quiet — the sexton!"

"What? — Seriously?"

"Go — go — here, I am holding the ladder, it is high time."

She pulls him to the exit.

He dips down unresistingly. And yet, how supple and full of grace all his movements are now too. Bent far forward, the girl remaining behind must follow this slipping down. Now a hesitation.

"What is it?"

"I will fetch you."

"Me?"

"And if it should be on the wedding day itself, I will fetch you, little one, you will see, I will come."

A leap.

A shadow bends around the corner, and at the same moment, six luminous white sails again swirl from the

Ah, but what stillness reigns from now on in the hay loft, how the freshly cut grass smells, and the little one sits all alone, holds her hands crossed, clenched in her lap, and stares at the white envoys floating into the cloud lands. Further and further, tinier and tinier. Suddenly, however, words crumble carelessly from her lips, "I will fetch you."

Then she shakes her head poignantly, lost in dream, "Ridiculous."

2

Thus the time at Werrahn elapsed, and only two days still remained until the engagement of Heinrich Kalsow would be celebrated, in an old fashioned way indeed, but yet sumptuously.

"Only twice more will the fireball sink there behind the yellow waves of the wheat fields," Hertha thought as she leant by the window of her room towards evening, in order to breathe in the cool air which now streamed in from the evening fields. "Twice more. And then? What will become of me then? Will everything be decided then? Everything restfully? Or is there still something else for me? Another path which leads into the heights, into the blue? Foolishness!" She placed her hand about her neck as if she wanted to strangle every word there at its source. Foolishness, it was certainly all only spoken thus, who could take her away from here against her will? And she did not want to at all, she wanted anyway to remain on the firm, certain ground from which peace grew like a grain crop. The wind carried the sweet smell of clover to her full and strong, and right before her, the massive lime tree shook itself gently, strewed blossom, and streamed with the scent of evening. Then the blond clenched her teeth, clasped the window's crosspiece, and what she murmured was barely comprehensible, "Just what am I doing? Who is giving me advice?"

Heinrich stood below in the yard, and his dark tanned face radiated with peacefulness as he now showed his mother, lingering next to him in an old-fashioned, plaid shawl, the just felled tree trunks which, adorned with colourful paper flowers and garlands, would the day after the next serve as an honour gate to receive the engaged couple as well as the guests.

"But why did you choose light blue tissue paper?", mother Lotte asked, pointing astonished at a heap of blue roses and loops, for this uniformity stimulated her misgivings.

"Oh," the giant apologised, as he smiled to himself embarrassedly. "Mother, I saw only how Hertha, how my fiancee", he corrected himself, "sometimes ties such blue loops in her plaits, and then I thought — —".

"Ah, so," the old woman interrupted him, shaking her head, "yes, then it half makes sense, my son, but —".

With that the lady of the house drew all sorts of figures in the sand with her stick, which she now almost always carried for her support, and as if suddenly her entire tenderness, which usually lay so deeply hidden, were pressing visibly for this good, needy man, she tapped her son quite unexpectedly with warmth and sympathy on the shoulder, but she said nothing out loud but the words, "Boy — boy!"

But as mother Lotte turned around, she sent a solitary look up at the window behind which the blond was leaning, and this look was so serious and admonishing, it contained such a strict demand, that the fiancee up there, overflown by the redness of shame, had to instinctively lower her eyes. Just why was she blushing?

Why?

Because at the same moment, the scent of hay was billowing about her, and because it seemed to her as if the instep of her feet were being kissed by a hot, trembling mouth. It was penetrating as far as her forehead.

Oh, who was giving her advice?

In the afternoon, when the lady of the house was having her nap, Heinrich's sister Anna secretly slipped into her room, and began hurriedly dressing. The best and finest she possessed, black silk. With her tall, towering figure and her gleaming, hazel hair, the girl looked proud and distinguished.

"What's happening?", Hertha inquired, having been lured by the noise from the next room.

The hasty girl just threw her a distrustful half glance, then her features again assumed that cold pride which had been burying itself in her countenance for weeks.

"You see, I am going away," she responded, seemingly heedless, as she set a broad-rimmed hat on her head with trembling hands.

Hertha's heart was pounding, "But where?", she breathed quicker, for the poorly concealed hostility towards the ever still and haughty girl also arose in her anew.

Now the decamping girl was already standing in the low doorway, the flowers of her hat almost thrusting against the lintel.

"To where I must," she threw back scornfully over her shoulder, but then it twitched about her mouth like fear, as if she were frightened to have already betrayed too much, and without saying goodbye, she swayed gently and inaudibly down the stairs.

The girl left behind, however, almost threw herself out the window as she peered after her future sister-in-law.

"She is going through the garden and across the field? She is only doing that to deceive me; whether she is really so crazy as to carry her shame amongst the people?"

For a moment, contented vindictiveness took possession of the little one. She bared her teeth, expanded her chest fully, and smiled cosily to herself. Only, as if a bolt of lightning had passed through her being, her narrow, pale face changed quite abruptly. Feverish sympathy, a full, indulgent pity painted itself on her countenance, and without knowing it, she clasped her hands to plunge to her knees at the next moment, where she groaned to herself, as it were in prayer, confused, disjointed syllables of understanding, of hope, and of forgiveness, "Give her happiness," she forced out in unbearable, cutting anguish. "Let her take everything, this nasty, haughty girl, everything. And if I don't like to tolerate her, nevertheless give her happiness so that she can live, and I can, and all of us."

Thus she struggled with the Almighty, but what she did not know consisted of the fact that the pity over her-self sought a way out from her in this hour of realisation, for an idea stood over her that Anna was born to hold up a mirror to her. And she already saw her scurrying image in the glass, and was horrified.

***

273

In the arbour in the garden, coffee should have been drunk. Mother Lotte had already been sitting quite a while on the bench under the broad bean and vine leaves, conversing with her son Heinrich in-depth over the preparations for the festivity which was to be celebrated in two days at Werrahn, when the long absence of her daughter finally occurred to the old lady.

"What is keeping Anna so long?", she inquired in astonishment. "At Werrahn, is it usually not the fashion that the youth press the sofa towards the table."

But hardly had her question faded away, and before Hertha had found time to leave the arbour, the firm step of the girl was already crunching on the gravel path. In her old, firmly close-fitting blue linen dress, the tray with the steaming coffee can in her hands, the daughter of the house stepped in calmly and without any of the signs of agitation for which the little blond eagerly lurked, offered the time of day, inquired how her mother had slept, and then presented them with the brown drink. She herself sat down with her towering figure right next to Hertha, and after she had thrown a dismissive and defiant look at her little sister-in-law, whose tension she surely must have noted, and thereby shrugged her shoulders barely perceptibly, she led her cup to her mouth, and looked out indifferently at the garden beds.

Then Hertha felt chilly, and shivered. And full of fear, a loathsome thought passed through her mind. The other girl next to her, the simple country girl, she was struggling, she was wrestling with the fate which was acting hostile to her, which had already placed a foot on the path so that she had stumbled and been bloodied. But the country girl remained tough. She rose and grasped her fate anew. Whether Anna really had been with Fritz Hohensee's parents? Would the proud girl have in fact humbled herself so much? And what sort of an answer did she bring home? A favourable one? That was impossible though. Would bourgeois attitudes prevail even in the Count's family? Unthinkable, not a chance. That is, she did not begrudge her future sister-in-law a redeeming, mild fate, certainly, that she must not, for that she felt herself obligated, but then — why must the plain, awkward person also directly cross her path? And even if it were just stray thoughts. Naturally only silly tricks of her mood from which any reality was lacking.

Strange, was this strong smell of hay coming from the nearby meadow? No, she could not bear that scent anymore, it numbed her, and caused her so much unease that she had to rock back and forth nervously with hot cheeks.

But then — praise God, then this family coffee was also finally dealt with once more. Heinrich went, after he had heartily kissed his fiancee, into the house with mother Lotte, where they worked on, planned, and performed the eternal preparations for the coming festivity. Hertha, gazing after them, pressed her finger into her wrist, and attempted to smile mockingly like before. Only, she succeeded all too weakly. Horrid, that these people did not notice how indelicate an effect their so loudly and publicly pursued preparations had. If everything would at least be agreed upon in peace, coyly, covertly, somewhere in a secret corner, so that nobody could speak about her and her decision, yes, so that no eye and no ear could espy her stifled sighs and her reluctant gestures. Instead of which an exhibition. She would be shown to all the people whom she suddenly hated, Uncle Ludwig Wippermann, the rich uncle of the Kalsows, sexton Vierarm, and mercilessly the entire farming community of the district. She started with indignation, and at the same time, she noticed all of a sudden that Anna still sat motionless next to her.

Oh, that this woman could remain silent so patiently.

"What's upset you, Hertha?" the country girl asked urgently, as if she had been observing the little one the entire time, and it was as if all the loud and screaming voices which were making a racket in the blond's breast had been overheard distinctly and unanswerably by the clear, sober girl. "What's upset you? Why do you gaze after Heinrich so strangely? Are you perhaps ruing your word? And you don't want to plunge him into misery?"

"How? — What?"

There it was, this clarity before which the rococo figurine was terrified, there was the burning white, sandy, unswerving path which she hated, for she intended only to stroll through covered brush, sometimes to the right, sometimes to the left, in wavy lines on which no goal was to be sighted. Only not this blinding clarity.

In full fury with flashing eyes, she turned entirely to her besetter, "You should not always ask me such a mistrustful thing," she tossed at her, hissing like a teased snake. "I am as honourable as you. I've had enough!"

The other girl nodded cold-bloodedly.

"Good," she replied, "but we are here for clarity."

"So?", the little one mocked. "If that is the case, where were you before?"

The country girl calmly rose, and placed the coffee can on the tray. "I told you," she replied dismissively, "where I had to go."

With that she cleared everything away, and an unpleasant, pressing silence occurred again. But when Anna towered under the arbour entrance, already turning away with her crockery, she fetched a deep breath once more and, half against her will, it slid out of her, "It is right well organised with the old families."

Hertha ears perked up, "What?"

"Well, the awe before the parents, and the old family laws which obligate the individual. That is good."

But, as if she had already revealed too much, she seized her tray more firmly, and strode confidently and erectly, yes, almost triumphantly, down the garden path. How proudly and calmly she walked away, in the certain feeling of possessing some confederate, or having achieved something decisive.

Hertha clenched her teeth, "Where? — Where? — Who will give me advice? Two days yet. Oh, this uncertainty kills everything that is decent and maidenly in me. — Advice — Lord in heaven, advice!"

***

In his bare study one Sunday afternoon, Professor Oskar Rogge was sitting at his desk, which was covered with the unpretentious green leather, and reading with pleasure Simrock's Nibelungenlied. Impetuous and full of contented sympathy, he threw his black-hair right and left against his shoulders, for what excited him so was the place where the grim Hagen strikes out from behind for the death-blow against the unsuspecting, kneeling Siegfried. And then — he seemingly saw the swishing throw — the little birds fall silent trembling in the forest, the giant roars so that the clouds in the sky quiver and hold still, and the court servants are thrown apart to all sides, drained of blood.

Oskar Rogge grasped the coffee cup which his Agnes cautiously put down for him, and slurped excitedly a full swallow of the fragrant drink. "Yes," he said in a raised mood to himself, as his chest expanded and he stroked the page of the book smooth with a decisive movement, "You must confess, a murder, but also a deed which originates from a decisive, never wavering will; amidst a crowd of un-German, floundering doubters, a man finally acts. And the deed leads constantly to an aesthetic pleasure. Over this, my schoolboys could actually write an essay."

After he had clarified this to himself, he grasped cautiously for the piece of cake which, beautifully strewn with sugar, his Agnes had placed next to him on a plate, examined the taste with a connoisseur's tongue, and as he ate and drank, he descended, reinforced with iron, into the traces of the Germanic past.

Opposite him, the yellow afternoon sun was playing on the red cap of the Pomeranian tower. On the ledge projection, however, four of the tiny kobolds crouched translucently, as if made of bright glass, for they could not bear the sunlight, squeaked and squealed to themselves, and struck their wooden clogs against the brickwork.

"Look," the most crippled of them miaowed, "him over there, that is a little man."

"Yes," the second one coughed, his mouth reaching from one ear to the other, and who thus constantly bit into his crooked nose for fun, "that is the proper philistine with the great man's vanity. If we could breed more of the brood, then —".

"Hey," the third hissed, turning here and there like an earthworm, "then this beautiful land, which is much to wholesome, would clatter together quite by itself."

"Leave off — leave off," a fourth voice cried, whose owner was so tiny that his own brothers could not see him anymore. "Those down there are helping us themselves. They want to be completely different to how they have been created; that is already suitable. And see, here comes a carriage driving up. Do you recognise the two brown country horses? There one sits within who will certainly send such a pair of halves to their doom for us. Merely needs pricking. Hurrah, she shall live, the little blond. It is good for us when the women are stronger."

The four swung their red caps, and cried out with all their bodily strength. Only, the citizens strolling past just thought that the midday sun was reflecting on the red stones.

Since the day when she had been dislodged from this town with bare, sober words, the commandment of decency and of good bourgeois life for its own sake, Hertha had not entered the residence of her relatives again.

"Shall I wait, Miss?", Johann, the coachman, asked, whereby he respectfully lowered his whip before the little one.

"Yes, I will only stay a few minutes."

"And where to then?", the old servant allowed himself to add.

"Then?" Hertha stared across the lifeless market square between whose bumpy stones the grass was sprouting, and so empty and homeless was everything in her that she had to first remember where the next hour would find her. "Then? — Then home of course."

"Beautiful, Miss."

With a heavy resolve, the little one sprang up the broad, well-worn wooden steps. What strange shadows even drew back and forth in the house this day. They rode on the handrail, they crouched on the steps, and clung onto the feet of the girl ascending the stairs.

"How tired I am," Hertha thought. "It feels like there's lead on my ankles."

But then she took heart, and knocked on the first door behind which she supposed her sister would be.

No answer.

Hertha was taken aback. Would Agnes perhaps be running errands, and hence have left her home? Then it would certainly be better if she also hurried away immediately herself before she had mentioned and revealed something of what had driven her here. But as she was still considering this, her finger was already tapping on the study of her brother-in-law, and her hand was already seizing the handle as if she could not expect at all to confront a strict and indisposed judge.

A sharp, impatient "come in".

Even as she turned the inner baize-covered door, the quick slipping-in was dominated by the feeling that she was degrading herself. She thought nothing of herself anymore. She did not believe in herself anymore since she had been wandering about in a dream, since she did not know anymore what she wanted, nor what she loathed, since she was running alone through the world to beg for advice from a stronger, hate-filled man.

"Come in."

There she stood again in the bare, uncarpeted room. In the corner, the plaster Venus de Milo towered, and from his desk at this moment the black-haired, broad-shouldered man rose whose forehead was now over-flown by distinct signs of astonishment, yes, of petulance, but who had at one time overcome his protesting conviviality only arduously opposite her.

Quite right, quite right, that had befallen at the time, but now the same sombre, uncertain eyes again flamed towards her half in shock and aversion, and hence, hence Oskar Rogge was straightaway the man who would feel sympathy for the straying, thrown-about girl, and say to her full of pity something palliative, resolving, liberating.

Really, the little one hoped for that.

"Oh — oh," the kobolds cheered screeching, as they kicked their legs up high; "how well it is going for us since the cleverest down there wore black glasses on his nose. — What joy we are not making for our mother and our high father."

***

"Come in."

The Girl Who Lost Her Way

Oskar Rogge abandoned the Germanic forest only with distaste. In his home, a precious calm, a soundless comfort had actually reigned for a few months. Everywhere lurked the readiness to serve and to obey him, the crowned lord. He lived quite like a king who indeed pressed and tormented his folk for the sake of his mood, but who now, after he had apologised at the first rumblings of revolution through a pair of resounding proclamations, was being regaled, even idolised by the appeased subjects yet more than before.

Really, the conventional, constitutional bourgeois life contained something good. It befitted the citizen who had arrived at a certain age, and it must be defended against the unwarranted demands of youth. In that his superiors were undoubtedly proved right. At heart, he shuddered when he now recalled the unease and the hounding of that past in which all manly dignity had been so difficult to maintain.

And now the arsonist who had misdemeaned herself on him and his property stood before him again.

Very unpleasant.

How large and insistent, even fearful, the expressive blue eyes of the little one adhered to him. Certainly, she did not induce the least in him, but the one thing remained yet horrifying and puzzling, for as he rose next to his chair, he felt with rising anxiety how that ill-fated, enticing danger which he had kept distant from himself with indignation again climbed up in his chest again. As if for protection against himself, he threw the skin of the bristly hedgehog about himself.

"Hello, Hertha," he began, as he stroked back and forth on the arm of his chair with lowered head, and, so as to cut short the conversation at the outset, he added straightaway, "What leads you to me? Agnes is not at home, she is making a few errands for the festivity at Werrahn tomorrow."

Thus, with that it was implied from the start that the little blond was induced by her own impulse to a life circle alien to him, and that their mutual relations could consequently only be looser and more incidental.

That was more distinguished and clever.

But, how obtrusive and unmaidenly she was behaving. She hurried promptly to him, and as she hastily began turning a button of his green loden jacket, she burst out with hot cheeks and trembling voice, "Oskar, I would like to talk with you about my engagement right now."

"Why?"

The Professor stared at the floor on which he constantly sought for something lost, and kept to himself. What did all this mean? Was the little one, now so deathly pale, bringing the unrest with her again? For God's sake, just not that. Such irregularities must be avoided above all.

Hertha was still fingering his green jacket. And the uncertain movement slowly made the man's blood rise to his head. "Just away — if she would just go away," he thought secretly, and he instinctively added, breathing deeply, "This ample, light hair is — yes, it is loathsome."

"Oskar, what's wrong?"

"Me? Nothing at all."

"Tell me outright, don't you know what I have to ask you? — What advice I desire of you?"

Then the Professor raised his dark head fitfully, pursed his bearded mouth helplessly, and shook his chair in rising fury, "No, I know nothing. Dear child, do me the single pleasure, no puzzles and no equivocation. You know how much I despise such things."

"Yes, that is well-known to me — but, have pity on me, see, I beg you — I am experiencing nothing but equivocation."

The Girl Who Lost Her Way

Oskar Rogge did not need to hear any more. In his rising fear, he had grasped completely the girl's story, but precisely as a result, he knitted his sombre eyebrows still more darkly, and pushed the pleading girl's hand away from himself. No, no, she must remain entrapped and shackled, otherwise he would unbind with his own hand the evil spirit which apparently wanted to disarrange his house anew; and then — he was also offering her a good deed through his resistance. — Subordination, thus read the highest law for average people, why should the little one, the wild one, possess something better than had been given to him himself?

And in envy and hate, he continued, "Let us look the matter in the eye. Are you perhaps bristling now against the place and man whom you have chosen?"

"Oskar, Oskar," she lifted her hand, and stroked imploringly his hairy cheek as if she wanted to attune the hard man more mildly to her helpless position. "I beg you, think about me for once."

"Yes, yes, I know, do you consider yourself too good for the steadfast, proven man? Or are you horrified at giving up your conceited freedom?"

"Oskar — dear, good Oskar —", she attempted to cling to him, but was shaken off by him, "I know, you do not think at all like that at heart — you suffer yourself under shackles which you had placed on yourself alone, and yourself by others."

"Me? Shackles? Don't come to me with such phrases. No, dear child, I have, praise God, realised at the right time that subordination and obligation depict for us everyday people alone the modest space in which we are able to become useful to both ourselves and our neighbourhood. You don't place a carp pool in the open sea. Look at me yourself. Since I humbled myself, I have fulfilled my teaching office in all directions punctually. I am a model to my students because they learn from me to resign themselves to the needs of the day, and my family believes in me."

Did the little one hear right? All the sober words which she heard hurt her, yes, they were causing her a torturous pain in the head and heart, and yet something compelled her to lean on the ungovernable man who wrestled intellectually so grimly with her, to hide her silky head on his shoulder so as to then ask and plead.

She was so forsaken, and here stood the only man who surmised and guessed something of her innermost wishes.

She lingered so close to him again that he felt the trembling of her delicate limbs. A quite indefinite, agreeable perfume, which the man unaccustomed to it secretly loved and craved, played dispersing about his shaken senses.

"Oh, Oskar," she stammered tearfully and without proper consciousness, "being modest falls so heavily."

"Yes, certainly, it is not easy," Oskar Rogge murmured, the light tremor of these tender limbs secretly overwhelming him, as if a new, stronger life were flowing over into him — "but," he added with violent coldness, "all the greater and more beneficial is the effect then of the final victory which we experience over the like in unclear contests. That you can hear from every pulpit. And it remains eternally true."

"Oskar — don't speak in such a commonplace way — you can't guess —"

"But — but — do you consider me perhaps to be so stupid and inexperienced? A so-called 'great passion' is driving you again."

Now the girl driven by despair grasped the man's hands, and though he wanted to defend himself, he could not shake off the hot, quivering clasp anymore.

"And if it were so," she cried fervently, and over her pale countenance spread more decisiveness than she had shown up until then, "if it were so, would you, — could you directly condemn me if I indulged in such a tendency?"

The Professor sank ponderously onto his chair, and buried his head in both hands in aimless despair. Though he did not like to confess it, this open courage of a struggling human child tore at him, yes, him, the unfree, the thousandfold shackled man. But it also remained just as clear that he must not on the surface follow such bewitching churning. Already because he himself was enslaved below ground in a mine. Hate and envy prevailed again.

"Oskar, would you condemn me?"

The Professor aimlessly grasped a pen, and began, as if for his protection, or to be able to collect his thoughts properly, to scribble about on a sheet of paper. A sharp, etching noise screeched through the room as a result.

"Above all, Hertha," he rose arduously, "I request of you once more that we don't lose ourselves in the mist. So, if you want to suggest to me what I don't hope, that you intend to call off your engagement, and indeed, as I unfortunately must assume, because you at the present are seized by a different inclination, then admittedly the only respectable thing would have to be if you informed your hosts at Werrahn about it today. It seems to me, you have hesitated already for a somewhat long time with this revelation, for the people have certainly already outlaid greater expenditure. The further details must then be arranged, assuming of course that it can happen with decorum and without all too great a furore for you and your fiancé. I mean thus, if the respective 'unknown' man depicts no imaginary greatness, but is determined to keep you honourably and conventionally. He conducts himself thus hopefully, does he?"

When the little blond heard this clear dissection of her position and her hopes, her eyes coloured darker and more menacingly until they displayed completely the appearance of the angry heavens. A short laugh of contempt erupted from her. Yes, now she knew it irrevocably, her wish, her secret yearning would tolerate daylight nevermore, for what drew and enticed her was an abyss surrounded with green.

Nevertheless, she inquired once more with proudly raised head, "And if I now left without any certainties, Oskar? — Then I would be the lost daughter, wouldn't I? Destined for nothing else but sinking, and you, you would then throw the first stone against me?"

"Me?" —

Oskar Rogge balled the paper together in his fist and tossed it away. He wanted to keep himself utterly safe from being drawn into such a heaving catastrophe. This ungovernable creature, she knew though that he did not want to think through the problems of youth, but those pitifully dying or ill ideals in him which were wasting away suddenly cried out from him in rebellious fury, "Leave me, leave me, I could perhaps admire you —".

"Yes, could you do that?"

"But I must condemn you though, yes, yes, I would turn you from my door."

"You would do that?"

"Yes, quite certainly, because —".

"Well, because?"

"Because —." Then he groaned like a wounded animal, "Because there must not be any people who, for the sake of an hour of happiness, or better, for the sake of an hour of sated senses, may throw an entire life cheerfully down the slope, while another — —. I — I hate these people, I despise them."

The little one in the white dress stood calmly after this outburst, yes, motionless, and just looked the speaker sharply in the eye. Then she reflectively buttoned up a button of her light jacket. The Professor, however, as if he must not at any price allow the girl to achieve the freedom she was hoping for, tore at his beard, and added in menacing zeal, "And the end? Have you forgotten that? Abandoned, shunned by all the world, for you dumb, infatuated women always foot the bill. And then being pushed around, hardship and perdition, and finally perishing in a corner."

"Yes," Hertha said quite still, "you must think of that. Ugh, only not hardship and tormenting sorrow. That digs creases in your face. Can you imagine how I would look with wrinkles, Oskar? No, brother-in-law, you have convinced me completely. You are a clever man. And tomorrow I will expect you with Agnes at the festivity at Werrahn."

3

"**S**exton Vierarm, have something," mother Lotte thus commanded her religious friend, behind whose chair at the upper end of the long white table, she was just then appearing with a wine glass in her hand to clink glasses with her trusted advisor. "You will have something proper too?"

Now the religious man was chewing at the moment with all his strength, his wrinkled cheeks had rounded out so frighteningly that he had to pour down a hefty swallow of the heady red wine before he could at all emit an answer from the depths of his stomach, and even then only after a few heavy breaths, "Oh, Madam," he puffed crimsonly, "are you absolutely serious? Look, I speak of God's bounty which stands here before me in the figure of a beautiful, pink ham which an expert feminine hand —", here he stroked reverently the fingers of the smiling mistress of the house, "has cooked in beneficial burgundy, I speak of it, God the almighty knows, certainly according to my modest powers. But see there, Mrs Lotte Kalsow of Werrahn, does this remarkable ham perhaps dwindle? No, I look at it thereupon incessantly, it claims the field. And that despite overground and underground efforts. For, don't take it wrong, Mrs Lotte, here under the table in fact sits my poodle Sus, you see, it now stretches its snout out. I do not know what has again passed into this demonic beast, but it wanted as it were to take part in our magnificent feast, and hence be confined under no circumstances. And you can recognise by that, worthy friend, that Sus is no common dog and guest. No, observe rather how my poodle constantly raises its paw to the middle of the beautiful table — ah, much too beautiful a table, Mrs Lotte, despite the heat — as if the beast wanted to greet our happy engaged man in his new well-fitting frock coat, and above all the little, golden engaged girl with her radiant heavenly eyes, or even give them a sign. Heaven knows what that may mean."

"Now, perhaps old friend," Mrs Lotte responded, and her thick, black silk dress rustled like a poplar in the wind when she now bent her goshawk's head down confidentially with its white muslin bonnet towards her confederate, "perhaps the clever dog thinks you would like most of all to give us a little toast."

"A toast?" the sexton cried stricken, and let his fork drop.

"Why not?" mother Lotte affirmed in a whisper, "you must offer the people something. And since it did not work out so well with the singing together —".

"There you are right," sexton Vierarm interrupted grumpily, "a four year old kid would have noticed that, Professor Oskar Rogge is too distinguished for that, — the teachers from the town, Mrs Lotte Kalsow of Werrahn, you can note in general, are everywhere too distinguished for that —".

"Certainly, and that I must sit Uncle Ludwig Wippermann right next to him — —".

The sexton nodded, and whispered emphatically now in the ear of the mistress of the house, "Have you surely observed, the Professor did not enjoy that Uncle Ludwig Wippermann always beat time with the pint glass as the singing rang out. And when he told him with the bouillon about his manure which he mixes in with a new sort of coal dust for the sake of savings, the Professor pushed his plate away."

A falsetto voice intervened from above. Uncle Ludwig Wippermann jumped up with his scrawny, tiny figure from his chair, and tapped on his glass. In his short-tailed coat, the wrinkled and furrowed little man looked as rattly as if you had just struck the black cloth about him to hold his bones together neatly.

"Quiet," he commanded, and raised his forefinger earnestly.

"Hello? What is it then?" it sounded from various sides.

"A new course, my attendees," the rich uncle crowed, as he propped his knife up on the table before himself with his other hand.

"Hm, the tablecloth," the Professor sitting next to him jibbed offended, but was as soon induced to silence again by his Agnes who stroked his arm, imploring and placating.

"A new course, my attendees," the rich uncle cried importantly. "Something quite extra fine. Snipe in jelly. Have you eaten this delicacy before, Professor?"

"No," the scholar cut him off sharply.

"Sexton Vierarm," mother Lotte tapped her friend now on the shoulder, a little unsettled. "Now give us your little talk for the couple. It is high time. I will re-member you for it."

The sexton wiped his mouth awkwardly with the ser-viette, and patted his poodle Sus under the table on the head, "Why not, Madam Lotte?" he considered. "Since Professor Rogge has already spoken for your house, and our pastor is also not present because of his flu, so such an honour would come easiest to me on account of my spiritual position. In addition, however, Mrs Lotte Kalsow, a pair of strong admonitions to be addressed to the little golden, engaged girl could not exactly harm. For, as you know, I once considered her to be demonic, and if this dangerous addiction has been driven out for the great part from the maiden, you must yet also think of relapses." He pushed up his scrawny, overly tall fig-ure slowly from behind the table. "So, if you allow, I will begin now."

"Quiet," the lady of the house ordered, satisfied. "Our sexton has some words to say."

Only, the rich uncle had not understood.

"Why?" Uncle Ludwig Wippermann crowed in-between, being reputed to not like to suffer the sexton's calling, presumably because he had to bear significant schooling charges on his farming estate, and was sus-pected in addition of urging free thinking. "Why, Aunt Lotte? We don't need any long marriage speeches though with an engagement!"

"Uncle Wippermann," the orator intended to strike him down indignantly, and brandished his long serviette as if he wanted to shoo away an overly irksome horsefly. "In your manure, you may perhaps — —".

"No, no insults," the lady of the house admonished, still lingering behind the sexton, irritated.

"Quiet — quiet!"

"Begin," they urged laughing from the other end of the table where the young folk were placed. But suddenly, a bright "woof woof" echoed through the large room. The poodle Sus had in fact sprung into the sexton's empty seat, shaken itself, and turned menacingly towards the enemy of its master.

"Has a dog also been invited here?" Oskar Rogge, taken aback, inquired of the engaged girl who was white and pale, but drawing with feverishly sparkling eyes all sorts of figures on her plate.

But then sexton Vierarm was already letting his blaring Isaiah-like cry ring out with full throat. The windowpanes rattled from it, and it became momentarily still.

"I have the chair," the religious man roared, as he let his serviette flutter in the air with a jerk.

"Bravo — bravo!"

"Hurrah, sexton Vierarm."

"Well, then at least a glass of punch," Uncle Ludwig Wippermann wrinkled venomously, "he will steam away otherwise, — well, and now you can begin for my sake."

"Yes, now I will begin," the sexton intoned reproachfully, and at the same time, he directed a flaming pair of eyes as eerily at both the Professor and the rich uncle as if he had to now establish in a short talk the deserved death sentence of them both. "You see, my dear devout people, you hear it yourself, the world is depraved, so like Sodom and Gomorrah that it will not accept anymore the voices of religion and its official servants."

"It's also not necessary," Uncle Wippermann added here impatiently, and began riding his chair back and forth, "The Church history leaves no doubt. But here we are celebrating, as I am told, an engagement, and here we want to hear something lighthearted. Best of all something with allusions."

"Please, allow the speaker to express himself," the Professor determined, gradually taking pleasure in the cheerful side of this argument. "Silentium for the sexton."

"Thank you, Professor, but I am obtaining a hearing already quite alone. For even the old knitting women in the church will wake up at my voice even if they are fast asleep. So, now to the business. You want allusions, Uncle Wippermann? Good, you shall have them. What are we celebrating here? We are celebrating an engagement." Here he shook his fist, and looked about challengingly at the circle as if a bold person should even contradict this claim.

"Almighty," Uncle Wippermann murmured into his glass.

The sexton struck the table thunderingly. The plates leapt high.

"I have heard well what you lisped there. And you are quite right, the Almighty has much to do with it. For, my dear engaged girl with the golden hair, the engagement time is for a chaste and lovely maiden nothing more than a very serious preparation for the final wedding, quite exactly like the school days form the entire human life for the final shifting to the other side. Is that so, Uncle Wippermann?"

"I have nothing against that," the rich uncle growled indifferently, and whistled softly through his teeth.

The sexton grew a few more inches, and stretched his hand towards the apparently defeated opponent almost in blessing, "Beautiful, we will speaker further up there. And now my dear, maidenly engaged girl, you have probably noted already, dear — for I will call you dear in this celebratory hour — you have probably noted already, dear, that we out here in the countryside talk the raw, pure truth."

"Bravo — bravo — up with the countryside! Hurrah for Werrahn!"

"And because it is so, I must tell you that when you arrived here as a fine girl in a half-length dress and with see-through black silk stockings — —".

"Eh, eh," the rich uncle crowed, "that is a pretty allusion."

Only, the sexton just threw him a killing look. "When you drew up here thus — not to forget the black velvet coat — Mrs Lotte Kalsow at Werrahn, who is the cleverest woman and lady there is, whom I know anywhere —". Here the sexton folded up like a pocket knife, a motion he called bowing though, and he was answered blustering from all sides, "Hurrah for mother Lotte of Werrahn. Cheers!"

"Long shall she live," Uncle Ludwig Wippermann sang in-between, intending to use this pause by all means.

But the sexton just moved his hands, as if he intended to accompany himself on the organ, and boomed onward, "I wanted to say, for I will not let myself in any way be interrupted, when you arrived here, lovely engaged girl, Mrs Lotte Kalsow at Werrahn and her daughter and I myself and my poodle Sus — behave, Sus, you are being spoken of — we looked at you with expectation and suspicion. For in our current time, you must get a good bite of the youth to see whether it suits you, like the beautiful raspberries on the bush. From the outside, this very inviting fruit always looks appetising and juicy, but within crawls the worm."

"What?", sexton Vierarm's adversary now hissed. This picture seemed to the rich uncle to be too tangible. What? The schoolmaster also wanted to smear a maggot in his sandwich? Such an ink stain? "A cognac," he flailed, as he stepped heftily on the Professor's foot. "Did you just hear that, it ruins one's appetite."

"That it should too," the sexton drowned him out. And Heinrich leant over, tapped the rich uncle on the hand, and suggested to him, "It is only a parable, Uncle Ludwig."

"But a quite infamous one, Heinrich, ugh the devil."

"I have the chair," the religious man again invoked, having fallen gradually into utter fury through the interruptions of the little wrinkled fellow, for he rightly considered it sinful to mangle a beautiful, well-worded talk in that way. "And I will not be discouraged by anything in the world from my oratorical path, for not everyone can hold a talk with main clause, subordinate clause, predicate and object."

"Bravo — bravo," Oskar Rogge then applauded with approval.

"Thank you, Professor, I know you are a learned man and understand the difficulties. And if Uncle Wippermann is spoiled by my toast —".

"No, just by the maggots, ugh the devil!"

"Then it is because of his jaundiced stomach, and he should take a little elderberry drink more often."

"Excellent — bravo — bravo — elderberry here!"

"And now to you, you dear sweet engaged girl, with your golden-spun hair and your blue eyes which can gleam and sparkle like our Baltic Sea in May."

"That I enjoy," the rich uncle suddenly squeaked as he brandished his champagne bottle. "All the pretty little girls!"

But the sexton nodded seriously, and continued, "I said we would have strictly fitted you to the service as if you were a bush which we could plant without worry in our garden."

"A raspberry bush," a pert voice called from below.

Uncle Ludwig Wippermann rubbed his hands.

"But see here," the sexton continued speaking, no longer paying attention to such insignificant trifles. "What happened? You gradually put away the black velvet coat, and also the see-through black stockings —" But the much tried toast maker did not succeed in continuing straightaway.

What was that?

The rich uncle turned and shook to and fro on his chair with laughter, and when, struggling for breath, he was finally brought to life again by a glass of water, he was only able to wheeze quite weakly to himself first of all, "Ha — ha — excellent, — the black stockings on the table of the house — that is an allusion though."

"That fellow is a smutty one," Superintendent Hartmann scolded clearly across the table.

"My devout people, let us hold to morality," sexton Vierarm's trombone voice blared in that dangerous moment, and he brandished his serviette as if he wanted to wipe away all the smut from the world with it. "Let us not worry about the habits of those of other faiths who pray Our Father's differently. So, my beautiful blond engaged girl, I want to close with something uplifting. We have seen that you set aside the coat and the stockings, and with them at the same time the entire modern existence, and became that which is called an obedient, innocent maiden. And the cuckoo knows how it happened, but through the change in your girlishness, we have all become fond of you, my dear little one, right from the heart. Mother Lotte and Miss Anna, and I and my poodle Sus, and finally also your fiancé, our Mr Heinrich. Dear little one, with this Mr Heinrich, however, we grant you a happiness which you cannot measure beforehand. And hence, dearest daughter, the worm in the raspberry, if it should still be there — Uncle Wippermann, don't twist your face, I will not be discouraged from my worms by you in any case — hence, my dear daughter, you must for the sake of the great and ample fortune which is placed in your lap inwardly conquer the worm until it dies. We humans must all conquer our worms. And hence, my daughter, you must constantly be a submissive maid for your future husband, for he will keep all hardship and worry far from you, because he lives in blessed circumstances. And you must foresee every wish from mother Lotte's eyes, and you must not ever behave haughtily towards us others, but amiably and loving, for otherwise, engaged maiden, Jehovah, the Lord, will smash you to pieces with his best lightning, and he will strike you with infertility, leprosy, and all sorts of bad ulcers, just like he once maltreated the Jew Job. And hence I toast you, in this godly mind you shall live, hoorah, and once more hoorah, and once more hoorah."

Both the violin players sitting next to the musicians by the piano started up ringing and jubilantly, the entire company rose to clink glasses, and a racket occurred so that nobody could understand his own voice anymore. But all were agreed that sexton Vierarm's speech had been good value. The sexton himself, however, wiped his forehead modestly. Then he took his glass, and held it thankfully towards his poodle, who, still crouching on his chair, followed all his movements tensely, "Your health, dear Sus; I have well noted that an enlivening demonic power passed into me, otherwise I would have not been able to finish this difficult piece. Cheers!"

Thus the meal continued for a while yet. One delectable dish, well-tested and expounded on by Uncle Wippermann, followed the other, the young people at the lower end of the table again began singing and giggling, and Mrs Lotte's maids, looking appetising in their white aprons, ran around, and placed ever new champagne bottles on the table, on which hardly an empty spot was still to be seen.

And yet a little, unnoticed disturbance had eerily interrupted the cosy festivity.

"What is happening now?", Uncle Ludwig Wippermann wondered, as the young girls, all in bright dresses and with natural floral wreaths in their hair, closed a circle around the couple. "What is Anna doing there in the middle? Does she perhaps want to make some poetry?" And turning to the Professor, the scrawny little wrinkled man chirruped delightedly, as he tapped his neighbour most familiarly on the knee, "Just look at the neckline on Anna. Oh God of France! Plump — plump! Yes, the beauty, Professor, inherited in our family."

Meanwhile Anna Kalsow had stepped up close before the engaged girl. In her right hand she carried a pair of white lilies. Now she made a short, timid curtsy, but even if her mouth was compelled to smile, her eyes remained immovably riveted to the floor so that a sharp observer would have had to have discover how much and how fiercely the daughter of the house secretly bristled and resisted the attention which she was now meant to show the engaged girl.

But only Hertha sensed this antipathy. She instinctively clasped firmly the arm of her fiancé as if only a weak protection could be had at his side, then she bent forward hesitantly, and her gaze was directed as anxiously at the slender, luscious figure of the country girl as if she surmised that the artificially enthralled peace must be thrown now from this table to make room for the restlessness and the tormenting, gnawing fear which was filling her entire being ever anew.

What would yet happen today?

Yes, what? What?

Redness and pallor alternated incessantly on her narrow face, and again and again she peered out the window furtively and unnoticed.

Nothing.

A golden, hot summer afternoon was slumbering outside in transparent calm, the leaves of both the mighty lime trees barely curled, and over the entire farmstead stretched a soundless peace, as mother Lotte had ordered.

But there?

Out there?

Now — now — if her surroundings had not spoken so loudly for all the world — she must listen though, and then, if her intuition did not betray her, then, yes, then they would spring up and hide.

"What's wrong, my little sweetie?", her fiancé then inquired.

It ran over her back like drops of ice. She shivered with a chill despite the heat, and her teeth quivered against one another.

"Do you not hear the carriage outside, Heinrich?"

The farmer raised his head serenely. "It is already past," he remarked then heedlessly.

Hertha grasped his fingers.

"Dear little one," the giant murmured once more, touched.

"Now my daughter Anna will recite something," Mrs Lotte Kalsow announced, and moved her pointed countenance reflectively. "The poem was recited to me at my eve-of-wedding party, and hence I have sought it out again. Now don't make a fuss, daughter, the company will already know how it is meant."

"Yes, but complete quiet," Superintendent Hartmann called, looking with pleasure at the tall figure of the daughter of the house. "Hm, that would actually be a sturdy wife. Just what in all the world did she recently seek out the old Count for?"

But the girl still did not release her eyes from the white stone floor.

"Well, Anna, now courage," her brother encouraged her, and plucked at her arm.

Then she raised her head, and the gaze of both the girls was buried in each other for a vanishingly brief moment.

And again Hertha groped for the arm of her fiancé.

The daughter of the house began:

> See, these lilies, white and pure,
> From a pure maiden's hand,
> They shall be a symbol to you,
> A greeting from the forsaken land.
> A sign of what you lose
> When you turned your heart to he
> Whom for breeding you — —
> you — — choose — —

A soft cry was heard. Hertha sprang up. At the same moment, the three lilies slowly slid down the dress of the girl speaking.

"Anna — Anna," mother Lotte cried, and pushed through the rows of those standing around.

"What's this about then?", Uncle Wippermann started, but sexton Vierarm was already shooting over with a leap, and slung both arms around the swaying girl.

"What's is this meant to be about?", the religious man growled. "Nothing, absolutely nothing at all — merely the great heat. Pass over a glass of water please, Uncle Wippermann — our Anna has in fact become a bit faint."

***

In the afternoon, the guests were strolling in pairs or in groups through the garden, or they had settled down chattering at the white-covered little tables which were strewn everywhere, in the arbour, by the hedges, even in the middle of the paths, because to them the coffee was be taken without hurry. In the midst of those invited, the daughter of the house was already striding about again, having all sorts of crockery placed cleanly on the round tables, and was able herself to joke amicably when she was teased about her little mishap which nobody would have trusted of the strong girl.

But everyone knew how to explain it, and the view of sexton Vierarm, who meanwhile was with some young fellows hanging a few colourful Chinese lanterns on the trees, cut right through it. Namely, when, standing on a ladder, he stretched his bushy iron-coloured shock of hair wildly and unexpectedly from out of the tips of the maple, and cried down in terrible tones, for he was carrying the Chinese lantern on a wire handle in his mouth, "A laugh — laugh — with such heat — 25 in the shade — at the same time someone recites a poem. That I wouldn't even dare."

"Why actually are you hanging those garish yellow things up?", Uncle Ludwig Wippermann flounced, having placed himself with his cigar in a folding chair under the maple, and now fearing any moment that one of the large lemon-like things could plunge down skittishly into his digestive business.

"Why?"

"Yes, we don't find ourselves in Italy under the lemon trees?"

"No," the sexton mocked terribly, determined to give no more consideration to his enemy here in the open, and hence he pushed his glowing red, furious countenance, which resembled a beautiful crimson lantern more and more, down dangerously far, "Not lemon trees, Uncle Wippermann. This maple shall merely suggest jaundice; you understand, the tree is to be such a little allusion."

"Oh," the rich uncle got annoyed, and rolled around in his chair so that the cover creaked, "You inked-up son-of-a-bitch, you shall just be mine! How I want to get you."

Meanwhile mother Lotte was approaching her son, who was striding with his fiancee arm in arm on secluded and overgrown garden paths. Hazel shrubs planted opposite each other had formed an alley here, the bright daylight fell only weakly and muted through the unmoving leaves, and the couple strolled in the green twilight, happy to have escaped the loud swarms.

Filled with thanks, the giant stroked the little one's arm as gently and tenderly as his coarse hand allowed. Oh, what good, what warming words she had just spoken. He could not prove himself appreciative and overzealous enough at all for it.

"Come," she had uttered neatly and timidly as she attempted to draw the tall man away, "there — there in the dark paths — come, there nobody can find us, nobody, there we are safer."

"Safer, my sweetie?", Heinrich wanted to repeat half proud, half amused; only to his astonishment, he found himself straight afterwards drawn away with a power which he was hardly capable of explaining.

"She is just affectionate," he thought, touched, and again he stroked her split sleeve, felt vaguely the smooth, silky skin, and all his consciousness was veiled by a dashing cloud which lifted him and the wondrous creature up to abduct them both into the blood-red rose garden.

There, at the end of the path, mother Lotte stepped up to them. Once more she measured the couple with one of her estimating looks, as coolly and certainly as the old lady was accustomed to fixing the weight of sugar and coffee with the merchants, she contemplated once more why the little blond was alternating her complexion so frequently today, from the most pallid paleness to the most feverish blaze, and the goshawk's head rocked back and forth, finally reaching the result that the girl might surely also feel today the pain and the burden of love differently than it had been the custom in mother Lotte's time.

"Well, let it be," the woman of Werrahn thought, as she stuck her smooth-combed, thin hair with her palm more firmly to her temples under the white bonnet, "Cool love — hot love — she may well be no worse for it."

Slowly, solemnly, and momentously, she fumbled, half bent under the narrow hazel roof, through which dancing, green splotches were strewn over her old-fashioned magnificent dress, she fumbled a misshapen key reflectively from her pocket, "Here, my boy, here I bring it to you. Now show your future bride where she will rest her head in sorrow and happiness. You know we have ordered everything to the best of our knowledge, but now I hand over the key, for from now," — here the voice lost something of its calm, unclouded ring — "for from now on, a greater one must keep guard over your threshold. Right?"

"Yes, mother, yes," it poured forth fervently from the giant. His hand clasped powerfully the narrow, blue-veined hands of his mother, yes, he pulled the modest, helpless figure with full strength to his chest.

"Mother," he stammered once more, deeply struck in his soul.

"My boy," the old woman murmured, mildly and forgetting herself.

With downcast eyes, a chill in her limbs, and unheeded by both of them, the engaged girl stood next to them.

But then the young farmer pulled the key violently to himself, brandished it over his head so that the iron lost itself in the leaved branches of the bushes, and as he emitted a cry from the depths of his chest, so exulting and triumphant that it was carried far over the flat countryside, he drew his chosen one away with himself in senseless haste, spraying utterly good, incomprehensible words.

"Come — come — now you shall see — oh, you will be wide-eyed."

Soon they had both reached the side-wing of the house which had almost completely merged into the overhanging foliage of the three ancient, wide-branched lime trees which had formed the landmark of Werrahn since time immemorial. A flock of young starlings, just ready for flight, hung like a bluish black gleam on the branches, and twittered in sharp notes songs of flight and roving spirits. But in-between they shot into slanted flight. They were the house swallows and they chirped clearly:

> Hold tight — hold tight,
> Your own nest
> Is best.

"Yes," Heinrich stuttered blissfully. "Do you hear my only one what the good, old things are singing? My mother taught me all that as a child. Own nest is best. And now come; you shall not walk over the threshold in fact, I want to carry you here. My father did it thus. And his father surely too, and that is passed on thus."

Without waiting for an answer, he lifted the light load into his arms, and carried the trembling girl, who hid her luminous crown of hair deep and forcibly on his broad giant's chest, carefully and cautiously through the dull, red-floored hallway; it smelt strangely here of dried rose petals, the strong smell of old linen mixed into it, for the rooms had long been used as stores, and when the strong hand of the farmer now opened the first door expectantly, that remarkable, biting sharpness which tends to rise from new carpets streamed towards them at first.

Then they both stood wordlessly.

In the rising red glow of the evening sun, that which in purity and uprightness should be altar and fountain of youth of every family was unveiled before them. And in this space, alone from all the others, the wholesome, natural countryside had prevailed. Two massive beds stretched along the wall, with earthy, colourful, rural paintings at the heads; firm, colourful chairs and chests stood about, and, in the place of a graceful canopy, there was a beautifully embroidered house blessing, and the cosy mirrored commode made from oak had received an old-fashioned dressing of white tulle, without whose embellishment mother Lotte would not have looked on her son's fortune as being fully established.

Now the tulle, however, also flaunted itself in all sorts of artful puffs and pleats. Timidly, only in pinched embarrassment did the engaged girl dare to look at all the solid splendour. She remained wordless, trembling next to the giant, and as she tore at her handkerchief, she traced with concern the smouldering sunset which floated back and forth like a pool of blood on the white covers of the beds.

Where had she ever seen the like? And was it not as if the round splotch of blood was enlarging to rise, swelling more and more, gradually to the heads of the beds?

"Heaven help — give me peace," she murmured instinctively to herself.

The giant caught the cry of fear in astonishment, only, he interpreted it differently.

The Girl Who Lost Her Way

He firmly clasped the little one's hand so that she would have liked most of all to have cried out, then he drew her to himself, "You are right, my sweetie," he agreed, arduously pulling himself together. "Peace must reign here, and pay attention please, it will also happen if dear God gives only a little of his blessing. Oh, you don't know at all how beautiful I think it all is."

And once more he led the sleepwalker, who was frightened by her own steps, away with himself, and opened the second door.

Strangely, here they found themselves in a little circular room; all the furniture originated from the time of the great Napoleon, unchanged and untouched. Wonderfully darkened mahogany pieces, covered in faded green silk quite as if left behind by a wondrous female ancestor who had worked the farm alone and mannishly in mother Lotte's way during those dark times.

"Do you see," Heinrich explained with pride of ownership, "on this long sofa and behind this round table, that Mrs Kalsow hosted General Vandamme. Marshal "von Damned", our lads called him in their language. And there across the narrow writing table, there still hangs behind glass the obligation which the Frenchman left our female ancestor. You understand French, my clever sweetie, read it."

And when Hertha stepped up, there she found in a chamfered cardboard frame a deeply yellowed page which, signed with the seal of the commanding officer, displayed in scribbled letters the following receipt:

> A madame Jeanette Kalsow à Werrahn.
> Nous avons reçu de la part de Madame Kalsow par l'ordre de Monsieur le maréchal.
> vingt-et-une bouteilles de vin rouge,
> cinque cheveaux
> et une carosse.

And underneath stood mentioned expressly:

L'hôtel de Werrahn est très misérable.[†]

The little one had to laugh over that.

"It surely always was quite strictly done at Werrahn," she suggested.

That Heinrich had to confess with a grin, but then the young farmer drew his love with great seriousness onto the narrow Empire sofa, sat down next to her, and as he clasped her hands in his own, he gazed almost devotedly into her fine countenance.

Was it only the deep-red glow of the evening sun which made the dear, pale little face blaze so hot and crimson?

One of those hours arose whose traces can never be extinguished anymore in a human life because they have such a defining effect, like that of birth, and because from these quite rare hours, a fine, barely graspable melody streams out, which accompanies us into the land of promise. The engaged girl felt vaguely how the giant gently and carefully slung his arm around her hips. But how tenderly, how reverently, how sparingly. So entirely different than how her entire being had been enslaved and degraded recently in the fragrant hay. And when she realised this, she had to, as if forced, sling her arms, from which the slit sleeves had slid back against her intention, lightly about the neck of the honest fellow so that now her expressive sky-blue eyes hung on his like two timorous, child's fairy tales.

The farmer began. His voice quivered with suppressed excitement. "My dear little one."

"Yes, you good man," she whispered, collapsing.

[†]   To Mrs Jeanette Kalsow at Werrahn. We have received from Mrs Kalsow at the command of the Marshal the following: 21 bottles of red wine, five horses, and a coach. [...] The place at Werrahn is very miserable.

"See, my only sweetie," he continued with his deep good nature, "now we are sitting for the first time here all alone, and it seems to me as — as if a third one were still sitting next to us."

"A third one?", Hertha changed colour, her mouth opened, and her lips trembled against each other.

Could the giant be seeing ghosts? She peered distractedly to the side, only nothing lay next to her but the crimson light of the evening sun.

"Whom do you mean?"

"Do not be frightened, my child, I mean only the truth."

"The truth?" A hurt sigh flowed from her. "Yes, but what has the truth to do with both of us?"

"But — but —," he became eager, and nodded ponderously with his short-cropped, hulking head, "it seems to me as if I must tell you finally for once in this hour that I can recognise the truth quite well."

Then the listening girl was seized anew by a shivering which she could not stop to begin with in this quiet hour. She huddled fiercely up to her man. She just wanted to warm up her chill against him, to just not freeze in the midst of the red, sunny deluge, "What? — What can you recognise then, Heinrich? Reveal it to me."

He smiled melancholically, "Straightaway, my child, but don't look at me like that; look, I have wanted to tell you for a long time that I know quite well how to decipher your thoughts."

"Yes? Can you do that?", the little one repeated with a leaden smile.

"Oh yes, we country people must contemplate so much in silence, we are used to waiting patiently for the ripening and harvest, and I think that carries over into our innermost being too."

"Yes, but —".

"You see, and then I was actually clear in my mind from the beginning," — here the speaker cast his large boyish eyes down as if in shame, and did not dare anymore to look up — "yes, from the beginning, that you, my little one, with consciousness bear a heavy sacrifice, or — no quiet — shall we say, bear an open good deed into my house."

"I beg you, Heinrich, don't say anymore, not so — you have no idea at all how you are tearing apart my heart."

"My God, I don't want that," the giant murmured as he noticed her disturbed being, "no, that I certainly don't want, for I love you far too much for that. Yes, I love you beyond all measure," he stammered trembling afterwards, and the giant figure ducked down for a moment, "and now look," he continued, fumbling, "this certainty which is so holy to me, like the supper which finally gave me the courage to accept your gift, your condescension, — yes, so it is. For you see, little one, I have such a feeling, even if you furnish me with such an infinitely beautiful thing, really with far too much, but I have a calm certainty, I believe, which I can offer you. At least no rough breeze shall come near you, which I have not tried to hold off from you."

When he then pronounced this with his rough voice, faltering and stammering as if he were betraying something forbidden, Hertha at first moved away from him a little. Then she suddenly threw herself against his chest. There something was springing apart, there something collapsed with a sharp rattle.

Strange, how absolutely wonderful, as she now propped both hands against his chest to look at the giant curiously and astonished at the same time, she had to constantly shake her little blond head as if she could not apprehend herself or her companion at all. But that was quite natural, for in that moment, it seemed to her as if she were seeing the powerful man for the first time.

"Heinrich."

"Yes, little one."

"Stay sitting like that so that I can look at you."

"But there is nothing to see in me, sweetie."

"But yes, yes, it is such a calm, secure feeling. I want to see you and the beautiful old furniture here of Mrs Jeanette Kalsow, our female ancestor, for she is also mine now too, isn't she? And we will look at the beautiful quiet room together — oh Heinrich!"

"Yes, Hertha."

"I would like to ask you something. But I must be permitted to whisper it quite softly in your ear."

"Well, what then?"

"Place your arm around me again like before. It is so peaceful then, so full of blessed calm, like it can only be with you, with your family. Oh you, that I have learnt now. And it will remain so. You big man, you will never let fear near me again, will you?"

"Fear?" The farmer at first bent his head a little to the side as if he had to think about it, then his eyes sparkled good-naturedly. "Fear?", he finally erupted. "Where should that surely come from, little one? No, I would surely want to usher it off the premises. But what are you yourself imagining actually?", he continued thoughtfully. "What do you need to be afraid of anyway? I don't understand at all."

Only, the engaged girl, whose movements during his brooding were becoming hastier and hastier, shut his mouth anxiously. It was a peculiar image, when the powerful fellow was now so quickly and securely reeled in by this small, charming figurine, and pushed away from his thoughts.

And then they sat again by each other, hand in hand, and, what the blond head had never done before, she began, with hurrying mouth and with eyes from which imagination flashed, to paint their future together. Oh, how she was able to form everything.

Heinrich's heart pounded.

No, by God, it sounded like a fairy tale. It was almost all not possible when he imagined it thus.

"See, Heinrich, this room is set up so well for winter evenings. Don't you think?"

"Yes, if you think so, sweetie. Everything as you wish."

"Then we will bring out a beautiful book here, and I will read aloud to you. You don't know at all how well I can read."

"But that I well believe, with your clear voice."

"And we will also buy agricultural books so that I am able to then orient myself a little as it were."

"But little one, that would not be necessary at all."

However, she insisted on it. And here in the Empire room of Mrs Jeanette, they would always only go alone. When they had already taken their leave of mother Lotte and Anna. And on the narrow sofa, they would then always sit next to each other, just like today. And every day, it would have to become more and more homely and cosier.

"Certainly, sweetie, but it is already as beautiful today as it can almost ever be."

"No, let me," — she did not like to be removed even a step anymore from the images of calm and of sinking into comfort without a care in the world. And with gleaming eyes and sketching hand, she continued de-scribing. Now she had all sorts of important questions to bring up. Whether he wanted to smoke his cigars in the dining room in future, with her, or with his mother? Or whether he intended perhaps to stay with the old-fashioned, pleasant pipe? The smell did not disturb her in the least. Quite to the contrary, she had already become quite accustomed to the dreamy blue clouds. And then, with whom would she associate? Best of all with the simple, splendid people whom Heinrich had gifted his heart and his trust up to then. Yes, that would be the most proper. In this way then, the rushing and roaring of the great world would go past almost quite unnoticed at the house at Werrahn. And when Heinrich wanted to insert here with interest that there were also estate owning families in the district whose friendship they could seek, the little one knitted her brows again anxiously, and staved it off stormily and with energy, "No, no, not that. Don't you notice, you big man, that we will have to remain alone?"

Then he breathed deeply, and folded his hands. Only now did he grasp that he himself could perhaps be coveted. No, that was too much. He would have liked most of all to stammer words of thanks, mad, incomprehensible syllables of an intoxicated gratitude.

Thus they sat.

Meanwhile the red of the sunset was climbing up the walls, the dusk slid across the floor and stroked the rapt couple with soft fingers. But everywhere, in the green-covered furniture as well as in the red-shaded wood, it crackled, yes, in the air breathed by dried rose petals, whispered voices rose, and when the sunset had died out and grey shadows hung on the white ceiling, the engaged couple would, if they had paid attention, have certainly recognised the old Madam Jeanette as she strode rustling through the stateroom in her stiff crinoline skirt to look over at her progeny seriously and shaking her head.

But they both perceived nothing, for at the same moment, a many-coloured light blazed through the room. Colourful beams shot in towards them. Sexton Vierarm had lit his Chinese lanterns outside.

4

Heinrich later recalled that it had been the wizened little man, the rich uncle Wippermann, who had torn him from this gentle, blissful dream. Truly, when the flouncing little fellow stepped into the doorway, the last pinkish cloud in the youthful heavens of the giant had just fluttered away, and that iron-hard time began in which life at Werrahn hung like a rusty weapon which must be gradually ground sharp, bluish, and shiny for the cool and late vengeance.

Uncle Ludwig stumbled in and looked around everywhere into the corners uncertainly. Finally he seemed to have recognised them. "But children," he crowed with a suppressed grin, "just what are you doing? It is far too early for that surely." He flailed with his arm, and waved at the same time energetically, though without pulling his left hand from under his tail coat, "Do you not know at all then? A splendid illumination is waiting for you, bright red apples and yellow lemons. Fine, fine. But what remains the essential thing, you have received a really distinguished visit, truly, no-joking, something grand. I did not know that you were on such amiable terms with such noble people. But now come quick, children, otherwise it will look disgraceful, and I am as an accessory responsible for your tidy manners."

Gesticulating and urging them, he tore the door open. Only, Hertha sprang up, and turned for the back exit of the dark room as if seized by horror. The desire had befallen her with irresistible strength, "To hide, to crawl away, the animal is here, the predator who will tear you apart, who will lap your blood, for fun, for sport, and no saviour will leap in this time to strike him with the axe."

Why she was permeated and shaken by such a despondent fear, although she dwelt under the most devoted protection, was something she was unable to account for in the moment of approaching danger. She knew only one thing: it was awaiting her there, it stood before her and called, she heard how the voice talked frivolously, and how the sound could not awaken a trace of assurance, oh dear heaven, help, it all seemingly blinded her in its clarity, and yet in feverish shivering, she felt at this moment only the one thing, that this voice was poisoning her blood, that it awoke in her all the badness, wildness, and outrage which suspicious men, like Oskar Rogge, had long since recognised in her.

The legacy of her generation rose against her, and she defended herself, she did not want to succumb.

"I don't want to," she stammered, and sought to free herself from the hand of the giant.

"What?", Uncle Wippermann repeated, dumbfounded. And Heinrich too, over whom his unlucky star was shining, he did not let her go, no, he drew the bristling girl more strongly to himself, and had to ask in honest disappointment, as he saw his fiancee urging senselessly towards the bedroom they had just left, "Yes, where do you want to go then, little one?"

"Me? Me? I want to remain alone with you."

"Look," Uncle Wippermann interposed suggestively.

Heinrich's brow darkened. The presence of the stranger seemed bothersome to him, "But it does not suit," he reminded a little unwillingly.

Then Hertha stood still.

"Does not suit?" she repeated, awakening. And then once more lamenting, "Does not suit?", And suddenly her movements, which had been up to then marked by a stiffness, received something wreathing, supple, defiant, and reluctant, and she agreed firmly and strangely, "Yes, that is something else. Of course, if it does not suit, then come."

It had sounded like ringing mockery in her voice. Impatiently and furiously, she tore herself free, and strode ahead of both men. But in the hallway which led out into the garden, she clasped anew the powerful figure of the man striding out, and stammered something.

Darkness reigned in the narrow hall so that those passing could not recognise each other's features.

"What do you want?", Heinrich had to ask haltingly once more, for he was already rueing having opposed a desire of the little one in such an hour. Only, what he received for an answer exhibited no sense, and was unable to be construed by the simple-minded man in his haste either. They were just confused words, "You must not abandon me — must not take your eyes from me, do you hear? Think of it, Heinrich, it is now of extreme importance. Your hand must not be removed from mine, and even where we are called, we will go there together. For God's sake, don't forget that."

Then a whirl of blissfulness overwhelmed the hulking man again. Yes, that was affection, genuine, stormy desire, as honest and binding as he himself felt. And with a powerful squeeze, he enclosed her fingers, which, cold and shivering, sought his own, and in the triumph of assuaged hope, he drew the unresisting figurine away with him, into the garden lit by hundreds of colourful Chinese lanterns.

"Only a few moments, my sweetie," he whispered comfortingly and intimately, "then we will return again, and then everything shall be as you wish."

The round, luminous balls dangled from all the trees, and gave the leafy trunks a fairy-tale and fantasy look. Here a giant, sparkling lemon tree grew from the dark earth, there an apple tree glimmered in steady brilliance with enormous, flaming fruit, and all the splendour stood against the deep-blue evening sky in which the shimmering points seemed to fade away. Surrounded by the wavering red and yellow light, groups of laughing people strolled up and down on the gooseberry-edged paths, or they stood in great circles around an especially sparkling tree.

Right at the back, where the gorse hedges and thorn bushes reared up against the surrounding fields, two people stood alone. As if by chance, they seemed to have faded away from the colourful streams of light into the darkness here. Full of the dry scent, the evening wind swirled over from the fields, and at the feet of the solitary pair, an incessant, whispering cricket song swelled, rising and ebbing again until a desultory night bird, fluttering noisily against the disc of the large, still moon, interrupted the shrill song for a while. The daughter of the house gazed for some time after the black creature which overlaid the night-star with its outspread claws menacingly. But then her purposeful, honest way, which so often recalled mother Lotte, prevailed, and as she snapped about at the little roses of the dog rose bush, she took a step closer to the slender man in the fluttering, grey travel coat.

"It is wonderful, Count, that you have come to us once more before your departure," she said calmly and gratefully.

The man addressed, who remained turned away from the moon so that his countenance remained veiled by the darkness, looked at the shapely figure of the young woman for quite a while. But then he breathed deeply, and seemed to pull himself together.

"Certainly," he responded with his fawning voice, to which the simple country girl had succumbed from the

Now the young woman was plucking more excitedly at the bush. Her hand rustled in the branches, "Yes," she finally brought out reservedly, "I expected that."

From the garden, the quavering notes of a harmonica came across to the reclusive pair. Sexton Vierarm was crouching on his table, and the distant pair could discern how a swarm of people dancing and singing moved about around him. The swaying couples accompanied their circling with loud, lyrical sounds:

> Don't be angry,
> It cannot be,
> Don't be angry,
> Give in to it.[*]

Then a severe, reluctant trait slid over the serious, pale countenance of the girl. It was as if the trivial text of the song hid in itself an extra meaning for her, and with an appreciable effort, she began anew, "I — I am still in your debt — I should surely in fact ask you for forgiveness."

"You? Me?", the aristocrat asked, seeming to gaze over at the happy people under the yellow balls. He lingered with his thoughts certainly no more exclusively than with his companion.

"Yes," she sought to compel herself, as the poor, torn-up creature strove to hide the sudden flames on her cheeks under the night, "because I let myself be misled — by your kindness — my God," she continued quite incoherently and almost in tears, "I was not clear myself over what I was doing."

It all sounded so broken, so disintegrating into a wild, overflowing sorrow that these self-tormenting re-

---

[*] From Carl Zeller's operetta "Der Obersteiger" (1894), libretto by Moritz West and Ludwig Held.

proaches could not possibly flutter past the fundament-
ally good-natured cavalry officer.

He stepping up to her consolingly, and caressed her
beautiful, full arm comfortingly.

"Eh, let that be, Anna," he suggested amiably, "you
have — truly, you have perhaps behaved all in all entirely correctly."

That was again one of the moments when the easy,
dashing man, who liked most of all to strive to spread
mirth and joy about himself, was filled above all by the
intention of gliding away smoothly and ingratiatingly
over something unpleasant.

Which amounted to a few insignificant words. But
for the woman foundering in sadness, the phrase immediately brought forth an enlivening effect.

"Really?", she cried so loudly that he was startled,
and a light came into her eyes. But straight afterwards,
the practical sense of the Kalsows supplied her with a
still more important turnabout. Oh God, if he now just
wanted to answer back, she, the tall, proud creature,
would throw herself down before him, about him, unconcerned about the many strange observers, to
embrace his feet.

"Quite right," she stammered, waiting yearningly for
a dismissive hand gesture from him. "But I have delib-
erated, I possess actually no — no — oh, how does one
say it — it is all so difficult for me — no compelling
claims at all — I'm actually reliant on your kindness —".

"Oh, not that — not that, dearest child."

Fritz Hohensee stared at the ground, pinched, then
he let his gaze glide out expectantly to the dark farmstead over which the lanterns of his carriage threw a
fleeting light. Accursed once more, the beautiful tall girl
whose passion could blaze so seriously, so dangerously,
she was naturally right. It was not to be denied, he felt
bound, harnessed by strange claims, of which he had

317

never thought seriously, hampered by arms and legs. Well, and fetch the devil finally, at that moment, he was dominated entirely by a noble, self-denying feeling of fulfilling everything which was expected of him. Certainly, postponing just a little only to bring his duty to a certain conclusion. And then the current evening was spoilt for him anyway, and because what had driven him here in the intoxication of champagne would never ever take place — all these fervent, wild, fairy tale things — and then in addition, ugh the devil, it was doubtless because finally his wonderful, enormous expectation for all that formed a sort of crime, well, yes, in that the ad - monishers remained altogether unified, hence, for no other reason, he wanted to steal quickly and if possibly unseen into the waiting carriage, after he had shared with this beautiful, excited creature beforehand at least a few of his good intentions to which she could cling later.

Not exactly a vow, but a promise though.

"Listen, Anna," he began trustingly, and at the same time, he again grasped for her hand which was ceded to him so willingly. "I wanted to confide a few things about my further plans to you." And when the girl had said half contritely, that it would all not be necessary, she certainly did not want to intrude on his confidence, he continued his opening with easy condescension, "So, first of all to the war academy; now, immediately." — Out there, as she could see, his carriage was already waiting to take him to the station. After a holiday spent in Tyrol, a year of diligent work in Berlin. "No, no, really, a quite solid, grim swotting, well, and then, then the old gentleman wanted to retire, and I shall take over the estate with drums, pipes, and trumpets."

She looked at the ground, but the talking man sensed how the girl was suppressing her breath as if any sound from him would be a revelation, for now, at this moment, the miracle must follow. The impossible which could never happen, of which only lunatics were able to believe, and which the miserable girl nevertheless carried in her thoughts with rustic tenacity.

And the young Count felt the inescapable question. He caressingly stroked the cheek of the daughter of the house until the hounded girl could not control herself any longer, "Will you return?", she threw in breathlessly and in racing fear.

"Yes, of course."

"Oh, that is good."

"And then —".

She started. The decision was here. Now the black womb of the future was opening, and life and death were beginning to talk.

"Yes, and then," he concluded beset, and sought for the most harmless expression possible, "then we will speak to one another, dearest child."

His voice had cajoled so warmly and heartily; hence it could happen that the pursued girl only heard the kindly tone of this promise.

What further proceeded around her, she was unable to grasp clearly anymore.

Had she not bowed low over his hand which was withdrawn in fright? It seemed so to her. And why did all the colourful balls begin turning until they swayed like luminous planets through the leafy paths? See there — it hissed up from the earth, slanted flashes shot into the night and sprayed in colourful sheaves.

Fireworks.

Steps approached, figures emerged, and then a sharp, displeased voice spoke, awakening the country girl from her self-absorption.

"Anna, is that you?", the lady of the house at Werrahn asked.

"Yes, mother."

"Excuse me, Count, but go then into the house, dear, and have wine brought out. It is lacking already. Uncle Ludwig has already demanded it in vain. I don't like that."

Strange.

So much happiness and assurance adhered to the proud figure of the girl that she let herself part without argument from the place of her improbably, supernatural success.

Measured and formal, she offered her hand to the young man in the grey travel coat, "Until we meet again, Count."

"Until we meet again, dear Miss."

A handshake, and dreamwalking she strode to the house. When she caught the radiant light of the lanterns before the carriage which would carry the Count from there in a few minutes, she shut her eyes, blinded.

***

The nocturnal festivity at Werrahn had reached its climax. All the hedges and bushes, the great light-radiating trees, but also the still flowers on the silent lawns had come to life.

What a wondrous, iridescent summer night pregnant with secrecy. Do you see the tiny, bluish torches which were lit on the nodding leaves? Are you thinking they are luminous little beetles in their phosphorescent armour? Good, it can well be. But why do the red berries in the bushes glow so hot and fervently, why do they urge forth as if they were seeking eagerly for the voluptuous hand which plucks them? For what reason do the still flowers open their cups and infatuate, overflow mutually in intoxication and scent? Why do the crickets not want to fall silent? And to what end does the hidden nightingale lament with such lurid earnest?

The Girl Who Lost Her Way

You know quite well, although you like to feign it in this case. All parts of creation in which life circles, all the becoming in which the clockwork of the world's will ticks, all that is familiar with it, the deathly-sweet hour when the power of the strange, of that taking effect outside us, must become greater than our own. And it is given only to the beings venerated by God to not be mastered by the blind urge.

Under the trees of Werrahn, the young people were not singing anymore, they were rejoicing. On the small, white-covered tables which shimmered here and there between the bushes, the cooled sparkling wine beaded and sprayed. It once ripened on the slopes of Champagne, but now mother Lotte wished that it would spark delight, an honest, earthy, loud cheerfulness. For the honour of the house wants it thus.

Even the sexton and rich uncle Wippermann have made up. The power of the foaming juice which the lady of the house has dispensed profusely works so irresistibly. You should have eavesdropped on them, the pair, as they sat at one of the tables, before them two glass lanterns, and surrounded by an excitedly staring crowd, to play the most outrageous game of cards which was ever dared in this district. You notice, it is a demonic game, even if you put aside the poodle Sus who accompanies every success of his master with a hellish growl.

Just where did the sexton obtain the courage?

He began with a single taler, certainly only seduced by the beading wine as well as the fury of his Isaiah-like nature, and now he can already not count anymore the heaps of hard taler coins he has won.

"Quiet Sus, now we come. Forty, dear Uncle."

"Pity — pity — he makes every trick," his opponent crows. "That does not happen with proper things. It is sleights of hand. But here, king of trumps!"

"Ace of trumps," the religious man trumpets. And again you hear the laughter of the dog under the table.

Under the more weakly burning Chinese lanterns, the youths are dancing. They do not shuffle anymore, they do not circle anymore, no, their breath wheezes its own melody. Special arts are shown by the bolder girls, you see white and black stockings which jerk forth and vanish again, and occasionally a cry rings out which stimulates the blood for a moment in a more blustering way than the most fervent wine. The summer night lives and whirls. Even the stars in the night sky sparkle down like wild eyes.

"Here I am finally, Count," the engaged man announces himself, his girl led firmly by his hand, "and here is my fiancee."

"Yes, here I am," Hertha also repeats mockingly, as she presses her free right hand provocatively into her hip.

And now — take note! Convince yourselves all by it, you guests of the night, all those for whom the haze of wine has not veiled your eyes, all who will puzzle over it, and mutter and interpret it later, you stand quite close, nothing is concealed from you; to your own astonishment, it is revealed how the young, charming woman whose blond adornment is illuminated in the shade of the uncertain light brighter than the golden disc of the moon, how she mocks in consciously scornful intent the aristocrat almost with every word, how she smiles at him, injures, humiliates the same man who came only to offer his hand to the couple in congratulations.

He came just for that reason though?

The young people are dancing.

At the tables, the champagne corks are popping, and everywhere, both on the quivering grass and in the bushes black as night, it glitters and burns and stirs.

But those standing next to each other can hear it. There the little blond sways at the side of the giant, and describes her happiness to the Count.

But why does she toss all the goodness with such garish delight in the face of the man concerned? As if every sentence were a pointed knife which she throws? Does it not sound almost like fury?

But no, that cannot be assumed, if you ponder with what burning haste she describes the calm, the unassailable security which lingers for her in the house at Werrahn. Now she speaks also of the wealth of the Kalsows. That is not right, mother Lotte does not love that. Now she moves her own rhapsody for the rural life into the proper light.

"Right leg — left leg," the dancing people cheer.

And carried away, she steps closer, and gazes from below with clenched teeth and contemptuous eyes into the face of the teased man whose blood is poisoned by the shame of being spurned.

"Heinrich, give me your hand."

Oh, and cheerfulness would always reign here. Always like today. No musing, not a trace of fear, why should there be? Only jubilation and cheerfulness.

"Right leg — left leg!"

"Yes, we must dance it — right leg up, Heinrich, you are so strong, you must swing me through the air — but for God's sake! Where have you gone? Why have you abandoned me?"

It is right strange that the engaged girl suddenly turns as if she wants to flee. But only for a flashing second. Then Oskar Rogge walks past, and points the girl to her fiancé who has fulfilled the duty of man of the house at one of the covered tables where the champagne flows most abundantly, and at which they drink to him with all sorts of lighthearted, allusive expressions.

"You can laugh, Heinrich — cheers!"

"Boy, to have such a pretty soft blond in your arms."

"You can laugh, Heinrich — cheers!"

Then the little one gathers her skirts. Why yet the holding back? Fear yet of whom? She feels confident. Surrounded by many earthy men, who will leap in as soon as the young aristocrat, who gnaws darkly at his lip, should take some liberty towards her. Oh, it is so glorious to show someone who desires you passionately and achingly that strength resides in you. To mock him, scorn him, that is the vengeance for it, because he causes her so much consequential sorrow, so much trembling pain. Even just a short while ago, even just now.

"Right leg — left leg."

See how she gathers her skirts? This little foot which rises to dance is glorious.

And there, the journeying man in the grey coat stirs. Now he has stammered something, has he not? But — but, she has caught it with her eager ears, even if still so unclearly, "Dear Miss, will you allow me the honour?"

"What are you thinking? If not with my fiancé, then alone."

"But outside my carriage awaits, it would be as it were in parting."

She laughs and dances, "Knock that out of your head. Really, it is advisable. You see, I do only what gives me fun."

"And does it also offer you fun perhaps — —?", he wants to push out between his teeth, as he points over to the distant son of the house. But the little one does not hear anything anymore. She does not want to. Shuts her ears, and dances.

Never again has the Werrahn earth seen such mischievous, enticing, ardent movements. And at the same time, the supple limbs do not stir wildly and unattractively, no, a flexing passes through her body barely different from that when a cobweb is rocked by the wind.

"Right leg — left leg."

Only, how does it happen that the dancing girl nevertheless — against her will — is caught by the arms of the more and more enrapturedly staring man?

None of the many who patronise this wonderful dance scene found anything special or even incongruous in it. God preserve, they all invoked it later. And they were serious people.

"She tumbled," they adjudged, "or she lost her breath. And Count Hohensee wanted to support her. No, there was nothing in that. Anyone of us would have done likewise. But that she danced with him onto the dark path, laughing and crying at the same time? Eh, nobody heard that, that mad Professor made it up afterwards." — But, what then followed, for that there were again irreproachable witnesses, a good number of the Werrahn guests observed it, and, in the following days and nights, it was arduously and adroitly joined up and explained by them.

The Werrahn girls speak in such a way when they want to warn each other about it even today, "Do you not remember?"

"She came plunging out of the bushes, red, haggard."

"And the Count followed her, he wanted to hold her back, for he had kissed her in the bushes."

"How do you know that? They haven't told anyone anything about it?"

"Of course — it could not be explained any other way. And why had her thin gold chain been torn, the one which carried a flat, pretty little heart right below her neck?"

"For sure, he wanted to hold onto that."

"And he warned her also, as she ran half senseless to her fiancé, who was sampling the wine with the Superintendent Hartmann and the other men under the maple on which the great, red Chinese lanterns were still swaying."

"Oh, that was bad, you girls, you should have right seriously warned your loved ones, your brothers and fathers, about it, for really, Heinrich Kalsow had drunk too much. Such giant bodies are directly rooted to the spot by it. 'And it comes down to the roots', as Jochen Tobis tends to say."

"But what the Count, half while running, said to her, that we again caught clearly."

"You see, that cannot be denied. It is good that you retained that. He muttered as if to an impetuous child, or like someone who is certain of his cause. He urged her while he tried to hold her back, "Hertha, I will wait for you. Believe me, I know better what you will do."

"But didn't he also say something about a new will?"

"Certainly he did, you girls. He said, 'the new will which burns in you, you glorious nature, it will burn down the house over the good people's heads. Believe me, it must be extinguished another way.'"

"For God's sake, sexton Vierarm, just explain to us what the new will means?"

"Hold your beaks, pert brats. That even I don't know. It is one of the phrases which they have taken to now. One person means it always in a different way from the next."

"Continue — continue. Did nobody stand by when the engaged girl now reached her fiancé under the tall maple? What happened then?"

"Oh, that I can share with you, I, Superintendent Hartmann, for I was sitting with Heinrich unfortunately behind a bottle of champagne. And it was already the fourth. He was making large, glassy eyes — very large — when the little one appeared so agitatedly before him. Then he wanted to lift her up, you see, so, but the first time he sank back again, and when he brought himself onto his legs finally the second time —".

"Take pity, Superintendent, what happened then?"

"Oh God, that I did not guess at the time — but the damned bucket full of champagne — yes, what I wanted to say, when he finally stood on his feet the second time, you see, he probably did not comprehend the broken words which she tried to throw at him. We all noticed that he tried hard, but he did not succeed in doing anything but entice a half leaden, half violent laugh into his good-natured features, which lent them a quite strange, bloated look. And then incomprehensible sentences flew back and forth between the couple just like we throw snowballs at each other in winter for fun. 'Heinrich — Heinrich —', the little one thus cried, and tore wildly at her dress so that the broken gold chain fell to the ground."

"That is true, I saw it myself, the chain fell into the damp grass."

"'Heinrich — Heinrich — listen to me, now I want to share something with you, I want you to give you me a sign.'"

"Quite right, she screamed it, but her fiancé did not recognise her voice, no, he groped about in the air rather, and asked, 'Good — good — a sign? I hear, who is calling here?' Then she burst out once more timidly, 'It's high time'."

"Oh, and then the awful misunderstanding occurred. Do you know?"

"Of course, who could forget that? We see the giant still before us as he approached the little one slowly and with uncertain steps to seize the shocked, retreating girl's arm with his massive hand now swaying so.

'Let me go, what a sight you are.'

'Calm sweetie, — ever calm — high time you say? You're right, that I feel too, I feel quite strong. Come —'

'What do you want then, where are you dragging me?'

'Where? Strange little thing. Where? Back into the dark room which you did not want to leave before. Truly, you were right. Come quick — we are engaged now and need not care about the others anymore.'

'Let me go.'

'You should follow, I say.'"

And then the Werrahn girls whisper something in each other's ears. Mysterious, timid, for they surely do not wish strangers to be privy to the terrible event.

Oh, it was also too awful as sexton Vierarm and the rich uncle Wippermann as well as the Superintendent carefully led the intoxicated man with words of comfort to a bench far from the guests to impel him to sit down there. But still worse was the effect of the look with which the abandoned girl followed her fiancé as she stood quite alone on the lawn under the maples.

"And did you surely observe, you girls, in what way she clenched her hands, opening and closing them, how a trace of disgust flew about her lips, and how she suddenly turned to the Count, who was still waiting behind her, and offered her hand in parting?"

"That remains the most inexplicable of all, doesn't it? Wordless and unmoving, the two stood opposite each other. We still see them, for the light of the Chinese lanterns fell garishly and colourfully down on them. Then the engaged girl offered her fingers wearily and with lowered head to the young man."

"Yes, and then?"

"Then? Who could have guessed it at the time? Who suspected in the least from the quick affair? For the Count also at the same time shook the right hand of mother Lotte once more, before he curtly and indifferently waved a farewell to the guests, to then hurry to the yard with light steps, where he climbed into the waiting carriage."

"Do you not still hear the rattling?"

"Yes, certainly, quite clearly. We see the red light of the lanterns leave the yard and float out onto the country road. We hear the regular and easy clip-clop of the horses. The carriage travels slowly. Quite smoothly and without haste. The noise only fades away after some time. And the festivity continues."

"How long, we do not know. It may well have lasted another hour or two. The sexton plays with the rich uncle again. The young folk dance, right leg — left leg, mother Lotte's girls run about with the champagne bottles, and quite far away on the bench under the tall sunflowers, which bend their heads down to him sleepily, Heinrich rises and stretches."

"Has he recovered?"

"Presumably, he is probably again as of old, for he looks about, and asks something, 'Where is Hertha? Where is my fiancee?'"

"Strange how it just happens that his question is repeated through all the arbours and hedges, on all the paths and ways, as far as the most distant nooks and crannies of the garden."

"Hertha?"

"Where is his fiancee?"

"Yes, where has she got to?"

"Do you recall, you girls, one whispers, one asks, one searches, men run to and fro among the extinguished candles of the globes, it becomes animated in the yard, insistent cries are heard."

"But who brought the news?"

"Nobody."

"Truly no living person."

"Why, it was whispered, muttered, and later claimed with pale and cold lips, who wants to establish it still today?"

"God forgive us the sin — we do not want to affirm it, but the Count's carriage did not travel far. It stopped at the Werrahn gatehouse. And inside sat a white-dressed young woman."

"That is not true, you're lying. I will strike anyone down who claims that. An axe here, for I will strike the hound dead!"

"Calm — calm!"

"Where is Hertha — where dwells my fiancee?"

"Oh my boy, pull yourself together, nothing bad need have happened to her, we must search."

"For mercy's sake, search — search — the stable lanterns shall be lit, lads shall walk the Schwarzbach stream. A light here and my axe!"

That was the festivity at Werrahn.

The festivities are over.

***

A lonely wanderer strides over the field paths. Sometimes he pushes his woolen top hat back over his neck to stare up filled with hate at the garish disc of the moon which floats over the paths with its pale light. Other times he peers down, and seems to count every single blade of grass.

It is sexton Vierarm, in his creased worn-out frock coat, and with the misshapen knobbly stick in his hand. Right before the place where the willow brush gives way about the Schwarzbach stream and the lime trees stand against the night sky like massive black heads, the wanderer stops and shakes his stick with demented strength up at the cavernous, mightily stretched vault of the heavens.

He is probably intoxicated, for his words are sounding confused. He roars, he screams, "Come down Virgin, you daughter of Babel, sit yourself in the dust, sit yourself on earth."

And then again it rings out lamenting over the nocturnal fields, "There was nobody from all the children who led her, nobody, who took her by the hand."

"Ugh," the old drunken Isaiah cried, and swung his staff against the space sown with stars. "Whom will you call guilty? Am I? Is she? This tiny little thing that a breath of wind tears from the ground, who flees from the bite of a midge? Oh the stinking lie. Ruin across the world of whores. It is the times which made it up. The ruinous wicked times. Come down, see, I want to smash you."

But the old man tumbles from the weight of the blow which he deals swishing to the air. He sinks dully into the willow brush so that the bleak, black water murmurs past only a foot away from him. The fallen man grasps painfully at his forehead. Then he gazes about with concern. Pale cloudy mist is floating out under the thin swaying stems. It dances across the water, and the moonbeams glitter on its ridges.

"Is it not strange," the sexton murmurs. "Did I not even say that evil demons have surrounded us? How else could it happen that at the same time as our dear little blonde — she is accursed, the girl of Babel — but how did it happen, I ask, that at the same hour my poodle Sus disappeared with her? Where did he flee to? Had he completed his work, the beginning of the darkness, and now leaves us alone? Woe — woe — we who are abandoned must mourn."

The low mist thickens over the water, it curls and billows more and more. Like steam on burning fluid, it rolls sad and ghostly towards the staring man, creeps up to him, and sneaks damply over his gaunt, aggrieved countenance. The willows tremble and rustle at the same time. Right next to him, a toad plops loudly over the bank.

But see there, something in the midst of the crawling white swirls must have taken hold of the man quietly grumbling to himself.

"Is a wonder of the bewitched night drawing near?", the sexton worried as he spread both hands straining on the damp meadow ground.

Then he presses his head ponderously through the willow brush, and stares unbelieving into the pale haze which has sucked in the moonlight and now carries it on green and silvery.

Then it flows over the stooped man. He clearly feels how cold drops of sweat bead on his forehead and run into the gurgling water.

"Lord of the fortress of heaven and of earth," the waiting man stutters, his tongue swilling and sticking in his mouth. "You made the world and all that crawls and flies there in seven days. — Alright, very good. The Elohist praises you. But horrors, dear Father in heaven, I am afraid. Scourge not with rods my poor sinner's brain, do you hear? Oh God, almighty Father — I am hopefully only a bit drunk, am I not, for you know, mother Lotte's champagne was genuine. Or if that does not behove a religious man, then shall we say intoxicated. Ah yes, gracious Lord, we shall say so. But for the sake of your eternal justice, why is a wreath of nut-brown hair floating before me there? And behind it this pale, calm face which looks up so still into the green moon? Who is that? It seems familiar to me. I am horrified. Lord, Lord, what are you doing with your weak creatures?"

And the white mist crawls closer and closer. And with it glides the pale countenance, sways up and down a little until, right beneath the sexton's position, it is seized by a tree root which has tangled itself in her float-ing hair.

Then the suddenly sober man tumbles back a dis-tance. His nervous hands clasp the rustling brushwood, for he is unable to hold himself anymore otherwise. And from his wheezing chest, he slings across the silent heath, so that it penetrates full of accusation to the all-seeing thousands upon thousands of golden eyes in the vaults of heaven, "The only daughter of mother Lotte? Of mother Lotte at Werrahn? Lord of Sabaoth, you are the King in Israel, and we men are like only worms un-der the feet of your stool. But now I ask you, I, sexton Vierarm, I myself am a man of God, I ask you though eye to eye, Lord, why have you slaughtered this new vic-tim? For this was one of the old breed, and the old breed walks, as one knows, your paths, not to your sorrow, to your joy. Has the new idol also shaken this lovely blos-som from the secure branch so that she could no longer hold herself, and had to plunge into the black water? How long, Lord, do you want to let the bedazzled in So-dom drink from the flute of dizziness? How long shall the altars stand which false prophets have erected in your land? Oh Lord, I am your weak labourer, and how I must confess, at the moment I am also drunk, which is very wrong, and hence it surely comes about that my stupid mind constantly cries that all the new being which nestles now amongst us was not worth this silent sacrifice. And look, as I now want to attempt to pull the poor woman onto dry land, I cannot restrain my senses, I must ask you again and again, Lord of Sabaoth, why — why?"

And the sexton bent and grasped into the water.

5

It is a hard race, that folk which draws the plough on the flat land through the fields. They strew the seeds, silent and taciturn, and after they have waited in obstinate resignedness, then they harvest it without passion, in order, as soon as autumn passes over the stubble, to dive anew into the fields. Hailstones and floods strike, and often wash away what hope already sees in the barns, and yet this hard tribe does not complain, at least not outwardly. Their miens remain turned inward, their mouths closed, and if they open, then it is only for a calm, specific command, "Collect the chaff and thresh the grain."

The man in the town acts differently.

When hostile shells whirr into the townsmen's houses, spewing fire and smashing the furniture, then the citizen plunges down into the dark cellar with his family screaming and lamenting, and hides himself from the light, as he bewails his life and fate. The country residents also look darkly at the barns in flames, the horse paddocks blasting apart, but wordlessly, closed off, grimly, he bows the head over which the black shots cleave their path, and then he begins to extinguish the flames and build up again.

Ever anew, constantly from the beginning. He is calm about it, he is incapable of anything else, and knows no other way.

***

It turned autumn on the property at Werrahn.

The Girl Who Lost Her Way

On the country road, the cool wind was scrimmaging about with swarms of yellow leaves, the strong breath of fresh manure was coming across the fields, while the long drawn-out laments and groans of the cows rang out from the stalls which now closed them off from the open meadows. The dogs started up brightly when a wagon rattled past, strong maids stood in the farm buildings making butter, light smoke curled from the low chimney of the house.

The leaves fell from the three lime trees. Everything rolled on as before, calm, still, and full of order. Death had certainly stridden with both his pale dogs, horror and dismay, through the large living room, his scythe had swished, his dogs had howled, both the old ceiling beams had trembled at their seams so that you now noticed how worm-eaten they had become, and yet the house had not collapsed.

It stood.

No, both the people who resided in it, and all the furniture, they looked at themselves with deep, astonished looks in which a dogged pain curled, but the living as well as the immovable, they were too much accustomed to the house motto of the little woman with the goshawk's head, even if she had not shouted it daily and hourly, "Stay tough!"

On the main road, a miserable wicker vehicle was toddling. And although the autumn rain, which swept the land in short, grey blasts, splattered into the open chaise with vehemence, its owner, the old country doctor, general practitioner Abraham, nevertheless leant out to offer his hand to the rider trotting past just then at walking pace. In the middle of the streaming rain, both men stopped next to each other. From their gestures, which went in the direction of the Werrahn residence, you could extract that they were conversing over the residents of the strung-out building.

"Well?", Superintendent Hartmann inquired, as he pointed under his damp waterproof coat covertly with his shoulder towards the deserted entrance.

"Yes," the old doctor responded monosyllabically, and rubbed the stubble of his beard. For it was well-known that Doctor Abraham still practised that highest virtue of old-established family doctors; namely he did not like to gossip about the suffering of his charges, but could become right solidly coarse if you afflicted him all too much in this direction. Even today he raised the bamboo cane with the ivory knob to his mouth, sucked a little on it until he finally emitted very amicably in parting, "Yes, so, as I said — good morning, my boy."

For an additional fashion also pertained to the old practitioner, that of being informal with everyone who was somehow known to him. But, the rider grasped from his horse the cushions of the carriage so that there was an audible, creaking jolt, and the old doctor was thrown up angrily.

"Is there something else, my dear Superintendent?", he grumbled suspiciously, whereby he squinted with his somewhat dripping eyes at the other man from head to toe. "Do you perhaps have some aches? Or is it hurting, my son, in your big toe? I stand at your service. You look quite affected."

"No, no, doctor. I beg, do not blame me for my question, you know, the purest sympathy for the people over there propels me entirely."

"Wonderful, wonderful, but what else?"

The Superintendent wiped the dampness from his face with his hand, then he bent lower into the carriage, "Is it true," he whispered with muffled voice so that the coachman, who crouched on the front seat as if completely impassive or drowsy, could not hear, "tell me just the one thing, is it true?"

The country doctor struck his knee, and pushed petulantly at his worn leather cap from which the drops trickled down slowly and melancholically. Then he coughed and wrapped himself tighter in his grey fleece coat.

"True?" he growled. "Well, yes, it will surely be true. I have in fact still much to do, my good boy. A child-birth. And the worms don't wait for me, do they? Adieu as well, and get well soon."

"Oh please, doctor, just one more word. Is it really true, what is said in the district here, that Mrs Lotte Kalsow after — well yes, after that ill-fated time — is lame in the hand and feet? And that she, it is terrible, shall even have lost her speech? The people in fact are saying such things."

"So, so, they are talking? That's nice. Well, then it will surely also have some truth to it."

After this answer, however, the good-natured Super-intendent let the reins go for a moment, and struck his hands together so loudly that even the coachman was startled out of his paralysis.

"Shall I travel on, sir?", the hunched man turned his insensible, dumb servant's countenance around.

"Yes, Krischan, travel on — good morning, my boy."

Meanwhile the rider was not letting himself be dis-lodged. It was clear this miserable vehicle could not evade him, and so he remained at a tidy trot by the side of the rattly casket.

"Oh please, doctor, just one more trifle," he contin-ued the conversation in the middle of the rain and in full motion.

But the country doctor was becoming angry, "Thun-derbolts, my dear boy," he now blustered in full fury, whereby he rubbed his grey prickly beard spasmodically as if this could give him some relief. "You want perhaps something for purging? Plum puree, castor oil, magnifi-

337

cent. You are a right amiable, bold man, my son, that I must say. And curiosity, it plagues you surely never, eh?"

Meanwhile the rider just shook his blond, dripping head obstinately and indifferently the way all country people of that district do when they want to obtain something.

"Doctor," he suggested curtly, "you know quite well how much all of us here in the district are attached to our Heinrich. He is also the nicest man you can ever find."

"He is," the doctor nodded reluctantly. "But, what else?"

"And since I too," the rider continued insistently, holding onto the side of the carriage constantly and seemingly without effort, "was at Werrahn on the god-forsaken evening as a guest, and because we anyway, either way, are involved in this miserable story, you guess certainly what I am suggesting — —"

"Heavens, yes," the little Abraham cried, having to wipe his eyes for fury, "it runs neatly from you like from a leaking barrel. God, you should tell these country people. Heartbreak, what else now?"

"Doctor," the other man stuttered out half in fear, "the people say in fact that Heinrich has turned odd."

"Odd? I see, I see."

"Yes, and the lads say he is almost walking around as silently as his mother. But, what remains the most fear-ful, is the story about the axe."

The doctor struck the wicker carriage. "Aha — there we have it. What is it then, if I may ask?"

"Well, that he at midday and in the evening hour, when he finds some time, stands in the cartwright's workshop, and grinds an axe there."

"Look at me now, does he do that?"

"Yes, and, when the sparks are spraying, he sometimes roars out like a wounded animal thirsting for revenge. Doctor, for God's sake, tell me for my reassurance, what do you think of that?"

But the county doctor's patience seemed to have been completely exhausted. Once more he squinted at his besetter, peering from head to toe inquiringly, then he licked with vehemence at the ivory knob of his bamboo cane, and suddenly it erupted from him, in a very considered and serious way, "What do I think of it, my boy, you want to know? Yes, look, I only got to the bottom of it myself after careful contemplation. But now I want to reveal it to you, because you are such a nice, obliging man. Why does Mr Heinrich grind the axe, you ask? Because the thing will probably not be sharp enough for him, don't you think so, my son? And now adieu."

With that, the little, wrapped-up man rose berating and swearing, and since he intended to free himself now by all means from the undesired accompaniment, Superintendent Hartmann had to realise with surprise and displeasure how the general practitioner tore the whip from its place to hew with it single-handedly at his tired, broken nag.

And really, the animal bucked and stormed away.

"Get well soon," the country doctor called to the man left behind.

Then the vehicle vanished behind the curve of the main road. Rain and wind ruled again on the main road, and the yellow leaves rustled in clouds up the walls of the house.

***

Day after day elapsed in the house at Werrahn. Both the old ceiling beams in the large room, who had often laughed heartily when mother Lotte haggled with a stubborn dealer over a groschen, now no longer gave notice of their delight with crackling and crunching. The old, faithful supports of the building had become mellow, just like the mistress there below who looked at them immobilely, stiffly erect, and with her accustomed white bonnet on, sitting in the armchair before the sewing table. But the hard, pointed voice of the little woman never penetrated up to them under the ceiling anymore, the bearers listened in vain for the scribbling of mother Lotte's pencil, which had been the secret regent of the entire property. For oh, the talk of the lady of Werrahn had fallen silent to never be raised again. And the hand which held the pencil was struck with paralysis. Only one consolation remained to both the old friends up above, and they groaned to each other in the twilight hours of evening as they looked down on the woman sitting erectly below them, "Look, her eyes are alive. She blinks. They talk still more understandably than other people do when they open their dumb mouths. The dear old eyes still rule the house. Stay tough."

And the brown, sharp eyes of mother Lotte did that. They made themselves understandable, they spoke their own language clearly and distinctly, so illuminating and heart-penetratingly that Heinrich, when he returned home from the fields in the evening, could manage a short and yet exhausting conversation with the still woman there in the chair. Whom would not have been amazed by it, if they had not seen such an incident? Was it not strange that the old lady turned her head only a little, and only needed to encompass the man entering with a short, examining look to have immediately comprehended how it looked outside in the fields and deep down in the closed off mood of her only one? Her eyes were capable of greeting. They spoke clearly, "Good evening, my boy. Now you have worked yourself tired, and now sit yourself down. There behind the round table on the sofa which I occupied earlier. Now I can't anymore, my son. But the place shall not stand empty."

And then such a strangely bleak light flew through her eyes, which added, "Two places remain unoccupied anyway, that of your sister Anna, which gives us so much sorrow. But it is good though that she went. And the other one, whom I don't want to name, and of whom you should not think, my boy."

And when her son then hastily and alone took his modest meal on the sofa by the light of the lamp, the unchangingly peering eyes of the old lady then noticed how the farmer enjoyed without consciousness, yes, almost without tasting, the few morsels which a strange hand set before him. But the silently waiting woman considered it still more dangerous when her son sank brooding into himself, and his gaze, which seemed empty and hollowed out, was directed brooding into an empty distance. Then it happened that mother Lotte turned her head back and forth for a long time until the attention of her companion was excited by the barely perceptible noise. Or when she did not succeed in this, then her countenance gradually reddened, and after an enormous effort had worked in the stiff body, then the startled man heard with fright how a strangely whistling sound was thrown out from the narrow lips of the struggling woman. That always penetrated right to the heart of the attentively listening man, "Yes, mother, what do you want?"

And then the gleaming brown eyes again spoke softly and with tenderness. The representational concreteness with which the worried mother gave news of her wishes was indescribable. And likewise, it remained full of wonder how the hulking farmer knew how to interpret these fine signs.

"Stay calm, mother," he tended to reply in such cases, "I — yes, I am already entirely with you again.

Everything is in order in the fields. Today I have had the fallow land turned over. And, think, the marl pit still stands full of water, I must have it scooped out. But it is bad that I unfortunately had to dismiss our top farm-hand today."

Again a look.

"He drank," the son responded.

The mother nodded, and gave her approval.

But after the dishes were carried out, the farmer tried to entertain the paralysed woman. He almost always grasped then for a book which mother Lotte had previously esteemed highly because it had always excited her to an honest, kind-hearted laughter. Dicken's Pickwick Papers. And it remained stirring to see the eyes of the old lady express a bashful cheerfulness as soon as one of the old-fashioned jests which were familiar to her brightened her mood a little. But straight afterwards, she again turned her narrow goshawk's head back and forth anxiously, because it not infrequently happened that Heinrich, for the sake of the paralysed woman, likewise sought to charm a weak smile onto his lips. Oh, what a forceful, bleak cheerfulness that was. At such times, a tear forced itself into the eyes of the old woman.

Both the solitary people had long since given up the traffic with their neighbours almost completely. Only sexton Vierarm was not turned away. With a decisive sovereign movement of his hand, he fended off all objections which attempted to deny him ingress, bowed, and stepped with his violin case through the low door. And after he had ranted, thundering and formidable, about the constitution of the world as well as the behaviour of humanity, then he planted himself close before his old friend, bowed as pertains to the artistic manner, and began playing them chorales of Bach, the lieder of Mozart and of quite common musicians. All colourfully mixed together. But if he ever caught a look of the old lady between such artistic efforts, which glided over bleakly and furtively to the now always closed piano, then the religious man struck his violin bow through the air vigorously so that it gave a whistling sound, and as he made a pretext of not grasping the meaning of this ambiguous look, the old raging Isaiah undertook to belittle the importance of the piano accompaniment most abusively, "What are you saying, Mrs Lotte Kalsow of Werrahn?", he cried. "Such a miserable tinkle-case? Even Socrates, who was a very wise man among the classical authors, and invented a famous poison, or something else, he already expressed the clever maxim that such an instrument was actually only the half-brother of the barrel-organ. This I have myself already felt for a long time. And here your desire from me that I should admit to such an accompaniment? No, Mrs Lotte Kalsow of Werrahn, the distinguished man stands alone. Ever noble."

And then the iron-grey Isaiah set off on his ballads with desperate strength.

Quite right, the old man cried, he raged, he invoked his spirits, and boxed about with Satan himself, all as before. And yet, anyone who peered more closely behind his being must have discovered that it was no longer really serious for the old devil invoker. From his powerful strokes, the old elementary pleasure did not laugh anymore, and when his gaunt mast-like figure was seen sneaking across the country road, then even the farmers who had been frightened of him before recognised how his limbs had shrunk, and that the man, turned into himself, tended to conduct bleak conversations with himself. But he almost always seemed to be seeking something, turning to the right and left, raising both fists, murmuring to himself, then finally stopping and emitting a deep sigh. Then he would open his eyes terribly wide, and after he had shaken his head uncomprehendingly with its wild, iron strands, he would send an astonished, discontented look up to the heavens.

What was the sexton missing?

Truly, he was quarreling with his heavenly Lord. It seemed unbearable to him that his dear, blond plaything, in which he had thought to find the epitome of all demonic powers — it occurred quite inconceivable to the oppressive servant of the Church that that tender and fine creature, for which he had already successfully struggled with Satan in a raging battle, had been snatched from him. Oh, this knave, such a wicked rogue. A Count? How was that possible? For such privileged men are deemed to be chosen by God so that they should deliver models for the others. And now though? And now despite all that a murderer? For that this scoundrel was. And a secret seducer? And in a weak recollection of his prophetic patron saint, the religious man began during his walks in the fields to boil over in seething fury.

"Oh, you stagnant mire, covered with splendid green lentils! You nest of snakes, you house of mad dead! Rubbish on silver dishes, you blemish, you spittle, you oppressor! If you are also hard, your neck an iron cord and your forehead brazen, look, my boy, that will not help you at all. The time which formed you so full of quiet treachery, ha, I hear it already sneaking up. For reward, it will pulp you in its hundred throats, and spit you out into perdition."

Only, the sorrow also befell the growling Isaiah that such beneficial outbursts did not soothe his misery anymore. He strode petulantly about rather than stay in his house. To the great displeasure of his pastor, he frequently forgot to pull the bell rope over the table, and the old campaigner's mood finally became so embittered and brooding that even Satan, who was his oldest friend, did not seem to take pleasure in interacting with the aggrieved man. He broke off his visits. As a result, however, the sexton seemed more and more forsaken. Wherever he walked and stood, whether he was sleeping or awake, everywhere he saw the blond head whose hair shimmered like bright ears of grain, and however much he bristled too, he constantly heard that soft voice through which something like quiet excitement had always trembled; eyes reflecting the light blue of the heavens looked at him from everywhere.

"I must surely have been her father in another life," the sexton said musing. "The lecherous Magdalene also had a sire, and the adulteress likewise. For where else would they have originated from? So there must surely have been a special relationship between us both. For that the devil infused me with such a funny desire which burns there as if strong grain spirits had been lit there, that I don't believe. For as I realise now after all these long years, he does not occupy himself with such lovely and yet heart-rending caprices."

And now even the disappearance of the poodle Sus, that most teachable and cutest of all dogs, who had straightaway become quite indispensable in the religious sphere of the sexton. Who now woke God's campaigner punctually at six o'clock in the morning now that the black animal had escaped who had felt obligated constantly at this early hour to snuffle about encouragingly by the the resting man's big toe, which always peered out a little from the red and white checked pillows? Pity, for pity! Who now growled so strangely as the sexton finished his secret sermons which had openly jibbed at the demonic nature of the dog? Who performed at the table and during the long walks the drollest of tricks which a dog had ever practised? Who made somersaults, stood on its head, caught mice and rats, and bit the passing farmers so trustingly on the calves? None. Only Sus was capable of that, whom hell had lent for a period to the friendly sexton as a sign of its high regard, and now, after the work of darkness had been completed at Werrahn, had demanded it back again jealously. For, it was clear, and sexton Vierarm dreamt every night about it. The poodle Sus had at the Werrahn festivity, when the hellish enterprise seemed to have succeeded, sprung into the largest of the red Chinese lanterns, had dissolved in a whirl of fire, and had passed thus hissing and laughing as a red ball under the earth.

Gone — gone.

But this last parting meant complete loneliness for the sexton. His house became empty, and the only pleasure which still filled the religious man with a grim delight consisted in determining and following the noble seducer's tracks as well as his victim's with a po-liceman's gaze, thirsty for vengeance. Indeed, he must not ask about it in the Count's castle, respect forbade that. But the sexton got his bearings nevertheless, and wrote the individual stations with inch thick letters in a black notebook which he had acquired expressly for this purpose. They had been seen in Munich. "The Lord toss his lightning into the hotel. It must burn down to the ground." They were thought to have resided by Lake Starnberg. "He must drown in it like a cat or like the pharaoh in the Red Sea. The Lord choke him." And the last traces pointed to the amiable bishop's seat of Ber-chtesgaden. "How might it surely look there?", the sexton thought. For he had read that at this blessed site, a salt mine extended deep under the earth. And in his attachment, he wished fervently that the Lord in Heaven would want sometime to make an example. Per-haps the dishonourable fellow who seduced the little blond could solidify into a pillar of salt down there, just like Lot's wife, so that he would later be shown for money. That would be wholesome for him.

But it remained conspicuous that with all these curses, little Hertha came out completely untouched, and that the sexton sometimes caught himself as he skimmed in spirit through the mountain streets of the old bishop's seat to seek and to find the lost girl.

"Nonsense," the old Isaiah then grumbled. "That is of course nonsense. Such a woman. And it all comes down to my having received a kiss from her. That struck at my disposition, and I must overcome it."

Only, that he was incapable of. His gaunt figure shrunk even further, he neglected the bell rope more and more often, he sang at church with wailing voice blatantly wrong verses, and his yearning for the poodle Sus, as well as for the little blond, grew ever more painful.

"I must perform an incantation sometime," he thought finally in complete despair. "The great exorcism for me and for Mr Heinrich. For it may well prove still worse for him."

Only, if the sexton had guessed at what his companion in suffering was driving towards, and for what his mistreated soul was yearning, then he would have surely put off his formula of invocation in sincere horror so as to inform the old general practitioner Abraham right urgently about it.

For Heinrich Kalsow did not always sit so calm and motionless with his uncommunicative mother, and read to her from 'The Pickwick Papers'. No, the labourers were right with their tales. Since the calamity had befallen him, since his belief in friendship and in womanly loyalty were destroyed, a mutinous, explosive mania had broken over him. He did not lament, in no way did he mourn for what was lost, no, the dull, unspoilt, and simple nature of the giant brooded only on revenge. His being cried for that, and all the rambling thoughts of the hulking man sucked fast to red, bloody ideas. How grisly. The image of the large dog which he had struck dead at Hertha's feet did not leave him anymore. When he felt especially well and strong, then his inner eye saw spraying blood in sparkling circles, he heard a hissing, yawning noise, and the next minute brought him a lan‐ guishing release. Yes, yes, that was it. One blow, one lunge, one scream of death — and then he would again be well.

"But the law, the state," the inner voices warned.

He shrugged his shoulders, strode to the cartwright's workshop, and, as he set the treadle of the grinding stone in motion with a firm kick, he grasped the axe which had once already done such a good service, and began to hone it. Then he shrugged his shoulders with a short laugh. What did laws bother him, or the state? he must wash the taint from himself and his house, bring his dead sister a sacrifice. Thus sounded the higher law, thus desired the ancient rites which had reigned in the Mark of Werrahn since the days of the old gods. And the day would come, that he knew exactly. And if it did not approach him soon, then the brooding man must strike out himself to seize his moment. And then the wheel whirred, the red sheaves of sparks singed his hands, and again the labourers heard that avid roaring before which they drew back shuddering.

"Mr Heinrich is grinding his axe," they then said.

***

At the same time, when the clouds hung down so low and threatening on Werrahn, the old Count Karl Anton one day put on his plumply-sitting frock coat silently in the Wildhagen castle, and after his servant brushed his top hat, which the countryman only tended to use on very serious occasions, the estate owner fastened the

Iron Cross in his buttonhole, and threw one more glance at the mirror in his simple bedroom to see if the parting of his grey hair was running neatly and martially. He did not complain, he did not moan either over the impeding clothing to which he was so unaccustomed, his ragged brow hung heavily and drearily down over the usually lively sparkling eyes, and he frequently turned his head to the adjacent door to see if his wife Anne-Marie were not perhaps surprised at this behaviour. Only, everything remained calm, and after a short time, Karl Anton travelled in a simple country chaise, which he always preferred for himself, into the town. During the entire journey, he looked down at the tops of his patent leather boots, or he folded his hands to press them tightly against his chest as if he had something to hold firmly there. Only once, when the nobleman travelled past the house at Werrahn, did he breath deeply, press himself timidly into the cushions of his carriage, and pull the stiff top hat far down his forehead as if he must not show his honest face freely during the day. And then he murmured to himself, "Mr Heinrich is grinding his axe."

For this saying of the labourers had also reached the high-born aristocrat, and it filled him with shame and horror at the same time.

"Travel on, Johann," he cried agitatedly out from the inside of the carriage. "Past here. Whip the horses, it is going too slow."

"Mr Heinrich is grinding his axe."

And again the man pressed his clasped hands against his chest, and again he looked uncomprehendingly at the tops of his gleaming boots. Thus he arrived in the town.

Before one of the gothic houses by the market, which with its peaks and points was erected entirely from red bricks, a cuirassier was marching up and down with drawn sword, guarding the standards of his regiment. Karl Anton ordered a halt before this building, and left the carriage ponderously. But the old gentleman remained for some time yet standing on the footpath as if he had to listen to himself inwardly once more or as if he were shying from really carrying out his plan to its conclusion. The cuirassier also stopped, and examined in astonishment the Knight of the Iron Cross who lingered so lost in the street. And again the estate owner, struggling heavily for breath, pressed his clasped hands against his chest until he, forcibly pulling himself together, climbed up the few stone steps. He did not have far to advance. Directly on the right in the high-vaulted hallway, a brass plate flashed, and on it stood "Lieutenant-Colonel von Henning". A few moments had to elapse yet, in which the estate owner handed his card to a military fellow in a simple, blue liveried jacket, but straight afterwards, he was led into a narrow gentlemen's room which was filled on the walls with the most select foreign weapons, for Colonel Henning was deemed to be an avid collector and knowledgeable antiquary. You could see old Japanese suits of armour of the finest work standing around, lances and bows of long died-out Indian tribes adorned the corners in bundles, and from a pillar behind the desk, a caparisoned saddle even greeted you, of which it was believed that from it old Fritz had directed the battle of Leuthen. This was the principal sanctum of the Lieutenant-Colonel before which he performed his prayers in serious hours, which happened only seldom with the cheerful man. A fine cigarette smoke was curling through the air when Karl Anton entered with a deeper bow than he had intended. And this testimony of honour also appeared so odd to the Lieutenant-Colonel, who with his improbably tall figure had just shot up from his rocking chair, that he broke out first of all, as was his custom, into a cheerful, jarring laughter. But then the officer, who let his grey jacket dangle open over a crumpled white vest, grasped both hands of his old acquaintance, and gave blatant expression to his joy at seeing the rare visitor.

"Hohensee, truly, you are here with me?", he laughed full of delight. "Boy, that is magnificent. You are the nicest fellow this entire goddamned region here has spawned. Well, now don't say one more word though, we will first drink a bottle of Liebfraumilch with each other. And then I will call my wife so that she can likewise look in on the strange, miraculous animal. Not so? Hard out, Hohensee, you are really giving me a phenomenal delight. Well, and now you land yourself first in the rocking chair here. Respect, dear friend, it is in fact no common vice, but rather my blessed rich uncle, you know, the Hanoverian Uhlan, brought it with him from Verdun." And with newly erupting cheerfulness, he added, "Pilfered you think? Very well, okay too, but you don't look a gift-horse in the eye, you know. So as said, I am barbarically pleased."

With that the cheerful amiable man was already stretching out his hand to ring for his servant, who would probably fetch the wine waiter, when he found himself unexpectedly restrained by his visitor.

"Dear Henning, a word," the Count stammered, embarrassed to a high degree, and having not completely won control over himself. "I am in fact — you must know — I am in fact — Lord God," he suddenly burst out, and stamped his foot, "that it all falls so heavily on me. I find myself in fact purely on private business here with you. Do you understand?"

Only, the other man did not comprehend anything at all to begin with. Astonished and soundless, he stared for a moment into the worried countenance of the stately man, from which he now read how deeply serious and wrinkled it had become. But straightaway, the

military man was compelled once more by his indomit-
ably happy nature to find the remarkable introduction
of his friend to be funny and amusing. Without any fuss,
he thus pressed the old gentleman down into the rocking chair, and as he mucked about in the corner to
finally haul out a bundle of misshapen cigars, it rattled
again disjointedly from him like a firing squad, "Private
business is good, Hohensee. You were yet again a quite
peculiar number. But what have I always said? The little
prince at Wildhagen is the only original fellow from this
entire soul-destroying province." And while he sat down
with delight astride a simple wooden chair, he added insistently, "Well now Hohensee, now first clench my
forest fire between the teeth, and then explain to me in
the devil's name why you have brought your splendid
farmer's mask into such a desperately serious shape.
What is wrong actually? Man, you can fetch a horror!"

Karl Anton slowly dusted off his cigar, and then he
blinked, uncertainly and from below into the smoothly
shaven Don Quixote countenance of the Cavalry Colonel, who only consisted of skin and bones. But when he
noticed with what sympathy and honest esteem the
other man replied to his look, the estate owner turned
blood-red, and it remained undecided whether the
smoke of the cigar or inner torment had enticed the
damp veil before his eyes.

"Jesus, Hohensee," the Colonel now cried, a fearful
apprehension being placed on his heart. And with a
quick movement, he grasped assertively for the hand of
his friend, which he did not let go of anymore. "Nothing
has happened hopefully out at your place though?
Everyone is healthy, well? Dear old man, for God's sake,
make it quick, no hound could bear it!"

The Count scraped about with his patent leather
boots on the soft carpet for a while yet. But then he collapsed entirely into himself, and as he bowed his grey-

parted head so low, as if he had a pin to look for on the colourful Persian carpet, the tormented, and in his pride so wounded father began with barely audible, groveling voice to report the hardship which his only son, the heir to an immaculate, old noble name, had thrust into his house. He kept nothing secret. And it gradually seemed to the honourable, upright man as if he were in fact speaking about a stranger, an unworthy man who did not belong to his distinguished caste, and over whom now two impartial men would have to hold a knightly court. The cuirassier had long since let his cigar fall into the ashtray, and as he drew up one of his stork's legs ever higher, his bony countenance became from second to second sharper and more angular, until he finally let with badly concealed excitement the monocle, which hung down over his crumpled vest, whirl hastily and in wide circles about his forefinger.

"But that is hideous — inconceivable — a quite base story," he inserted now and then.

And when Karl Anton had finished, and now sat there, sunken and like a man who, without guilt of his own, must not dare anymore to step as an equal before his peers, the Lieutenant-Colonel hurriedly buttoned up his grey jacket, scratched his martially trimmed black hair, and strutted with his scrawny legs silently up and down the narrow room. Finally he stopped before the Japanese suit of armour so that he could turn his back to his visitor, for not at any price in the world would this noble soldierly character have wanted the man who had fallen into misfortune to now have looked in his face, and hence he traced with his forefinger, seemingly with interest, the finely chiseled lines of the armour's ornament.

"So now listen please, dearest, best Count," he began finally, as if he were negotiating an affair like they oc-

"Honest confidence?", Karl Anton swallowed, moved tormentedly back and forth, and wiped his forehead with his handkerchief mechanically.

The Colonel, however, bowed lower over his armour, and traced still more concentratedly the improbable flowers and dragons of the Japanese armour.

"Well, now listen please, dearest, best Hohensee. Of course, you were right at your entry when you remarked that you intended only to make a friendly visit to me. You are simply a clever, practical man, and your attendance takes place naturally entirely in purely private non-official bounds. You understand me, old friend!"

The visitor nodded, stuck his handkerchief in his breast pocket, and drew it out again nervously.

"Well now quiet, old man," the Colonel continued rattling, whereby he raised the Japanese armour up to give it a somewhat different position. "What I now say to you, is of course not perhaps from Lieutenant-Colonel von Henning, but from your old skat brother who is appropriately irritated over your godforsaken rogue. Understood?"

"God," Karl Anton groaned anew, and again passed his hand over his forehead.

"Calm boy, calm. Now it is essential for both of us above all things and quite alone by it, that no shame comes to the name Hohensee, the old race, the family. In a word, to the man who first received the iron at Mars la Tour, right?"

Only, instead of an answer, the estate owner, who thought he could no longer possibly hold the inner urge closed in his labouring chest, sprang up, and planted himself turned away before the window, where he rattled back and forth at the bolts in brooding impatience.

"Henning," he murmured, "dear friend, do not speak of me. What do I make from my fate? That is a nullity and of no mind. But the boy, the boy. Believe me, he is not bad, but the women, the damned women are differ-ent from our time. And they are to blame for him."

A half ill-tempered twitch passed over the bony countenance of the Lieutenant-Colonel. The idealistic man who lived in a happy marriage, and found himself constantly in a devoutly enthusiastic mood with respect to everything feminine, because he held every single one to be a special gift of grace from heaven, the nice man was displeased by his friend's view most thoroughly. And so he just shook his sharp Don Quixote head curtly, and, in his antipathy, prodded the Japanese rider quite roughly under the ribs.

"Well, now listen please, Hohensee," he diverted, "that stands now on a different page, over which we can converse by chance sometime. Above all things though", he burst out candidly, "the possibility of a spectacle must now be prevented."

"The disgrace," Karl Anton repeated, the sweat breaking out on him anew, and he tapped mechanically on the windowpanes so that the guard strolling outside peered in with astonishment.

The Colonel then continued, "The precondition for everything else, dear friend, consists of course in that your dear filius — hm yes, don't take me wrong — I mean thus, you must take the proposal to your son as quickly as possible that he aim to drop out of the army once and for all and permanently. He will emigrate, you understand?"

Karl Anton nodded. "Yes, yes," he murmured, "that is the form."

The Colonel, however, threw half a side glance at his depressed guest, and began messing around for the sake of variety with a pair of old cavalry pistols.

"But quick, old friend, uncannily quick. For tomorrow, the day after tomorrow, it can happen to me that the affair is reported to me by one of my officers, and you know how the course of the business continues then."

"Yes," Karl Anton said, "that I know. But that must not happen."

"Of course, quite naturally, hence we act with one another, friendly, conversationally, without any officiality, right? And now my best Count, dear, old fellow, straighten up a bit. It is a disgraceful story, and you understand that I, from my personal standpoint, whatever happens, disapprove and des—", von Henning wanted apparently to say 'despise', but he swallowed and turned it into a more amiable 'discountenance'. "Certainly, your boy is a gifted subject, and when we have just got him safely out of the army, then I hope quite confidently that he will again become under your thumb an honest, practical man. Assuming of course that you are capable of teaching the boy the essential things of respectable life."

There Karl Anton suddenly turned around. With uncertain steps, he approached the scrawny officer, then he placed both arms unstably on the shoulders of the man towering so far over him, and as thick tears fell down over his broad, good-natured face, he murmured choking, "Tell me that, Henning. State that to me. For you are such an upright fellow, and I am myself so bewildered that I cannot distinguish a pitch fork from a tablespoon anymore. What do you think that I must teach my Fritz when I have him before me again? I have no idea what that could be."

Now the cuirassier Colonel also turned around animatedly and torn up. "Dear, good Hohensee," he rattled forth again like a large firing squad, and at the same time, he stroked his visitor like a tender mother on both cheeks, "don't work yourself up, it must get on track again, and it will all get on track again too. Just for that reason, because such sins with women are considered in our time to be interesting and harmless. The boy will become a farmer, and the strong air out there will again bring him to reason. But what you must funnel into him — you see, I mean of course only from my old-fashioned standpoint, which the blind idealists of today certainly find most absurd, for which I don't give a damn though — what you must funnel into him consists of the following: of you and your example, old friend, he must learn that our women and girls are put into the world by the old Lord up there not as means of delight — thunder-bolts, that they are not, that would be still more beautiful — but that they stand as stars in the heavens which show us poor mariners the course on our odys-seys. A great number of good men have considered it thus with me, praise God. And we have not done badly as a result, and have laid down a mighty empire. So Ho-hensee, and now wipe the tears from your eyes, for now I'll, despite everything, have the bottle of Liebfraumilch fetched. And I will also call my wife. You don't see a real nobleman every day as guest, and such a one must be celebrated. For that, however, Liebfraumilch is directly the proper drink. Sit yourself down, old friend."

6

Black and dreary like a storm cloud that has sunk to the earth, Lake Königssee stretched between the dark, treeless rocks which surrounded it. The dinghy which ferried him across was black, the oar strokes with which the boat was steered were soundless. And even the rays of the sun which had clambered over the tall rocks did not conjure forth any colour from the dead water. The birds fled this place, all around silence brooded, and, in the little Salzburg fishing village which sat by the lake, that accursed soundlessness likewise resided. Even the children of that world-forsaken spot held their fingers to their mouths and looked with serious eyes across the black world of the water. A place made for turning within, and for thinking.

And truly, who is that charming, slender creature who has chosen the colour of the lake for her clothing, and now rests stretched out irresolutely into the most lost, most rapt brooding in a folding chair on the balcony of the respectable hotel, "The Golden Dolphin"? Why has she covered her eyes with her beautiful arm, since the rays of the sun have not reached her place of rest, and why does she let the old Frenchwoman, who serves her for society, chatter and gossip, without dignifying the lively woman with an answer? And is it not strange that she only then gives a sign of life and starts fearfully when the page of newspaper which rests old and crumpled on her lap is moved by the wind, rustles once more loudly, and crackles?

The lake lies there as if the angel of death were bathing its pale limbs in it. And it is also death and de-

cay which besets the mind of the taciturn blond. How
long is it — barely a few weeks — since she unsuspectingly grasped this mellow, crumpled page of newspaper
in the Berlin hotel? Since then she has not parted from
the paper anymore. Surely someone has attempted to
take it from her; her companion as well as the adroit
Frenchwoman, how often they have sought to tear the
page away from the blond rococo figurine. But they have
not succeeded. No, they could not succeed, and all the
living and dead who squint at her with pale faces from
the short newspaper notice, it has flushed them up, and
with them the others which they now must protect like
invalids. Far across the artist's city on the Isar, far
across the lake where the fairy tale king drowned*,
through forests and mountains, behind them joy and
calm must rest. But strangely, joy and rest spring up before her, like flushed game, and don't let themselves be
chased. Instead the narrow Schwarzbach stream, overshadowed by trees, gurgles unchanged behind her.
What does it mean? Why can she not exorcise this
noise? What concern to her is a village stream from the
North German Plain which only serves to water the
fields of a hulking farmer?

Onward, onward. Through Salzburg's sparkling,
white lanes. Here the South is already nearer, you see
dark-eyed Tyrolese, and in the middle of autumn, little
donkey teams bring mountains of the most colourful
alpine flowers to the city. It is beautiful. Here she can
smile again, and occasionally she also hears the mocking talk of her companion as he seeks to cheer her up.
Every moment it meanwhile rings out from the Frenchwoman, "Oh, mademoiselle, voyez donc, c'est drôle,
vraiment, c'est très drôle."[†]

---

* King Ludwig II of Bavaria died mysteriously in Lake Starnberg.
† "Oh, mademoiselle, see there, it is amusing, really, it is very
amusing."

But why does the green Inn whisper so sadly and admonishingly when she strides along its banks? Then it compels her to stop and listen. And already it is not the fierce mountain stream anymore. Away, away, for it gurgles behind her with the familiar weary sound which she cannot bear. For God's sake, pack up, and then onward. Onward up into the mountains. For if she remains for a single moment yet, then the Schwarzbach will wash over the pale face which follows her and by which she is always caught. The living one is reached by the dead one. Must she then also yet see how sexton Vierarm bends down in the moonlight to stretch his hands into the cold water?

Take pity, do not leave me here, onward, onward!

No, do not settle down in Berchtesgaden, the old bishop's seat.

Why not?

Because there so many North Germans live. They could have read about it. They could point their fingers at us. Back there, beyond the forests, there calm will be enthroned.

But beyond the forests, there the black lake stretches between the lustreless rocks which clench the water. There the angel of death bathes its pale limbs, and sometimes it whirrs into the air, cruel and cold, as if it were shaking its feathers. And the angel of death stands down there and looks up at her. Almighty God, why can she not laugh over such webs of imagination? Defiant and pert like before when it was valid to mock old venerable customs? Many people have already drowned themselves. And she was not the one who pushed that taciturn, secretive girl over the edge into the stream. Why does she not laugh then? Why in all the world does she not read the vapid books which her companion brought to her so that she could free herself from all worry? Why does she not act like him, and go for hours across the lake to fish and cluster amidst the crowds of sightseers?

And as she lies on the balcony, her arm drawn close over her eyes, she broods really over these obvious questions. She needs only spring up, and the spell is broken. For a period at least, enjoyment would again reign about her. And over the time — there you do not need to think it over.

"Oh, mademoiselle, voyez donc, c'est drôle, vraiment, c'est très drôle."

But when the little one catches the French prattle, it again runs like a shudder over her resting body, and her right hand presses the page of newspaper in her lap so that it crackles and rustles. Yes, now she knows, now she feels for the first time inescapably what power has broken and changed her rebellious mind. Certainly that is it. She lived too long under mother Lotte's roof. Since she sat in the good room at Werrahn, cut off from the stormy wind which unleashed the new times, quiet and unnoticed forces had broken in over her, forces which she had not known before. They were the heavy, conventional ideas of those people who formed the unspent kernel of the common folk, ideas whose paramount law read: you shall be good! And in addition: you shall humble yourself! And again: you shall step back behind the common people, and fetch and act without reward or finery.

Woe to her! That took power over her. And now it cries out in her because her existence is dissipating without goodness and in heartlessness, and that she could not humble herself, and because she tempted herself and others thereby to an aimless decadent life.

Oh, she should never have entered mother Lotte's good room. For in there under the roof beams, such a fresh, wholesome air reigns, and she breathed it for too long to not feel loathing and tedium for the atmosphere by which she was now fanned. Truly, she lived too long in the strung-out house at Werrahn under the three lime trees, and hence it surely occurs that her eyes as well as her mind are directed backwards, and that she must imagine so frequently what the two people left behind might be up to in the quiet home. For now there were only two. Horrors, the third is missing, who strode so towering through the room like the little one had earlier surely pictured the king's daughters in Homer to herself. She was missing. For the powerful female figure slowly glides down the narrow Schwarzbach and directly at her. All merciful one, it is already gurgling again next to her. And with a loud cry, the burdened woman starts from her resting position, and looks around, deathly pale and disturbed. From her eyes, the peacelessness implores, "Madame Dufournier, pack up, we cannot stay here."

"Oh heavens, I don't know why not? It is so beautiful here, si joli, and your fiancé is coming along too right now."

"Who? My fiancé?"

"Oui, votre fiancé, monsieur le comte. Does mademoiselle not hear the barking of the little dog?"

And really, from the lake a loud, powerful bark rings out, and right then, the disturbed woman sinks back for a moment with more reassurance. The poodle down there who already seems to greet her from afar, it is the only one of her old friends who followed her into exile. How strange! Did not the dear old sexton Vierarm always maintain that some mysterious kobold was hiding in the black animal? And now the scattered creature must think about the strange way in which the dog attached itself to her person. And of the Werrahn festivity where her engagement was celebrated — again she was startled, and held the page of the newspaper flushed and mistrustfully to herself — yes, from the garden where the many Chinese lanterns burned, the poodle chased after the Count's carriage. He had not wanted to leave her at the branch train station either, as often and as energetically as the animal was driven off. And after he sprung after her with a mighty leap into the carriage, and bedded his head between her knees wheedlingly, from then on the little one had clung to the ragged friend like a last protection. Oh, she knew right well how often the young Count had already supposedly lost sexton Vierarm's poodle. For her companion nourished a secret antipathy towards her favourite. But every trick rebounded from Sus. He had swum through the lake for hours, and not drowned. He must have strayed for entire days through mountains and forests, and yet he had found the tracks of the little blond again and again. And when she then slung her arm around the homing dog to press the animal to herself, it offered her a weak satisfaction when she noticed how the Count bit his lip ill-temperedly.

Thus sexton Vierarm's assistant became her last hold.

***

They both sat alone in the humble room which the landlord of "The Golden Dolphin" had raised magnanimously to a lounge because the room was adorned by two worn, red velvet-covered fauteuils. They reclined in these chairs opposite each other. The young Count smoking a cigarette, his brow a little knitted, like someone in sympathy or gnawing a quiet reproach. His blond companion, however, in a tight fitting, grey English cloth dress, from which a narrow, white man's collar peered at the neck. Her hair, which she now wore in the Greek style, had been placed by Madame Dufournier in a golden clasp, and it would have shimmered and sparkled as usual if the light in the extremely modest room could have managed a sufficient entrance. A weak twilight, however, reigned about them both, as if the lake might not tolerate any colour in its territory as it were. Then the young Count stirred for the first time, and after he waved away the cigarette smoke with his hand, as if he feared that the blue clouds could bother his audience, he fetched a deep breath, and began with sparing restraint, "I believe, my dear child, we will visit today the table d'hôte, you promised. And I must confess, I looked forward to it actually."

"Yes, I promised," Hertha responded hastily. Then she passed her hand uncertainly to her pocket, and when she had felt that the page of the newspaper which she guarded so fearfully was in her possession, she tossed out in bursting excitement, "Yes, I promised. But I'm sorry, I cannot keep it."

"Not keep it? Oh, and why?"

"You know. I regret it. Quite especially for your sake and for us all. But you must not be angry with me because of it, I cannot force myself. We must leave here, Fritz."

In the few words that flushed up hounded state nestled again, the entire hidden sorrow of a soul fleeing from itself, so that Fritz Hohensee decided in his genuine good-naturedness to proceed still more carefully. Without moving himself especially or even opening his eyes, he continued the conversation in a kindly tone. Only, hardly had he objected that the doctor from Berchtesgaden prized directly the solitude in the region of the lake as quite especially curative for the nervous excitement of the little one, and that they could at least wait a few days yet, the slender figure in the light grey dress shook her narrow head in a wild motion so that the golden jewellery made blood-red sparks spray in her bright hair, and from her pale face, her eyes burned in an unfamiliar dark fervour.

"We must leave here, Fritz," she whispered despairingly, and looked around as if the image from which she constantly fled stood right behind her. And in shaking fear, she rushed onward, "I have already had everything packed. Madame Dufournier is informed about it all. And if you do not want to accompany me, then I must travel alone."

"But to where, my dear child? Think about it, where do you want to go from here?"

"That I don't know. Or, though, now it is becoming clear to me. I must go to the big city. In amidst the existences of thousands, amongst whom you aren't observed, and aren't seen because they are all hurrying and rushing and working."

Only, hardly had these words escaped her than she suddenly faltered, and directed her darkening gaze insistently and admonishingly at the handsome red and white countenance of her companion. It was obvious that she had finally found what she had sought so long in avidness and fear.

"Listen, Fritz," she began, as her hands again stroked her dress uneasily until they reached a momentary halt at the crackling page of newspaper in her pocket. "Dear Fritz, you must not misjudge me, I know, I have fallen as a burden on you up to now, and the intoxication and free life which we promised each other — oh, dear God, what has become of them? Through my fault, I want to confess, entirely through my ill-humoured being."

"Continue, little one. You can do nothing about your shock. You wanted to say something else?"

Then she bent forward, far over to him, and the young officer could discern how her breast quivered up and down.

"Fritz, now I know what constricts me so. What makes me so unemployable that I cannot carry on this existence any longer."

"Yes, what then, what?"

"I know, I will hurt you by it. But see, even if I should not be recalling my former residence, I have lived simply lived too long amidst perpetually active people, so that our languorous lack of any occupation — yes, I mean also your own — this sated, aimless vegetating seems to me to be a direct sin against our best intents. Formerly, I only saw men around me who had a goal before their eyes, even if also such a modest one. And you, Fritz? And me? What do we want out of life? Where shall it all end?"

At her reproach, the aristocrat had turned blood-red in his elegant dinner jacket. Why? Should that be the final straw, that this charming creature, from whom he up to now had collected only complaints, gave him standards of behaviour, and tossed reproaches in his face which recalled quite clearly the powerful admonitions of his old lord, Karl Anton? But quiet, quiet. The guilt which he had loaded on himself closed his mouth constantly. And even now, he was driven only by the desire to help the agitated woman to find some rest. And suddenly he rose, grasped the little one's hand, and pressed it to his heart. She was herself in her illness still so wondrously lovely and noble. This little, charming apparition stirred him again and again.

"Hertha," he said with his innate lovableness, "do you want to know where that shall lead? Child, of that you cannot seriously have doubted. But since you urge me there, you shall experience it today. Good, we will hurry now to Berlin, since you want to have it so, and there, little one —".

"There now?"

The young man looked around helplessly. "There I will simply fulfill my duty to you."

"Your duty? Don't speak such false words, Fritz. What do you mean by it?"

"That you will take note of. You will be at peace with me."

The elegant aristocrat had surely expected that at this revelation which yet again sounded a little dark and confused, a liberated, exultant cry would follow. Only, he was deceived, everything remained still. The large dark eyes from which the tears slowly and arduously struggled remained rigidly directed at him, and the hand which he held in his own turned ice-cold. Finally a scared question released itself anew from her lips, "And then Fritz? What do you then intend to do after you have fulfilled your duty towards me," — here she smiled almost imperceptibly — "what do you then intend to undertake?"

The young Count clenched his hands involuntarily. So there it was again. His resolve, which she must have guessed, had created no further impression on his demanding companion than that she continued in her schoolmistress way.

"Then," he erupted somewhat more vigorously, "well then, if it interests you so, than I will take up my studies at the war academy to the best of my abilities, for I am simply a soldier, and wish to remain one for the time being. It has been the basis of my class since time immemorial. And now little one, don't examine me any further, go turn yourself in."

After that it remained silent between them both for a while. But after Hertha had a few minutes later removed the damp drops from her eyes, she leapt up, threw a short, despairing look at her companion, whereupon she was startled again, and opened the adjoining door hurriedly.

"Madame Dufournier!"

"Oui, mademoiselle."

"Hold yourself in readiness. Tonight we are travelling to Berlin." And with trembling lips, she added,

"Just away from here. Away from the black lake, and to where German people work and do things."

And she bent down, and under the disapproving look of her companion, she began tenderly stroking the poodle Sus's coat.

"We are going homewards, Sus. We are going home."

***

It was a day later. In the dawn light, the young Count made his entry into the distinguished Berlin hotel on Friedrichstraße. The gold-laced porter was just assisting the alighting of the two ladies who were accompanying the distinguished guest when an envelope was passed in the vestibule to the arrival who had just given his name. He casually tore it open, and blanched. It contained only a few words, which he read, "Submit your permanent resignation today. There is no other way. Father."

With a timid movement, he stuck the form in his breast pocket so that it would not be noticed by the others. For he did not wish for a renewed discussion. For God's sake, that must be averted. First sort out his own thoughts which were once again pricking him like sharp needles. Now the end was waving. And the end meant being chased from the circle in which life flowed along so easily and smoothly and glistening. Ugh the devil, who would have thought it? And why this monstrous punishment? Because, with a zest for life and openly, he had achieved what all his comrades desired in the bold exuberance of their existence. Love and glamour.

"Stop it, stop it, remain at bay. I know quite well that these are damned phrases. I have always guessed that something else, something serious must be stuck behind life."

An enormous dejection, like that which his easy-going nature had to struggle with in strange opposition so frequently, overcame him, and when he was first sitting alone in the broad hotel room, and catching the acting and deciding of both the ladies from the adjoining room, his fate, to which he did not feel grown, pulled him unresistingly to the floor. He sat sunken, and stared before himself. Whether this thoughtless decadence had not incapacitated him from realising and mastering the true conditions of a replenished human life? And slowly, like a large, black snake which turned to him, the idea arose before him that he had fallen victim to ridiculous words. Nothing but words. He, as well as a great number of his friends who had not been capable of tearing the tinseled rubbish from the bodies of these polished wordsmiths.

"Intoxication?"

He laughed bitterly. What sort of mendacious construction was that? What did intoxication mean? What did it give? He had not been able to fathom it. It remained a mendacious word like so many others. But had not the few syllables driven him out over the borders of decency and honour? Had they not even demanded a blood sacrifice? And for the first time since it happened, the easy-going man shuddered in dull shock, for now, since he himself must suffer, the same phantom emerged before him which was making his companion restless. The carpet at his feet was transforming. The colourful floral pattern became a stream, and the disfigured female figure which he once desired so fervently was drifting along it. She like so many others. And the last was the little one in there, whom he did not love, whom he feared because she had outclassed him.

"Go, what do you want from me?"

What was that?

On the other side of the Schwarzbach, the blond Hertha towered before him. It was really her. She must have

"What do you want?", he erupted suddenly, curtly and defensively, for he was not capable of feigning it anymore.

"Fritz, you received an envelope."

He shook his head, and grasped instinctively for his breast pocket.

"Give it to me, let me read it. I know you are called homewards. Follow the advice, Fritz, let us depart straightaway. What is wanted there may yet come to nothing."

Only, then an unfounded, hot fury seized the irresolute man, who saw no path before himself. The little blond before him was to blame for everything. She alone had seduced him. She possessed the power for it. And with a mocking laugh he put on his creased felt hat, and plunged out the door as if a blaze were advancing towards him and already threatened to singe his chest. Now he was still lingering in Berlin. The great laughing city must bestow her best on him. Some joy, a pleasure which would help him overcome his hard future. And were it also only that he must hurry through the cheerful, din-filled streets to be able to imbibe new events, new pictures.

With long leaps, he flew down the hotel stairs.

And the mighty city took the helpless man in her arms.

***

It has turned evening. An autumn evening. Through the blue-grey haze, the numerous moons of the electric cupolas are shining seriously and evenly. The bustle on the streets thereby receives something of the ghostly.

"It looks like when ants are given brandy to drink and they stagger about because of it." Thus a strange figure grumbles, which pushes through the jostle up-right like a wandering mast.

Here and there the doddering brown frock coat is marveled at, or someone mocks the misshapen, fleecy top hat which lends its wearer the look of a masque. But all that does not bother the apparition. Without turning its head left or right, it strides onwards, for this crying, roaring Babylon does not deserve a look when a real prophet gives it the honour of drawing through its lanes. Only when something especially obscene in the shop windows attracts the figure's attention, then it raises its rough knobbly stick up, and swings it for a moment above the heads of the crowd.

"Oh, you quite miserable place," the wandering man murmurs in such cases. "You are a desert of sin, and your entire pride consists of being unable to count any of your grains of sand. One is like the other. Where shall it be possible then to find such a blond atom? It is spiritual pride which came over me because I could not bear it any longer. But I give up, and will travel back fourth class. For your delights, oh Babylon, do not charm me, you whore amongst cities, and the drink which you offer me tastes bitter."

With that the brown figure turned around on his heel, and strode back without further ado to the nearby train station at Friedrichstraße. His path led him past one of those slideshow theatres established in a store, in whose window a half clothed girl shrouded in colourful rags sought to obtain passersby for admission. There the sexton stopped, tore open his mouth, and since a red wave of blood completely robbed him of any clear thought, he flailed in an outburst of rage with his stick against the young woman in the shop window. But after the following words, the passersby on Berlin's main street would have been able to establish and guess the delicate thoughts of the man of God.

"Down with you, you excrement, you vomit! What does the prophet say? You shall not be happy anymore, you defiled maiden, you daughter of Zion! Get up and move away, for you must not stay there."

Someone roared, someone laughed, someone shouted, and just as the powerful campaigner wanted to seize one of the mockers by the collar to make a closer acquaintance with him, a strange noise made his pause.

He knew that tone. It sounded lovely to him, like the cymbals of Saul's daughter at the victory feast.

A black poodle suddenly sprang up to him, and when the sexton, as if fallen out of the clouds, slung both arms about the animal as if he wanted to embrace his beloved assistant or prevent a new escape of the fugitive from hell, the perplexed watchers saw how the dog began licking the smooth-shaven cheeks of the man.

"Oh Sus, how is it possible?", the sexton cried, quite distraught as he pressed the rediscovered dog tightly to himself. "Are you appearing to me as a sign? And here in Tyre and Sidon shall a still greater miracle follow? From what abyss have you emerged? But come, dog, come, we want to get ourselves out from the swarm of Sodomites. And after I buy you here, my dear Sus, des-pite your disloyalty which surely adheres to you because of your hellish birth, a piece of sausage in this butcher's shop, for my heart rejoices over your return, then you shall run ahead of me like before. For I want to follow you to where you have your place. And now come, my poodle. And if you want to bite the calves of these Sod-omites, good too, I will close my eyes, and notice nothing."

Sexton Vierarm had appraised the arts of his assist-ant correctly. The poodle stopped before the vestibule of the massive hotel, and refused to follow any further.

"Aha," the religious man said to himself, "looks to me, now I have you. The thing goes entirely according to plan."

Straight afterwards there was a light scratching at the door of hotel room number 23. Madame Dufournier opened it.

"Viens donc, mon petit chéri,"* she wanted to command lovingly. But the next moment, before the strange brown figure who doffed such a strange top hat before her, she emitted a soft cry of fear. "You are mistaken, monsieur, this is the wrong room."

Only, what could stop the religious man now? Had he recognised in there, bedded on the chaise longue that little blond figure who had cheated him of any rest day and night during this entire time. With a powerful step, he entered, but the next moment gave him the certainty already that he was dwelling before an ill woman. Oh, dear, great God, what had become of his pretty, blond, little demon! How Sodom and Tyre had mangled the delicate, graceful figure! With a deathly pale countenance, he saw her lying before him, her blue eyes directed darkly and imploring at him as the still red lips attempted to smile in shame and embarrassment. And the intentions of the old Isaiah to hold one of his forceful sermons here were immediately also blown away in the wind like chaff. Dear heavens, that could not be any use anymore. Here certainly only words of good, religious comfort would help. And since the old exorcist was not accustomed to the like at all, he unwittingly did the most rational thing which he could have done in this situation. He silently moved a chair before the little one's place of rest, sat down as if his presence were the most natural thing in the world, and stretched his hand towards her grumbling as if they had both only parted the morning before. Then he passed his hand through

---

*   Come then, my little beloved.

his iron mane, and after he had once more thrown a short, inquiring look at the trembling woman, he tossed out a sentence from the middle of his train of thought. It sounded as if they had already been conversing for an hour.

"Yes, and you see, little one, Mr Heinrich has now also got his harvest in. The potatoes had become somewhat spotty though, bluish, you understand? But the wheat earned him a nice piece. Almost as much as the old Wildhagen Count."

Then the tormented woman sat up, and gave her lady companion a signal. She wished to be alone with her visitor. And when the Frenchwoman had vanished in astonishment to the adjoining room, the blond threw herself about, shaking with fear, and grasped with both hands at the arm of her old friend. Her eyes implored in a sorrow which the hardened Isaiah did not think he could withstand. Hence he closed his eyes.

"And Heinrich?", the little one cried shrilly. "And mother Lotte? Don't keep anything secret from me. I am not at all as ill as they surely assume. I am not afraid of you in the least either. You see, I am fond of you, oh, so terribly fond, like you could not at all believe."

She convulsively buried her blond head in the man's chest, but straight afterwards, flushed up, she repeated her questions anew, "And Heinrich and mother Lotte?"

The sexton pushed away with his foot his dog, who sat before him and waited, and he directed his gaze bashfully at the ceiling.

"Eh," he growled, "how should it go? Mr Heinrich is grinding his axe."

"His axe?", the listener repeated apprehensively, that far-off, bloody incident abruptly coming alive before her inner eye again.

"Eh, that is just such a Werrahn phrase. You must not imagine anything special by it, little one. And Mrs Lotte Kalsow? Yes, now that is a special matter."

Only, Hertha was not to be held back any longer. With wild, senseless words, she implored further for news until the sexton continued with extreme reluctance, "Yes, look, the lady at Werrahn has become very quiet, that happens thus with age. Eh no, you must not excite yourself. I have known many women who have become old and grey. And such a paralysis does not the slightest damage to clarity of mind. And Heinrich's mother possesses it thank God to the fullest extent."

And since he could not contain himself finally from asking a side question which had to scrape and stab, he added harmlessly, "Well, and how goes it then with the young Wildhagen Count? The cuirassier Lieutenant? Hopefully good, well?"

But Hertha had straightened up, and as her hands slowly slid down from his chest, she embedded her fingers trembling over her eyes. The image of the paralysed woman stood so clearly and sharply before her that she saw Heinrich's mother sitting hard and angular right next to her on that chair in which the sexton had sprawled himself. No, no, it was her, and she was directing her large brown eyes chastisingly at the godforsaken little person who had made the mistake of rattling at the gates of her house. And behind her, who was that threatening so contemptuously behind the paralysed woman? With the full nut brown hair from which the water of the Schwarzbach was dripping down?

Oh, just not that, just not that.

And with a whimpering croak, she moved her bright head close to the sexton's, and whispered something curtly and disjointedly into his ear.

"What do you want little one? Are you serious?"

She nodded. And her straying eyes remained riveted to a small travelling bag.

"I must," she responded wearily, "I cannot endure here any longer, something is stalking me."

"Who is taking that liberty then?", the sexton filled with indignation, and grasped his stick.

Only, the little one shook her pale head painfully, "It climbs out of the Schwarzbach daily, sexton Vierarm, and then it sits next to me, and eats with me, and sleeps with me, and walks behind me wherever I may turn. And it will not stop until I have seen and spoken with Heinrich Kalsow and his mother."

Then the sexton rose, and stroked the disordered woman's bright hair which had always delighted him so much. Even today it shimmered like gold which had been polished.

"You see, little one," he said, as he quelled a strange swallow. "Now the sparks of purgatory which burn in every human are near to being extinguished in you. And that was also the reason which led me here. For see, between us both something special surely exists. I just haven't worked it out yet. And now I will lead you, praise God, back home again. And you and my poodle Sus, you can live with me. For although I am a bachelor, I am also a religious man, and I will make nothing of the stupid farmers' talk but muck. But I want to ask you one more thing in closing. How will the high-born young Count take it when he learns that I have fetched back both my blond and my black-haired property?"

The little one had meanwhile risen fully from her place of rest, and now stood by the hotel room's window, from where she stared down at the din-flooded street of the capital city. She did not turn as she impassively and indifferently tossed back over her shoulder, "What will he undertake? He will certainly not notice straightaway. For the Frenchwoman saw him sitting drinking wine half an hour ago with a lady — yes, with a lady —", she added with the light excitability in her voice which was peculiar to her, "down there on the platform of the large specialty theatre which is found in this hotel. And it is also okay thus. I don't want it any other way. And now sexton Vierarm, dear, old friend, if my company really does not appear too painful or too unworthy to you, then take me by the hand, and lead me away. Away, away," she suddenly cried shrilly afterwards, and wrung her hands, "for it is whispering next to me again, and spraying ice-cold drops at me. They are penetrating my bones to the marrow. Take pity on me dear sexton, offer me your good, pure hand, and then come what may."

7

Life is a greater writer of tragedies than Sophocles and Aeschylus and Shakespeare, and all those like them who stand at the threshold of existence and scoop with their hand from the well of God. But life gives itself wastefully. It sits like a sorceress by the great cauldron, and heats it so that it foams and hisses and wants to boil over. But before heaven and earth can be reflected in the colourful bubbles which swell up there, and balloon and stretch, the shape is burst asunder, and new spheres bubble up which interest the old witch more.

Life surely gathers up tragedies, and ties them up, but before these reach their end, she throws them away into the dust of the ordinary.

"Lie there!"

And thus we would certainly have barely received news of what happened in that small corner of the earth at Werrahn — for the witch also took her plaything there, and threw it in the dust — if one of those secret sermons of sexton Vierarm which he wrote shortly before his retirement had not been kept preserved. One written at nighttime and by the round table over which the bell rope hung down.

Here is the sermon.

He wrote it down on the large yellow sheets. And it is introduced by a text of the prophet Isaiah, for the old gentleman remained faithful to his patron saint even after his retirement.

Isaiah 29: 14

Therefore, behold, I will proceed to do a marvellous work among this people, even a marvellous work and a wonder.

See, anyone who denies then that our dear old Lord sits up there on his golden chair of worries, and looks down at what every single one of you is doing, you miserable worms, whether he now be a horse groom with dirty boots, or a fine baron with lavender stockings and bows on his shoes, which these days is meant to be the finest of all for men; anyone who denies in his stupid, fatuous, and intractable mind; and all those who would like to make of our highest master such an old, breezy, lapsing element, some sort of ethereal stuff as you find in stinky rooms of sick people, all such blockheads who have donned glasses made of the soles of shoes, I want to give them a sign and a lesson here.

Listen!

The Girl Who Lost Her Way

I will give you an example of what our Lord is capable of, for through an example, which also originates from the district, you make more of an effect than through a hundred books, may they even be written by the most learned professors who received payment for them. I, sexton Vierarm, experienced all this myself, and stand by it with my word. That is why to anyone who would like to shrug their shoulders perhaps with noble-mindedness and in disbelief over my testimony, to them I would pass disgustingly under their nose what I herewith send ahead merely in warning. I know quite well little Hertha, and Mr Heinrich Kalsow at Werrahn, and the young Count who — who — but I don't want to scold here, but rather talk with the tongue of an angel — they were for a long time the subject of your immature, godforsaken gobs. But you don't know the truth, only the Lord of Sabaoth knows, and one of his servants whom I do not want to name here from modesty.

The matter, however, was conducted thus.

I had travelled through the entire night with the little one, of course not in fourth class. And when we finally arrived in the town, she suddenly uttered the wish to look up her brother-in-law, Professor Rogge. It was now early in the morning, and I discouraged her insistently from it. Oh, how miserable and affronted she looked. And during the entire journey in the night, she had constantly asked me, as I tried now and then to take a small pinch of sleep, when we would finally be in her home town. It was a proper worry, and I could distinctly notice that the phantom which chased after her must be even quicker than our train. But when she now wanted absolutely to go up to her relative, whom I could never really suffer, I finally conceded, whereby I myself waited before the door to the house for her. It was still quite cool, and on the red cap of the old Pomeranian tower it lay like white frost. But I had not been walking up and down for long when the little one plunged out of the house towards me. And I merely needed to look at her, her tear-stained eyes which were not blue at all anymore, but appeared black, and the fine lips which constantly trembled, to know that she must have been chased away by the fine gentleman up there who constantly mouthed such mighty talk. No, no, there is no other interpretation, my devout people. The Professor, that is one of your sort. They surely approach the sins and squint at them, but if they then should ever have boldly pledged themselves to them, then they had not and did not want to. It would be better for such people if they lay with a millstone — but stop, such a fellow should not disturb the charm of my talk. I thus hired now Krischan Guhlen's open wicker carriage, for I could not obtain another vehicle because the horse market was on in the town. And really, right before the gates, we saw all the animals tied up, and many officers and estate owners from the district were there. I mention this circumstance only because it becomes important for the following, and because you can see from it that our Lord himself did not forget to put such a common thing as an animal market in his calculations.

From there we travelled out into the countryside. The air of the turned fields wafted preciously towards us. Truly, quite another thing than what you breathe in these so-called capital cities. And from now on the cheeks of the little one also coloured more deeply, and as she bent forward in fear and apprehension, she held my hand fast as if I were really her proper father. This was a very beneficial feeling for me, and I advise you not to laugh about it. Only, the closer we came to the boundary of Werrahn, the more restive the little one naturally became, and she asked me a few times to stop the horses so that the carriage stood still. She was surely very scared at heart. At one such pause, it happened then also that she asked me, "Oh, tell me, what will Mr Heinrich do with me? Don't you think, sexton Vierarm, that as soon as he thinks of his dead sister and of his paralysed mother, that he could take his axe up to strike me dead?"

Strangely, it did not sound at all as if she were frightened. Then I answered her as she held the poodle in her arms, "Little one, that I don't know. The man surely plans many a thing against the other man, but if they then stand eye to eye opposite each other, then to my knowledge between the enemies will rise as much custom and tradition as habit and past friendship, and also fear of possible punishment, that the wildest intentions will remain undone." But I added as well, "Indeed with Mr Heinrich, I am unable to say, for he is a quiet and inwardly turned man. And before them you must be careful. But be quiet, little one, I will stay with you."

Thus we arrived, my devout people, at the house at Werrahn. It remained conspicuous to me how lightly and adroitly my ward sprang down from the carriage. Yes, even when she was striding across the yard, I had to admire her floating, feathery gait.

"Look," I said to myself. "That is almost the same old. Where does it come from surely?"

But oh, it would not remain so for long. And now comes the worst that I have to report. We walked through the red-floored hall, the little one in front, and myself always behind her, for I bore qualms about leaving her alone. With a quick resolve, the blond opened the door which was always much too low to let me through. But for the little thing, it seemed yet too high to me. And then — I am an old man, and have attempted many things between heaven and earth. But I must honestly confess here, before that which I now saw, my heart faltered in my chest, and I would have most liked

There Mrs Lotte Kalsow of Werrahn was sitting in her chair before the sewing table, as ever. Only rigid and stiff. And before her stood Mr Heinrich, holding a plate, to infuse his mother with one spoonful after another of the soup. For she was fed thus, I'm afraid. It was a dreadful picture, and I was seeing it for the first time. But still more terrible and heart-clenching it must have been to throw a look at the returning woman. There she stood namely in the doorway, pale, like a lily in the field, and you became aware that she would like to have stepped into the room — no, not stepped, but rushed — had only a good word been directed at her. But it was not forthcoming. It was an infamous, a properly shattering silence which now occurred, and it seemingly choked one's neck. At least it did so for me. But here I saw how it was possible that in a single look the fate of three people can lie decided. For Mr Heinrich and Mrs Lotte Kalsow noted the little one quite well. But do you believe surely that the paralysed woman stirred? Not a movement came from her. Only her eyes began burning like smoking pitch. It was terrible to look at. But still much worse was the effect of her son's look. It was as if his blue eyes froze and iced over. Do you think he let the plate with the soup fall even by an inch? No, his hand with the spoon did not tremble once. But then he straightened up, pushed his neck forward a little, and called loudly, quite loudly so that the sound broke against the walls, "Sexton, what do you want? If you have something to say to me, then come in. Otherwise you know that we let in no strangers."

Thus he called out brightly and penetratingly, and at the same time, it seemed as if the ill woman had imperceptibly nodded to it. Truly, it seemed so to me. And then the son turned, and fed his mother further with her nourishment. You could clearly hear the swallowing of the old lady. But I did not wait for anything more. I thought the little blond, my daughter, would fall down. But to work out such young women is difficult, and I was only beginning my studies. She stood there with lowered head namely, held her hands clasped, and looked incessantly up at the paralysed woman over in her chair. She moved her lips constantly at the same time, and although nothing could be heard, it seemed as if she were murmuring inaudibly to herself. Only, nobody paid any further attention to us. Like something superfluous, we were left standing in the open doorway. There, my devout people, you will bear me out, there I could not endure it any longer. You see, I bent down in fact, slung my arms about the blond who probably did not comprehend what was happening to her, and then I carried her without further ado down the hall and to the wicker carriage where my poodle Sus was already waiting for us. And when the little thing sat there on the leather cushions, still wordless and murmuring to herself, I spoke these words up to her, "Dear little one, now we will go to my bachelor's home, and then I want to step up to the threshold, and call out to you a welcome. Also I still possess a bottle of old red wine which my pastor gifted me for my anniversary. We will drink it together. And then we must wait for what the Lord of Sabaoth in heaven has planned to do next. For God's mills grind slowly, and there is nothing he likes to suffer as little as impatience. I know that about him. And now, giddy-up."

With that we departed. But when I turned around once more, it seemed to me as if Werrahn lay behind us hard and cold like an imprecation or a curse.

Now I look at you, however, you dumb farmers, I see that you are not yet capable of drawing the practical application. That lies, however, only in your nailed-up

skulls in which it looks like it does in my hay loft at wintertime. Quite congested and dense. For see, I want to
reveal it to you. Now, only now has the time approached
when the Lord came down on his chariot of lightning
and surrounded by light and smoke.

Now you will see him.

For in the same hour as we both — I, the sexton Vierarm, and the blond — stood before mother Lotte Kalsow
at Werrahn, the young Count Fritz Hohensee had arrived in the town.

Why, that I can explain to you only poorly. Only later
have we arduously worked out and whispered together
his intentions and plans. But as much is well established, that he had arrived in fury and rage because the
little one, my daughter, had fled from him. Who will
know what the ill-fated, reckless man was thinking and
had in mind? Perhaps he wished to fetch her, perhaps
also he had received a new despatch from his high-born
father. As much remains certain in any case, that he ran
through the streets in mad haste, as does not behove a
lieutenant at all, to suddenly, dressed in his grey overcoat, emerge at the horse market. You see, now the
significance of this place will stab you in the eye. At the
animal market in fact, a number of acquaintances and
comrades of his must have been present, and by these, I
later learnt, he was from all sides told that he should be-
ware of the Werrahn district. There Mr Heinrich was
standing and grinding his axe. Meanwhile, the Lord of
Sabaoth poured contempt for such warnings into the
soul of the young man. And the last that his good
friends caught of him consisted only of him borrowing a
horse from a comrade to at least not cover the long
stretch on foot. And now it is as if bolt after bolt of lightning is thrown from grey clouds, and the heavens turn
black, and the thunder rolls so that nobody is able to see
about themselves anymore. God knows how Heinrich

Kalsow learnt of the approach of the young man. I don't know, and you don't understand. It remains only to assume that heaven sent out a black angel so that it was announced to the waiting man. But Mr Heinrich remained quite still. He just slowly stretched out his fist, and then he looked up at the dark heavens, sombre and imperious, as if he wanted to reveal beforehand what would now happen. He wanted probably to do nothing in secret, but act openly. With a firm stride, he strode into the cartwright's workshop, and fetched something. It flashed blue and glinting when he returned with it to now place himself under the three lime trees. Such a man had never waited in the yard at Werrahn before. Just think of this connection. Inside in the living room, the paralysed woman who sent her eyes about in circles fearfully because she guessed that something remained hidden to her, and outside, the man who stared into the storm clouds and into the dust of the country road for the desired, the so fervently longed for thing which did not yet approach him. But next to him, the angel of the Lord lurked in its black armour.

And there — there, my devout people, do you hear how it gallops along? The young Count must have become anxious in his soul. For he sits bent far forward, and rides like someone who wants to redeem himself. Clop, clop, clop, the hooves of the unfamiliar horse strike. Before him, however, a cloud of dust billows. Whether the rider thought at this moment of the girl whom I heretofore pulled out of the Schwarzbach from under the willow brush? Or whether he recalled the other whom he led away from the red Chinese lanterns and into the nobleman's carriage? And whether he perhaps asked himself in this last moment what it had all been worth, what the life which consumes itself like a flame, in vanity, greed, and idleness, showed in the way of a meaning? All that I do not know, for he was incapable anymore of revealing it later. But it is known to me that Mr Heinrich, when he saw the rider close before himself, emitted that terrible roar which was then already heard so often at Werrahn. Only it sounded louder, more terrible, and more violent, as if the ice across the lake were breaking and the element roaring up.

See, you dumb and contemptible people, in that last endangered moment where it was still a matter of whether a good and honest man should fall forever into the claws of Satan, the miracle happened like can only be performed by the magnificent one in his blazing chariot about whose wheels the lightning fizzes. The rider had rushed up quite close. Mr Heinrich stepped forward, already both men were staring each other in the eye, and suddenly something shot up which flashed blindingly like a blue beam.

There in the last adversity, there the black angel, which lurked next to the simple man, and yet was only a tool of the Lord, stretched its hand out. The hand, however, must have towered up an invisible wall, or torn open a grave in which bloody snakes writhed in confusion, or from its fist a vulture must have shot forth which with brazen beak put out the eyes of the rider's horse. For before Mr Heinrich could move the raised weapon even the width of a thread of sunlight, and hardly had his shrill cry died away, "Scoundrel, scoundrel, defend yourself, for now we settle up."

Before the words had even been chased away by the whistling wind, the end befell.

What is it? Open your eyes, you dumb farmers, and be appalled. For the Lord himself looked out from the clouds, and held judgement.

The steed reared. It seemed to straighten up high with two feet, and wander like a giant figure across the country road. Then a shrieking whinnying, a stifled cry, and a human figure swished like a swimmer through the air until, crashing into the trunk of the lime tree, it plunged into the dust. Did you surely hear the dull, soft, clapping noise? Don't hide yourselves away, you cowards, for it is only the brain which can think the seven deadly sins, and which now floats in the yellow sand which covers it. The beetles of the fields will nourish themselves on it. And do you want to know still what Mr Heinrich did? Mr Heinrich again emitted that never sated roar when he saw the man who escaped him lying before him, and the black angel of the Lord struck the axe from his hand so that it clattered before his feet, and covered him in passing with night and darkness.

Of that I now want to report to you further. Do you need to know how the little one sat three whole days with me, and how the contempt towards her climbed in the district, since there was muttering and whispering like only tends to happen in the countryside? And why should I reveal to you that on the evening of the third day, Mr Heinrich knocked on my door, from where I, however, turned him away because I found his visit to be unsavoury. But I want to remind you, rabble, of that Sunday which now followed. You surely still have it in your minds, you thick-skinned mob, how you distanced yourself from the little blond in the church where I brought her with me, because I wanted to play the organ comfortingly to her, how you distanced yourself from her there as if the plague shimmered from her. Are you now ashamed at all, you puffed-up asses? Are you perhaps proud of your flesh, just because it flaunts itself too fat and too potbellied to be able to be led into temptation? I tell you, keep and raise your daughters so that they can feel contrition just like mine. For contrition is the most precious property of humanity. It is like a silver bath which the Lord of Sabaoth gifts in his kindness so that we can climb out from our dirt and appear before him washed clean. Have you bathed even once in such a tub? I say no, and therefore hold your tongues. Be rather deeply ashamed that you distanced yourself from the little one who cried silently to herself as your yellow pride demanded. But is it not true that you flung open your mouths when someone at the back by the church door rose and slowly approached. Always one row after the after, until he stood next to the shunned woman and remained there. But on the evening of the same day, Mr Heinrich again stood before us at the round table. He said nothing more than, "The Lord has held judgement, and I don't want to continue. But what becomes of you now, Hertha?"

Then the little one looked firmly at him, and stretched out her hand bravely towards him, which the man did not spurn.

"That I will tell you, Heinrich," she answered confidently, and a shimmer radiated from her hair so that she almost appeared in her humility like the Magdalene in the Holy Scripture. "I have now clearly recognised myself and all my sisters. Words have seduced us, words which we wanted to savour because they were received from everywhere with such an alluring sound. See, I am one of those who did not shy away from attempting the test of whether behind those flickering ghosts of words the land of promise would really receive us. But, like everyone before me and everyone after me, I have returned with sore feet, and I have plucked nothing from the tree of life than the recognition that there is only one intoxication, the intoxication of self-education. And men and women, only one thing educates them — work. See Heinrich, when I saw your mother sitting motionless in her chair, then the paralysed woman suddenly showed me the path which I want to walk with joy. I want to learn to become a help and a support to the ill and the burdened. I want to be the eyes for the blind, and the right hand for the lame. Not perhaps in humility and remorse, but as an independent disposition which is proud of being able to gift and contribute to everyone else."

Then she looked at the hulking man for a long time. And he unexpectedly placed his hand on her head, and spoke with lowered voice, "Go your way, Hertha. Meanwhile, I will provide, and get ready at home. For the countryman does not like to have torn about by the storm what he can surely raise up again, although I don't know how that shall happen. But, since man cannot wait for the next hour, so it is perhaps possible that you will at some time bring light into mother Lotte's good room."

This, my dear congregation, memorise in your ungovernable and darkened minds. Man is only thus. He shall not pound, neither on his virtue, nor his knowledge. For the prophets who scream in your ears today, tomorrow they lie already on the manure wagon. The best which God has given us is the quite common, wholesome, human understanding which says to such servants of Baal, "Keep a step away, and then we will choose what appears respectable and useful to us from your junk."

And may the Lord of Sabaoth hammer into you such understanding with hammer and nails. Amen.

About the Publisher

Our mission is to provide translations into English of the complete works of neglected major European writers. We do not cherry-pick works that seem the most marketable, but rather seek to provide a complete collection of each writer's works so that readers can follow the writer's development and decide on its merits for themselves.

http://www.facebook.com/KANitzPublishing

http://www.kanitzpublishing.com

Lightning Source UK Ltd.
Milton Keynes UK
UKOW04f2056041217
313878UK00001B/5/P